RODERICK ANSCOMBE is Assistant Clinical Professor at Harvard Medical School where he specialises in schizophrenia. He has also worked at a maximum-security prison facility where he interviewed over one hundred murderers within forty-eight hours of their committing the crime. His first novel, *The Secret Life of Laszlo, Count Dracula*, has been published in nine countries around the world.

ALSO BY RODERICK ANSCOMBE

The Secret Life of Laszlo, Count Dracula

SHANK

RODERICK ANSCOMBE

BLOOMSBURY

First published in Great Britain 1996
This paperback edition first published 1997

Copyright © 1996 by Roderick Anscombe

The moral right of the author has been asserted

Bloomsbury Publishing Plc, 38 Soho Square,
London W1V 5DF

A CIP catalogue record for this book
is available from the British Library

ISBN 0 7475 3095 5

10 9 8 7 6 5 4 3 2 1

Typeset by Hewer Text Composition Services, Edinburgh
Printed in Great Britain by Clays Ltd, Bungay, Suffolk

for Jean
my beloved nurse

ONE

D ear Sandy:
    I'm writing to you because you've always seemed like a fair person. I've watched your program all my life, it seems. You're always professional—of course, we expect this—but there is another quality I count on, and that is the kindness I see in your face and the compassion I hear in your voice. My side of the story—as a prisoner on the run—is not easy to take to. That's why I'm hoping you'll withhold judgment until all the facts are in. More than that, it takes a generosity of spirit to look at what happened from a point of view that I know won't be popular. When we move on tomorrow, I'm going to leave this letter in the envelope where the management asks you to put your comments, and sooner or later it will land on your desk. I know, because you're a fair person, that you'll find a way to read at least some of it on TV. I want the truth to be told.

1

For now, I'd like to correct some statements that appeared on your program last night.

First, the whole thing was not my idea. I did not plan it. It happened, and I went along with it. That may sound like a funny way of describing an escape from prison, but it's the way it was. I really can't say much more about that aspect now, for obvious reasons, and because it's not entirely clear at this stage, strange as it may seem, how it turned out the way it did or what my role in the break was supposed to be.

The part of your program I object to most was where the reporter made me out to be some kind of mad dog. "Armed and dangerous," he said. What kind of cliché is that? It's obvious the words come from some spokesman for the state police.

Yes, I am armed. But that doesn't necessarily make me dangerous. A gun is a tool. Like any tool, it can be used responsibly—defensively, unavoidably—or irresponsibly. The truth is, I had to get out of Denning. If I hadn't escaped, I'd have been killed. It's as simple as that. So you could say the escape was an act of self-defense. I expect you don't buy that. It's difficult to overcome prejudices. Inmates are guilty. Convicts are bad people. This is the point of view from which members of the general public start. I don't blame you for it. People are conditioned that way. They've been taught to expect that every time a convict opens his mouth a lie is going to come out. "The con is only going to try to take advantage." "All he's about is seeing if he can put one over on you." "He'll push it to the max to find out how far he can go." And so on, and so on.

Maybe so. But that's the way you have to live in prison. I wasn't that way before I went in, I promise you. I was a decent man who tried to make a difference in his community. I was a high school teacher, as a matter of fact, and pretty well respected. Whatever I am now, prison made me.

All I ask of you is this: Judge for yourself, Sandy. I think, by the time you get to the end of this letter, you'll feel differently. Suspend mistrust. Hear me out. All I ask for is a chance to prove my point. It's my hope that you'll be able to see beyond the convict stereotype. I'm going to write straight from the heart—no second thoughts or attempts to paint myself in a good light. You'll find no crossings-out

2

here: Once I write it, I stand by what I've said. I believe, in the end, that you'll see the real me, the real Dan Cody.

Second, I am truly sorry about Officer Fairburn. I wasn't aware he was married, and I was devastated when you showed the picture of his little boy. From what I remember of Fairburn—and I didn't know him well—he wasn't much more than a kid himself, hardly old enough to have a family of his own. But perhaps that's more indicative of my age. He had fair hair. He was eager. You could tell that his first impulse was to be helpful; then he'd remember he was supposed to be cold and stern. He was the sort of man who had difficulty hiding himself inside the role. He wasn't going to last long as a guard. Controlling human beings didn't come naturally to him. I don't remember seeing him in Denning more than a couple of months before the detail, so he must have been new. Why they put a rookie on an outside trip I do not know. Perhaps, if someone more experienced had been in his position, someone who hadn't panicked or tried to be a hero—who knows?—maybe it would all have turned out differently and he'd be at home now playing with his little boy.

I'm not trying to shirk responsibility for what happened. I'll make no bones about it. I was the one who pulled the trigger. All I can say is that my mind was in a whirl. I hardly knew what was going on. One moment I was quietly eating lunch, the next I was being hustled along a corridor while an officer informed me in unsympathetic terms that my mother was dying and that I was going to a hospital to see her for the last time. While I was trying to come to terms with this, stumbling into the civilian clothes that were tossed at me, Fairburn was crouched at my feet fastening leg irons and Sergeant Baruk was yelling at me to hurry up, ratcheting on the handcuffs before I'd had a chance to knot my necktie, yelling at me to hurry up because there isn't much time because she's in Intensive Care and going downhill fast.

I can't think why they had Sergeant Baruk assigned to the detail, either. Baruk is the sergeant on Medical, where I worked. He didn't do outside details. He was edgy on the way to the hospital and kept looking in the rearview mirror. At first I thought it was standard procedure, making sure no one was following us. Then I wondered if I was being set up, but I thought, if I was going to be hit, they wouldn't have gone to all the trouble of getting me out of Denning. But Baruk wasn't looking out the rear window; he was looking through the steel grill that separates the front seats from the back of the car, and every now and then I'd catch his eyes on me. And the way that works, once you notice someone looking at you in a mirror, you check the mirror again to see if they're still doing it; and on the other side, they see you're looking at them, so they start checking the mirror, too, and it goes from there. After a while I just stared out the window. I wasn't going to get into mind games with Rich Baruk.

At the hospital, I saw visitors come and go and a few nurses leaving to run errands during their lunch breaks. After four years inside, you forget what normal life looks like, people going to work, women walking without fear, without a hundred pairs of eyes catching the swish of their thighs, memorizing every little jiggle of their breasts as they do that little jump, women in a hurry, when they cross the street and come to the curb on the other side.

You see? This is an example of what prison does to you. It corrodes your thinking. I personally hate this obsession with sex. It's degrading for everyone. It's like the itch of a gigantic mosquito bite. It fills your mind until you can't think of anything else. But if you scratch it, it'll get worse. If you scratch it again, the urge will get out of control. The need takes you over. Prison is an environment that brings out the animal side of a man, there's no doubt about that. Then, when he's released into so-called normal society, what can you expect?

Baruk parked the car in the lot and tilted the mirror to comb his hair and touch his eyebrows into place. He is in his early thirties and handsome in an obvious sort of way, but he is vain about his looks and does not realize what a weakness this is. When he'd finished preening, he told Fairburn to get me out of the car. Baruk stood like a god, shifting the gun on his hip, looking around to see who noticed him, and flexing his cap between his hands so the peak would stand up like an SS officer's.

I felt the morning sun on my face when I stepped out of the car. The whole world felt full and bright. I wanted to linger so that I could enjoy the illusion for just a moment, but I had no say in

4

that. Baruk put a hand on my back, and I had to shuffle forward quickly just to keep my balance. Then they each took one arm and marched me through the sliding glass doors, Fairburn with a grip like his job depended on it, Baruk with a hand resting on the back of my arm to show he's the sergeant, he's in control.

We entered by the main lobby. We could have gone in through the emergency ward, or the goods entrance, or some little side door where there weren't people hanging about gawking at me and nudging one another as I tripped along in my leg irons. But this was the way Baruk had decided it would go.

There's a part in bullfighting where the matador turns his back on the bull to show the crowd he's defeated the animal even before he plunges the sword into the beast's heart. The matador takes a stroll in front of the bull who's too confused by all the fancy cape work and the psychological duress to toss the bastard into the air. That's what Sergeant Baruk was all about, strutting through the lobby as the Protector of Society, while I shuffled after him, struggling to keep up, as People's Exhibit A.

We stopped and waited at the elevator bank. Baruk made a show of looking around, as if he had to maintain himself in an acute state of vigilance, always alert to the possibility that there could be someone in the immediate vicinity who posed a threat to public security. He glared at some teenager who had wandered too close to where we stood. All of a sudden the kid caught on to who we were, looked me up and down, and took three hasty steps aside. Now that Baruk had the response he wanted, he nodded reassuringly at the boy, as if to say, "Don't worry, son, I got this dude under control."

Baruk is so handsome, there's a stupid look about him. You see that sometimes in very handsome men. Baruk looks like Rudolph Valentino.

With the chains, I didn't have much option but to slouch. I was the con in funny, out-of-date clothes, with the salt-and-pepper hair pulled back in a ponytail, and the sixties mustache. I'm Rip Van Winkle who's been asleep in his cave for four years. I kept my eyes lowered, away from other people's faces. It wasn't that I was afraid to see what they thought—I don't care for their estimation—but I didn't want them to see the fire in my eyes. I have not been broken, rehabilitated, or tamed. By the time the elevator finally arrived, there were a dozen people waiting in the lobby, but when the doors opened, not one of them got in with us.

Baruk stepped out in front when the doors opened at the third floor. He checked left and right, then strode ahead. He seemed to know his way around. With the shackles, I couldn't keep up, even when I waddled along on tiptoe. I felt Fairburn grow nervous that Baruk was going to leave him alone with me. He tightened his grip on my arm as if he was hanging on for dear life. Baruk turned a corner ahead of us, and when we got there, we saw he'd already disappeared through the double doors of the Intensive Care Unit. I turned casually to see what Fairburn wanted to do; his eyes were big and he licked his lips uncertainly.

"We'd better go in," he said. It was more like a suggestion.

I don't blame him for being nervous. The Department of Correction has regulations for every procedure, and Sergeant Baruk had just broken one of the more important ones when he'd left me alone with Fairburn. That's not important. Really, what do I care about a correctional officer's career, one way or the other?

We went into a hallway that led to the ICU proper. Baruk was wearing a mask and was already half into a yellow gown. He made a show of having his handgun stick out so it didn't get caught up in any of the paraphernalia. The nurse was wearing a mask. She could have been anyone. In the mask, Baruk was condensed down to a basic element. You saw only his intent, dark eyes, crinkled in expectation, or a threat, or a smile.

"My mother's dying," I said. "Wearing a mask isn't going to make any difference."

"Just put it on," Baruk said.

"I want my mother to see my face," I told him.

"You want what she's got?" Baruk asked me. I thought he might be laughing at me. His eyes were narrowed down to slits.

"You told me she'd taken a stroke."

Baruk's eyes swiveled to the nurse.

"She's developed pneumonia," the nurse said.

"Suit up yourself, then put the mask on him," he told Fairburn.

The nurse had already figured out how to get the gown on me with my hands cuffed together and was fast at work with her scissors slitting open the sleeves along their seams. She came around behind me to tie the gown, and for the first time that day I enjoyed a moment of peace as I felt her fingers turning, tugging, pulling the knot, gently, just right, behind my neck. You have no idea how men who are locked away crave a woman's touch. For one precious moment, things seemed to fall into place and make sense.

"I'd hate for her to see me this way," I told them, holding up my hands to show the cuffs. I thought, with the nurse there, there was a chance they'd make an exception. "This could be the last time."

Fairburn looked to the sergeant. There was a softness in his eyes he'd never been able to get rid of.

"What do you say, Sarge?" he asked.

"Forget it," Baruk said without hesitation.

We went through the next set of double doors into the big white room. There were machines everywhere. More machines than people. They had the curtains drawn around one of the bays. The nurse drew one back for us to go in, but I had to stop and get a grip on myself, because I'd had no time to prepare for what I might find inside.

My mom was peaceful. There was a spotlight on the wall above her that put a soft light over her head and shoulders. The rest of us, in the shadows, seemed more substantial. She wasn't able to respond to my voice. She was in a coma, the nurse said. In inner darkness. All her energy went into breathing. At the end of each breath she gave a little grunt, as if it was a major effort to push out each lungful of air. I looked down at her face. She hadn't been able to bring herself to visit me in prison, so it had been a long time since I'd last seen her. She had aged, of course, and sickness had taken its toll. Still, I had to look hard to find the outlines of the woman who had raised me.

I was having trouble reaching through the bed rail to take her hand, and the nurse leaned across the bed to show me how the bed rail folded down. I touched my mom's hand and felt the thin white skin covering the bones, and I'm not ashamed to say I was overcome at that moment. I knelt on the ground and took her hand between mine. Mom's hand was cool and indifferent, and I knew death could not be far away.

There didn't seem to be any point in prolonging the scene. I raised the gun and cocked it. Fairburn was standing at the foot of the bed to my right. I motioned him to the other side. He looked to Baruk for a sign as to what he should do, even though I had a .38 a few inches from his head.

"Just do as he says," the sergeant told him. "Don't do anything foolish." He looked more afraid of what Fairburn might do than of me.

I had the three of them standing in a row, at point-blank range. I want you to know that I had them in my control, totally, and that I didn't get off on any power trip, humiliation demands, brutality, or any of that cliché con nonsense. I hope the state police told your reporter that. All I did was to ask Sergeant Baruk for the keys.

He tossed them on the bed. I asked the nurse to please come around behind the officers, staying inside the curtains, and unlock my cuffs and leg irons. Which she did. Then I asked her to loop the leg irons through some hardware on the bed and put one clasp on Baruk and the other on Fairburn.

Baruk put his boot up on the bed.

"Excuse me, ma'am," he said to Mom as he hitched up his pants leg so the nurse could hook the iron around his ankle. He loves these moments when he can show off his swashbuckling charm.

I was distracted by Baruk's paisley sock and the ratcheting of the irons when Fairburn made his move. He lunged across the bed at me. Baruk tried to get a hand on his shoulder to stop him. Before I knew what was happening, I'd pulled the trigger. There was an empty click, and nothing else. I put a hand on Fairburn's face to block him, and he lost his balance and twisted sideways, but his hands kept clutching for the gun. I cocked it again and fired.

We were deafened by the sound. I saw Baruk mouth "Oh, shit!" and look at the nurse as though she was supposed to set everything right. My ears were ringing. Color disappeared from the scene in front of me and it seemed to have lost any depth. The nurse went to Fairburn. He was lying face down on the bed. There was blood coming out of his mouth.

I heard someone on the other side of the curtains making for the door, stealthily at first, then a mad dash to safety.

I said to Baruk, "Fix the other end of the leg iron to the bed." He did it. "Put on the cuffs."

He had trouble locking the second cuff around his wrist. The nurse squeezed it shut without my even having to tell her.

Everything around us had gone very quiet. I heard only the soft regular thump of a piece of equipment.

"Come here," I told the nurse. I didn't want to hurt her. "Do as I say." She nodded. "OK?" She nodded harder.

She had a stethoscope hung around her neck, and I hooked my hand around the tubing so that I had her.

"You're going to come with me," I said.

When we came out from behind the curtain there were a few people hiding behind beds. We went through the double doors fast. I heard someone in an office off the hall trying to get security to understand what was happening. She stopped in midsentence when she caught a glimpse of us, but I didn't pay her any mind.

I ripped off my mask and the paper gown and told the nurse to do the same, and I released the stethoscope and let it hang loose around her neck, balancing up the ends on her chest. I wrapped the gun in the gown as though it might be some kind of bandage around my hand.

"Come on," I said.

I took her by the arm. She didn't struggle. We went right through that hospital and out into the new morning.

I don't like the word "hostage," as if I'm some kind of bully. You make it sound like I'm hiding behind a woman. That isn't so at all. She is with me to ensure that there is no more bloodshed. I haven't harmed her. I would never harm her.

Yes, Officer Fairburn is gravely wounded. I'm as upset about it as anybody watching your program. Probably more than anyone else watching your program, because people are going to blame me for it. I accept responsibility, but I insist that his death was avoidable.

Here is the third statement I want to correct: I am not "mentally ill." You have no idea how hard it is to shake that "psycho" label once it's been pinned on you. Convicts are the most prejudiced people in the world. Hate comes easy in prison. It's the most natural feeling in the world—in that world. Cons hate everyone—blacks, whites, Jews, homosexuals, rapists, child molesters, informers, retards, anyone in Segregation—even if they're a member of that group themselves. Especially if they're a member of that group themselves, just to prove to the guys on the tier that they're not really like that. Not like the rest of them. Not one of "them." It is not easy doing time with a "psycho" label hanging around your neck.

I am trying to be reasonable about this, though the truth is it makes me mad as hell. *Yes*, as your reporter said, I tried to cop an insanity plea. But I didn't get it, did I? Doesn't that tell you people something? The jury heard all the evidence of every shrink the lawyer could muster, and where did it get me? Denning! Life! Natural life for murder in the first degree!

I have to get myself calmed down before I can go on with this.

The only reason I went along with the insanity plea in the first place was because my lawyer said it was my only shot.

"The way the evidence stacks up, Dan, if you're not willing to try an insanity plea, it's the moral equivalent of pleading guilty, which by the way you can't do anyway."

That's what he told me. I did it, not because I believed in it, but because I thought it was the only chance I had. And for a time it looked like it might work. The jury stayed out for two days. They kept sending notes out to the judge asking him to clarify this or that. I thought, at the very least, I was going to get a mistrial. I was stunned by the verdict. *Then* you could have said I was crazy.

Remember also, I was devastated by my wife's death. Yes, I know. Cynical people sneer at that. I can well imagine the snickering among the sophisticates in the TV studio as you read this part. *I loved that woman.* Janie.

Everyone who knew us knew that I adored her. One so-called friend who became a prosecution witness even got up on the stand to say my love was excessive. Isn't there something wrong here? I know the jury bought it. But think about it. If you love someone—I mean *really* love them—how on God's earth can that love be *excessive*? How can any human being be the recipient of

10

too much love? How can that be possible? I haven't allowed myself to become bitter about it, even though, during the last four years, I've gone over the trial in my mind time and time again, witness by witness, fact by fact. I have come to this conclusion: Few people are capable of understanding what I've just written.

I want to tell you about Janie, because I want you to understand what she meant to me, and that will give you some idea of what kind of person I really am. I met Janie when I was touring with a band. You could say I got my midlife crisis over with in my mid-twenties. I'd finished college and got my first job teaching at a junior high, and I was thoroughly panicked at the thought of settling down for life. It felt like death. A friend from high school got me on my first tour. I knew something about stage lighting, but I also had to do my share of humping equipment out of vans. One tour led to another. You never spent more than a week in any town, and you always knew that in a few weeks the job would come to an end. I'd been touring for two years when I met Janie in Boise, Idaho.

Janie was a lot younger than I was—still a teenager, really—and at first she was more or less using me to get close to somebody famous. I suppose I was using the same kind of angle to get close to her: "Sure. I know Mick. You want to meet Mick?" But I never told her she had to be nice to me first if she wanted to be introduced to him. I asked her if she wanted to have a drink with me after the show, and she didn't say anything and looked away. I thought she was turning me down, not realizing that she was too embarrassed to tell me the driver's license she carried said she was underage. Instead, we had a cup of coffee and a donut. Of course, Mick Jagger didn't know me from Adam. She caught on to that pretty quickly, but by then it didn't seem to matter.

She was shy at first. I suppose because I was the older guy, because I'd been around. I was glamorous, in her eyes. In those days—this was the seventies—she had long blond hair and wore lots of mascara, which made her eyes look big and always wide open, as though she was permanently amazed. She had the look that all the girls wanted then—lean and leggy, all straight lines.

11

Later she filled out a bit, and I don't think she was ever happy with that more womanly look. I couldn't take my eyes off her. Sometimes she'd find me looking at her and she'd ask, "What?" pretending to be annoyed, though she knew very well the spell she cast on me. And when I didn't say anything, a small, secret smile would appear at the corners of her mouth.

Everything was a thrill to her. It was all new. After our first stop, when it came time to move to the next town, she was quiet, sitting thoughtfully on the edge of the bed. I thought this was it, I'd lost her. She wanted to know if it was all right for her to take the little bottle of shampoo and the cardboard package that contained the shower cap, and when I said it was, she brightened right away and jumped up and gave me a big hug. It's funny, the little things people really want.

It's weird to think of Janie as a kid. A kid in the candy store of life. She wasn't a whole lot more than a girl and looked to me to guide her, though I wasn't so very experienced myself. I never knew how long it was going to last—whether at the next town she'd decide she'd traveled far enough from what she knew and head for home. But she stayed on until we reached L.A., and at the end of the last concert I asked her if she wanted to fly back to Massachusetts with me, and she said she did. Somehow, each one of those days on tour stands out more clearly in my mind than the eleven years of our marriage.

The sense that something was wrong came to me gradually. She was losing weight before my eyes. Janie liked that at first. I think, unconsciously, she wanted to regain the girlish figure she'd had when we first met. During the trial, one of her friends said that she'd lost weight intentionally. Janie was dieting at the time she died, but she was always on some diet or other, mostly halfheartedly. In reality, she wasn't an ounce overweight. I told her I loved the way she was. Then one day I noticed how skinny her thighs had become. Her cheeks were hollowed out, and she began to look like a concentration camp inmate. That's when I learned she'd gotten infected with the AIDS

12

virus from a blood transfusion she'd had after a road accident years ago.

With this virus, some people live on for years, in perfect health, it seems, and others go quickly. Janie was in this second category. What bothered her most was that she was losing her hair. You can imagine what that does to a woman. One morning I caught sight of her staring at her hairbrush, slowly plucking at the strands caught in it. She saw I'd noticed and she reached out her foot and hooked the door so it slammed more or less in my face.

She was a proud woman. She didn't want to wither in front of a mirror, in front of her man, and end up some weak, pathetic creature neither of us recognized anymore. I couldn't stand to watch her die. I know also she wanted to exit this life with dignity. There came a day when she all but asked me to help her go. You can't expect people to say the very words. It's too much for them. I never asked her to spell it out to me. Does a husband tell his wife he wants it in writing? When people are as intimately connected as we were, that's not how they communicate. I knew what she was thinking from little things she'd let out. That was Janie's style. She'd use words in particular ways. Phrases, tossed out casually, took on special meanings.

To someone on the outside, it might have seemed that Janie was just complaining about the Social Security deduction on one of my paychecks she was waving around.

"For God's sake! Who cares about being sixty-five? Who cares what money they'll have when they're sixty-five? We want the money now! While we can still enjoy it!"

If you live day in and day out with a person for over a decade, you understand things which other people, hearing the same words, wouldn't get. It's all in the eyes. Janie stopped her tirade for a moment and our eyes met in the pause. She softened. She was on the verge of saying the thing that had gone unspoken. Then she turned, frustrated it seemed, looking for a way to move back from the chasm that opened before her. But there'd been that moment of significance when our eyes locked.

13

I made no attempt to hide what I did. I believe what I did was right. I know also that what I did is against the law, and the law must be upheld. I have no argument with that. I was willing to plead guilty, but the law won't let you do that when the charge is murder. That's why my lawyer got me caught up in that not guilty by reason of insanity nonsense. Was it premeditated? Of course it was. I *had* to think it out. I had to plan what I was going to do. I had to think of a way to ease Janie's passage, the woman I loved, a way which would cause her the least pain.

Do you have any idea what it takes to put a loaded gun to the head of the woman you love? Let me answer that question: You can have no idea. I did it, though. And pulled the trigger. I don't remember pulling the trigger. Some other part of me did that. At the last minute she pleaded with me, but there could be no second thoughts. I had to be strong for both of us.

They say I took off. Yes, I "left the scene of the crime," if you want to put my reaction in its most cold and legalistic light, although I didn't think what I did was a crime in any ethical sense. The law's not big enough to encompass an act of mercy. The law can't make allowances for individual circumstances. I understand that. I'm not bitter.

I did take off. I drove. I didn't know where I was going. I don't think I was going anywhere. I had no destination in mind. A state trooper stopped me in New York. It could have been Vermont for all I cared. I was just driving. They made a lot of this in the trial. The DA asked the jury, "If he was so disturbed in his mind that he didn't know what he was doing, how was it that he tried to make a getaway?" I have never tried to get away with it. I have accepted my fate. Though I don't believe anyone can really accept a life sentence. In their innermost heart, no one can really live with the thought that he will be incarcerated forever, until the end of his natural life.

Denning State Prison is the most terrifying place on earth, even if, as almost all of the inmates have, you have spent time in other prisons, jails, boot camps, or juvenile detention centers. A middle-class person like myself, an educated man, knows immediately that all those social and intellectual skills that you have so carefully acquired over half a lifetime will not help you. They are a hindrance, baggage. Your natural emotional reactions—compassion, empathy, a willingness to see both sides of a question—cripple you. You have no street smarts. Your reflexes are wrong. You don't learn until it's too late how to place the adjective "fuckin' " before every fuckin' noun. Countless inmates delight in chanting: "This is jail. It ain't Yale." In Denning, something as basic as your choice of words marks you as prey.

Denning is shaped like a cathedral. Its body is a central corridor a hundred yards long, forty feet wide, which soars three stories high. At intervals, partitions of steel bars stretching all the way from floor to ceiling, divide the main corridor into sections: the maximums, the minimums, the segregation unit, the chow hall. At one end, the corridor turns a corner to workshops, the hospital, the chapel, the gym. At the other end it leads to J Block. "Movement" is a specified period during the prison day when all the inmates except those on the maxes can walk through the main corridor to where they have to go. That's when I first arrived.

A prison is an anticathedral. Where a cathedral soars upward, lifting the spirit, lifting the medieval man beyond himself, full of hope, to a union with his God, a prison keeps us braced against the concrete. It presses us deeper into ourselves. Prison contains an atmosphere so dense that it compacts the soul. It may crush it out.

The noise is enormous. It's not just loud. It's alien. It's the shouts and cries of another kind of life going on. It invades your head. People call to each other in words you can't at first understand. It's another language. Some men aren't yelling to anyone in particular; they're broadcasting. They're singing at the tops of their lungs. And in the background is this constant buzz of deals going down, or sports scores, or bets, or threats. A background rumble, like the bass part of rock 'n' roll. It's the backbone of the music, but you don't hear it until you stop to listen, until you try to find the sense at the bottom of the noise.

15

All this is the sound of men together. Men without rules. Men left to come up with their own rules. Men with nothing but time on their hands. Taunting, selling, ass-licking, snagging, wooing. Raw emotion without regulation. If loneliness is the ache that comes from being alone in the world, Denning is pain of the opposite kind. Denning is the agony of being with men every minute of every day for the rest of your fuckin' life.

They put me in A6, a minimum block. The cell block was a huge shoe box with cells on three tiers on either side. I stood on the flat with my personal belongings in a garbage bag hanging over my shoulder and waited for the officer sitting at the desk to sign off on the papers. Inmates leaned over the railings of the tiers above to check me out, assessing what I might be used for. They called out to me—they already knew my name and what I'd done. They taunted me with the details of my crime, and I was terrified. I did my best to ignore them. I thought anything I did would reveal how terrified I was.

The officer at the desk handed the clipboard to the one who'd brought me from Transport.

"Cody," he said.

"Yes," I answered. I thought he was asking me a question.

"I know who you are," he said coldly. "The point is, who I am. I'm Sergeant Baruk. You got that?"

"Yes."

"Yes, Sarge," he said, looking up at me for the first time.

"Yes, Sarge."

"You got an attitude, Cody?"

"No, Sarge."

"That's good, Cody. Don't fuck up in my cell block, because that makes me look bad. OK? If you do fuck up here, you'll go to J Block. Then, you'll go to the maxes for attitude adjustment. You understand that?"

"Yes, Sarge."

"Yes, Sarge," someone on a tier muttered, simping.

Baruk acted as though he didn't hear this. "You're number five on the second tier," he said. He nodded his head in the general direction, and even before I'd turned to go he'd returned to the newspaper open on the desk in front of him.

Someone came up behind me as I walked along the second tier. I felt his hand on the garbage bag.

"Hey, easy!" he said when I turned suddenly. He was a slim young man with fair hair. "I was going to help you out." He looked harmless, helpless even.

"I'll carry it myself," I said.

"What've you got in there?"

"Nothing much."

"Anything you want to sell?"

"I don't have anything," I told him.

That was advice my lawyer had given me after sentencing: a five-minute lecture on how to get along in prison, without ever making eye contact. "If you don't have anything they want, they'll leave you alone. Eventually." Having nothing—that's quite a trick! Having nothing anybody wants is hard to arrange. In fact, it's quite an achievement.

There was someone in cell five. He had heated some water on a hot plate and was pouring it into a mug to make Tang. He looked like he'd moved in some time ago. I checked the number painted over the door.

"The sergeant said I was in five on the second tier. Is this it?" I asked him.

"Fuck off," he said without looking up.

I wasn't sure what to do and hesitated in the doorway.

"I said fuck off!" he roared, like an animal defending his cave, and came at me.

I took off quickly down the tier and bumped into someone. He shoved me hard, and I thought I was going to go over the rail and fall to the concrete of the flat below.

Baruk shrugged. "Take what you can find," he said.

The only empty cell was on the first tier opposite the officer's desk. It reeked of urine. The mattress was torn. There was no chair, and the table wobbled so much you couldn't put any weight on it. When I used the toilet, it overflowed on the floor. While I was trying to clean this up, the inmate who'd tried to get his hand on my belongings when I arrived came and stood in the doorway.

"Sammy Shay," he said, pointing to his chest.

He didn't look more than twenty years old, with pimples and

17

a wispy mustache. He was going to come in, but he saw the mess on the floor and beckoned me to the doorway.

"You need anything?" he murmured.

"Like what?"

"Valium, Talwin. Grass. I can get you heroin, but supply's tight right now."

"I don't use that stuff."

He shrugged. "It passes the time. You pop some pills, the day goes right by you. You should think about it. You've got a lot of time."

He eased past me into the cell and looked around. What I had was laid out on the bed: a razor, soap, prison-issue white T-shirts and a change of blue work shirt and dungarees. I wanted him to go, but I was afraid to make an enemy.

He wrinkled his nose and made a face. "You're going to have to get that toilet fixed," he said.

"I know."

"I could get someone to do it for you." He waited for me to say something. "It won't cost much."

"I don't have any money. The lawyer got it."

"You could borrow. You want to borrow some?"

"I don't have any way to pay it back."

"There's ways," he said. "People do it all the time."

He was turning over the T-shirts, holding them out, one in each hand, between two fingers, shaking them delicately as if something small and light might be caught in them. He let them fall. First, one onto the mattress. Then, as he turned, watching my face carefully, arm out stiff, he let the other float down toward the mess from the toilet, then swooped and caught it at the last moment. He was pleased with himself. He laughed.

"I don't need much," I told him.

I was scared half to death by this punk with a wispy mustache. I didn't know then that etiquette required me to take a handful of blond hair and smash his fuckin' face three times against the concrete floor.

"Maybe your family can bring some in for you?" he suggested.

"I don't think so." I smiled wryly. A Yale smile. Sammy looked at the smile as if it was a smear of lipstick on my face.

"Find someone," Sammy said. "Mom. Grammy. In a place like this, you got to have money."

That night I lay on the stinking mattress and thought of Janie. Someone on a tier opposite was having a nightmare and cried out as though he was being beaten to death. I thought I could never have felt more alone, but I was wrong. One thing prison teaches you is that normal experience is only one small segment of what it's possible to feel. It's like the hearing of dogs. They can pick up sounds we haven't the slightest sense of. Or the vision of insects, tuned to colors beyond our range. In prison, you learn that normal experience is only a narrow band that lies within a far, far broader spectrum. In prison, you learn about ultraviolet.

The next day, in the metal shop, I was raped. I don't want to make a big deal out of it. Fortunately, I knew enough then not to report it. It was one of those things. I know now it was arranged to make a point. Some men jumped me. They caught me unawares, even though I thought I was being careful, always watching my back, always staying within view of an officer.

I fought them. They had hold of my hair and pulled my head back over my shoulders. One of them held a shank made from scrap steel in front of my face; the spike was six inches long.

He said, "You want this up your ass instead?"

Sandy, I know this kind of stuff is hard to take. I know it's not part of your average TV newsmagazine, and I'm not telling it to you to shock you or to get your sympathy. People on the outside don't want to know. If bad things happen in prison, they think maybe that's part of the punishment. After all, the inmates do it to themselves, right? They create their own hell.

All this is true. I'm not going into the gory details. That's not what this is about. As any woman can tell you, it isn't so much what happens to your body. Flesh heals. A man, a woman, it doesn't matter who's being raped: The bodies are different, but the mind is the same. In my previous life, when I was still a teacher, I went to workshops on sexual abuse, so I knew what was happening to me. All the time, I told myself, "Rape is about power, not sex," until I didn't know what the words meant anymore.

I think, if anything, the physical pain is helpful, because it gives

19

you something to latch on to. Otherwise, what can you make of what's happening?

Sometimes I felt indifferent. I thought, what does it matter where he puts a piece of his body? Why is it so different from someone putting a finger in your mouth? What's the difference? I thought a lot about that.

But it didn't really matter what I thought. There was something forming inside me, something hard and sharp, which had its own existence but lived inside me. It began when I entered the walls of Denning, though I didn't know it then. It was too subtle. It was the rape that brought it forward. Like a woman who says she feels the instant her baby is conceived, the first jolt of life starting within her body, I felt this something begin in me at the moment the first one withdrew. This being inside me was a science fiction monster. It fed on ultraviolet.

Before my second day in Denning was over, I'd learned who Ralph Mandell was. He'd sent Sammy Shay when I first arrived, to scout out how I might fit into his scheme of things. On the day after the incident in the metal shop, Sammy came to fetch me. Ralph's cell was the last one at the end of the top tier, the farthest from the officer's desk. He spent most of his day in the top right-hand corner of the block, leaning over the back of a chair pulled up to the railing so that he could survey every movement in his kingdom.

Ralph was a big man with reddish hair and mustache, in his mid-thirties, I would guess. Every day, for several hours, he worked on his body in the weight room. He wore his muscles like body armor, the warlord of the minimums. When he walked, bracketed by arms, ponderous, grounding each foot carefully in front and to the side of the other, you were aware of the weight he hefted on his body. The bulk was an alien thing he carried about him. His thickened neck and shoulders and chest were a container in which something slight and fearful lived. Can you imagine a man lost inside his own body, buried by muscles, suffocated by ferocity?

His eyes were small and set close together, so that he often seemed to be peering, as though irritated that he couldn't bring the situation into the proper focus. Ralph had a very deep belief that the world, unless deliberately fucked up by someone, would tend to work to his benefit. It was a dangerous sign if he happened to be talking to you and this puzzled, angry look came into his face, because it meant you'd started him thinking that things weren't the way they were supposed to be. To see his face at that moment of turning was to see a man fighting off darkness. The world was tipping, opening, threatening confusion. As my own fear receded, and I became able to see, I glimpsed flickers of panic in Ralph's tiny eyes at these times.

But it was hard to see Ralph's weakness when his strength was so obvious. He was infuriated by opposition, and his fingers curled back on his wrists, and his forearms fanned out in wedges of muscle. Then, it was moral outrage that filled him. When he dealt with offenses against his natural order, Ralph was pitiless. He did not lose sight of the fact that the body he dealt with was human, but he not handicapped by this sense. Soon after I arrived, people told me he was responsible for the murder of an inmate who was found with his head cut off. They were proud of him. A local hero. I'm sure Ralph was capable of such an action. It was in his style: shocking, brutal, flamboyant.

Ralph Mandell was my ruler. On that first occasion, Ralph hung lazily from the ledge above his cell door, sagging on his feet with his hands above and behind him, using his weight to stretch the muscles of his arms. The undersides of his arms were soft and white like a child's legs.

"Well, schoolteacher," Ralph said.

"We should call him 'Mister Cody,' " sneered Eric McKenna, his lieutenant. Eric was in his twenties. Institutions had formed him, and he understood them with the quick, intuitive cunning of a man moving in his natural habitat. With his fair hair cut short and pale skin, he seemed colorless, as though he'd never been exposed to sunlight.

"Cody's fine," I told them.

I didn't know how to talk to them. It took me a year to learn the subtle diplomacy these men had mastered in the school yard. The way you stand, the tone of your voice, where you look: You walk a knife edge between confrontation and cowardice.

Ralph pulled himself up and grunted. He breathed out slowly

21

through pursed lips. "I'll call you whatever I want," he said. "I run things here."

I said, "Someone told me."

"Who told you that?" Eric asked quickly. He took a step toward me.

"Everyone knows," I said.

"Yeah, but who told you?" he wanted to know.

"I think it was someone in the metal shop. I didn't know him."

Ralph let his hands float down. He held them out in front of him. "We don't like rats," he said.

"You're not going to have a problem with me," I told them.

They stared at me, Ralph with his little, angry eyes, Eric sharp and cold behind the lenses of his wire-frame glasses. Ralph turned to see Eric's reaction, and Eric nodded yes in answer to a question they'd discussed before.

"We want you to go fetch something for us," Eric said.

"Sure," I said. "Be glad to." I thought they wanted me to carry out an errand. I felt relieved. I was grateful they were giving me the opportunity to be of use to them. "Where is it?"

"It's a little package a visitor's bringing in."

"What kind of package?" I asked stupidly.

"A little package of good stuff. Some for you, some for us."

"I don't do drugs."

"If you can't use it, we'll sell it for you."

"I don't know."

"It'd be like a partnership," Eric explained. "One of our people on the outside delivers the goods to one of your people on the outside."

"My people? Who do you mean?"

"Anybody." Eric shrugged. "It could be anybody you want."

Ralph watched him take me through the steps, leading me gradually to what he wanted. It was a remedial class. Ralph nodded when I'd understood a point and Eric could move on to the next one.

"I don't have anybody on the outside," I said.

"Then your person, when they come to visit, passes it over to you in the visiting room. You're going to have to swallow it, because

22

that's the only way you can get it past the body check outside the visiting room."

"Then the next day," Ralph interrupted, "you're the goose that lays the golden egg."

The phrase pleased Ralph. He couldn't resist a glance to see how Eric appreciated it, though he must have heard it before.

"I don't want to get involved in drugs," I said.

"You have to give a little, to get a little. We want you to do this for us," Eric said.

I started to walk away, but Ralph caught hold of my neck from behind and tossed me back onto the tier. He had my head wedged against the bottom of the rail and his foot on my throat. Eric bent over to look at me upside down. I couldn't breathe.

"I want the name of the person who's going to bring the stuff in."

I could have struggled. I could have clawed at Ralph's leg. But I was afraid if he pressed any harder something in my throat would break. Ralph loosened the pressure at the moment I felt myself starting to pass out.

"Give us a name," Eric said. I saw him glance down the tier, but I could tell from his expression that I couldn't expect any help.

I had to work to get the words out. "No visitors."

"Everybody's got somebody," Ralph said.

"I don't have anybody."

"Just give me a name you'd bet your life on."

"After what I did, I don't have anybody."

"What about your mom? Or your dad?" Ralph suggested.

"They're dead."

"Brothers and sisters?"

"Don't have any."

"Listen, Danny," Ralph said. He took his foot off my neck and crouched beside me. He might have been my high school football coach. "You got to come up with a name. Otherwise . . . bad things happen. You already know that."

The next day I had a letter from my sister. I hadn't seen her for two years. She hadn't even come to the trial. She wrote to say she'd stand by me. She'd found God. She'd come to visit me.

23

I don't know why she wrote to me now. I wrote and told her she was to think of me as dead.

A hunted animal can run away. In prison you can only circle. There are no places to hide, because that's the way prisons are built. Every minute of every day, they know where you are. I kept away from the showers and tried to stay on the flat in view of the officer as much as possible, but I knew it was only a matter of time.

You didn't know who it would be. The job wasn't important enough for Ralph to take care of himself. Enforcing discipline on a nobody like me would have lowered his status. He'd send someone who couldn't pay his debts, somebody under the same kind of threat as I was and running just as scared. For that person, too, it was a matter of survival. Him or me.

I lived in terror for three days. I was alone. I trusted no one. I thought anyone who started a conversation was going to hit me up for sex or simply hit me. After lock-down at ten o'clock was the only time of safety. But at night I couldn't sleep for thinking about the next day. The day had its trouble spots, times and places where I could be ambushed, or shanked in the midst of a crowd, or out in the open where no officer could see. At night, I lay awake trying to figure out how I was going to get past each trouble spot.

At chow hall the officers stood against the back wall and looked on while the inmates went at their food, too far away to intervene if a fight started or even to notice someone passing with his tray in one hand while the other put a shank into the back of an inmate hunched over his corn flakes. In the metal shop men moved around. People you'd never seen before came by on some errand or other; the place was full of dead ends, blind spots, and dark corners. Then there were the showers, which had to be avoided at all costs. The officers never went there. A professional courtesy. That was where men soaped up and got it on in the steam. It was a place where you could be tortured for an hour without anyone noticing. Ralph disappeared in the mists of the showers. It was his natural habitat. He'd turn up the steam till it was impossible to see more than two feet in front, and sit for hours after a session in the weight room. The hiss of water forced through nozzles and the splash of the jet on the tiles hid sound. No one talked about the showers.

24

It was in the afternoon, in the exercise yard, that they got me. Some guys were throwing a football about. Not a game really, just tossing the ball from one to the other. Sometimes, if one of them felt energetic, he'd run, and the man throwing would lead him a bit. I was watching, standing alone, feeling very conspicuous. I knew I was visible to the guard in the tower. One of the guys said, "Hey!" and threw the ball to me, so I caught it. It seemed harmless enough. In fact, I was childishly grateful to be allowed to join in.

I threw the ball back. It arced in a tight spiral to the man farthest from me, and I felt good that I hadn't lost my touch. They tossed it back and forth among themselves, keeping it from me, building a hunger in me for the ball; then the same guy threw it to me again. I had to move a bit to one side to catch it. I threw it back, the same tight spiral. I felt, seeing that, that they'd let me more into the game. And they did. The ball came back to me more quickly this time, but badly thrown, and I had to run hard to catch it. My guard was down. I was calling to them, pointing, "Hey, over here!" but the passes all seemed to be slightly off, in a different direction. I wasn't suspicious. I didn't stop to wonder whether I was being maneuvered into position. From their point of view, I must have looked eager, easy.

He threw the ball again. I was running backward and to the right, with my hands up ready to catch the ball. I was timing my jump. I thought this new man who was coming from the side, who hadn't been part of the game, was going for the ball, too, and I wasn't going to let him get it. I'd been a wide receiver in high school—if he wanted to take a shot at it, I didn't mind the competition. I said to myself, "No, this one's mine." I was showing off a little, I guess.

But he didn't have his hands up for the ball. He had his hands down, and it wasn't until the very last minute, as I committed myself to the jump, that I saw his hand come out of his shirt with the shank. I turned as he tried to stick me in the belly, and he lunged past me, ripping my shirt.

I came down to earth. Time seemed suspended. We were moving in slow motion. The ball passed over us. My feet landed on the concrete. He was regaining his balance, centering his body for another thrust. I was trying to get my hands down, like in one of those nightmares where you have to run but can't move. I saw his elbow come back for a second shot, and I tried to get my right hand down first. The shank came forward to slash at my face, and I couldn't move my feet even though I knew I had to, because they'd just touched down and there was no bounce in them. I got my hand up and blocked the shank, batting it away from my face, and then I felt the bounce come into my feet and I kicked him in the knee and he went down. We were back in normal time. I could pick my shot. I kicked him as hard as I could in the middle of his face. Nothing personal, simply survival. Someone hooked me from behind and shoved me away before I could do anything more to him.

Two officers took me to the infirmary. I hadn't felt the cut on my hand. It wasn't until we were in the main corridor that I saw a lot of blood had spilled down the front of my pants. When I opened my hand, I saw the skin was opened up across the palm.

A nurse came to the door when we rang the bell on Medical. The sergeant swung open the door and she came forward to us.

"Let me see," she said, and took my hand in both her own. "I'm the nurse. My name's Carol Ambrosino."

I knew then that she was as new as I was, because staff in prisons don't want you to have their names anymore than they want you to possess a piece of their clothing or to know where they live.

"The doctor's going to have to suture this," she said.

We went with her to a room that said "Treatment" on the door, and she had me set out my arm under a lamp. After a while she came back with a doctor. He looked at my hand, but he never looked at me.

"They dip their shanks in urine before they use them," the doctor told the nurse. "They believe it poisons the wound." He laughed. He was pulling up something into a syringe. "If they knew any physiology they'd have known that normal urine is practically sterile!"

The doctor talked all the time the nurse was getting things ready for him. He seemed to like using her name. Every opportunity he got, he'd add "Carol" to what he'd said. He talked to her about the inmates as if she was a lady from a cruise ship who'd helicoptered ashore to look at the natives. She dipped a cotton ball in some antiseptic and squeezed it out.

26

"This is going to hurt a bit," she said.

I didn't think she'd look at my face, but she did.

"They make these things out of anything. You'd be amazed how ingenious they are," the doctor said. "They're not unintelligent, some of them. Just watch out you don't underrate them, Carol. They'll take advantage if you do."

She looked to see if I was some kind of aborigine, and our eyes met. The doctor prattled on. Carol was looking into my eyes to see what kind of thing I was. I smiled at her, and she looked away.

At first, she cleaned up the palm of my hand well away from the damage. I think she was apprehensive about how I might react when she touched me with the antiseptic and it stung deep into the cut. She dabbed firmly at the edges and let the antiseptic flow into the wound and looked into my face again. She was curious, I could tell. Face-to-face with a murderer. "He was as close to me then as I am to you now." Dinner-table talk. Did she think she was looking into the eyes of the tiger? Some rough beast. I let her look into me. I'd kept my eyes down the whole time I'd been in Denning, and now I raised them to her.

Baruk was the officer leaning against the wall, playing with the toothpick between his lips, taking it all in. He looked lazy, but that was his style. He watched everything, except the doctor. Everyone wanted the doctor to shut up, but we couldn't say anything to him, least of all me.

"They sharpen up the aerials from their TV sets, or the knob that changes the channels."

Carol flushed out the cut and dried off my hand. The doctor had me make a fist.

"He's lucky. The tendons are intact."

He injected some anesthetic into my hand, but he was in a hurry and didn't wait for it to work. I felt the pain moving away from me. The thing I was becoming inhabited my body, and looked on with indifference to what was being done to it.

When he'd finished putting in the stitches, he sat back to look at his handiwork. Then, without speaking to me, he got up and walked out of the room, leaving Carol to put the dressing on. Baruk nudged himself off the wall then. He nodded at my hand.

"You want to go to Segregation?" he asked.

27

I'd only been in Denning two weeks, but I knew enough to know that a lifer couldn't go into protective custody with the child killers, the skinners, and the rats. Once you'd been in Segregation no one would ever trust you. And sooner or later, on someone's whim, or because of an administrative mistake, you'd be moved back into general population.

"I'll put in a request, if you want," Baruk said. "If you request it, chances are you'll get it."

The nurse was taping up the dressing on my hand. In front of her, Baruk might as well have asked me, "Do you want to be a coward?"

"Forget it," I said. "I don't want it."

"You're going to the maxes, then," he said.

He waited for me to protest, but I didn't know enough about the maximum units to argue.

"He assaulted you, sure. But you didn't have to kick him in the head." He waited again. Then he shrugged at Carol. "So you're going to have to do some time on Max One. You play your cards right, you could be out of there and back on the minimums in a couple of weeks."

The maxes were a world apart. People thought of them as the outer circle of Hell, only one step from J Block and the blue rooms. But when Baruk told me I was going there, I was glad, because it took me beyond the reach of Ralph Mandell.

There's a lot of talk about victims nowadays. A lot of your reports are about people who, through no fault of their own, have had something terrible happen to them. I'm not going to pretend to you that I'm a good person. I couldn't have survived four years in prison being a good person. I've seen too much and I've done too much to leave me with a conscience that's entirely clear. In prison you have to turn away from things you see to get along. You're forced into situations where it comes down to you or the other guy. But I'm not a bad person, either. Whatever I've done, I've had to do in order to survive. I'm no worse than an animal living in the wild that has to kill for food. We don't condemn it for that.

I'm not making excuses. I'm not looking for vindication. I don't expect anyone, hearing this, to start up a collection to pay for my appeal. It's too late for that. All I want is for someone to understand what I've gone through in order to keep my spirit alive.

The hostage has not been harmed. Nor will she be. I swear this on my mother's grave.

TWO

D ear Sandy:

Yes, I'm still "at large." When you used the phrase in your report tonight, how romantic you made it sound! But it's not much of a life, really: moving from place to place every day, each time in another car, everything up in the air, temporary. It's prison of a different kind. The food isn't much better. I can't say much more about it, for obvious reasons.

It gave me a lot of satisfaction to hear you read my letter on your program. I know you had to let the state police see it before you put it on the air. I accept that. But I'm disappointed by what was left out—the parts you referred to as "thinly veiled appeals for sympathy." I'm not appealing for anything! I thought I made that clear. Not sympathy, not pity, not vindication, not a pardon. Just plain, vanilla understanding. I'm not asking you to take sides. You don't have to take a side to understand.

I did not lie about the old woman at the hospital. In my letter, I

30

put everything down as it was told to me. What else was I going to say? Believe me, I was more surprised than anybody when they told me I had to go to a hospital to see my mother for the last time.

My mother's been dead ten years! She left my father and my sister and me when I was a kid. My mother went her own way. Even when she still lived in the house with us, she lived within her own life. She didn't notice much. It was hard to get her attention. She hummed a song to herself as she rinsed dishes in the sink, her eyes on some far off place, and when I spoke to her she seemed to turn to me in a startle. A beautiful woman. I hardly remember her.

Who the old lady was in the bed in the Intensive Care Unit, I have no idea. She came from a nursing home and had no family, as you say. That woman was in no way harmed by what happened around her and passed on simply because it was her time to go. She was unconscious throughout the incident, and as far as I am aware didn't come out of her coma even when the gun went off. You complain about my pleas for sympathy, but your hinting that I am somehow responsible for that old woman's death is a low blow, Sandy!

So Officer Fairburn died. I am genuinely sorry. I never really knew him until that day. A rookie. Perhaps, if they'd had someone more experienced on the detail, someone who'd been in the job long enough not to care so much about doing it right, he'd still be alive today. The film you showed of the funeral was very affecting and brought home how precious life is. A hero's burial, with brother officers at graveside. He deserved that. I know this makes me sound like a hypocrite. His wife looked so young. I can only hope that in time she'll get over it and be able to love again. And the little boy.

You are dead wrong about Janie. The idea that I killed my wife because she was having an affair is sick. That was the DA's line at the trial, and frankly you've gone way down in my estimation by repeating the story. I loved her. The last thing in the world I would have done was to take Janie's life because of an emotion as trivial as jealousy. I cherished her. I wanted her to live forever. But she was a proud woman, and she did not want to endure the indignity of dying from AIDS.

The reason there was no proof was that the state medical

31

examiner never thought to save a sample of Janie's blood to test for the HIV virus. I never said anything about it because I was too distraught and wasn't speaking to anyone about anything, even my own attorney. I didn't trust anybody, for good reason as it turned out. I have never lived down that aborted insanity plea.

The reason I know Janie was HIV-positive is that she told me. We discussed the whole situation, and that was good enough for me. Why, then, couldn't the defense locate the lab where her test was done, you ask? Because it's all highly confidential. They won't break the code. What were we going to do—subpoena every hospital and blood-testing lab in New England? Because Janie never told me where she'd had the test done. I never asked her. I trusted her. If she told me she was HIV-positive, then as far as I was concerned she was HIV-positive and we were going to deal with it the best way we knew how. I helped her exit this life. That's how much I loved her. Is that really so hard to understand?

I have been paying the price of that love every day for the last four years. I don't believe I belong behind bars for what I did, but there it is. Feeling the way I do, you can't blame me for trying to escape. If you could understand what I faced in Denning, I think you'd agree that any other man would have done what I did, if he could. And to understand what I faced in Denning, you have to understand Max One.

Max One is a box built to contain men, with a gallery of mirrored observation glass facing three tiers of cells. The front walls of these cells have bars instead of doors, so that at any given time, any action can be seen. The space is intensely psychological. Everybody keeps track of movement around them. You can't walk the few yards across the flat from one side to the other without it having significance. It's as impossible to avoid implications on Max One as it is to avoid ripples in water.

It's an enclosed space in the most profound sense. Inmates on Max One don't go anywhere. They have only themselves to deal with. Everything anyone does affects everybody. Actions ricochet and come at you from new and unexpected directions. It's such a dangerous place that the intention behind any movement has to be understood at once, before it's too late. A man rises slowly from the picnic table in the middle of the flat; an inmate stretches, turns as he stretches to glance at the first man; the others watch to see if there is a connection between the two; they look lazily around to see who has noticed. All action is reflected endlessly, mirrors reflecting reflected images until the original image is lost. All this in the midst of endless noise, all movement occurring at speed.

They are suspicious, defiant, hard men on the maxes. They are troublemakers who must be segregated from the inmates who only want to do their time. They aren't allowed the privilege of work. They can't go to the chow hall to eat. They're not allowed in the exercise yard. They go to the gym a couple of times a week when the general population isn't there. They can go to the law library. If they have to, they go to counseling. That's it. All they have is each other.

Baruk signed me off to the sergeant on duty. Garbage had been tossed all over the floor. It looked like a pen at a zoo where more evolved beings could view specimens of the human race: the Human House. There were piles of candy wrappers and milk cartons accumulated in corners, and, randomly on the flat, Styrofoam food containers that inmates on the upper tiers had tossed over the railings with leftovers still in them. It was hard to tell what some of the mounds were. They'd changed color, or they had fungus growing on them. On the left-hand wall, they'd thrown feces, which had stuck to the glass of the observation gallery. Even to notice the smell would have been to lose status.

Sullen men twisted around to see who I was. They stared with a dispassion that showed no possibility of mercy, following me with their eyes across the flat.

Sergeant Lombardi showed me the cell I'd been assigned. It was obvious to him I didn't belong there.

"Look," he said, "do your time and get back to the minimums. Don't get mixed up in what goes on here."

"I won't."

"If you want to volunteer for a job, I'll see what I can do to get you back quicker."

"I don't want to go back to A-six," I told him. As if I was in any position to bargain.

Lombardi nodded sarcastically. "You clean this place up, I'll see what I can do."

33

He gave me a broom. There were no instructions, or hours of work, or expectations. I pushed the broom with my good hand, using it like a snowplow to gather the garbage together. The inmates jeered. Some of them threw trash from the upper tiers onto the area I'd cleared. I didn't care. The work kept me busy and I was always in view.

For a week, I endured the fear and harassment. I was running scared every waking moment, but I didn't get hurt. I would do anything not to get hurt, not to get killed, even though my life was meaningless. The other inmates despised me because I worked. They spat on me from the upper tiers. I made it my mission to get the block clean, and they delighted in thwarting me. I told myself I wanted to accomplish something beyond merely staying alive, but in reality I was only distracting myself from the fear of being killed.

I kept four feet between another inmate and myself and only went into the showers when Randy did. Randy was confined to a wheelchair, a casualty of the Denning drug wars. His nastiness was more than simple human nature, and I think it went with the head injury that had paralyzed him. Handicapped though Randy was, no one messed with him. It may have been a perverse and desperate bravery that steeled him to go after big men who stood securely on their own two feet, but the truth is more likely that Randy didn't appreciate what he was up against. The only concession the prison made to his handicap was that the officers would go into the showers with him to prevent the other inmates from stealing the wheels off his wheelchair so that they could use the spokes to make weapons. So while a stream of brain-damaged macho poured out of him, keeping the officers busy, I had some precious moments of security.

I don't know if you can imagine hiding out in a bathroom while a brain-damaged man yells obscenities, without a friend, without anyone you can count on, knowing that there isn't a single person in the world who gives a damn if you live or will miss you if you die. And it stretches on for the rest of your life. I'll admit, I came close to suicide during one of those moments of safety. I felt the prick of the urine that some one had thrown on me earlier that morning drying on my back, and I think that was what tipped the balance between killing myself and killing someone else. The anger had been there all along. It made the fear worse, because I knew how close I was to rebelling against Ralph and Nando, an act of suicide in either case. And in a sense, during that moment of peace, sitting fully clothed on the lavatory, sensing the salty itch of urine in my skin, I did kill something of myself. I let myself go. I let the humanity float away. I felt suddenly stronger, because I didn't care about myself anymore.

Nando ruled Max One. To look at him, you wouldn't think Nando was the most dangerous man in Denning. He was a small Hispanic man of about forty, with a head that was bald and smooth and brown, like the mahogany ball at the bottom of the banisters in my grandparents' home. He didn't strut. He was polite, more or less. He didn't shout. He didn't need to. I rarely heard him swear. He wasn't distracted by the rhetorical flourishes of violence. There was a quickness and a directness about him, like a piranha, darting in and burrowing with its tiny razor teeth into the entrance to one of your body cavities, not letting up till it found its way to your liver or whatever place it had set as its destination. His will was so strong that it overcame any centrifugal force, the weakening tendency to reach out to others. Nando was sufficient unto himself, or so he seemed.

Every evening at dinner, Nando ate my dessert, and I wanted to kill him.

There wasn't much to break up the day on Max One. The arrival of the chow wagon was the big event, and by five-thirty most of the men on Max One had come down to the flat and were standing around waiting for the wagon to arrive.

The wagon was late, and the men were hungry and bad-tempered when it stopped outside in the corridor and the officer unlocked the gate for the workers to wheel it in. Immediately there was scuffling for position. The officer opened up the cart and told people to line up, but the smell of the food made them restless. Sno-Cone, with his hair tied up like a woman's, his arms and eyebrows shaved, slid between jostling bodies. Randy barked shins and ran over men's feet, swearing left and right all the while, to get to the front of the line.

Nando wasn't part of the crowd. He waited, leaning over the

railings on the third tier, and surveyed the scene: a little Napoleon of crime making his battle plans.

Dinner that night was baloney sandwiches and baked beans, with chocolate pudding for dessert, a big favorite. It wasn't until the men had more or less formed themselves into a line that Nando ambled down the stairs and took his place at the front. No one thought to question his right to do this. It was routine. Next came an enormous black man named Bentley. Randy jammed himself in fairly high in the pecking order. Sno-Cone insinuated himself close to the front, too. I was last in line.

You'd think one baloney sandwich is pretty much like another. But Nando had to look over the whole pile, even turning back the top slice on a couple before he could decide which was the one for him. He looked at the puddle of beans on his plate and asked the officer for more. Then he casually placed two chocolate puddings on his tray.

Sergeant Lombardi said, "There's one chocolate pudding for each man." He looked to Bentley. "You giving him yours?"

"Hell, no," Bentley said.

Nando jerked his head toward the back of the line. "He's giving me his."

The officer looked to me. Nando was moving off with his tray.

All I had to do was nod. It would have been enough simply to look away. But I wanted that container of chocolate pudding. I wasn't looking ahead. I didn't measure myself against Nando and calculate my best shot. I didn't care what it cost. I shook my head. I wasn't scared anymore. I was free to kill for a container of chocolate pudding.

The officer looked at me hard, as if I had made a mistake and needed an opportunity to change my mind.

"Hey, Rodriguez," he called to Nando.

Nando turned, but didn't come back to the chow wagon.

"He wants it," Lombardi said.

"So?" Nando asked. He didn't look at me. "He can have it tomorrow morning." He rubbed his stomach. "I'll give it to him first thing."

The men in the line thought this was funny.

The officer looked at me again. I saw him swallow. I did nothing. Nando walked toward the tables as if none of this concerned him.

"Put it back, Nando," he said quietly. He was making a concession, conferring status on Nando by calling him by his first name.

Nando sat at the table in the middle of the flat. He was adjusting the things on his tray and didn't look up. Everything in its proper place.

"I said, put the pudding back, Rodriguez," the sergeant said, more loudly, with snap in his voice.

Nando went straight to the dessert. He finished off the first container of chocolate pudding quickly. He dabbed it into his mouth like a cat, businesslike and methodical to the last smear around the bottom rim of the container. He held the spoon and twisted the container around in his hand. We waited and watched. Some of the men were smiling.

"I'm giving you a direct order, Rodriguez." The officer looked up at the gallery behind him. He had to be praying his buddy up there was paying attention. "Put the pudding back on the cart."

It was inevitable, what was going to happen next. Looking back, I can see now that at that moment I was entering a kind of funnel where destiny narrows and I would go forever down this road and not one of a thousand others.

Nando picked up the second pudding and ate it tenderly, as though he loved it. He took a scoop and looked at it all the way to his lips. Then he twisted the spoon around so that it came face down on his tongue and stared off dreamily into space as he pulled the spoon slowly down and out of his mouth.

"Hey, let's move this line," said Randy in his wheelchair. "Come on. Serve it up."

"That's it," Lombardi said. "I'm writing you up."

Nando exploded. I have never seen a man get so angry so fast. One moment he was spooning chocolate pudding into his mouth, the next he was on his feet hurling the container with all his strength. Lombardi jumped aside and the plastic container cracked on the side of the chow wagon.

37

"You tell us, 'Clean up your act, we'll move you to the mini-mums,'" Nando yelled. "You want us to kowtow to you—fuck it! We do everything you say, we're all set—and you jerk it away!"

"I'm warning you, Rodriguez," Lombardi said, but it was way too late for threats to have any effect.

Nando strode across the flat. He got right in the officer's face. "You goin' to write me up?" The officer took a step back, but Nando came after him. "The hell you are!" I thought he would hit him.

"Step back."

"I'm not stepping anywhere. You're going to write me up over a lousy, stinking chocolate pudding?"

"You heard what I said. Step back."

"I want to hear it from you."

Lombardi glanced aside to see what the rest of us were going to do. The men at the front of the line were helping themselves to sandwiches—three each. The guys in the middle were shoving to get to the food before it was all taken. Randy was shouting; someone had spilled baked beans on him. Bentley threw Sno-Cone out of the line and then dove in as though it was a football scrimmage. One of the trays with the chocolate puddings fell on the floor, and men got down on their hands and knees to go after the containers, which had landed bottom up. Randy rammed the crowd with his wheelchair to get in. An elbow caught a man in the face, and that's when someone threw the first punch.

Distant, running footsteps echoed in the corridor outside. The chow wagon went over. Someone was caught underneath it, screaming because hot water was spilling on him. I didn't help him. I didn't care. I watched Nando and waited for my chance.

The officers in the corridor all arrived at the door at once. Their faces were pressed against the bars, impatient to get at us, while one of them worked the lock. They burst through the doorway and ran onto the flat. Two of them took hold of Nando and pulled him back from the sergeant. Nando broke one arm free, and two others grabbed the arm and slowly bent it around and behind his back. They took hold of his legs, but he stayed upright, and they couldn't stop him arching and bucking with the whole strength of his body. With the arm that wasn't bent behind him he had hold of an officer about his neck. He wrenched himself one way, then the other.

He didn't care about keeping his balance. They lifted him off one of his feet. The cluster around Nando leaned slightly to the left. It shifted and lurched. Very slowly, with destabilizing jerks from its center, the press of bodies, like a single thing in slow spasm, twisted and toppled and fell. It loosened when it hit the ground. Nando worked a leg loose and was booting any parts of the guards he could make contact with. The rhythm of the pile changed to a series of staccato movements as the guards gave up attempts to secure his limbs and instead used their hands to punch into the center of the heap where Nando lay.

If the inmates hadn't been preoccupied with dinner, some of them would have pushed aside the two officers who faced them in front of the melee. I ran around them. I jumped onto the pile and hooked my arms around a guard's neck and pulled back until he came loose. I threw him aside and started on the next one. I caught hold of an arm that was pumping blows into the heap in a gap between a pair of legs, but the officer swung around and took me with him to the floor. I crawled back to the heap. I used my fists like hammers trying to get to Nando. Someone had me around the neck, but I didn't care. I was thrown to the ground. And then there were the black boots of the officers everywhere. Hands took hold of me and pinned me to the concrete so I couldn't move at all.

It wasn't till then that I realized I was yelling. I had my head back and let the sound pour out of me. I don't know what I was doing. I was lost. I was less than human, enraged beyond reason.

The block seemed full of officers. Some hoisted me to my feet. They held me captive in front of the lieutenant, who looked at me strangely.

"What's his name?" he asked. No one knew me. "What's your name?" he repeated.

I told him over and over.

He leaned closer, as if that was the only way he could make the angle to see into a dark corner of my head.

"Cody." The lieutenant jerked his thumb. "J Block," he said.

Darkness is not neutral. It is not nothing. It is not a simple absence, any more than silence is. I have never known such a cruel darkness. In J Block, they locked me in one of the blue rooms. The room was not dark in the sense that there was no light—the dim blue light in the wire cage high in the ceiling stayed on all the time. But after a few days, the unchanging, featureless surround began to fade. I have never known such harshness to the spirit.

A guard told me, "Once you get out of here, you're never going to come back."

I think that was their intention, but it's hard to tell what part a person plays in the greater scheme of things. They think they're doing one thing, and all the time they've been part of an entirely different process where their mistakes and missteps have been essential parts of the action. I believe there is a greater purpose to all things, and I cannot believe my suffering is meaningless. I had to go through J Block to get here.

The blue rooms contain nothing except a mattress on the floor and a steel toilet. There is a barred door, and outside that a steel door with an observation window. There is one hour a day in the exercise cage, fifteen feet long, ten feet wide, ten feet high.

J Block is solitary confinement. You can have no idea of the loneliness, Sandy. The blue room is to being alone what the North Pole is to winter. It's an absolute. Nothing moves but your thoughts. And you think and think and think until you're afraid you're going crazy. You want to sleep, but your mind has a life of its own. It won't stop. Your thoughts trickle through cracks and into pockets of memory you thought had been lost long ago. You pull yourself back, with more and more of an effort. After a while, your mind goes where it wants.

I let myself go, I admit it. After a few weeks, even the officers—and they have tough hombres stationed in J Block—were concerned about me.

"You ought to eat better. Keep up your strength, Cody."

Someone would say something like that to me in the morning, and I'd think about it for the rest of the day. It wasn't exactly thinking. More like an echo in my mind. Reverberations, far off, of thoughts. But not like an echo, either, because distortions would creep in. And it wasn't exactly the physical sound that was getting bent: Somehow the meaning got warped in the process. It took on nuances I couldn't quite catch, suggestions that might be important, and then again might not. I'd repeat the phrase in my head and strain to catch the other meaning before it fell away, but my mind wasn't fast enough.

I'd rub my face with my hands to stimulate the circulation, to get the feeling back that I was in the here and now. I sat on the floor and scooped water out of the toilet and let it run across my forehead and down the channels between the eyebrows and the nose. And when I pressed the water from my eyes, I felt how insubstantial the flesh was between my hands and skull. The skull was solid. It had substance and definition, while the face was little more than a surface that moved with the moment. I knew I had to stick with what was hard and enduring. I had to find the hard, enduring purpose beneath the appearance of things and press my hands to it.

One day, after breakfast, they came to my cell earlier than usual.

"Hands out, Cody," the officer said.

I put my hands through the slot in the bars ready for him to put the handcuffs on my wrists, but he said, "No, you're not going anywhere. Put your hands through the bars," so that, with one hand on either side of a bar, I was anchored.

"Someone to see you." He looked sideways, down the narrow corridor that ran in front of the cells, and nodded to someone I couldn't see. "All clear, Doc."

A little man edged in front of me. He had a goatee beard and watery eyes.

"I'm Dr. Goodman."

He was nervous. He talked in a soft voice and kept looking at my hands as though he couldn't decide how far I could reach if I decided to make a grab for him.

"What kind of doctor is that?" I asked him.

"I'm a psychiatrist," he said. He was looking straight into my eyes to see my reaction.

"What makes you think I need a psychiatrist?"

"I don't."

41

"Then what are you doing here?"

"To see if you do."

"Is that strictly logical, Doctor?"

"I think it is."

"I think one of us isn't making sense," I told him.

He smiled quickly. It looked like something he practiced. "Let's start again, shall we?" he suggested. "I'm Dr. Goodman, and you're Dan Cody."

I looked at him as though he was insane. "I already know who I am," I said.

He didn't try to be nice anymore. "Do you want to go to Haverford?" he asked. "It might be good for you for a while. Give you some time out. Get yourself together."

"I was there before."

"Yes. I know that."

"I was evaluated there before I went to trial. They said I'm not mental."

"It might help you get into a frame of mind so that you can do your time . . ." He held his hand out to indicate J Block and found himself looking around like a tourist. "More easily."

"I'm here for life. Life without parole." I could feel myself losing control.

"It doesn't have to be this hard, surely?"

"There's a reason for everything."

"A reason why you won't cooperate enough for them to let you out of the disciplinary unit?"

"If I'm here, there's a reason for it. I have to believe that."

"And what is the reason?"

"I don't know it yet. Maybe it's none of my business. All I know is that there is a reason."

"But it hasn't been made clear to you?"

"That's what I said."

"Not even a hint?"

"Not that I've noticed."

"No special sign?"

He must have seen in my eyes, as soon as he asked the question, that he'd gone too far.

"I'm not paranoid, if that's what you're asking."

42

After that, they left me alone for a long time.

Did I go a little crazy? Probably, yes. It happens to most people, eventually, in solitary confinement. It doesn't matter how tough you are, or how stable. You may think you're too well integrated, that you're too strong, but you can't say it wouldn't happen to you until you've been there.

I didn't take care of myself. I spent a lot of time trying to understand why this was happening to me. I began to talk to myself to pass the time, arguing back and forth. I got very involved in this, although it was always under my control. I suppose that last part isn't entirely true.

I had conversations with people from my past. I talked to Janie, explaining things to her, trying to get her to imagine how it might have been if things had gone differently. I couldn't get these conversations to turn out right. There were times I hardly recognized her. Her voice sounded different, as if some harpy or avenging angel were impersonating her. She wouldn't listen. She kept on talking, accusing, in this barking voice. I tried to shut my ears to her, but she was inside my head, of course, and there was nowhere I could escape to. Solitary can do that to a man, anyone, in blue, unreal light.

I think that was when I began to bang my head against the wall. I didn't notice I was doing it until a guard pointed out I had blood running down the side of my face. I put my hand to the wetness I had thought was sweat, and when I tasted my fingers there was the rusty taste of blood on my tongue.

"You're definitely losing it, Cody," he said shaking his head as though I'd disappointed him. "You want to go to Haverford?"

"No," I said.

"You look like you're ready."

He went off down the corridor, and later that day I heard more than one pair of footsteps coming in my direction.

"Put your hands through the bars," he told me.

I could tell there was someone else there, but they wouldn't step forward until I was secured.

"Put your head forward," he told me after I was anchored to the bar, and I put my head up against the bars so that my nose and almost my eyes stuck through.

43

I must have looked like an old-fashioned convict from Devil's Island, with my hair grown long and a scrubby beard covering most of my face. I don't know how bad I smelled, because I lived with myself day after day and couldn't notice it anymore. I was hanging my head in a dazed sort of way, and I looked up because I had this sense of whiteness and I smelled scented bath soap.

I'm trying to communicate how strongly she affected me. To say it was the nurse, Carol, isn't entirely correct. The light was behind her, and I couldn't make her out. She wasn't so much a person as a figure of loveliness in the J Block filth. I thought she was a hallucination. Even though my eyes stayed open, I hadn't used them in days.

She was dressed in white. I was dazzled. She wore a white dress and white stockings and white shoes with thick soles so that she moved without a sound, like an apparition. Her hair was black. It glistened. It was pulled tight back from her face and gathered behind her head, so that this part of her was sleek and sculpted and sharply defined. Her lips were red with a vermilion lipstick. White and floating. Black and tight. Hypnotic red.

I couldn't get my eyes to focus. I couldn't see her face. She was a being from another world who smelled of bath oil or scented soap. Her life was charmed. I could never understand her, her cleanliness and flavor.

When she spoke to me I saw only the pursing and stretching of her lustrous red lips, and the sound passed me by.

"I want you to put your head forward."

I was fascinated by the way in which the pigment of the lipstick lay thicker in the tiny clefts of the skin on "want," then thinned to the point of transparency when I tilted my head the way she wanted: "There."

The words could have been notes on a piano. I heard them as pure sounds, without meaning. The animal part of my brain knew what she wanted.

"Yes," Carol said. "Like that. Now turn a bit, so I can see the side."

I thought she would bring me to life. I thought when she touched me I would feel a warm, filling wave spread through my body. I was afraid her influence would take possession of me. I was afraid

44

I would let it. All my sensation was focused on the side of my head. When she touched me, I flinched. But she was wearing gloves, and I wasn't prepared for the chemical smell and the tacky surface of the material.

Carol was pressing along the eyebrow and the cheekbone, gently probing to see the damage. I held my head lowered for her, and took in the way her stance stretched out her legs. I heard her every breath. As one ended, I listened for the next soft sigh.

I was sucking the reality of her into my mind, like a man who has almost drowned coming up to the surface and sucking in air. I was greedy for every tiny aspect of her existence. I stored these sights and sounds in my memory. There was a small, sharp fold in her blouse—no more than an inch long—where her iron had nipped the fabric that morning, and she hadn't noticed to smooth it out. The clean, clear, sharp edge. The tiny, crisp shadow. I hoarded them in memory. I carried off such small scraps that no one could have noticed. But to me they were a feast. I gorged on the reality of her.

Sometimes reality is too strong. I was dazzled. I was looking into a floodlight and couldn't see in front of me. When for weeks everything had been floating in and out of my mind, when it had been insubstantial and untrustworthy, this real woman was precious beyond anything I could possess. I felt the world's hook catch inside me, the tug as it pulled me back inside it. I almost cried. And I was scared, too. I was like a child, awestruck, brimming with gratitude, surrounded by sensation too big for me to understand.

She asked, "When did you do this? This is old."

"I forget," I said. I felt foolish, not knowing something about myself. I was about to explain, "I did it when I was dead," but I knew it would sound crazy. "Maybe yesterday," I mumbled. "You lose track. Maybe two days ago."

"How long has he been here?" she asked the officer.

"A few months."

"It's too late for stitches. They won't help now."

"I'm OK."

"You can't go hitting your head on the wall," Carol said.

The tone of her voice made me look up. Her eyes had come

45

down from the cut on my head, and she was regarding me. You become suspicious of kindness, because you want it so badly. Nothing makes you more vulnerable in prison than a hunger. We can smell it a mile off. I looked away, but she looked on.

"You'll get brain damage," the officer said. "If you haven't got it already."

I looked up at Carol, and our eyes met. It was only for half a second, and she quickly looked away. You don't show kindness to inmates. "Please do not feed the animals." It only makes them hungry. But I fed on that moment for months to come.

I think, until Carol came, I'd given up the desire to live. I'd lost my will. I existed. I drifted in and out. I'd let go of my body and shrunk down to a speck behind the eyes. Very small and hard to find. I think I was becoming like one of those black holes in the universe that contract into themselves until eventually they disappear. In the blue light, I was about to go through and out the other side of myself into nothingness. But Carol brought me back.

I was in no hurry to go back to the Max. I didn't want to be hunted again. I thought of Nando waiting for me there. Nando would be transferred before me. He knew how to move through J Block quickly, and I wasn't even trying. I was uncooperative. They treated me like an animal. I think I acted like one. I was trying not to matter to myself. If you don't care what happens to you, there's nothing you can fear. I challenged the officers. Once they brought a fire hose and turned it on full blast so that I was pinned to the back wall of the cell. After a few minutes of fighting the brute force of the water, blinded and suffocating, I was so exhausted that I couldn't do anything but curl up on the concrete floor beside the toilet and pull myself in and became like a pebble in the sizzling torrent. Then they directed it to the rest of the cell and swirled out the filth I'd been living in, and it swept around my elbow and past my forehead and between my fingers to the grate.

Even when I wanted out, when I wanted to show the officers good behaviour, I'd slip into the old defiance, and that frightened me, because I thought I'd been putting it on. I discovered that what I'd become wasn't entirely under my control. Something inside me had hardened and set solid.

I began to go out to the exercise cage, which I'd refused for weeks. The daylight had a strange tinge to it. Some halogen street lamps, the kind you find in mall parking lots, have an orange tint; they shed light, but it's light of an eerie, defective kind. When I went into the exercise cage and looked up at the sky for the first time, I sensed something similar, that the outside world had changed while I'd been away, though I couldn't see what it was that was missing. Just that same effect of strangeness, or being underwater.

In the cage two over from where I was, someone was shooting baskets. When he turned to take a rebound, I saw that it was Nando. He must have seen me, too, but he didn't react and took several more shots at the basket. I thought, because of the changes I'd gone through, he hadn't recognized me. He bounced the ball, short and quick off his fingertips, as he stood with one foot forward waiting for the right moment to come to him, the right moment to make his shot. But he just went on bouncing the ball in front of him.

Then he turned to me. He seemed to stare at me for a long time, the basketball in his hands. Nando said, "Get back to Max One. You stay here too long, you'll lose your mind."

I started to say, "I know what you mean," but he ignored me and went back to shooting baskets.

He hadn't said, "Get back to Max One. You tried to kick the shit out of me while the officers were holding me down. I'm going to kill you." He was giving me advice. He was trying to help me. And I realized that, from the bottom of the pile, he'd misunderstood what I was doing: Nando believed I'd been coming to help him. After that, I went out to the exercise cages whenever my time came, but Nando was never there, and I found out he'd gone back to Max One.

Once I stopped struggling against every rule and check the prison put in front of me, it became possible for Administration to move me, too. It's hard for people like yourself whose comfortable lives have never touched this level, who have never lived a life that has been stripped down to the basic core of existence, to realize how this animal existence can become as much a habit, can feel as natural, as going to the office.

They cut my hair and let me shave my beard before I left J Block. I don't know if I looked different, but I was a different man. Back on

Max One, the inmates treated me as if I had never been away. I was an initiate, and they accepted me—as much as anyone is accepted on the maxes. Lombardi handed me the broom, but I didn't want to work. I didn't want to be part of the inmates' criminal activity, either. That may sound funny, coming from someone who's been sentenced to life in prison, but I still thought of myself as an honest person. I have my own standards.

I'd barely arrived back on the tier before Sno-Cone came to the door of my cell and told me, "He wants you."

Walking along the tier, I sensed an observing presence behind the mirrored glass who looked for signs in every step I took. After months in the blue room, I wasn't accustomed to the space and light around me, and I felt transparent. Inmates lounging on their beds stared at me as I passed by. I had no business there except to see the boss. I wasn't sure what awaited me at the end of the tier, but there was lightness in my step. My fear had lifted, like a fog. I was resigned, but I wasn't going to throw my life away. I didn't matter much to myself, but I wouldn't be used. In the back of my mind, I didn't think that being alive was a permanent feature.

Nando was sitting on the bed. He wasn't reading or watching TV or working out. He was simply sitting, staring hard into the middle distance. This was a man whose mind was always working, looking for new angles and searching the old ones for flaws. I thought he hadn't heard me, though I should have known better. I shuffled my feet, but he gave no sign that he'd noticed me. He was drawn into himself, compact and dense like the uranium they make antitank slugs from.

I waited on the tier outside, feeling conspicuous, but not wanting to interrupt him. Finally, I said, "Did you want to see me, Nando?"

He waved for me to come in, a quick, irritable movement. He pointed for me to stand against the wall opposite him. Then he stared at me for a long time, and I wondered how much he could see. He didn't have much stuff in his cell. Other inmates had pinups on the walls and all kinds of electrical gadgets rigged from the one electrical socket, but Nando's cell was plain and uncluttered, like the inside of his head.

"I got a job for you."

48

I didn't know what to say. His eyes had me nailed to the wall. "What kind of job?"

"What the fuck has that got to do with it? You think this is an interview?"

"I don't know if I can do it."

"Next week you get a visitor."

"I don't have visitors."

"You do now." He looked at me hard. There was a flicker in the muscles on either side of his forehead. There was an intensity to him that went beyond business. "Next week you're getting a visit from your girlfriend. The one no one knows about. The one you killed your wife for."

"There's no one—" I started to say.

"I know that!" he hissed. He was holding back, with difficulty, from attacking me. "You're getting a visitor, because I set it up! Understand? You treat this lady with respect. OK? You don't take advantage of the situation." He was choking on the words. I saw him struggle with the shame of a mysterious confession. "She's my family. OK? You do what she says. OK?"

"OK."

"OK, get lost."

Two days later I saw a man murdered. The inmates on the maxes had a two-hour gym period twice a week. Everybody went, even Randy in his wheelchair, to get off the block, to spread out in another space. Nando shot baskets by himself at one end of the gym. There was a pickup game going; I tried to join in, but it was hard to follow. People changed sides whenever they felt like it, without letting anyone else know. No one passed the ball; instead, they just dove for the net, sometimes not even bothering to bounce the ball. Bentley did body checks on whomever he felt like; no one called him on it. I saw men glancing around when they should have been watching the ball. Looks passed from one man to another. The game went on, but no one kept score. Something else was happening on the court that I wasn't in on. Everyone was waiting, going through the motions.

I didn't see the sign. All at once there was a new excitement to the game. Everyone was around the net, jumping for rebounds, shoulder to shoulder. There was some scuffling. Everyone on the

49

court got into it. They were all in a tight group beneath the net. The ball came loose and rolled in my direction. I scooped it up and ran. No one challenged me. I came close to the crowd. Out of the corner of my eye, I could see it was starting to break up. Faces were turning outwards. I jumped and made my shot in midair. No hands came up to block it. It was a perfect trajectory. I watched it tip the metal rim and catch in the net. It dropped right through.

No one bothered to catch it. The guys were walking away, each one in a different direction. The ball hit the court loudly in the silence. People were walking quickly away from the net with their heads down. The ball bounced again. Then it caught at the edge of the puddle of sticky blood and rolled toward the inmate with his throat cut.

At the other end of the gym, Nando stood with the ball between his hands, looking over his shoulder. Then he bounced the ball in front of him a couple of times to get focused for his next shot.

The officers ran onto the court. They made telephone calls. More came and rounded us up and counted us off and marched us back to Max One. But they were on the outside. They moved at the edges. They saw the results, but they couldn't know what was producing them. They were watching TV with the sound turned off.

I didn't know who the inmate was. Another casualty of the drug wars. Nando was consolidating. He didn't allow freelancers. Ralph was doing the same on the minimums. If anybody wanted drugs in Denning, they had to buy through them. It was all about controlling the market. This is what I found myself part of.

The visiting room is a long space with artwork by the inmates on the walls and some model ships and airplanes in a glass case. It's divided down the middle by a long table. Visitors enter the room on one side and inmates on the other. It's a wide table, so you don't get very close, and a wooden partition runs down the center to the floor to prevent people having sex underneath it. The rules say you can't touch, but most people reached across to hold hands. Usually they were allowed a good-bye kiss.

When the officer brought me into the room, I could see several visitors sitting patiently in front of empty chairs, waiting for guards to bring the inmate.

"OK, Cody. Go ahead," the officer said.

I looked down the line. Nando had said she was family, but he was dark, and I couldn't see anyone who looked like him. Of the empty seats, the closest one was opposite a Hispanic woman with hair dyed a kind of blond who looked about forty. When I came to her she looked up at me and smiled. I put my hand on the back of the chair. I'd even started to pull it out.

Someone down the table called out, "Hey, you, comedian!"

She was standing up, hands on hips, head to one side in a humorous pose. She was gorgeous, with big, dark eyes and fine features and a wide mouth with full lips that curled with all sorts of suggestions I couldn't begin to understand. I thought she was maybe twenty-seven or twenty-eight, but as I came closer, I saw she was older, in her early thirties.

"You forget what I look like, already?" she asked.

She talked loudly. She wanted people to hear. The men were looking at her, even the guards. When she sat down, all eyes followed her tight butt as it came in to land on the chair. She knew this, but she made it look as though it didn't matter to her one way or another. She had to motion with her hand for me to sit down.

"So." She put her head on one side again to look at me, to remind herself, as it were, of my face. "So Danny, how you been?"

I was bewildered for a moment. Part of me was still in J Block. The strange blue light was in my brain, and I was caught between realities, falling between them. No one ever called me "Danny."

"Good," I said. "I've been good."

She smiled at me and rolled her shoulders. "Aren't you going to ask me how I've been? It's been so long without you!" She pouted her lips as if she was taking me in.

"How are you . . ."

"Vera."

"How are you, Vera?"

"Not so bad."

She was losing interest quickly. Her eyes moved to one side, then the other. She tossed her head back and shook her hair loose. All the time she was watching, seeing who paid attention to us.

"Talk to me, Danny," she said. "You like basketball? Talk to me about basketball."

51

"I don't know much about it, really."

She was losing patience with me. "Look. I don't give a damn what we talk about. Just talk. OK? Make like you're having a conversation with your girlfriend. Tell me what you do all day— No, I don't want to know."

"I can tell you how—"

"No names!" She sighed in an irritated sort of way. "You're not from around here, are you?" I could tell she thought I was an idiot.

"I traveled a lot."

"Oh. What'd you do? Drive a truck?" She was examining her nails, figuring out which ones needed work. She didn't notice that I hadn't answered her question.

"You're very pretty," I told her.

Vera didn't even look up. "Oh, please!" she said.

She bent down to pick up her pocketbook from the floor. The guard at our end of the room took a step forward. Vera brought out a cardboard nail file and waggled it in the air for him to see. She held her pinkie straight out to the side. It was sexy and sarcastic at the same time.

Vera gave up the pretense of conversation and went to work on her fingers.

"Thumbs are ugly, don't you think?" she said without raising her head. "They don't look right. I think thumbs are the ugliest part of the body."

She looked up. She must have imagined she was talking to somebody else.

"You know," she said, "you wouldn't be so bad-looking if you was to fix yourself up a bit." She looked me over. "Get a haircut. Work out. Make something of yourself. You know?"

"I've been lifting weights," I told her. "I just started. I'm sore all over. I can feel every muscle in my body."

"What time is it?" she asked.

There was a big clock on the wall behind me that was in plain sight of Vera if she chose to raise her eyes.

"Almost two-thirty," I told her.

"Do you like French kisses?"

"Yes."

"That's good."

She stood up, and I started to get up, too.

"No," she said, "not you."

"I thought you were going."

"To the bathroom. You're ready for it?"

"Yes."

"When I get back, you're gonna swallow my tongue. The whole thing."

She wasn't gone long. She came back with a small, tight smile on her lips. She was wearing a short blue skirt and a white blouse. She looked almost professional. She might have worked as a receptionist. A dentist's office, maybe.

I stood up to meet her. She put the pocketbook down on the floor.

Overacting, she screwed up her face in an expression that said, "Sorry, got to go."

If anyone cared to notice, her hands were in plain sight on the tabletop, supporting her upper body as she leaned far across to kiss me. But all eyes in the room were on that tight body of hers, arched forward, the edge of the table at her crotch, her feet about to slide out from under her, the navy blue skirt stretched taut across her buttocks.

I wasn't ready for what was coming. Her lips pressed against mine. I was distracted by the smell of her makeup, her closeness. She was too quick. Her tongue snaked between my lips. It was an intelligent thing. I opened my mouth to it as she pressed her face against mine as if in passion. She was working the wad forward to the front of her mouth; then her tongue caught hold of it and pushed it into my mouth. It was huge. Her tongue pushed it deep into my mouth, and I thought I would choke. She felt my panic. I was drowning. I opened my eyes to find hers, cold and threatening, looking into mine.

I maneuvered the condom into the back of my mouth and swallowed hard at the moment she took her lips away.

"You always do this!" Her voice was raised, looking around, attracting attention to herself.

The package stuck at the back of my throat. I stifled a cough.

53

I thought I would suffocate. I bent over the table, trying to draw breath.

"Just when it's time for me to go, you get emotional!"

A spasm I couldn't control was starting deep in my body, and I knew I was going to retch. I swallowed hard against it, forcing the wad down against all the survival reflexes my body threw against it. I swallowed over and over, with my mouth suddenly full of saliva and my eyes tearing.

"Isn't that like men?" Vera was talking to the other visitors.

I tried to speak, to play along with her script, but I couldn't get the words out.

"They've got nothing to say for the whole visit, and then, right when you've got to go, they get all choked up." She patted my hand. "You'll be all right. Don't think too much. You think too much, Danny. You know what I'm saying? Just do it one day at a time. And I'll see you in a couple of weeks."

I looked emotional. I blinked to clear the tears and kept my head down. Slowly, the urge to vomit came under control. I could feel the condom behind my breastbone slipping gradually down to my stomach. When I looked up, Vera had gone.

Back on the max, Nando was leaning on the rail on the top tier. He didn't even turn his head when I came onto the flat. He sent Ramon to speak to me.

"How did it go, man?" Ramon looked worried. "Come on, how did it go?" he asked impatiently. I think Ramon was more afraid of Nando than anybody. "You have a good visit?"

"Everything went great. Piece of cake. Except, I have this feeling of indigestion."

Ramon looked at my face for signs of poisoning from a ruptured condom. He put a hand on my arm to feel my skin.

"You're kidding," he suggested uncertainly. "You're just kidding, right?"

I felt giddy with success. "I fuckin' did it," I said.

Ramon turned and nodded to Nando.

"I don't know," Ramon said. "Maybe you should take some Maalox or something."

"Prune juice would be better," I said.

When the chow wagon came that evening, Ramon had me right up near the front of the line after him. It was chocolate pudding.

Nando jerked his head in my direction. "He's having mine," he told the officer.

It was payday, because of me. I was a hero. I was the movie star cavalryman who rode through the Indians to bring supplies to the fort. People I'd never seen before gave me high fives in the gym or nodded to me on the flat. I was the man.

Nando offered me drugs. He wanted to give me money. He sent Sno-Cone down to give me a blow job. I didn't want any part of it.

I did it again, two weeks later. This time the wad was even larger. Practice wasn't making the job easier. If anything, it was harder, because I was more anxious, and that seemed to tighten my throat.

Then, a few days before Vera's next visit was scheduled, Administration decided I no longer needed maximum security and moved me back to the minimums, back to Ralph and Eric, and Sergeant Baruk, who gave me a mop and a job.

Maybe Baruk was looking out for me, although as far as status went, the job of cleaning up the block was at the bottom of the barrel, something like being an untouchable in India. But it gave me safety. Almost everything I did, except for when I cleaned the shower room, was in an officer's line of sight.

I thought I was safe. I was out of J Block. I'd passed through Max One. I'd made up my mind I was going to make some kind of a life for myself in prison. Vera was right: I'd let myself go; I didn't care how I looked. But I started to pay attention to my appearance, if only to rediscover some basic self-respect. I began to work out in the weight room every day. I became something of a fanatic with the weights, but that was all right, because it reconnected me with my body, and in recentering me, it helped to bring me back from the blue room. All I wanted was to be left alone. If I had just been left alone, I wouldn't be the subject of this manhunt that's playing out on TV.

One day while I was sweeping on the flat I heard something

drop behind me on the floor I'd cleaned. It was a soft sound, at the edge of perception, and when I looked around I saw an empty cigarette pack. Above, Eric looked down at me from the third tier. He waved for me to come up.

Ralph was leaning against the rail. Eric went inside the cell. As he went by, he took hold of my shirt and pulled me with him.

"I don't want to get involved," I told Ralph. "I just want to do my time."

"Your time is forever, Mr. Cody," said Eric behind me.

Ralph stretched out over the rail, looked down, waved to someone on the flat, always in view of the officer at the desk below. "All this homemaker stuff with the broom," he said, "you're on your way to being Inmate of the Year."

"Whatever it is, I don't want any part of it."

"We've been saving you. You're our ace in the hole."

"You are part of it," Eric said. "What you did for Nando, you do for Ralph."

Ralph said, "Tomorrow, you're going to have a visitor."

"Same setup," Eric said.

"Vera," Ralph said. "Very nice, I hear."

"That was with Nando," I told them.

"It's still with Nando. We're, like, his agents."

"Like a collection agency," Ralph said.

He stepped forward and put his hand on my neck. He let his arm hang with his hand hooked around the back of my neck, and I felt the weight of it.

"I can't keep doing it," I told him.

"Sure you can."

"It doesn't go down right. Sometime it's going to burst inside me."

"You should be so lucky," Ralph said.

The next day, when Baruk read out the list of inmates who had visitors, I stepped forward when he called my name, and when I caught sight of Vera in the visiting room, I was glad to see her in spite of myself. She was moody and scarcely glanced up when I took my seat. When I tried to make conversation, she pretended I wasn't sitting in front of her. But I wanted to engage her. I thought she'd be interested in hearing about Nando. I started to tell her about the intense concentration he brought to everything he did, even shooting baskets in the gym.

"What's the time?" she asked suddenly, in the middle of what I was saying.

"I can't do this," I said.

"I said, 'What time is it?' "

"I've got stomach trouble."

She looked at me as though I was an insect. "I'm going to the bathroom. You better be ready when I get back."

"Really," I told her. "Since last night. I can't keep anything down."

She didn't believe me. I knew no one would believe me, but I couldn't do it anymore. I was being dragged deeper and deeper into something evil.

"They really need this stuff," Vera hissed. She glanced left and right and leaned closer to me. "Don't you care about other people? What someone's going to go through because he can't get it? Withdrawal?"

"I can't help it. I'd do it if I could."

"What are you telling me?" she demanded.

"I won't do it."

"Are you fuckin' crazy out of your mind?"

"I guess."

I wanted Vera to understand, but I knew it was hopeless, trying to get her to see another point of view.

"I'm not doing it anymore," I told her. "I'm out. I don't care what happens."

She gave me a piercing look and shook her head at what she saw behind my eyes. Her lips were tight and unforgiving. "I don't think you're going to last long, Danny," she told me as she got up.

As she left, I had second thoughts. I got up and almost called out to her to come back. But it was too late, and I stood at the table with my hand out in a futile gesture as Vera went through the door and sealed my fate.

Then I really did start to have problems with my system. I

was afraid I'd lose control of my bowels during the walk back to the block.

Ralph was in the weight room. He lay on his back on the bench. He took deep breaths, preparing to press a bar loaded with about three hundred pounds, and he had just committed himself to the lift when he saw me come in.

"I don't feel good," I told him.

The bar had come quickly the first twelve inches off his chest and now slowed. Ralph couldn't do anything more than grunt between his teeth. His face was a dusky red, and veins swelled on his face, distorted with effort, as the load came to a stop only a few inches from full extension.

"I've been throwing up," I said. His eyes flicked over to me, then quickly back to the weights. "I didn't want to risk it."

Ralph's arms were trembling. He shook his head, denying the reality, enraged that the weights wouldn't obey. Very slowly, the weights started to slew sideways, like a skyscraper starting to collapse in slow motion.

"Fuck it!" Ralph said. He had to force the words out through muscles stretched taut.

Eric stepped up to take one side of the bar, but he'd sent Ralph's other helper away when I'd come in. Ralph's arms were shaking with exhaustion, and I watched fear come into his eyes as he fought the weights with all his will and still they descended slowly toward his face. At the last moment, just before his arms gave out, he glanced at me in a silent plea. I stepped up to take the other side with Eric.

Ralph sat up and turned away. He hung forward with his head between his knees, his huge body slack and defeated.

"You got the stuff or not?" he whispered.

"That's what he's saying," Eric told him. "It didn't go right."

Ralph turned and took hold of my arm. He was weak and his hand trembled.

"You haven't got it?" He couldn't believe it. "You have any idea how many people in the joint are counting on this?"

"I know."

"You are not going to be popular, Cody. When Nando hears this . . ."

Eric's eyes were locked onto me as his mind ticked off possibilities. Behind the glasses, his eyes seemed more remote than the rest of his face.

"How do we know he didn't pick the stuff up from Vera?" Eric asked Ralph.

The light flashed on his glasses as he turned from one of us to the other. One moment he was an opaque reflector, the next I felt caught in his lens.

"Ralph, what about the double-cross?" Eric urged.

Ralph glanced at me quickly. "He'd have to be crazy," he said. He looked worried.

"We can check it out with Nando," Eric said.

"And have him say we fucked up?"

"Not us. Cody. Cody fucked up. The guy Nando chose."

"We have to figure this out ourselves," Ralph said. He considered my stomach.

"At least Nando can tell us if Vera passed it off to him," Eric said.

"No."

"What if Nando doesn't believe it?" Eric asked. "What if he thinks we're trying to rip him off?"

"Shut the fuck up!" Ralph said. "We don't want to involve Nando. Unless we have to. Jesus! Couldn't we give him something?"

I saw a look pass between them and knew that, without the need for anything to be said, they were both thinking about cutting me open.

"Cody sits out on the flat till we can check it out," Ralph said finally.

"This is going to work out OK," I told them, but they weren't interested in anything I had to say.

At chow hall, I sat between Eric and Ralph.

"Eat," Ralph said.

"We should have made him throw up," Eric said.

"Too late now. He should eat. It'll come through faster."

After dinner, I sat at one of the picnic tables on the flat while Ralph watched TV nearby in a cell he'd commandeered. Eric disappeared to the gym.

When he came back, he pulled Ralph aside. They had a long conversation, which ended in an argument in which they looked often in my direction. When I walked over to where they were standing, they abruptly stopped talking.

"Vera still has it, right?" I said.

They didn't answer, so I knew they hadn't heard back from Nando.

"Get back to where you were," Ralph said, but I didn't move.

The time for lock-down was coming. We all knew that if I had the cocaine in my gut, they had to kill me now. Otherwise I'd pass it in the night and have it stashed before they could get to me in the morning. We all knew that to Nando's way of thinking, if I had it and they had me, they'd taken delivery.

Ralph looked over at the officer who sat at the desk; he was working something out on a pocket calculator.

"No one would double-cross Nando," I said. "You'd have to be crazy." I was calm. I wanted them to see how calm I was.

"If you're lying to us . . ." Eric started. But what was the threat? If I was double-crossing Nando . . . "Fuck it," he said, and turned away.

Ralph couldn't let it go. He glowered at me, his fingers clenching and unclenching, as if he could scare the truth from me.

"We should've done him straight after he came back from visit," he said to Eric, "but you didn't have the balls for it!"

The officer put the calculator away and looked at his watch. With ten minutes to lock-down, most of the other inmates were already in their cells. We three were becoming conspicuous. Eric was the first to move toward the stairs.

"It's your ass," he told Ralph.

As soon as Eric took that first step, I knew I would be all right, at least until tomorrow.

The next morning, I took out the nail I kept in the piping of my mattress and dropped it into the dirty water at the bottom of the mop bucket. I ate breakfast sitting between Ralph and Eric, but by then the situation contained so much uncertainty that their surveillance was halfhearted. Eric went to his job in the metal shop, and Ralph went on sick call so that he could remain on the block and keep an eye on me.

I know it sounds bad, keeping a weapon. And I admit I bought the nail before this problem with Ralph began. But I wasn't looking for trouble, only to defend myself. In prison, everybody's armed. Besides, a nail—a flat-headed nail only four inches long—isn't exactly a formidable weapon.

I went about my routine under Ralph's vengeful gaze. He pulled a chair up to the rail on the top tier and brooded with his head resting on his arms. I knew he wouldn't be able to let things go much longer before he killed me out of blind frustration. I knew I couldn't let things go on, either. If I hadn't taken a stand, I'd have been pulled into the drug wars, and then, sooner or later, I'd have been caught or killed.

It was after lunch when Eric hurried into the block, ran up the stairs to Ralph, talked to him briefly, and went out. I was mopping the flat when Ralph came up behind me.

"Vera says you collected," he said quietly, dangerously.

I thought I hadn't heard correctly. "What?" I asked.

"She says she passed you the stuff and you swallowed the whole thing like a fucking hot dog. Says you practically sucked it out of her mouth."

"That's a lie!"

"You tell that to Nando. 'Hey, Nando. Your cousin Vera? She's a lying bitch.' "

"She walked right out of the visiting room," I told him.

The officer at the desk looked up. He was new and didn't know who was who on the block. I put the mop in the wringer on the bucket and squeezed it out.

"She didn't even go to the bathroom," I said. "You can ask anyone who was there. How's she going to have anything to give to me if she doesn't go to the bathroom first? You tell me that!"

"No one gives a fuck. Nando wants his money. And I want the stuff."

"He's playing you off."

"Against who?"

"He knows Vera didn't make the drop. Nando's setting you up."

"You know what? If it's your word against Nando's, I'm going with Nando."

We were in plain sight of the officer at the desk. I took the mop and worked closer to him. I thought maybe the time had come to ask for Segregation, even if I had to live with pedophiles for the rest of my life. But then the signal for Movement sounded, and the officer got up and walked away from us to open the gate to the corridor. Ralph saw what I was doing.

"Forget Segregation," he said. "The only way you're going to stay alive is to give up the coke."

An inmate came to the gate. He was from another cell block, but the officer didn't know him and let him enter. Ralph stiffened when he saw him. The man gestured to Ralph, calling him over, as if he was giving an order.

"Have you passed it yet?" Ralph asked.

"No," I said.

He seemed childishly relieved. I watched them talking. The other inmate was setting conditions, emphasizing each point with a chopping motion of his open hand. When Ralph interrupted, he cut him off. When Ralph returned, he was sweating.

"You got till dinner tonight. Then I'm going to cut it out of you."

We went to the weight room. I pushed the mop and bucket across the flat. One of the wheels caught at the same point as it turned and let out a squeak at regular intervals as we traversed the open space in front of the officer.

Ralph went through his training routine. He worked hard. He worked every muscle in his body until his legs and arms and shoulders were so full of blood he looked like he'd burst. He worked a muscle until it couldn't lift anymore. Then he turned to another part of his body and went through the same process. Then he ran through the routine all over again, until every part of him was exhausted. He lay on his back on the bench and did a last set of flies with free weights in each hand, raising them from the horizontal so that they clinked above his head, more and more slowly, until he came to the point when his arms trembled and he let out gasps of air, but the weights wouldn't move.

"We're going for a shower," he said.

"I don't need a shower," I told him. "I'll clean up in there while you take one."

You have to go slowly with water in the bucket, otherwise it slops over the side. Ralph walked stiff-legged across the flat in front of me. His thighs were so thickened with exertion that they got in each other's way. The towel he'd draped around his neck unraveled, and he wasn't quick enough to catch it when it slipped off his shoulder. I saw the effort it cost him to bend to pick it up. He looked as though he could lift a mountain, but a kitten could have taken him down.

The shower room was filled with steam. There were two men in the end stall. Ralph stripped off, and I went about my work. I wrung out the mop and washed the floor in front of Ralph's stall. He sat on the tile floor and let the hot water splash on him full blast. He had his eyes closed, but every now and again he opened them to track me.

I moved the mop bucket past the stall, but Ralph was still able to see the head of the mop at the end of the sweep. Every time I moved, Ralph could hear the squeak of the wheel and know that I was nearby. Moving the mop back and forth across the floor, I unscrewed the cap on the top which held the metal loop for hanging it up. Out of view now, but still clattering the bucket, wringing out the mop, making noise that Ralph would identify, I fitted the nail through the hole in the cap and then threaded the cap back so that it held the flat end of the nail tightly against the end of the mop. Then I moved back toward the cubicle where Ralph sat exhausted beneath the hissing water.

I kept the rhythm, back and forth with the mop, working my way in front of Ralph until I had the angle on him I wanted. He held his head back to receive the flow of water, for his emotion to be worn down, for the contours of his face to be smoothed by it. He had an expression of repose. Hair, mustache, the lax muscles of his face, were streamlined by the vertical fall of water. When I came level to him, he half opened his eyes to check on me, and then he let himself go again, half in lethargy, half in pleasure. When his eyes closed, I speared him in the throat. His eyes came wide open and he looked at me in horror. He was totally silent. The only sound was the hissing of the water on his skin.

He couldn't catch up with what was being done to him. His mouth gaped and closed again. I hoped I'd done enough to kill

63

him. I wasn't sure I could bring myself to stick him again. The water fell rapidly on him, making a new Ralph who was glossy and obscure. I held the broom in place hoping for a shudder or limpness that meant death.

In slow motion, in extreme pain and fear, Ralph started to bring his hand up to the broom handle. I pulled it out before he could get to it, and the water around him suddenly turned pink with blood. He was trying to say something. His lips were working. I stuck him through the right eye, and he fell sideways and his weight snapped off the cap holding the nail in place.

I waited, not moving, for the sound of another person. In prison, there is always someone who lurks at the edges of action. One of the men in the last bay spoke to his friend. There was no noise outside the hissing of water and the patter where it puddled around Ralph's thighs. No one came into the shower room or passed to leave. I pulled on Ralph's arm to sit him up. The plastic cap of the mop had split. I took the pieces and left the nail in place. With some small adjustments, with his head slumped down on his chest, Ralph looked simply tired. The wound in his throat had stopped bleeding.

With the mop, I wiped away the blood that had run down the corner of his mouth and sluiced the pink tinge on the tiles at the edges of the stall. Mopping as I went, with the wheel squeaking once every five inches, I worked my way back to the flat, to the security and alibi of the officer at the desk.

Over the next half hour, several people went in and out of the shower room, but Ralph wasn't the kind of man anyone cared to disturb while he was having a nice shower.

Almost an hour went by before Eric returned to the block. He looked wild-eyed and scattered. I assumed he hadn't had a good conversation with Nando's people.

"Where's Ralph?" he asked me.

"He fell asleep in the shower," I told him.

"You were meant to stay with him!"

"I did. Then the guy said it didn't matter anymore, everything was OK. So I left."

"What guy?"

I stared at him. "The guy you sent with the message for Ralph."

"Who?"

"I never saw him before."

"Then how'd he get onto the block?"

"I don't know. Must have slipped in when the screw wasn't looking."

Eric was thinking fast. He was like a computer going mad with calculations even as more data poured in.

He grabbed my arm, then let it go. "Get in there," he said, pointing me toward the showers.

Ralph's body had undergone some change since I'd last seen it, and it was obvious now that he was more than sleeping. He was like a gray stone Buddha beneath a waterfall.

Eric reached out to turn off the water, then thought better of it. He kneeled down and angled his head so that he could look up into Ralph's face, and I saw him stiffen when he caught sight of the nail planted in his eye socket.

He looked shocked. "Did you see them do this?" He wanted to shout, and the words came out strangled. His mouth stayed open.

I shook my head. "I was mopping down the flat."

He paced back and forth: three paces, turn; three paces, turn. He made shoving movements with his fists. He didn't notice me anymore. I'd set in motion a chain reaction, and Eric would be too distracted ensuring his own survival to bother about me. I was irrelevant. It was all I wanted.

I was never charged with Ralph's murder. As far as I'm aware, I was never even a suspect. I am making a full confession to you now so that you'll know that I'm sincere. Obviously, I have nothing to gain from telling you this. At the same time, it's not a burden I have to get off my chest. My conscience is clear. I feel no more guilt about killing Ralph Mandell than I do about the cow that was killed so that I could eat.

It wasn't guilt that troubled me, but something else. Murder is a corrosive act. Violence corrupts. I have always been against it. I marched in peace demonstrations against the war in Vietnam. I know that seems like history now—in class, my students looked at me as if I was an ancient relic when I talked about the antiwar movement—but it used to mean something. My whole philosophy is based on a profound respect for life. I was afraid of what I was becoming, what prison would force me to be. The blue light of J Block brought me to a level of existence, to such a profound ruthlessness, that I was afraid I had died. Yet nothing less than that ruthlessness would allow me to survive. That's why I had to get out. This is the most important thing I'm trying to get you to understand: If I wanted to stay human, I had to escape.

THREE

D ear Sandy:
  I was disappointed how little you read of my last letter on
your program, though I understand that, compared to what
the police had dug up, it might have seemed like old history.
All the same, I think you exaggerated when you called the
new facts "startling revelations." The "revelation" was only a
matter of time. Anyone could—or should—have seen it coming,
otherwise how could the escape have worked? How did the gun
get under the mattress? Once you start asking these questions,
the police work doesn't look so spiffy. And what took them so
long? I know. You have your sources, and you have to keep
them sweet.

  Yes, the "hostage" is Carol. But you are so wrong to belittle
her motives! Contrary to what your pet psychiatrist thinks, this is
not the result of some syndrome in which nurses fall for convicts.
I resent the word "infatuation." You know nothing of our love,

though apparently that doesn't stop you from passing judgment. I'll tell our story, then let your audience judge for themselves.

On that fateful day last week, I stood between Baruk and Fairburn when the elevator door opened on the third floor. Baruk took off, and by the time we caught up with him in the anteroom to the ICU, he already had his mask on. A nurse came toward us. She was wearing a mask, too.

The masks bothered me. I didn't want to wear one, and I gave them a hard time about it. The nurse came and stood right in front of me. She was wearing blue scrubs and a paper cap that hid all her hair. A blue mask like a small bowl covered the center of her face. I still didn't know who she was. I wasn't sure. I hoped it was Carol. I was afraid to hope it was her. Her lower face, her hair, all her features except her eyes, were hidden. Without the rest of the face, the eyes are so expressive and so meaningless, like someone speaking a foreign language.

A designer stethoscope with magenta tubing hung around her neck. I suppose a thousand nurses have stethoscopes that color, but I fixed on it as if it revealed a certainty. The other two, Baruk and Fairburn, stood behind her. They were watching me, but Carol had her back to them. As if she were adjusting the mask to make it sit more comfortably, she pulled it down to reveal herself to me.

"It's better to wear it," she said.

The elastic held the mask tight under her chin. She pulled it out and over, covering her face again. But her eyes stayed on me. Even as she turned away, her eyes stayed on me until the last moment.

Fairburn stood in front of me to put the mask on. He was genuinely respectful of the situation, believing my mother lay dying in the next room. He was clumsy getting the elastic over my ears, because he was being overly careful not to cause me any pain. You see, he was a decent, mistaken man.

I watched Carol go to work on the gown with her scissors. Even then, I didn't know for sure what was coming next. The gown wouldn't go on over the handcuffs and she was cutting open the sleeves. She pulled it on and came behind me to tie the tapes.

"Is that too tight?" she asked.

I breathed in the familiar scent of the bath soap she used.

"No, that feels about right," I said.

She made a fuss of adjusting the gown around my neck, as if she couldn't get it fastened properly.

"Raise your arms a bit," she said.

I did as she said. The fabric crinkled and she whispered next in my ear, "Feel under the mattress," so softly that I wasn't sure I'd really heard. Then, "Take me hostage."

"OK?" she asked out loud.

I didn't know what was happening, but I felt myself being carried along, as if I'd been swept up by a river, feeling the current catch hold of me. When she came around in front of me to tape up the sleeves she'd cut, it didn't matter that she avoided my eyes. There was a secret bond that didn't need to be acknowledged, however hungry I was. When she moved around me, fussing with the yellow gown, every gesture from her rippled across my body as though we were standing in water.

We went through the next set of double doors into the Intensive Care Unit. Carol positioned herself so that it was natural for me to go to the left side of the bed. Fairburn would have followed me. It was his job to stand always within arm's reach, but Carol shook her head as if to say that it was better for me to be, at least in some sense, alone with my mother, and he took up a position at the end of the bed looking very uncomfortable.

For a moment I was afraid that the old lady in the bed *would* be my mother. I was acting, playing a part, and the make-believe had sucked me in. In that state of floating free, feeling yourself in the grip of somthing you don't understand, anything seemed possible. I took the woman's hand and put it between my own, and, eerily, I felt her unconscious fingers curl through mine and grip me. There was no change in her face. She seemed to stop breathing and then, just at the moment I thought she'd slipped away, she'd start up again.

I'd gone as far as I could, improvising. I didn't know what the rest of the script called for. Carol was standing slightly back from the two officers where they couldn't see her. She had her hands raised in the position of prayer and nodded for me to do likewise.

I looked around, but there weren't any chairs. It's not easy going down on your knees in leg irons and handcuffs. I lowered myself slowly and awkwardly, hanging onto the bed rail. The guards preferred things done slowly: You had to telegraph what you were about to do. I suppose I played it up a bit. Fairburn looked embarrassed; I expect he thought I was humiliated by their witnessing this private moment. At a time like this

I stayed on my knees for several minutes, with the strange, bony hand pressed against my forehead, and tried to figure out how I was going to get my hands under the mattress. I didn't dare look to see whether the guards were paying attention. I heard Baruk shifting on his feet, restless and bored. If I cried, would Fairburn look away? I gave a small shoulder spasm, waited a few moments, then gave two more close together.

Then, slowly but persistently, the old lady took her hand away from me. I let my head sink onto the bed rail. My hands, as it were, of their own accord, slid down to my lap. I hoped I looked like I had given myself up to grief. I let myself go for maybe ten seconds. Any longer, and I was afraid someone would step in to try to rally my spirits. I took deep breaths. I brought my hands up to the edge of the bed's metal frame to support myself in a more upright posture and worked my fingertips under the mattress. There was nothing there. I shifted position toward the head of the bed and swept my fingers beneath the edge of the mattress as I moved. My fingertips caught on something hard.

Hampered by the leg irons, I struggled to lift myself into a standing position, and with a clumsy forward shift, it was quite natural for my right hand to go all the way under the mattress and for my fingers to close around the stock of the gun. Even before I'd fully got off my knees, I'd released the safety catch, and as I stood up, I brought the gun out of its hiding place and cocked it with my other hand.

Baruk was cool, I'll give him that. I expected him to try to talk me out of it, given that he'd known me for so long. But I'm glad he didn't. He tried to get Fairburn to act realistically, but Fairburn had a wild glint in his eye. He couldn't do the sensible thing—just go with the situation, let it play itself out. He had to do something. I think he'd watched too much TV. On TV, cops routinely go for the one in a thousand chance, diving across a hospital bed at a man holding a loaded .38 on them.

The gun made an awful noise. Carol is marvelous in an emergency. Never flustered, always perfectly prioritized. She turned Fairburn over, but there was nothing she could do for him. I was so dazed, she had to help me secure Sergeant Baruk to the bed with the cuffs.

For effect, I took hold of the magenta tubing of the stethoscope and pulled her toward the door.

"You're coming with me," I said.

We went quickly through the doors of the ICU. The elevator was waiting, the doors open, and I sent it up to the top floor while we took the back stairs down to the emergency room. We were brisk. We knew where we were going. An ambulance had just brought in an elderly couple from a road wreck. No one paid any attention as we walked though. Carol's car was parked outside. We've been on the move ever since.

I am very much aware that I am free and Officer Fairburn is dead. There is no one who thinks that that equation balances, including me. If I could reverse events, if my returning to Denning would bring him back, I'd do it in flash. But my being a prisoner again won't bring him back, so I must go on.

Any attempt at justification would be an insult to his memory. There is no justification. But I keep coming back to the question: What would you have done in my position? Until this point, I haven't been able to say anything about Carol, but she is the reason for this escape.

Soon after Ralph was killed, Baruk was transferred to Medical, the hospital unit inside the prison. It was something of a promotion, though I don't know what he'd done to earn it. Medical had a terrible reputation in those days. Inmates who worked there made a habit of shaking down men who were too sick to look out for themselves, and they stole syringes and any medications they could lay their hands on. Baruk wanted to clean house, and he wanted his own people in the jobs. For some reason, he decided to give me the job of Medical

71

janitor. I was elated, because it kept me out of Eric's clutches all day long.

Janitor may sound like a lowly occupation, especially for someone who's been a teacher, but it was one of the plum jobs in Denning. It mostly consisted of running errands and keeping the place clean—and there was a lot of surface to keep clean, because Medical was spread out along three sides of a square around an inner courtyard. It was all on one level, with no tiers, and because it was in the older part of the prison, it contained all sorts of nooks and crannies where dust accumulated and that made it a security nightmare.

Medical had a different culture from the rest of the prison, even though Administration regarded the doctors and nurses as little more than a necessary evil. The officers looked on them as if they were civilians wandering on a battlefield. They saw them as bleeding hearts, possible sympathizers, and therefore security risks. But because the medical staff wasn't versed in security, because they were civilians, discipline was relaxed on Medical; rules got bent, or sometimes the small ones forgotten. And then some of the civilians were women.

The nurses' trap was located on the corner where the first side of the square joined the second. It was set up like the nurses' station you'd see in a regular hospital, with a counter for the nurses to do their paperwork and answer telephone calls, except that steel mesh shut it off from the counter to the ceiling and turned it into a kind of cage. The mesh was wide enough to stick a finger through. It didn't prevent you from seeing the people inside or speaking to them, but it was thick enough that you couldn't quite see, say, the person's face in its entirety unless you moved your head so that your eyes could fuse the mosaic into a single image.

I once saw a *National Geographic* program about the Great Barrier Reef. They lowered divers in a cage so that they could get close to the great white shark; the huge animals flashed by and crushed in their mouths the chunks of meat the divers pushed out. To a great white, those pieces of fish were just an appetizer, and the camera showed the beasts looming in and out of focus as they circled the awkward, more substantial meat inside the cage.

That was the purpose of the nurses' trap—to scare the civilian

72

into believing that she was safe only if she kept a layer of steel—steel mesh, steel bars, steel doors—between herself and the inmate. To make her scared enough that mistrust became a reflex.

The nurses came from a different world, a different medium. The prison world was made up of guards and inmates. They could never mix. There was no neutral ground. They were yin and yang. Spy and Counterspy. Master and slave. Screw and con. Yet in spite of the great divide, we were both of a common human substance, rough and raw. Call it mankind.

Even with the officers, the nurses maintained a degree of separation. The nurses were a breed apart. They were fabulous beings, like mermaids or angels. The nurses rose above us. They were kept in the purdah of the trap, and some would walk abroad only when accompanied by an officer to protect them. Baruk was puffed up with more than his usual swagger when he squired Carol along the corridor. The White Knight before a Genevieve whom no one may even dare to covet.

In this caste system we, the inmates, were not nothing. We called them "Carol," "Tanya," just as the officers did, because they existed outside the elaborate prison hierarchies. Like popes and kings who are known by their first names—like Evita—they were distant figures brought to an imagined point of intimacy by being so often in our thoughts.

Baruk didn't introduce me, on that first day, to any of the other people who worked on Medical. I mention this for your information, although the idea that he might introduce me would strike anyone who knows prisons as humorous. I was a worker. I was like one of those black servants from the Old South who moved about silently in the background. So Carol was able to pretend that she didn't notice me as I worked my way in front of her trap, mopping back and forth, getting the whole width of the corridor in a single swing.

An inmate could not look directly at a nurse unless she addressed him. And then only briefly. A glance, a sip, was all that was allowed. There was no rule in the books that said this, and no one told you that this was the way it was, but it was obvious as soon as you stepped onto the unit. An inmate knew at once how to behave.

But I did look at Carol. When you're mopping, it's natural to keep

73

your head down. You develop a way of looking out of the corner of your eye as you swing the mop from one side to the other. And then you pause, as if to rest your muscles for a moment, because no one can keep going at it forever, and accidentally, as it were, your eyes happen to be in the vicinity when, like two cars rounding a corner, both with their high beams on, my eyes met hers.

You can tell in an instant if someone recognizes you. Carol hadn't learned how to make her eyes lie. She remembered me from J Block. John the Baptist in an eight-by-ten wilderness.

"My head's fine," I said. "Good as new." I hoped I might make her smile. "Maybe better."

She went on with her business as if I hadn't spoken. She picked up the telephone, dialed a number, and swiveled on her hip, the receiver pressed to her ear, her elbow tight against her chest, to look at the clock on the back wall.

I'm sure she felt me looking at her. We listened to the telephone ring in the officers' trap at the other end of the corridor. Carol opened her mouth and let her head fall back and blew an imaginary smoke ring of impatience at the ceiling. She knew I was looking at her. She sighed with an edge of irritation, turning back and forth on her hips with the receiver held to her ear.

"Oh, Rich," she said, straightening suddenly. At the other end of the corridor, I could hear his initial gruffness soften. "We need some more towels."

"You got it," he said. Somehow he made the undertaking sound gallant, noble even.

A moment later, he stuck his head out the trap and barked, "Cody!" although I was in line of sight and a simple hand gesture would have been enough.

I left the mop standing in the bucket and ran to where he stood, hands on his hips, looking stern. I think he liked the fact that I ran. He seemed a little taken aback, as if he'd been preparing to give me a culture-shock talk about jumping to it. He snorted some moisture from the back of his nose and coughed. He tossed his head in the direction of the nurses' trap.

"Get the nurse some fresh towels," he said, and turned away from me almost before he had finished speaking.

I returned to Carol with a pile of towels in my arms. She was

74

sitting at the counter writing, and I stood in front of her with the steel mesh separating us. She let a few seconds go by before she looked up, and then she wouldn't let her eyes go all the way up to my face. They wandered slowly up to my chin, as if her mind were only beginning to engage in the process, then slid quickly sideways and curved down and away as she slid off her seat to the door.

She hadn't been in the job long enough to acquire the prison knack of using her body as a counterpoise to heavy steel doors. She unlocked the door to the trap and jerked at it with no more than her arm, as if she was opening her own front door, but it moved only an inch, and she had to take the handle with both hands and lean back to get it to swing smoothly open. She was awkward and cold with me. She went out of her way to show her indifference, which was self-defeating, because you don't have to avoid something that doesn't matter. As I held out the towels to her, I imagined her heart active and fluttering like a butterfly enclosed within cupped hands.

She reached to take the pile from me with difficulty, using her thigh to keep the door from swinging back. She said, "OK, I've got them," but still wouldn't look at me.

She put down the pile of towels at the corner of the counter and went back to studying the lab reports that had come in. She wore her hair the same way she had when I'd seen her on J Block, with bangs at the front and the rest pulled back tight behind her head. In the shadows of the trap, her hair had a dark, metallic sheen and curved around her head like a helmet. When Carol looks down, there is a lock of hair that falls forward over the corner of her eyebrow, and she has a mannerism of stretching it back with the first three fingers so that it hooks behind her left ear. On that first day on Medical, I watched her pull back that curtain of hair as she pored over a lab report; her fingers came up slowly while she read, setting shadows across her face from the desk lamp on the counter, and stretched the hair to the exact point of release where the strand could run off the tips of her fingers and drop into place.

We're changed by the simplest things. Once we've passed through a certain perception, we can't go back to the way we were, even if we wanted to. The gesture wasn't intended for me. I think she was genuinely unaware that I was still there. If she was aware of me, it had no intended meaning. It wasn't possible for her to predict an effect like that. She seemed momentarily vulnerable, and I was touched by this gesture. We can't help our feelings—they fly up, suddenly in flight, scattering in the air inside us.

The picture you showed of Carol doesn't do her justice. It's an ID photo from the Department of Correction. I know it well. It's on the laminated badge she wore every day, clipped to the lapel of her nurse's uniform. You say she's thirty-nine, but she could pass for early thirties in certain lights. Blown up to cover the entire TV screen, Carol looks tough: the full frontal face, the tightness around the jaw, lips clamped shut. She isn't tough, really. She didn't have a feel for it, especially at the beginning, when she was idealistic and harbored fantasies of rescuing inmates from their evil ways. Although she wasn't religious, there was a touch of the missionary about her then. I think she was looking for a place where she might tame her fears. She had her own reasons, her own demons.

Like a lot of people who struggle with a deep-down shyness, she didn't know who to keep at arm's length. She thought inmates who were sick wouldn't try to take advantage of her, simply because they were sick and weak and needed her. In prison, you have to put a certain degree of cynicism between you and the cons to protect yourself. She was naive about this. In the beginning, Baruk had to warn her about it several times. Then, with other inmates, she could be abrupt. At times she might have seemed cold and businesslike, but it was a surface she used to hide behind. Carol had many layers of surface.

"What are you staring at?" Carol demanded on that first day. She'd looked up suddenly from the lab slips.

"Nothing," I said. I was already starting to move off with the sly, inmate lope that was never too fast to attract attention.

"Rich, do I have to put up with this?" Carol complained.

Baruk was standing in the corridor behind me, watching the new man. I stopped in my tracks as soon as I saw him. He came toward us, taking his time.

"You got an attitude, Cody?" he asked.

He made a display of calm to demonstrate his mastery of the situation.

I knew that if I so much as sighed, he'd see it as protest. Just the inching up of your shoulders toward a shrug can be taken as sarcasm by a man who has to show his superiority at all times. The officers had a special sensitivity around the nurses.

"No, Sarge," I said.

"You can keep your eyes to yourself."

"Right."

I got to it with the mop. For the rest of the day, Carol ignored me, and Baruk couldn't take his eyes off me.

A good-looking woman in the midst of a thousand men attracts attention. Everybody, cons and screws alike, tried to take advantage. I think the fact that Carol was a single woman of a certain age made men think she was more vulnerable to their charms than might otherwise have been the case. They assumed she had fewer options. That if she'd come to work at Denning, she had a past, or lacked a future.

To look at Carol going about her day, you'd have thought she could hold her own anywhere, Denning included. But when you came up close to her, she really was vulnerable. I sensed this, but I didn't see it until I reached by her one day to stop the heavy door of the trap from swinging back on her. I had to move my hand quickly past her face to catch the door, and she flinched. Some old part of her assumed I was about to land a blow on her. She froze for an instant, and a look of pain came to her face that had nothing to do with the present.

"Don't ever do that again," she said. Her eyes came on to me for a moment, full of madness. Her lower lip puckered as she turned away.

"What?" I asked her, softly.

"Never mind."

She let the door swing shut with a solid thud then hurried about her business inside the trap. She was drawn into herself. She was removed from her surroundings. I don't think she was there even for herself as she moved absently along the counter, shuffling papers, shelving patients' charts, picking up paper clips and dropping them into a drawer. Tidying,

77

sorting, making the environment orderly, making the world make sense.

There were always people trying to take advantage. Carol knew how to take care of them. She brushed them off or complained to Baruk and had them sent back to population. When she wanted, she had a no-nonsense manner that deterred most cons from even trying anything. But her guard was down with people who were really sick. She let Diego manipulate her shamelessly. Baruk and the other guards couldn't keep her in view every minute of every day. She needed watching: At times she was helpless.

Sammy Shay was admitted with a mysterious fever. I knew he was malingering; he wanted to hide out on Medical for a few days to escape some trouble he'd got himself into on the block. I'd come out of the supplies closet and I was looking for Carol because I had to ask her to order some more cleaning fluid. I couldn't find her in the trap. When I turned the corner, I saw Shay and Carol together. He was standing unnaturally close to her. I don't know how, but he'd maneuvered her against the door of a patient's room and was leaning over her with his arm against the wall to block her exit. You could tell she felt trapped. Her face was turned away from him and clenched tight, as though she was refusing to breathe. He was whispering something disgusting close to her ear. All she had to do was yell for an officer, and they'd have come running. But she was trapped by her own fear. She felt helpless, and so she was helpless.

He turned when I came up to them. He told me to get lost. I took hold of the side of his face. I gathered his cheek and the skin under the jaw tight in my fist and pulled him away from Carol. He reached out to my face, but I shook him and that hurt him enough for him to keep his hands down.

Carol seemed to come back to herself. She took a deep, shuddering breath. When I looked back, she was gone. I took Shay to the end of the back corridor where there were offices no one used. I held him by his face and pulled him along to the end of the corridor. It would have been easy to kill him. I put him against a door. He was like a doll. I had the strength to do anything to him, but I let go of his face.

78

He said, "What the fuck?" He couldn't make sense of what I'd done. "So what? What's it to you?"

I beat him halfheartedly. I was afraid of what I would do if I let myself go.

It was a crazy notion, setting out to win Carol. It was as if the lowliest servant in the castle had fallen for the queen. But I had all the time in the world. As they say in prison, we've got nothing but time. Even if Carol was the queen and I was a servant, that relationship can't exist for long when a man and a woman spend their days within six feet of one another. Barriers break down, whatever they're based on. They wear away with the everyday rub of one presence against the other. And once the barrier's punctured, once two people touch, that hole gets bigger faster, because that's the nature of the human spirit, to flow through the smallest connection between two people and wash barriers away.

Carol had a lot of time on her hands. It wasn't a busy job, most of the time. She might spend thirty minutes sitting behind the steel mesh, turning her nails moodily beneath the desk lamp, examining them this way and that. Though there was a glow about her when she was with the patients, it wasn't difficult to see that she was unhappy. In repose, there was a slackening about her mouth that spoke of disappointment. Then, sensing I was in the area, she'd pull her face tight and look up with a small, absentminded smile that was like a reflex.

I was very conscious of not making a nuisance of myself. That's the risk when you try to get close to someone who has no need for you. I made small, legitimate requests. Before each one, I spent a lot of time deciding whether, on the basis of what I'd observed of Carol's mood, I'd let enough time go by since the last one. For example, I might push a pencil through the mesh.

"Can I ask you a favor?"

"Yes," she said dreamily.

She'd been staring into space. I'd startled her. Then she focused on the pencil.

"Sure."

She turned the handle of the sharpener a few times and examined the point. When she passed me back the pencil, I hadn't managed to become a person to her.

"Here you are . . . You're welcome."

It's hard to decide when the moment occurred, when I became a person to Carol. I think it was the first time I entered the trap. I happened to be passing, and when I glanced back I saw her shaking her head from side to side as if she was crying or in pain. She brought her hand up to her face, but wouldn't touch it. She made a clawing motion as if an invisible barrier stopped her moving her hand closer.

"You got something in your eye?" I asked her.

She nodded her head and fluttered her hands. "Oh! Oh!" Her right eye was clamped shut.

"Why don't you let me take it out for you?" I suggested.

"It's OK. Just let me get to a mirror."

Carol stumbled against a chair as she felt along the counter toward the locker where she kept her pocketbook. She groped in the bag and brought out a compact and tried, one-handed, to prize open the lower lid of her eye while the upper one fluttered painfully. She peered into the mirror and led the lid go again.

"You should let me do that," I called to her.

"I'm a nurse," she said. "I ought to be good at this."

"But you can't do it to yourself. It's like cutting into your finger to take out a splinter. It's the reflexes. It goes against human nature."

She put down the compact and stood perfectly still, her hands gripping the edge of the white counter. Her eyes were closed, not clenched anymore, and her face was upturned so that the light from the desk lamp caught the sweep of her throat and cast her face in shadow. She seemed at peace. There is a rare, smoothed beauty in such unguarded moments. I could look at her all I wanted.

"Sometimes they come out by themselves," she said.

"Don't hold your breath."

She smiled like a blind person, with an expression of rapture directed upwards. I waited. There was no one in the corridor.

"You want to let Dr. Dan take a look?"

She hesitated. Beneath the lids, she must have moved her eyes and shifted the lash. She shook her head back and forth slowly in pain and frustration.

"I'll have it out for you in a flash," I said.

She came along the counter, groping, one-eyed, for the big brass key. "OK," she said. "But you have to make it quick."

I guided her to a chair and angled the desk lamp so that it illuminated her face. She let her head fall back, and a calm surrender came over her. She gave herself to me. I took her head in my hands and tilted it toward the light. Her head was like the universe which I held in my hands.

"Let me," I whispered to her.

She flinched when I touched the side of her face, but then let herself go again. Trust is such an unnatural thing. It goes against all the reflexes. Her lids were clenched tight. I placed my hand against her cheek and ran my thumb along the length of her eyebrow to persuade the muscles to relax. Very slowly, I drew back the upper lid. Mascara was clumped at the base of the lashes and flowed onto the skin below her eye.

A tear broke loose and cascaded down her cheek—fast, then slow, then fast again, as it moved over the contours of the skin beside her nose. The exposed eye was a wild, scared thing, jerking from one side to the other, as if desperate to escape.

"It's a lash," I told her. "It's in the corner."

I took the tissue she held in her hand and reached toward her.

"Be careful," she said.

It was a bold, black lash, bathed in tears. I touched it with a corner of the tissue and it came away cleanly. Immediately, she pulled away from me.

"I didn't know you wore contact lenses," I said.

I looked up when she didn't reply and saw Sergeant Baruk standing on the other side of the mesh. I wondered how long he'd been there.

"She had something in her eye," I said.

"I couldn't see," Carol explained. "I had to get it out."

"You OK now?" he asked Carol. "Get back to your work," he told me, like an afterthought, before she had a chance to reply.

I was relieved when Carol came to work the next day, because it meant she hadn't been fired. I was surprised Baruk hadn't fired me on the spot. Later in the day, I found an opportunity to be alone with her in the treatment room. She seemed intent on ignoring me and went on with checking supplies off on a clipboard.

"I hope you didn't get into trouble," I said.

She looked annoyed. "No. Why should I? It wasn't a big deal."

"I was afraid Baruk would write you up."

"I don't report to him."

"I know."

I thought she was going to say something more, but she scribbled something on the list she was checking.

"This job," I said, "it really means a lot to me. If you put in a good word for me, I'd appreciate it."

"Like I said, it wasn't a big deal."

Carol didn't look up from the clipboard. She frowned as if she had to concentrate on a problem she saw there. I fiddled with the trolley until there was nothing left for me to plausibly do. I lingered anyway.

"I owe you one," I said.

She looked up as if she'd forgotten I was there. "OK," she said vaguely. "If you want."

Lying on the bunk in my cell, I thought about what had passed between us at the end of each day. Carol had smiled at something I'd said. Had that been the breakthrough I was hoping for? Had she seen me, finally? Had I put a hole in the barrier? I'd made her laugh. I'd made her stop and think. I'd recited a couple of lines from a poem by Blake that seemed to fit the situation and walked on, throwing away the chance to see her reaction. We'd gotten into the habit of stopping by each patient's room at the end of Carol's shift to see if they needed anything before she left. Was this intentional on Carol's part? Was she deliberately setting up an unobtrusive way in which we could spend time in each other's company? Or maybe it didn't matter to her one way or the other whether I went with her on these rounds? I lay on my bunk and analyzed each incident for signs of hope or despair. It's not too much to say that she was the whole reason for my existence at Denning.

If I sound like a teenager mooning over his latest crush, that isn't far off the mark. I couldn't approach Carol like any man would outside. This love affair was against the law. I had to woo her an inch at a time, invisibly. I pursued her in plain sight with ordinary words. No one could know what we were doing. Even Carol couldn't know it, in the beginning, or she'd have pulled away.

We evolved a private language. Like all the strongest secrets, we never acknowledged to each other that such a thing existed. We could never be sure what exactly had been said. The message was disguised in a tone of speech. It curled within a single word that had been picked out for emphasis. It hid within a hesitation. Our love letters were invisible. The sounds of our love were inaudible to anything but the naked ear. The meaning was a hint within a nuance, oblique, almost unknowable.

At first, the secret dimension was so subtle that I couldn't be sure the language even existed. I spoke it to her, but was she speaking it back to me? She seemed to be responding, but it was a code we invented as we went along. At least, that was my hope. Or were these signs just accidents of speech? Every night, I turned over every word that had passed between us during the day. I repeated sentences in my mind, searching for the accurate distribution of emphasis, the true meaning, until the meaning disappeared and the sentence became nothing more than a jumble of sounds. There comes a time when you have to turn a corner and find out for yourself what's real. It's a moment that has to be chosen with the utmost care.

Carol wasn't supposed to smoke in the trap, even though I could smoke, one foot away, in the corridor. I'd gotten into the habit of being on the lookout for her as I went about my work, and I'd warn her whenever Sergeant Baruk was heading her way. One day, I saw her sitting in the trap with a cigarette between her fingers and a faraway look in her eyes.

"He's not worth it," I said.

"Who?"

She smiled, carefully. She was wary, watching for the first sign that I might try to overstep the boundary.

"Whoever," I said.

"What do you know?" she asked, giving me a challenging look

that was supposed to make me bolder. Her elbows rested on the counter, and she held her hands tipped together as if she was praying, tapping the fingertips on her chin, her eyes screwed up against the smoke. I stood two feet from her, but Carol acted as if she'd already returned to her daydream. We both knew it was an act. Whenever there is an unspoken understanding between two people, there is intimacy.

"Give me a light?" I asked her.

Grudgingly, mocking, hooded till the last moment, her eyes came back to me. She was dainty, tapping off the ash. She took a pull to bring the cigarette to life and then held the tip through the mesh for me to press mine against. At the last moment, just before I pulled back, I looked into her eyes and saw there a loneliness and a hunger that seemed no different from my own. I took a deep pull, as if I was sucking her deep into my chest and held her there, held her with my eyes. She was looking sideways, but her eyes were wide open, and she wasn't hiding from me. I had the strongest feeling that she was letting me have her, that I could look at her and drink her in, that I could suck her down to the depths of my lungs, dive underwater, and hold her there until I became dizzy and couldn't think straight and had to come up for air.

"You're lovely when you have that dreamy, faraway look in your eyes," I told her, and I saw a shy, secret smile begin on her lips as she turned away.

I want her to know this. That she affects me down to the substance we're made of, the grounding that is deeper than quirks of personality or dreams for the future. Somehow, though I've got Carol all to myself now, without the barriers that have kept us apart all this time, I'm tongue-tied. I can't tell her how much I love her.

She broke me out of prison so that we could be together, and now she is distracted. She worries a lot about being caught by the police. I know this is inevitable, sooner or later, and I think she does, too. It's hard for her, being on the run. I try to get her to relax, to go with it, to accept each minute as a gift and to think of ourselves as lucky to have it. She insists we keep on the move. She tells me we can get new identities.

She has given up everything for me. She knew, when she put

that gun under the old lady's mattress, that she was taking a step she could never undo. Carol denies this. But it's a lot to come to terms with, and I think it would be too much of a shock for her to recognize all at once the implications of what she has done.

Our relationship has been turned upside down since the escape. In Denning, Carol was the queen of Medical. She controlled me totally. My body. My every move. Where I went. When. If I disappointed her, one word was enough to have me removed forever. No one would even ask for a reason. If she stamped her foot, I'd be packed off to A6 to wait my turn for an opening in the metal shop. If she wanted to punish me, all she had to do was lift the telephone ("Rich, do you know what he just said to me?") and Baruk would deliver a discreet beating before he personally dragged me feet first through the corridors for a few weeks in J Block. It's the closest modern-day America comes to the world of Marie Antoinette.

Once, after a tiff—I think I'd gone too fast and overstepped my bounds—she said to Baruk, "Let's give Cody the day off tomorrow." Carol wanted to make a point.

I was crouched in the corridor, scraping out the dirt that had accumulated in the seam between the floor and the wall. She had her back to me, but she knew exactly where I was.

Baruk looked at me doubtfully. "Yeah. Sure," he said, wondering how to square this with the lieutenant. Schedules don't change in prison. If an inmate's supposed to be at a certain place for a certain time, you can't change it just like that.

I could have spoken up. If I'd said, "I don't mind working," I'd have taken Baruk off the hook. But I could as easily have pleaded with her, "Don't send me away!"

"He's put in a lot of extra time," Carol told Baruk. They strolled together away from me, their shoulders almost touching.

At three o'clock, as he went off shift, not even stopping as he headed for the front gate, Baruk told me, "OK, Cody, you can take tomorrow off." He looked shifty, because time off is time on your hands, and that's no reward for a man in prison.

The next day I sat at a picnic table on the flat and pretended to read a book, but I couldn't sit still and went to the weight room as soon as the officer opened it. I worked on my body until I felt stuffed with muscle. I was swollen up with pumping the blood into my chest and arms and legs. I pumped and welcomed the burning pain. I imagined acid destroying the cells of my body. I worked the weights until I couldn't raise my arms above my head. I lay on my bed for the rest of the morning, then in the afternoon I went back to the weight room and did the sets again.

Somewhere else, life went on without me. I'd been shut out of the world of Medical, which had become my world, my entire world. You have no way of knowing what you have become (believe me!) until something essential is taken away.

The next morning I was up and ready long before the guard came to the gate. He looked at his clipboard.

"You're not down here, Cody," he said.

"That's because I had the day off yesterday," I explained. "I was off the list yesterday and never got put back on."

"Let the other men through," he said. He was already looking beyond me.

"Baruk'll go nuts if I don't show up," I told him.

His face was stiff. "Move aside," he said.

That was the extent of her power over me. She could banish me. Uniformed men acted on her whims. I raged at her and was afraid of what my anger might do. What's a day to a man serving natural life? What's a day in prison? That was the extent of her hold on me, that a day without her was a day of anguish and burning pain. I was doubly imprisoned. Yet I wouldn't have had it any other way.

The next day I was back at work. I wouldn't go to the nurses' trap straight away, though I could hardly bear the uncertainty. I was a volcano of fear and anger and love. I couldn't trust myself to go near her, and I couldn't stay away.

Need is corrosive. It eats away all the discipline and resolve you must have to survive. I craved her as I've seen other inmates crave cocaine. They say, "Coke owns me." I knew, as I mopped the floor, pulling the mop across my chest with enough vigor to feel a gentle burn, backing along the corridor a foot at a time toward the nurses' trap, that Carol owned me.

I slowed as I came level with the door. I flicked the mop into a corner to flush out particles of dirt that had never been touched

86

before. I listened for the sound of her. I worked furiously, back and forth, on one-inch strips and waited. I wanted it to be her who broke the silence. When finally I stopped and turned to look into the trap, it was Tanya sitting at the counter, daydreaming.

I gripped the mop handle as if it was a lightning conductor for pain. I hated myself for my dependence on this woman. I was a slave to my feelings, and she controlled them.

Then, down the corridor, I hear a key turn in the door of the treatment room, and as it opened, her voice. First, an inmate on crutches came out, followed by an officer. The inmate held a bandaged foot off the ground and looked down as he placed the rubber stumps uncertainly on my wet floor.

I wasn't ready for Carol's entry into the corridor. Almost always, she wore white pants and a uniform top that covered her whole body, but that morning she had on a navy blue cardigan over a white dress. Carol has lovely, slender legs that look good even in white tights and the shoes with thick soles that nurses wear. Her outfit was a stunning break from her customary style. It seemed to me too much of a coincidence not to suppose that she'd chosen it this morning for my benefit.

Carol turned and saw me, and my heart leapt because—I was pretty sure of this—I saw her hesitate for a fraction of a second before she walked, purposefully, toward the nurses' trap, toward me. I was already in motion, pushing the mop, pulling it across my chest, edging backwards with my head down.

I saw her feet stop at the door and her knees dip and swivel as she inserted the key. She paused, and I waited to hear the tone of her voice that would tell me at once where we stood.

"Hello, Dan," she said.

I'd played this moment in my mind a hundred times, each one a shaved nuance of warmth or rejection or apology greater or less than the time before. Lying on the bunk in my cell, staring at the ceiling, I ran through the tones of her voice like practicing scales on the piano.

"Hi, Carol," I said.

We spoke in neutral tones. Neutrality is not the absence of emotion, because prison is a place where emotion can never be absent. Neutrality is not a space or an area, but a point. A tiny

87

point of perfect balance. There is a Tao, while looking Baruk in the eye, in holding a mop in a stance, that is neither defiant nor submissive. There is an exquisite calculus involved in passing an inmate in the narrow space of a tier without facing him down or giving way. A neutral tone of voice is an achievement, like singing with perfect pitch. We sang to each other.

Carol went into the trap. I worried at something invisible with the mop. Carol shuffled papers.

"How was your day off?" she asked, barely looking up. Her question was perfect. I marveled at her control.

"Two days," I corrected her, lightly, without a trace of bitterness, without consequence.

"Was it really?"

"Yes. Two."

"Well, it was probably good to have a rest."

"I needed it."

"You earned it."

I wanted her to be the one to break, to overbalance with emotion.

I crossed the corridor and came close to the steel mesh. "Thanks for putting a word in for me," I told her, with perfect pitch.

She was standing at the counter with her head down. The trap was dark except for the desk lamp whose light reflected from the papers on the counter onto Carol's face as if she possessed an inner glow. One finger traced a line of print. When she turned the page, a lock of hair loosened and tumbled forward. With her other hand she hooked it back, and that hand absentmindedly continued to the steel mesh and the fingers went through it and curled in front of me. My heart was pounding. Carol leaned casually on the mesh as if to brace herself. I glanced right and left along the corridor. I was afraid a sudden movement would startle her deeper into the trap. I was afraid that at any moment, absentmindedly, she'd take her hand back, and I'd go spinning helplessly into space.

Scarcely able to breathe, I raised my hand to hers and brushed the fingers, crossed the joint, the nails, lingered with our fingertips end to end, and that was all. I was filled. Carol took back her hand and turned a page. She had never looked up. I stepped back, out of a magic circle. I had never touched her hand before.

I had loved her for three years and never once had touched her hand.

The surface world fell back into place around us. We'd been enchanted. Now we had to work to break free of the spell. Carol frowned, remembering something.

"Oh, Dan?"

"Yes?" I said.

I would have jumped into fire for her if I could hear once more the drawn out huskiness of the middle of my name. Could anyone else have detected within a syllable embedded in a casual request an entire world of promise? No one could have sensed the ridges of that smooth vowel unless they placed it under the mind's microscope; and then they would have seen how the sound shuddered, how the gaps within it were filled with the ache of longing and regret.

"Would you do something for me?" she asked, looking at me directly, really looking at me, with everything clear and out in the open, for the first time in two days. Then she smiled mischievously. "We're out of sheets. Would you get some from the laundry?"

Nothing could be the same again. Until that moment, our relationship had existed on nothing more than words, gestures, glances. Touch gave our love substance. It brought it into a new, physical dimension, with new actions and new emotions.

We had to be doubly careful to keep what we shared hidden from others. Everything is seen in prison. It's like movement in the desert: life is so scarce that the merest flutter attracts the predators' attention. We could scarcely reveal our feelings to each other. At any time Baruk might round the corner. Or the mirror's fish eye mounted where the walls joined the ceiling would catch me reaching toward her, expanding the gesture until it splayed across the center of the lens. I could love her only in tiny sips. I was a man in a burning building filled with smoke, sucking life-sustaining oxygen through a keyhole.

In the evening, when I'd returned to the block, I'd hear a song on the radio and wonder if, at that same moment, Carol was tuned to the same station listening to the same song. We lived in parallel universes, and in the beginning, I'd taken pleasure in imagining where she might be, what she was doing, at the moment I was thinking of her. But the physical element changed that. More often when I wasn't with her, my imagination tortured me with the most obscene jealousies. I was locked in my cell, while Carol was free to roam and take her pick of a hundred men. I couldn't sleep and instead tossed and turned while I wrestled with these thoughts.

Then, in the morning, my whole outlook was transformed. I woke with an emotional dawn: a smile came to my face, and the glow of happiness filled my chest when I thought of the day ahead. I imagined the first moment when I would see her, and the last part of the day when we talked in Diego's room. I schemed of ways in which we might have a brief moment alone with each other—it felt like stealing fire from the gods. Often, I counted myself lucky to be in Denning.

There were delirious instants when our fingers touched, but these were rare occasions that put the entire relationship at risk. It was a romance where everything happened in each other's eyes—that's where we loved and had our existence. Chastity is an old-fashioned notion. It's not something we would have chosen for ourselves—it's certainly not something we have to endure now—but it deepened the relationship and forced the feelings down channels far inside ourselves.

Once, she walked by me on her way to lunch and I couldn't acknowledge her because other people were present. I never raised my head. I watched the ground and noted the exact spots on the floor where she placed her feet. I'd mopped the floor five minutes before she walked by, and although it looked dry, it was still damp enough that at each point where her shoe had touched, she'd left a faint outline of her foot. I fussed with the mop, rinsing and wringing, waiting for the corridor to clear, and when I was sure I was alone, I knelt and placed my cheek to the place where her foot had momentarily rested.

I wanted to feel the warmth of her body. I was at the farthest stretch of my imagination. I closed my eyes and focused beyond the concrete's hardness and its chill, like an astronomer stretching out into the universe, at the limits of resolution, to detect the infinitesimal warmth left over from our coming into existence. And it was there. There is no absolute zero of human affection. I closed off everything; I focused all perception on that point of contact with cold concrete. In the darkness of my mind, at the farthest edge of feeling, I sensed the faint echo of the warmth of her body.

And this is crazy, of course. I'm sure you think that. A convict pressing his face against the floor where a woman has just passed by! Poor, sex-starved fool! After being locked away from women for so long, it really started to get to him! Perhaps it is extreme, in a sentimental, bedazzled kind of way. But who's to say what's normal, what's extreme, what's crazy, in the deserts of maximum security? In a place where so much is possible, is it crazy to set out to discover for yourself the farthest extent of what is possible where love is concerned? If you still think you know, consider this: Would you give up all hope of love for the rest of your life? Be honest with yourself. If you answer honestly, I think you'll find that you're not so different from me: I would do anything to keep that hope alive. I can't live in a world without love.

After our fingers had touched that one time, we realized that we couldn't go on the way we had. We'd set something in motion that had been held back. It's strange, the way two people arrive simultaneously at what needs to be done. All of a sudden, we couldn't put up with anything coming between us. The physical frustration had something to do with it. You can't live on hot looks forever. There comes a time when you feel you have to make love or go mad.

It's something a man can't hide. It got to the point where I was aroused whenever I came within six feet of her. Several times when I was in this state I caught a small smile on her face. Carol enjoyed her power over me. And I gave up trying to hide. The truth is, I wanted her to see me. My life in prison was made from glimpses, glances, hints. I'd existed on scraps for too long, and I wanted her to see the raw hunger I felt.

She pretended she didn't notice the effect she had on me. She glanced down and away. She turned away and busied herself with a patient's chart, holding it up so that I couldn't see her face. I thought she might be blushing. She could have been suppressing giggles. I was always touched to discover how thin her shell was. Catching sight of some hidden, girlish, aspect of her sent a pang of endearment through me that was like a physical sensation.

I told her, "Look what you're doing to me. I'm like this all

91

the time. Anytime I see you. Anytime I think of you, I feel it starting up."

"I know," she sighed. She gave me a sympathetic smile, as if she was hearing about a patient's symptoms. "For now, you'll just have to do what you usually do."

That "for now" was an itch that wouldn't leave me alone. Before, I'd been tormented by visions of Carol going with other men as soon as she was out of my sight; now, my night was spent with visions of how she'd give herself to me. Fast. Secret. Covered. Nakedly revealed in a flash and quickly clothed again by some clever Velcro in her nurse's uniform. Hands. Mouths. I was obsessed with this one speck of pleasure that could wreck everything we had slowly built.

I would never have asked her to break me out of Denning. I never did. It was too dangerous. Too irrevocable. It would have been unfair to Carol to ask her to take that on. I had nothing to lose. She was free to come and go, to choose how to lead her life. She didn't owe me anything, and I didn't want to put her in the position of feeling guilty if she refused.

I was not the first one to raise the possibility of escape. That wasn't at all what I thought Carol meant when she said "for now." All I was aware of was my hunger for her, my sexual hunger gnawing at me, as real as the hunger for the food necessary to sustain life.

"You have to be sure you want this," she told me.

She looked tight and scared. She kept glancing up at my face as if she might catch the truth there by surprise.

"You have to be sure," she said.

"I am," I told her. But I was afraid we'd lose the little we had.

"Because there's no going back."

"Just tell me what you want me to do," I insisted.

"You have to realize, once we take that first step, there's no going back."

"I don't want to go back," I said.

"I mean, for any of us."

"I know that."

I wanted to tell her how grateful I was, but I felt she was struggling to achieve some new balance in herself and that anything I might say would upset the precarious arrangement she'd made. I owe her my life, this new life.

We heard Baruk yell my name. I glanced up at the mirror to check that he wasn't nearby. He asked a lot of questions if he had to call me twice.

"Look," I said, "I have to go."

I grasped the mesh so that my fingers came through onto her side, but she was drawn in, still trying to rearrange herself around the decision that had taken up the center of her life. She stood very still with her head lowered, biting down hard on her lower lip.

"Oh, Jesus!" she said. "I can't believe I'm doing this."

That's how we came together, in snatches, over days with long, agonizing interruptions in between, inching closer. It's hard to be patient, even when you know you'll lose everything that matters in your life if you push too quickly.

"I want you to know I'm serious," she told me another day.

"I know you are."

"But I want you to really know it," she insisted. "I want you to trust me."

I thought how we wouldn't need to feel one another out so carefully if we didn't have to communicate through steel mesh.

"I'm going to get you out of here," she said.

"I know," I said.

I thought escape was one of those fictions two people keep going for years and years, plans that hold them together and never need to be realized.

"Once you're out of here, I don't want them to connect me to you."

"They'll never find us."

"Once you're gone, I'll see you from time to time—"

"—We'll be together."

"Not all the time."

"I don't understand," I said. "That's the whole point. So that we can be together."

"We will. We will. But first, things have to cool down. There'll be investigations. I'll be a suspect. Everybody will be."

"Then come with me. Get away from it. We can go south. Once we get to Mexico, we can go anywhere."

Even as I said it, it didn't seem real. I thought we were arguing about the rules of a game, about how the fantasy had to be played.

"I'm going to stay here," Carol said.

She looked at me carefully to see if I would respond to reason. I was surprised how sure of herself she seemed, as though she'd already had this conversation with herself, playing both sides of the argument until only this one point of view remained.

"I want to be with you," I told her. "That's the whole point. That's all there is to it."

"Then you can stay here, if you want," she said in a flash of anger.

It was easy for her to avoid me for the rest of the day. When, desperate, I went out of bounds to try to speak to her, she complained to Baruk about the state of the toilets, and he kept me there until they were spotless and Carol had left at the end of her shift.

She had a new quickness to temper and decision that worried me. Behind her facade of competence, Carol is often tentative and unsure. She looks to me for direction. I put this new independence down to a crisis in her life as she came closer to the ultimate decision. It's understandable that she would have a need for certainty, that she would want to feel in control of events that were being driven by emotion.

If escape was real, then Carol had a new power over me. I felt this change in the balance of power. I had no say in my future.

"I'm sorry," I told her the next day.

She peered into my eyes. "We'll be together just as soon as it's safe," she said softly.

"We'll go to the Bahamas," I said. It was like a story.

"But first, I have to stay here. I have to go on working here long enough for them to rule me out of the investigation. That's why we can't speak to each other for the next two or three months."

"Why? What difference does it make? No one knows about us."

"After you get out of here, I don't want anyone to even think about a connection between us. Nothing. There'll be state police all over the place. When they come to this unit, I don't want anyone remembering you even said hello to me."

"I'll be out in two months?"

"Two. Could be three. You have to be patient. It could be six months. I won't know when until everything comes together."

"Six months?"

"You can't talk to me. You can't hang around near the trap."

I thought about this.

"Don't ask me how," she said. "Don't ask me how it's going to work. When it's ready, it'll go off."

"I don't want you doing anything dangerous," I told her.

"You have to trust me on this."

I was silent, trying to decide if this was real, what it might mean.

"Can you?" she insisted. "Can you trust me?"

"Yes," I said.

"Because after today, I'm going to act cold to you. It has to look real. But it'll hurt, even though you know I'm acting."

I nodded, thinking of six months, doing time, time within time.

She touched my hand, but she wouldn't look at me. "I want you to feel sure of me," she said.

"You don't have to prove anything," I told her.

"I want to. I want you to be sure of me."

"You've done enough already."

"I want us to be together." She sighed, having to use words, a kind of failure. "To do what we've never done."

I could hardly speak. "It's too dangerous," I said, though I was ready to throw everything away to have her, skin to skin, for one moment. It was worth dying for.

"There's a way," she said. She looked away, with her shyness out in the open. I saw her lips begin a word, then hesitate. She looked at me again, smiling. She was lewd and mischievous and loving. "I'm working late tomorrow. I'll be in the old office at eight."

"I'll be there," I said. "I'll knock four times, and you'll know it's me."

"No, that won't work. What if they want you?"

95

"There's not much they'd want me for after dinner. By eight, everybody's pretty much settled down."

"Someone could call you."

"Then I'd go. I'd have to go."

"What if they didn't call you? What if they came looking for you and they didn't find you?"

"They'd give me a couple of minutes. They know me. They wouldn't turn the place upside down."

"They don't trust you."

"Sure they do."

"They don't trust you. I know."

"What are you trying to tell me?"

I was standing inside the door of the nurses' trap. It was a risky area. Normally, I wouldn't have lingered there so long. Carol touched my cheek. She let her fingertips brush the side of my face down to the corner of my mouth. I couldn't think. I had a tingling feeling in the pit of my stomach that I had to get out of the trap, but I was intoxicated by her touch, rooted to the spot. Then her hand fell away.

"We have to trust each other," she whispered.

"I'll do anything you want," I told her.

"You have to stay outside the office. It's the only way they'll know where you are."

That night I woke myself up just in time, almost at the point of no return, in the midst of a sexual dream involving Janie. It troubled me that another part of myself held onto the old loyalty.

I went under the shower the next morning, even though I'd taken one the previous evening. I cut myself shaving and worried about the blemish of the small black clot on the underside of my jaw. I felt like a young bridegroom. I put on a fresh shirt, then took it off again, because I thought I should save it until the evening. I was afraid someone would notice this activity. All of a sudden, I felt obvious.

Carol came in with the three o'clock shift and ignored me. Whenever I managed to work my way close to her, she moved on. Baruk didn't leave at three o'clock, which troubled me. I wondered if he was on to something. I was full of unreasonable fears. But even if he'd been ordered to work a double shift, he increased the risk for us. Baruk was always in motion about the unit, looking for things out of place, coming out of nowhere to ask me about something that didn't meet with his concept of a normal, everyday explanation.

I watched for signs that something might have gone wrong, and then worried that my watching might have drawn attention to the fact that something was going on. I was on a knife edge of anticipation. When I went around to the patients in their rooms my hands shook as I handed them their dinner trays.

Baruk was in a foul mood. I didn't get the brunt of it. He bawled out one of the guards—in fact, I think it was Fairburn—for letting an inmate into the TV room when he was meant to be on bed rest. The Red Sox were playing. Everyone wanted business out of the way early, especially the guards, so that they could lounge in the doorway and catch the game.

I worked at being transparent. When I saw Baruk haranguing Fairburn in the corridor, I tried to pass them like a ghost.

"And you!"

Baruk stopped me in the middle of his sentence. Fairburn took the opportunity to make himself scarce.

"Where are you going?" he demanded. There was an angry glint in his eye.

"To the supplies closet, Sarge."

"What for?"

"To fill the sprayer. The windows need doing."

"Damn right. If you think you're going to watch the game, forget it. You're cleaning windows."

"Right, Sarge."

"Don't give me that!"

"What?"

He leisurely crossed the five feet that separated us, his hands behind his back, his face ending up a few inches from mine. It's a standard intimidation tactic. Baruk is ten years younger than I am, and although he has a square, muscular body, he's two inches shorter and I'd built myself up with weights to the point that I could hold my own against any man who wasn't armed.

I waited for him to say his piece. When they're being bawled out, there's a way inmates have of retreating to the back of their heads, leaving only their eyes, dead and glazed, in front for the guard to talk to. But a wild defiance flared up in me, and I stared back. We stood for a long moment toe to toe, locked in confrontation. He wanted me to speak, but I wouldn't, even when I had everything that night to lose.

I looked down and away in time. Baruk stood unchanged for a second, then rolled back his shoulders to throw out his chest. I felt the tension in him slacken.

Fairburn came back.

"Sarge?" he began.

But Baruk, never taking his eyes off me, raised his hand, and Fairburn held the question he'd been about ask. Baruk tilted his head back, and his eyes narrowed.

"Don't condescend to me, Cody."

"I don't, Sarge."

Baruk nodded his head as if he were considering this, while his face rejected everything he thought I stood for.

"You don't think I notice what you're about?" he said. There was a small, bitter smile at the corners of his mouth.

"How d'you mean, Sarge?"

Baruk mimicked a superior tone. " 'How do you mean, Sarge?'" He snorted. "Give me a break!"

Fairburn shifted uncomfortably from one foot to the other, not knowing whether to stay or go. I began to say something, but Baruk cut me off.

"You think a Ph.D. makes you a better man than me."

"Sarge, I don't have a—"

"—I can hear it in your tone of voice. You sneer, Cody."

"I really don't, Sarge."

"And you know what gets to me, what *really* gets to me? It's you think you can slip it by me and I won't notice." He waited, but I knew better than to speak. "Do you think you can put one over on me?"

"No."

He considered me for a while. He'd wanted a crushing victory. Something that would prove something.

"OK," he said, as if he'd already lost interest.

I walked away, and I knew that his eyes followed me every step to the supplies closet. As I swung open the door, it would have been natural for me to turn and glance back, but I knew he knew I knew he watched me.

I started with the windows of the officers' trap, where Baruk would see me every time he turned his head. I thought he'd soon get sick of looking at me, but he ignored me. I moved steadily along the corridor, taking my time in squirting mists of cleaner against the Plexiglas. I spread the fluid across the surface of each window in a leisurely way and rubbed to dislodge invisible specks. Then, quickly and exactly, I cleared the pane with the rubber edge of the wiper.

I did all the windows on the inner rim of Medical's "U" and made a point of going to the officers' trap to ask Baruk if I could take a break. I wanted him to feel that he knew where I was.

He was leaning back in a swivel chair, his legs stretched out so that his feet hooked under the steel desk and locked him into position. His mouth was open in a fixed snarl, and he stared at a point high up on the wall in front of him as he worked between his teeth with a tool from his Swiss Army knife. He knew I could kill him. He enjoyed the power of being vulnerable, off balance, rocking slightly in the swivel chair, almost with his back to me, yet knowing I'd never touch him. Baruk thought it was his power, that it went with him wherever he went.

"OK if I have dinner now, Sarge?" I asked.

For a second I thought he hadn't heard me. He took the tool out of his mouth and pursed his lips and then slowly nodded, as if his thoughts were slow to return from that very precise point between hard and soft far back within his head. I waited in case he wanted to say something, but he didn't.

I sat on an upended bucket in the supplies closet. It was a quiet place, the closest thing anyone had to privacy in Denning. My mind was in a whirl. There were too many possibilities. I was afraid I was losing Carol. That was the possibility I feared most—that this was the kiss-off. I thought about the conversations we'd had. I reanalyzed the tone of her voice, her choice of one word over another for indications that she wanted to bring the relationship to an end, but I'd replayed the conversations so many times in my head that I wasn't sure that I could reach back to what had really passed between us, even though I had total recall of the words. But words aren't much more than bare bones.

There was a clock in the nurses' station, but I was staying away from Carol. I passed by the officers' trap to check the clock on the wall behind Baruk, but he noticed at once what I was about. Time isn't supposed to matter to me.

"What's up, Cody? You got a hot date tonight?"

It's a line he used every time he saw me look at his clock more than once on a shift. Once Baruk finds a chunk of language that appeals to him, he likes to get good use from it. Either he enjoys the repetition, or he knows how it grates on me. I'd heard the line every couple of weeks for a year, but that evening it threw me into a panic.

Time plays tricks when you want so much for it to pass. I worried I'd be early to the old office. Then, when I couldn't risk any hurry, I was terrified I'd be late. At last, I finished all the rooms on the right side of the "U," stood back from my work, stretched for the benefit of anyone who might be watching, gathered the spritzer bottle and the squeegee, and made my way leisurely along the corridor.

I couldn't walk naturally. When you're thinking about how your arm is supposed to swing with the added weight of the spritzer at the end of it, or the exact degree your knee should bend for walking naturally, the movement decomposes. I'd lost the knack of acting natural.

I passed the empty nurses' trap and risked a glance at the clock. I turned the corner. This corridor was darker. At the end there used to be another entrance to Medical, but they'd blocked it off and the corridor ended blindly, with the old office at the end on the left and the doctor's office on the right. The lights in the patients' rooms were out.

If you haven't made love to a woman in four years, you're a virgin again, scared and grateful. I wanted her like an animal. And yet this wasn't what I wanted, a sex act. I wanted to feel her truly with me.

I stopped in front of the door to the old office and glanced back along the empty corridor and listened to the sudden rise in sound from the people watching the ball game. I wanted to say something that would evoke her voice, but I kept to the rules she'd set. The door had a window with a pull-down screen on the inside, and the orange glow of the floodlights from the yard beyond the office leaked around the edges and through the ventilation panel set above. I touched my hands to the door and leaned my head against the surface of the window and concentrated on her presence on the other side of the door. She made no sound. I wanted to speak her name. I tried to sense her pressed against the other side of the door, two inches from me. I felt a fragment of her presence and I tried to catch hold of it and make it grow, but it slipped away and she disappeared and I was alone again.

I inched my fingers through the small slot in the door that had been used for delivering lab slips. I felt about blindly in the orange light on the other side, straining through the hole for an answering touch and at last I felt skin lightly brush me. My fingers curled and stretched hopelessly after it.

On the other side, I heard the creak of wooden furniture and I thought I saw a shadow of movement cast by the floodlights in the yard. Then nothing. I checked the corridor. I had forgotten the sound of the ball game, and at that moment it surged up, with guards and inmates cheering together. I hesitated. I felt close to panic with impatience and fear and animal excitement. I felt the urgency to act or let the opportunity pass forever from my reach. And at the same time, like a cool draft on the back of my neck, I had a premonition of another moment converging, as though in another corner of the prison someone I hadn't considered had started on a trajectory that would place him at this point, in time to prevent my moment from happening. Something brushed my fingers. It could have been a tongue. I hadn't realized how fiercely I gripped the slot, hanging on, afraid to let go, afraid to undo my hold and reach for the skid of the helicopter that was even now taking off, lifting up for the rooftop escape.

I unzipped. I checked the corridor. Standing on tiptoe, I guided myself, erect, through the slot. I clung to the corners of the door frame by my fingertips and held myself against the slot and waited forever, naked in the orange light on the other side, my heart beating, hanging out into plain air.

She touched me at last. She brushed a finger along the underside, and I was flooded with delight. She slowly traced a pathway with a fingertip that passed with agonizing closeness to the hidden points of greatest pleasure and stopped short where I begged her silently to go on, to begin again. She waited.

She held me lightly between finger and thumb and drew me farther into the room. I had to strain to follow her. I rose on my toes as far as I could go and pressed harder against the door, and as I levered on my fingertips I felt myself start to slip and swing outward and I grabbed the wiper from my back pocket and reached up to hook it on the ledge beneath the ventilation panel and hung from it.

I felt the lick of a tongue spiraling, moistening, each ridge picking out individual nerve endings with an intensity like pain. She pressed, and I felt myself taken in. Her lips yielded with a smooth, calculated reluctance that brought me close to crying out. I didn't dare move. I teetered on the ends of toes and pressed flat against the door and gripped the handle of the wiper as if it were an ice ax that was all that held me to the rock face. The lips moved so slowly that I wanted to beat against the door in frustration, anguish, delight. She held me helpless. She pulled back with the same control, all the way to the tip, and let go with a final squeeze that sent a quiver through me, dangling and bouncing in space, suddenly naked and cold in the unknown space on the other side.

She disappeared. In that pause, she demonstrated her power over me. To give and to withhold. She controlled every nuance of sensation. She gave pleasure one heartbeat at a time and stopped according to some secret rhythm of her own to leave me hanging by aching fingers hooked above the door. Every part of me strained through that slot. I was a dumb, blind, helpless thing that groped in darkness to find its place. She tortured me, and I raged against her. When she took me again, I almost sobbed aloud in gratitude. The muscles in my legs fluttered at the edge of exhaustion, scarcely able to obey. Their ache, the stretch of my body against the door, the agony of her pauses, all converged, closing on the moment of release.

I wouldn't surrender to her. I wouldn't close my eyes and give myself up to the sensation. And so I saw Baruk as he rounded the corner, though he made no sound. I unhooked the wiper from the ledge above the door and turned slightly from him as I stretched up

102

with great care to scrub at the ventilation panel. Baruk sauntered toward me. Half of me watched his approach; half of me was lost on the other side of the door where I was being drawn down in a rhythm that went on regardless.

I reached down for the spritzer hanging from the handle of the door. My fingers found it. With half my mind, I tried to concentrate on working the spritzer with my hand. I was lost on the other side of the door. I was separating. Spreading ripples of fear met ripples of delight.

Baruk strolled toward me with his hands clasped behind his back. He looked left and right into the rooms as he passed, as though I wasn't his destination, as though I happened to be only something along his route. I sprayed the pane above the door and caught out of the corner of my eye a change of direction when he crossed the corridor to check a door. And all the time those lips held me, extruded me, dropped me, in a progress that ratcheted closer and closer to the climax.

Baruk came to a stop ten feet away. He kept his hands behind his back, his feet apart, rocking his weight forward on the balls of his feet. I felt a shiver run through me, a foretaste of orgasm, as Baruk regarded me.

"You want to get a chair or something, Cody," he said at last.

All movement on the other side of the door stopped at the sound of his voice.

"You're going to give yourself a hernia, stretching like that," Baruk said.

"Yes, Sarge," I got out.

I reached up and drew the wiper in an arc across the pane above the door. I was hovering at the edge. The movement began on the other side. The wiper was silent and smooth across the glass.

"What's that?" Baruk demanded.

He was frowning. He took a step toward me.

"I said, 'Yes, Sarge.'"

My voice was strangled. I was being carried away. I was submerging. I was afraid I'd cry out as I began to drown. I burst into the unknown on the other side. I lost myself. I clutched with both hands at the ledge above the door, and the life went out of me in a gasp.

"See what I mean?" Baruk said. He studied my stance. "There's got to be a better way to do it."

"I know," I said.

Sweat broke on my forehead. I felt soft and weak, full of tenderness. My legs were about to let go on me. They quivered, and I felt my heels drop an inch and I couldn't pull them all the way up again. I wiped jerkily at the rest of the pane. Behind me, Baruk was silent, and when I next looked around, I found that he had walked away.

Carol changed to the second shift a week later, so I saw her only when one of the other nurses called in sick and she had to work a double, or when I came back to the unit at dinnertime. Even before the switch, she rarely spoke to me unless someone else was there. I was lonely without our stolen moments. She made a point of demonstrating to whomever might have noticed that she wasn't aware of my existence.

Then, out of the blue, while someone's back was turned, she'd flash me a shy, awkward smile, as if she'd all but lost the knack of how to move her lips in synch with her feelings. Then some of the hurt would melt away and my faith in her would be restored. These signs of love never lasted more than a moment, and they were gone so quickly that at times I doubted that it had happened at all.

I was stirred and uneasy. The sexual appetite was like a wound that Carol had opened and that wouldn't heal. I couldn't put thoughts of her aside. The desire for her possessed me. Sometimes I felt anger toward her, the idea of her. There are crack dealers who give out samples to hook customers, and at times when I was most frustrated, I felt I'd been had. I'd catch a glimpse of her in the corridor as she disappeared around a corner, and I'd feel a stirring that made my heart beat faster. It was body stuff. Animal heat. I hated that it dominated me. I felt defective that it so easily squeezed out finer feelings. And even the sex of it was confused. When Carol treated me coldly, in bright light, sheathed in a pristine white uniform, with the clear definition provided by eyeliner, blush, and lipstick, I had difficulty connecting this person with the sensual presence behind the door.

I understood why she behaved the way she did, but in my heart,

I never believed that she would really break me out. I felt that I was suffering for nothing. I had no idea how resourceful Carol was!

But I hope that what I have said makes understandable why, now that I have been given the chance, I keep her close. I know that she gave a lot of thought to the original plan. But it involved a separation, and I have no reason to trust in a benign fate to reunite us. Plans have a habit of going wrong. I was afraid that once we separated in the parking lot outside the emergency ward and I went to the safe place and Carol returned to work the evening shift at Denning, I'd never see her again. So once we came together again in the ICU, I saw no reason to risk another parting. That was why I took her with me.

Besides, the original plan entailed too many uncertainties. The police would have gone through the visitors' log and come up with a mysterious woman who resembled the ICU nurse: same age, roughly, same coloring, same height, and so on. Maybe they'd have chased after Vera for a couple of days. But sooner or later, they were going to look for a connection between the temp in the ICU and a nurse on Medical. The wig and the glasses may have fooled the temp agency, but would a borrowed identity based on the license of one of her classmates from nursing school really have stood up to scrutiny?

Carol was angry at first that I "kidnapped" her. In the heat of anger, under stress of the escape, hurtful things were said. Now I think she's come to recognize that this is the way it must be: all or nothing.

I really don't believe I've ruined her life. It's true that in a sense she has sacrificed her life for me. She can't go back now. She can't return to her life as a nurse, living in an apartment in a nice neighborhood. But what kind of life was that, anyway? If it was so precious, why did she start down the route she chose? Sometimes destiny is like bungee jumping: People need a small push if they're to find their way.

FOUR

Dear Sandy: You say that I've betrayed Carol. That's a lie! You want to manipulate us. You want to turn her against me. It'll never happen. We're solid. We are one.

You sneer at the story of our love. I'm sorry you think yourself so superior. The report you aired last night oozes innuendo. Why not come out and say it? That there has to be something wrong with Carol if she chooses to be with me: Is that what you're trying to get across?

Do you really think I'm some pathetic loser who moons around women hoping they'll fall in love with him? Do you think Carol broke me out of prison because she felt sorry for me?

I won her! I won Carol over to me.

Do you have any idea how difficult that is in prison? How hard it is, given our positions, for a man who is an inmate to win the love of a woman who is free?

Nothing is pure. There is no such thing in this world. Did I take advantage of Carol? Yes. I freely admit it. I don't like it, but I'll own it. Did I exploit her affections? Yes! Yes! Yes! God knows I am not proud of this. But I did use her for selfish ends: I wanted to escape from prison. I manipulated her. I hate that word! I did manipulate her. I would rather say it myself, clearly spell it out, than have you make suggestions on TV. Let's get out the whole story so there's no more hiding: I manipulated Carol, and I love her with every particle of my being.

I'm sorry that our love had to be on those terms. But if I hadn't used some small degree of coercion, occasionally, to nudge things along, there would have been no love affair. I would much rather that we'd simply fallen in love. Like falling out of a window, or off a log, or out of a canoe. I would much rather that something simple and irresistible like gravity had brought us together, but it could never have happened that way. I had to bring us together. I had to use my intelligence and my imagination. Frankly, I'm ashamed of some of the things I did. But they were to bring us into a kind of contact we wouldn't have known otherwise, a means to an end.

Carol hasn't been the same since the escape. Don't flatter yourself that I'm revealing any crucial piece of information when I say that she takes off for hours at a time without telling me where she goes. I'm well aware of the sly digs you slip in to provoke me. The fact is, she needs space. She needs to think. And I want her to know everything. It's the only way. For some reason my words carry more weight with her when she hears them on television. The only way is to make a clean breast of everything I've done. This is temporary. Our destinies are tied together.

In J Block, there is a yellow line painted on the floor. You must walk along it at all times when you're out of your cell. For the first six months on Medical, I walked some imaginary yellow line. I didn't push the rules. I didn't take advantage or liberties. I was always ready to work when something needed to be done, however dirty the job, even if it was during my break time. I was exemplary.

The result was that Baruk went easy on me, and Carol, seeing me cut corners in full view of the sergeant, didn't object if I committed a minor infraction when Baruk wasn't there. And when I did cross the line with Carol, I was always sure to step back again quickly, to show her that I knew my place.

For example, when I delivered fresh towels to her, she held the door for me so that I could put one foot inside the trap and place them on the edge of the counter for her. It was taboo for me to cross the threshold. In theory, if I had been the great white shark, I could have stepped all the way in, moved her from the door, and taken her into the tiny bathroom at the back and raped her. That was the fear the institution tried to instill in its civilian employees. But she knew I wouldn't do that. Anyway, what was one step? It didn't seem like a big thing. There was simply no need for Carol to struggle to take the pile of towels at the same time as she had to lean all her weight against the door to keep it open, when it was so easy for me to twist around the corner and put them on the counter in a neat pile for her. Why make a fuss about one step?

When rules are strictly adhered to, a small incident like this, which may seem insignificant outside the institution, is like a wedge. It means something. It means a lot. It sets a precedent. It means you can do it again, maybe push it a bit farther, a little more each time, until you have something more than a symbol, an advantage that is real. This is how I began. It was planned. Each step I advanced was deliberate. I am not proud of what I did, but you have to understand that everything I did was a matter of survival. The inmates looked at me and they saw someone soft, middle class. If you don't have the background of the streets, if you don't have that kind of schooling, you'll never be on equal terms with them. Once a man's natural, unreflective viciousness has been tamed, the reflex never comes back. I knew that. More important, the predators around me scented it immediately.

But Carol was drawn to me. I was the only educated person she had to talk to. To her credit, she didn't get along with Tanya, the other nurse. Tanya fit her environment because she was coarse and insensitive, but since it was just the two of them in the trap, Carol had no choice but to work with her as best she could. Tanya was maybe five years younger than Carol, with blond hair and big thighs that rubbed together when she walked so that her tights made a whiffing sound. Tanya generated static electricity. The way she swung her hips, thrusting out her big breasts, you'd have

108

thought she was the goddess of love. This crude stuff drove the inmates wild. Tanya pretended not to notice, but not very well.

When Tanya was in the nurses' station with Carol, I took no liberties. Tanya was very clear that there was a class distinction between herself and inmates. Unless she wanted me to run an errand for her, Tanya acted as though I didn't exist. I was a subhuman to her. If Carol became a little more flexible each week, Tanya was on the lookout for the smallest infraction. Tanya guarded the boundary.

I remember the first time Carol called me "Dan" in front of Tanya. They were sitting in the trap looking out through the steel screen.

Carol called, "Dan, would you check and see if Smith ate his dinner?"

I started off, and saw Tanya out of the corner of my eye with her hand half covering her mouth, her face screwed up as if she'd bitten into something sour, mouthing the question to Carol, "Dan?"

Around this time I started the rumor that Carol was working undercover for the state police. I know this caused her a lot of unhappiness. I hope she can forgive me.

After Ralph's death, Eric took over the minimums. He was convinced I had access to drugs on Medical, and I had a difficult time convincing him that I didn't. Every few weeks he'd have me up to the third tier for an intelligence briefing. Usually Bentley, who'd been transferred from Max One soon after me, was with him. It was obvious Eric and Bentley didn't trust one another, but they needed each other for political reasons.

"This nurse," Eric asked once. "Carol. She lets you talk to her?"

"Now and then. Baruk's on my case a lot." I shrugged. "She asks questions."

I saw his focus tighten. His feet came off the railing, and he let the front legs of the chair lower slowly to the ground.

"What kind of questions?" He stared up at me, scrutinizing me through the lenses of his glasses.

"You know," I said. "Life in the joint."

"What about it?"

109

"What people do."

"What do people do?" Bentley asked, looking away, surveying the flat. He seemed careless.

"She sees people brought to Medical messed up on drugs. She sees all the disasters."

"If she sees it all on Medical, what does she need to ask questions for?" Eric wanted to know.

"It doesn't mean anything. It's just her way of making converstion."

"She makes conversation?" Bentley asked. "Why is she making conversation with an inmate?"

"I don't know."

"Huh? You thought of that?" Eric demanded.

"I don't know," I said doubtfully.

"Does she ask you about drugs?" Eric demanded. "Huh? Does she?"

I didn't say anything.

Bentley, leaning against the rail, snorted. "Schoolteacher!"

"You don't get it?" Eric asked.

"OK," I surrendered, acting feeling stupid.

"What does she ask you about drugs?" Eric wanted to know.

"General things. Nothing specific. Like, 'Is it a big problem?' 'What are people using?' "

" 'What are people using?' That isn't specific?"

"Why is she asking you these questions?" Bentley asked. His eyes were pitiless.

"She asks me because I'm there. She asks me a lot of questions. About anything. She asks me about the guards."

Bentley looked interested.

"Stick with the questions she asks you about drugs," Eric said.

"No," Bentley said. "Tell us what she wants to know about the screws."

"What for?" Eric said.

"What does she want to know about the screws?" Bentley said. He came off the railing and took a step closer to me.

"I don't know—like, Isn't it terrible they can't stop drugs coming in?"

"And?"

110

"Are they conscientious? Do I know any of them who take bribes."

"She asked you that?"

"I don't know—once maybe. A while back."

I left Eric hunched over the railing staring across the void at the tier opposite while Bentley talked urgently into his ear.

Four days later, Sammy Shay sat down opposite me in the chow hall. He was very pleased with himself.

"That nurse you're so concerned about? The dark one?"

"What about her?" I asked carefully.

"You're wasting your time."

He smirked and waited for me, but I didn't say anything. He looked around. I suppose he felt relatively safe in the chow hall.

"At least I had the balls to treat her the way she deserved," he said.

"How's that?"

He stalled for maximum effect. "Because the lady is a cop."

"That's bullshit," I told him with no emotion. I collected the utensils together on my tray.

"She's fucking FBI," Shay said. He was excited by the thought. "Know what I was saying to her?" He giggled in spite of himself. "Oh, man! If I'd have known!"

"You don't know anything," I said.

"Everybody knows it. You take a look around next time. None of the screws talk to her. They know it, too."

"She's not FBI."

"Sure she is. Ask your sergeant on Medical. He had a buddy of his run a check on her."

"She's not FBI." I stood to go and picked up my tray. "She's state police," I told him.

I knew there was some risk to Carol in this, and when the rumor first got started I watched to see that no harm came to her. But there was no real danger. If the state police had had an operation going inside Denning, they'd be interested in catching some screws, and the guards weren't about to kill a police officer.

What happened was that all at once everyone stopped talking to Carol. Baruk kept his distance. Even chatty Tanya confined herself to the business at hand. Wherever Carol went, she cast a chill around her. Conversations stopped as she approached. Officers avoided her eye. People drifted away. Or they waited, nodding silently at anything she might say, staring into the distance over her shoulder, until she went on her way, and then she would hear behind her the sound of their conversation begin again. Or perhaps a laugh that could have been at her expense, or then again could have had nothing to do with her at all. I saw the look of incomprehension on her face, and my heart ached for her.

Baruk treated her with icy correctness. There was something girlish about the way she stood while she talked with him. She had a loose, spiral stance, with her legs crossed and one hand on a hip. She twisted slightly, making her seem tentative and insubstantial before Baruk planted solidly on the ground.

Once he walked away before she'd finished what she wanted to say. I saw her turn her face aside, the cheek exposed as if a slap had deflected her head. She gathered herself.

"Oh, Rich?" she called after him. "Rich?"

Baruk stopped. He held his back to her.

"I forgot . . ." Carol tried.

He turned to her slowly, as though turning to her required great effort and deliberation.

"Yes?" he asked softly, with perfect, neutral pitch.

He has a large mouth with thick lips, and he brought them to a small smile and held them as if he was sculpting them from the inside. I'd underrated him. An eyebrow arched to just the right degree—in inquiry, in irony—it was impossible to decide until you saw the glint in his eye. I'd thought Baruk wasn't capable of subtlety. He was a mask of courtesy.

Carol saw perfectly, and the glint withered her.

"It doesn't matter," she said.

"You're sure?" Baruk asked mercilessly.

She couldn't bring herself to look at him. I never saw her so wounded.

"No," she said. Her lower lip was slack. She was working to control herself.

Baruk stared at her and nodded to himself with satisfaction.

"No?" he asked. He was very patient, drawing out the pain,

taunting her with her loneliness. "No, it doesn't matter, or no, it does matter?"

Carol scoffed. "Forget it."

She seemed to find some reserve of defiance that took up the slack. Her body tightened. Her head came up. She pulled a smile, as if this was all part of a game, fun.

I watched it all from inside one of the patients' rooms where I was wiping down the door frame. I was proud of her.

"I'll catch you some other time," she told Baruk.

He shrugged as he turned. He sauntered away, once more disguised as the crude man, the alpha male: chest thrown out, hands clasped on either side of the belt buckle, masterful in the swing of his shoulders, his unhurried stride. Even in that macho world, the stance was pompous.

Sometimes I found Carol stuck in an image of isolation and confusion. On one occasion she sat alone in the trap with her eyes closed holding her hands cupped in front of her face. She exhaled slowly and carefully into them until she'd emptied her lungs, and at the fullest extent quickly inhaled her breath again in little spurts, testing it for odor. This occurred over and over again, like some hopeless circling motion of an animal.

No one told her what was wrong. She became very lonely. I was her sole friend. It was only a matter of time before she turned to me to help her understand the mystery that surrounded her.

She gave a nervous laugh, full of unhappiness. She didn't know how to begin.

"I feel like people are treating me . . ."

She moved her hands in an unfinished gesture. I thought she was going to give up. Then she ambushed me with her eyes, as if by looking up suddenly into my face, she might catch some sign that I was in the know.

"Like I'm supposed to have done something." She shook her head, not believing. "I don't know."

"They're a very tight group," I said.

"Sometimes I think I'm imagining it."

"They're OK, once you get to know them. Of course, I don't know them on a personal level. But they've always been fair to me, mostly."

113

"They turn away. Right in the middle when I'm talking to them."

"It gets to be their style, talking to inmates all the time."

"Have you seen that?"

I laughed. "They do it to me all the time. Welcome to the club!"

"I guess." I saw her lips relax at the moment before speech, then hesitate, then begin again. "I mean, have you seen them treat me that way?" She risked a look through the steel mesh at my face.

"You mean, treat you like an inmate?"

"Have you?"

"No," I said, wondering. "No, I can't say I have."

There it is right there: the betrayal. I betrayed the woman I loved. I caused her suffering. But I had to do it. I had to contrive a situation that would make her turn to me. The only way was if she reached out to me. I didn't see any other way to bring her within reach. There are times when destiny needs a nudge, like when the needle got stuck on one of those old 45 records, playing the same chopped-off fragment of song over and over, which is like life in prison.

The news got around quickly. The question of which side you're on is the most important one in prison. And here was a whole new side no one had considered up till now. She was instantly defined, categorized. Carol was a gang of one.

The guards were much more antagonistic toward her than the inmates. They put her through every petty, calculated harassment they could think of. You can justify anything in the interests of security.

She came onto Medical one day clutching her head. I thought they'd beaten her. She had her head down, almost running, with both hands spread over her hair. I tried to speak to her, but she hurried by me, shaking her head, fighting back tears.

I thought, "I started something. I've caused this."

I was ready to smash my face through a window if that would have made it up to her. Her tears were acid that burned me far worse than any pain of my own. She went away from me and wouldn't speak. I couldn't bear to see her cry. I couldn't bear the slow ache of her pain inside me. I thought of breaking surface through a pane of

114

glass, something thin like they use in picture frames, something that forms naturally into thin, curved shards. I imagined swimming from the depths, upwards toward glittering light, and breaking surface through the glass with my face streamlined as if by water, except by blood and cutting, features sheared away.

I held this image. It steadied me, and I felt a center forming again as I walked after her to the trap. She hadn't switched on the overhead lights, and with only the light of the desk lamp, it was difficult to see what she was doing. She made quick, desperate, wafting movements at her head, then shook her hair loose again. It tumbled down around her shoulders in disarray, with wisps sticking sideways and dark coils bouncing. She was loosened and disheveled, as though she'd just stepped out of bed. She turned away so that I wouldn't see her.

"What happened?" I asked her.

"Not now."

"Maybe I can help," I begged.

She sat completely still with her back to me. Her hands clasped her head with the fingers spread and the palms over her ears as if she couldn't bear to hear anything more. I waited for her, hoping she would speak or turn around. She moved a hand suddenly, as if she thought she might be naked.

"What did they do to you?" I asked.

She let out a deep, shuddering breath. She turned around, and I saw her teeth were clenched; her whole face was clenched tight to hold back anger and humiliation.

"They took my hairpins," she said at last. She let out a bitter little laugh. "How petty can you get?" She started to raise her hands in a gesture, forgetting about her hair, so that it cascaded about her face and down her neck.

"I thought they'd hurt you," I said.

I was transfixed by the wild nakedness of her hair fallen about her head. She was new to me. In the glance she shot me, through the dark tunnel of hair that had fallen about her eyes, I saw another person concealed within her.

"I'm crazy if I let it get to me," she said.

"Don't," I said. I watched her shoulders rise and fall. She made small movements of her head as if she was trying to

115

shake herself loose from the hold of emotion. "Don't let them get to you."

"I can't help it." She tried to make the words suggest that she was nothing more than exasperated, but her eyes glistened with rage. "They made me take them out one by one. They ran a metal detector over my head."

"It's just harassment," I said.

"It's never been a problem until now." She shook her head, smiling, as if the strength of her reaction had surprised her in an amusing kind of way. "Now all of a sudden, hair clips are a security risk. They say they can use them to pick locks."

She kept forgetting herself, talking to me as if I was simply another person. Then she'd remember that I was an inmate and try to make light of what had been done to her. She went back and forth, including me, pushing me away.

"You know what we should do?" I said. "I've got an idea."

Right away she was wary, as if she'd seen it coming, that I'd make some move on her. But she hesitated. It wasn't clear anymore what side she was on, or even whether she had a side to be on at all.

"All right," she said. "What is it?"

"I have to show you," I told her, grinning as if this was going to be a joke and pointing inside the trap.

"No," she said flatly.

She wasn't angry with me. She'd known all along I was going to try to get into the trap. This was in the beginning, when I was first getting to know her, before I learned how to maneuver in the gulf that lay between us. I was going too fast. Even if she was no longer with them, she wasn't yet with me.

I coached her through the mesh.

"Open the drawer in the desk," I told her. She humored me. "Now take out a paper clip."

"No," she said, seeing where I was leading.

"Take out a paper clip," I insisted.

"It'll never work."

I coaxed her. "Try it. Go on."

"I'll look stupid."

"Never."

I was too ardent. I felt her cool.

116

"Anyway," she said, "they can say the same thing about these."

She rubbed two clips between finger and thumb, considering them, and I knew she'd try it.

"How can they be a security risk if the Department of Correction supplies them?" I asked.

"I suppose so."

"And they'll look great with your hair. You could start a new fashion."

I hadn't realized how many clips she'd need to hold her hair up. I was her mirror. She watched my face as she tilted her head at an angle to reach a particular spot with both hands. I encouraged her and almost made her laugh. Finally, she scooped up a handful of paper clips and went into the bathroom at the back of the trap to finish the job.

When she came into the trap again and turned this way and that to show me what she'd done, the effect was magnificent and strange, with individual clips catching the light of the desk lamp and glistening silver like drops of dew formed in her hair.

"What d'you think?" she asked, though I think she could see the adoration in my eyes.

"You'll do," I told her.

She spun around, vamping. She dazzled me. She was renewed, dressed up, on her way to a New Year's Eve party I hadn't been invited to.

She leaned over the counter, closer, and I thought she would grasp the mesh between us, to break with her fingertips the plane that separated us, but she changed her mind at the last moment.

"Hey." She broke into a smile. "Thanks for helping me out." She looked down to pick up a folder of lab results from the counter. "Really. I appreciate it." She flashed me a smile, then opened the folder and turned away.

She wanted me gone. I was crushed, but I shouldn't have been surprised. A role is like a mask: nurse, inmate. With one word, with a particular intonation, she was telling me that the roles remained intact, that the masks were back in place. Whatever I thought may have happened, she defined the moment by giving me a tip: "Thanks."

117

Around this time, I suggested to Carol that I help out by doing the vital signs. The answer should have been no, but she needed the help. Tanya wasn't speaking to her then and communicated by leaving messages on scraps of paper in the nurses' trap. This gave Tanya all sorts of opportunities to avoid her share of the work and placed a greater burden on Carol, who felt that she had to take care of any chore that didn't get done.

Baruk was doubtful for the correct reasons—it gave me an excuse to be in all sorts of places I wouldn't otherwise have a reason to go—but it was hard to turn down an inmate who seemed intent on rehabilitating himself. Besides, with a police informer on his unit, he had more important things to worry about. He kept himself at his end of the corridor and only occasionally patrolled as far as the nurses' trap.

My new task brought me into closer contact with the inmates who were sick. I would take my time measuring the blood pressure, counting the pulse and the respirations, reading the temperature off the digital thermometer, and we'd talk. I liked to listen to the stories of an old bank robber who'd shot a cop. Other inmates on Medical were drug disasters, who'd infected themselves or overdosed. Mostly, I spent time with the patients who were dying of AIDS.

It wasn't long before I'd made myself indispensable. Tanya soon caught on that I was willing to be used. Rather than work, she preferred to sit all day at the counter in the nurses' trap, waiting unhappily for her shift to be over, for her life to go by. Now and then some frustration would build in her to the point that she'd abruptly storm off down the corridor to pull something out of the vending machine in the staff lounge. She had me doing everything I could safely do, except for handing out medications.

It was Tanya who got me working evenings. The first time I arrived on Medical after dinner, I was surprised to see Nando waiting outside the treatment room. I could tell from the way he tightened up when he caught sight of me that he hated the idea that I knew he was there. That small, dark brown man was pure, concentrated attentiveness, yet as I walked by him on my way to the officers' trap, I might as well not have existed.

Baruk was working late. Since the regular evening sergeant hadn't said anything to him about me, he didn't know what I was doing on Medical at that hour, and we had to go in search of Tanya so that she could explain it to him. She wasn't in the trap. Nando had disappeared from the corridor. Baruk knocked on the door to the treatment room.

"Tanya in here?" he asked.

"Yes," she called out. "Who wants me?"

He opened the door hesitantly, held back by a sense that he was intruding into medical space. Tanya must have just handed Nando the syringe. Baruk was going to say something, but he was taken with the image of Nando sitting on the edge of a stainless-steel stool in white underpants, dungarees around his knees, the syringe sticking out of his thigh.

"What?" Tanya demanded.

"Can I have a word?" Baruk said.

He was out of place. His eyes kept going to the syringe sunk into Nando's thigh. Baruk hung on the doorjamb and the handle and leaned into the room so that he wouldn't set foot inside and waited for Nando to inject the insulin before he could say what he'd come for.

Nando pushed the plunger, backhanded, with his thumb and held it there. He stared at us staring at him. Then he flicked out the needle with a professional flourish.

"What's the problem?" Tanya asked.

Nando looked aside as if none of this could matter to him. He inventoried the medical supplies along the counter. His hands hung loose between his thighs, and I didn't see the syringe anymore.

"A question about Cody here," Baruk said, gruff and formal in front of the inmates.

Tanya's attention was on Baruk as she came to the doorway. Nando was pulling up his trousers. Someone called Baruk from down the corridor and he looked away. Nando had his wrist crooked and was about to tuck the syringe up his sleeve, when Tanya remembered and held out the red plastic container.

"Cody's working evenings now," she said.

She rattled the container in front of Nando, still engaged with Baruk, challenging him to take me away from her.

"This man is my worker. He works days."

119

"He does both. It was cleared through Lieutenant Silva."

Nando looked up to her face. His dark eyes were still and without malice. Then he dropped the syringe, and I heard the needle make a dry, scratching sound against the plastic as it fell.

A few months after I started work on Medical, the superintendent died in his office. No one shed any tears for him. No one would have thought much about it, except that the department dragged its feet in appointing a replacement, and so his deputy became the acting superintendent, and his assistant became the acting deputy, and so on down the line, everyone in charge of anything in the prison an acting something, provisional, unsure of his powers, looking over his shoulder.

"Makes you think," I said to Carol. "Going like that, without any warning."

"He had a heart attack," she said. "He was a heavy smoker."

"I'd give it up myself, except it helps pass the time."

"I should give it up. I keep meaning to and I never do it."

"I will, if you will," I told her.

"What, just like that?"

I took my cigarette between finger and thumb, let it fall to the floor and ground it out with my toe.

"Just like that," I announced.

She smiled, her head to one side. There was always part of her that hung back, watching, assessing, wary. "Cold turkey?"

"It's the only way to go."

"I don't know." She shrugged.

"I could be saving your life right now," I told her.

I thought she was going to tell me it didn't matter. I caught a glimpse of weariness and disappointment, then she was quickly hidden again.

"I suppose," she said.

"I've done it."

"You haven't done anything!"

"Sure I have. I've stopped smoking. I'm not going to have another cigarette."

"It's easy to say."

"It's easier if we both do it. Then I won't have to watch you smoking."

120

"All right," she sighed.

"Make a commitment."

"I'll try. I'm not making any promises."

I could see that Carol was careful of getting herself entangled in the slightest way. Even a promise let her into a situation where another person held something over her. But I never saw her smoke another cigarette in Denning. The next day we compared notes.

"How do I know you didn't sneak a few puffs at home?" I asked her.

"You'll just have to trust me," she said, and there was a lilting, teasing, flirting tone to her voice that filled me with hope.

At some break in the morning's business we'd come together to talk about our common craving, the tricks of mind we'd almost fallen for, and the tricks we'd played to outwit the temptation to light up another cigarette. It was safe to share with each other our longing for one last lungful of smoke. It was safe, because it seemed to be about cigarettes. But beneath this surface, it was about keeping faith with each other, of being true. A metaphor can become real.

That was too much to hope for so soon. About this time, there was a change in the way people around Carol treated her. The suspicion that had surrounded her as a police informer melted away. I noticed officers nod to her when they passed. Then one day I came around the corner to find Carol and Baruk laughing together.

"Well, I got to do some work," he said.

He turned, but he didn't go. Carol lingered.

"I'd better be going, too," she said, but she didn't move, either.

There was a new, open configuration in the way their bodies stood in relation to each other. Carol with hands spread, feet apart, twisting at the hips, wavering, turning back; Baruk planted more solidly, hand gestures originating at the chest, eyes intent, holding her in his vicinity like a powerful magnet.

One day, around this time, I caught up with Carol as she was backing into the trap. She had her hands full with a clipboard and some IV equipment, and I jumped to hold the door open for her. She moved sideways and backwards and pirouetted. It seemed a very complicated, self-conscious way of moving past me. Instead of letting the door swing to behind her, I held it open with my foot. In my hand I held a Coke Baruk had given me.

"I'm not going to finish this floor for another half hour," I said.

I raised the Coke in my hand, hoping she'd be the one to suggest keeping it in the refrigerator.

"Would it be possible?"

I didn't want to make much of it. We both knew it was against the rules, but it was hot. Anyone has a right to a cold Coke after stripping a floor. The refrigerator was for medications like Nando's insulin, but if Tanya kept her Weight Watchers stuff there, what harm could a can of Coke do?

"It's unopened," I said.

"OK," Carol said, "but don't make a habit of it."

As soon as she said that, I knew I'd pushed too hard, and for several weeks I didn't try anything new. But I let Carol see at every opportunity what it was like to drink warm Coke. Once when I knew she was watching, I took a sip and then in disgust started to pour away the rest of the can, catching myself, as it were, when I noticed that she was watching. A Coke may not seem like much to you, but in prison a can of soda is something of value.

The next day, Carol called out to me, "Here, I can put that in the refrigerator."

I hesitated. "You sure it's all right?"

"Let me know when you want it."

After that, it was easy to make a habit of it.

From then, I started working my way deeper into the nurses' trap. I'd been inside plenty of times to clean the floor, but Baruk was there to watch me, half sitting on the counter, shooting the breeze with Tanya, his eye on Carol all the time. When Tanya was there, she didn't mind me taking a few steps inside the door if it meant that she didn't have to get out of her chair to take the supplies I'd brought. I made a point of doing this when Carol was there, too, so she didn't get the impression she was the only one letting little things slide.

One day I went into the trap after Carol. I slowed the door as it swung back and walked right in behind her and then let the door click shut behind me. I was so quiet that she was startled when she turned and caught sight of me.

"Oh, God!" she said, pressing her hand to her heart.

"Hey, easy!" I said. I kept on going to the refrigerator.

She didn't say anything, and I knew I'd taken a wrong turn. I stopped. I started to say something to reassure her, but she cut me off.

"Dan, what are you doing?"

I spread my hands and looked stupid. "I was just getting my Coke from the fridge?" I guessed.

"I mean, in the trap. What are you doing in the trap?"

"I'm doing what I usually do."

I looked around, playacting, for something that had changed the rules. Carol looked uneasy. Her lips were tight and set. She could have ordered me out of there. She could have said, quietly but sternly, eyes fixed distantly over my left shoulder, "Get out of here, please." She could have picked up the phone ("Oh, Rich") and had Baruk throw me out of the trap, never to return to Medical again. It was as simple as that. Or, rather, it had been as simple as that. We'd turned a corner. I'd become a person, and there are things you can say to an inmate you can't say to a person without a sense of betrayal.

"Look," I said, "if there's a problem, all you have to do is tell me."

"It's not a problem, necessarily—"

"—because, it's your trap."

"I know. What I'm saying is, it'd be nice if you asked before you come into the trap."

"OK. Sure. The only reason I didn't was that you'd said it would be all right if I put a can of Coke in the refrigerator."

"Right."

"And if you want to change your mind, that's your prerogative."

"That's not what I'm saying."

"We'll do it your way."

"It's my job on the line, Dan."

"Whatever you want."

I wanted to get inside the trap, but there was nothing I wanted

123

there. It was all about emotion—about crossing boundaries, about claiming a place in her life.

"Let's give Cody the day off tomorrow," she told Baruk later that afternoon.

I spent the next two days in a hell of uncertainty. I thought I'd imagined the whole thing between Carol and myself. The more I thought about it, the more the relationship seemed a sham. It was a dance of appearances—nothing but nuance, tones of voice, the choice of one word rather than another. I had nothing of substance. I told myself that any sign I'd had from her was something extorted, not given freely. I thought I'd seen beneath the mask, the necessary mask, that Carol had to wear to exist as a woman in prison, but I'd fooled no one but myself. I'd based my life on an illusion.

I felt myself disappearing. I spent the time in the weight room, using my body to change anger into mere physical pain. I considered joining Eric in the drug trade. That would have been a kind of suicide—not in the trivial sense of being murdered in the wars, but in killing off what I'd tried to preserve. I wanted to empty myself of anything that mattered.

But despair is grounding. You come eventually to a hard, solid core. I refused to give her up. I hoped against hope. In the end, it's not a decision. It's not rational. You make an act of faith.

It was only a matter of time before Eric talked to me about syringes.

"Let's do this one step at a time," he said slowly.

He had me sit on his bunk while he paced up and down in front of me, thinking aloud. A fly circled above us, colliding from time to time with the whitewashed ceiling.

"The used syringes go in the red plastic containers, right?" he asked.

"They have to put them there."

He waved me aside impatiently. "All of them, right? Every syringe they use?"

"Because of AIDS." I could see he was getting irritated, but I wanted him to know what he was dealing with. "These syringes have virus all over them."

"We can deal with that," he said impatiently. "We'll make sure people know to clean them. It's these red containers I want to know about. What happens to them when they're full?"

"They're never full. The nurses aren't meant to fill them. They're only half full, a third full when they send them out."

"So a container disappears?"

"They'll turn the place upside down."

"They count the containers?"

"Yes."

"But they don't keep track of how many syringes there are in this container or that container."

"It's not that easy," I told him.

"If it was easy, we'd all be doing it, right?"

"They never leave me alone in the treatment room."

"Nando says you have the run of the place."

"If it's so easy, why doesn't Nando steal his own syringes?"

"OK. You don't want to do it? Tell him yourself."

I could have balked, but we both knew that in the end I'd do what he wanted. I rigged a wire hook to dip into the red container and fish out a syringe. I tried it out when Tanya and the doctor were busy working on an inmate who had been stabbed in the stomach. No one questioned my presence in the treatment room, or even thought about why I would be there. It was easy to snag a syringe, lift it out, and drop it, needle up, into my underpants.

I thought there was something right about this method of transporting the deadly thing. If I bent over, if an officer decided on a spot check and patted me down with heavy hands, the contaminated needle would go into me. There was justice in this risk. It kept me from stealing syringes too easily, and it kept me close to the risk I was exposing some unknown inmate to in order to save my own skin. One wasn't enough, of course. They wanted more of the deadly things. All they could get, until I was caught. I didn't matter to them. I was an instrument, to be used until I was used up one way or another.

I don't know how Nando and Eric communicated with each other before they latched onto me. The routes must have been slow and roundabout, passing through several people with all the insecurity that entailed. By stealing that first syringe, I earned something that outside prison you'd call trust, although it's comical to apply the notion to professional paranoids like Nando and Eric. In their eyes, I had beaten the system, even a high-tech system—for some reason, Eric was especially impressed that I'd outsmarted the red containers. I'd shown that I was "willing to face reality," as he put it, meaning, that I was willing to be part of the most sordid kind of business, recycling virus-infected needles, to save my ass. If I could be reduced to operate on the basis of motives like their own, that made me understandable, therefore predictable.

The quickest, surest way to get a message back and forth between these men was for me to make contact with Nando when he came for his evening insulin. Most of the messages I carried consisted of no more than a few words. In the beginning, they were like pieces of a jigsaw puzzle that had no meaning when you didn't know the larger picture.

Nando would say, "Tell him he'll get it tomorrow." For some reason he never wanted to say Eric's name. Or Eric would say, "Ask Nando if he'll take five," and Nando would shake his head impatiently and tell me, "Seven. That's it!"

Gradually, I filled in the blanks. I began to get a detailed understanding of their business as they negotiated prices for drugs, or Nando wanted Eric reminded that he was behind in his payments or notified him of the day of the next delivery. Some of the business went on outside the prison walls: This was Nando's organization. Inmates who wanted drugs placed their orders with Eric, then Nando's people paid a visit to the friend or the relative who was going to put up the money. Inmates who didn't have anyone outside bought directly from Eric and Bentley. Nando had the system, but he was stuck on Max One; Eric had the distribution network he needed.

I worked to become invisible, like one of those translators seated in the background when heads of state meet, an out-of-focus face in the shadows of the newspaper photograph. As they came to forget about me, the messages got longer.

"Tell Nando that last load was cut to nothing," Eric would say. "The customers are complaining, for Chrissake! No, don't say that. Say something—I don't know. Tell him the quality has to improve. You say it. Find a way to say it to him, you know, with respect."

126

Or Nando might say, over his shoulder as he was on his way back to the maxes, "He's late," and I was supposed to know, from the curt way he's spat it out and the cold backward glance, that Eric better pay up quickly or there'd be trouble.

They expected me to be human, to be able to interpret the sense beyond the words they sent each other, but they also assumed that I'd be inert, like a piece of telephone cable.

Sammy Shay ran errands occasionally for Eric. He was a busybody, and he talked a lot. I'd had nothing much to do with him after the incident with Carol, and then I found myself dropping his name into messages.

"The last stuff was good, but we can't move the quantities you're talking about. Shay bears watching. Maybe we should lower the price to increase demand," I told Nando in the deadpan, newscaster voice in which I delivered all messages.

"Shay who?" Nando asked irritably.

I never answered Nando's questions. It was part of the role I had established. I was the messenger only. So now, when he asked something like this, he was thinking out loud and the fact that I, a nobody, was present at the time was irrelevant.

"Tell him the price is the same," he said. "The quantity is the same. That's the deal he made."

That night, just before lock-down, I reported to Eric's cell. Bentley was there. They were on edge.

"Nando was pissed," I told them. "He says the price is what it is." I stopped and waited, as if I could say more but was holding back. "The quantity is the same, too. You made the deal, you stick to it."

Looks passed back and forth between Eric and Bentley. There had been discussions before I arrived. They understood each other. They could compute the implications and arrive at the same answer.

Eric let out something like a nervous laugh. "The problem is, the guy doesn't understand economics."

"He say anything else?" Bentley wanted to know.

"He said, 'Who's Shay?' "

"Shay's nobody."

"I didn't know what to tell him," I said.

Eric jumped up off his bunk. His eyes had a wild, distorted look

127

to them. "You tell him nothing. You tell him fucking nothing we don't tell you to tell him."

"I didn't say a thing."

Bentley came up close to me and stuck a big finger in my face. "You are the messenger. Got that? Nothing else."

"We control the message," Eric hissed. "I'm the fucking spinmeister here!"

He paced to the back wall of the cell, and Bentley moved out of his way at the last moment. I don't think he liked the disrespect of Eric almost running into him.

"What's Nando doing asking about Shay? Why'd he want to know who he is?"

"He was pissed. That's all I know," I said. "You want me to ask him tomorrow?"

"No. Tell him Shay's OK. Tell him we know Shay, and he's OK."

"What if he's not?" Bentley asked.

"Scrub that. Tell him Shay's under control." Eric turned to Bentley, and I started to go. "Ask around. But don't let people know we're interested. Wait!" he shouted at me. He was starting to look distracted, his eyes zigzagging. Too many things were happening at once.

Inmates are very particular where they sit. I studied the seating of the inmates in the chow hall the same way the CIA used to study the reviewing stand for the Moscow May Day parade. I'd memorize the seating order at the main table: who sat next to who, who was in, who was out. If you remembered the order from the previous day and compared it with the seating arrangement the next day, and if you kept track of these changes over time, you could anticipate shifts in the balance of power. In the drug wars of Denning, this intelligence could be the edge that enabled you to survive.

The next morning at breakfast, I sat opposite Shay. People know when they're being watched. Shay knew it. If you know you're being watched, you can't act natural. You get in your own way. You calculate when you should be intuitive. You hesitate when you should be spontaneous. You notice things that shouldn't matter.

128

You act suspiciously. Shay looked around, grinning, and men looked down into their corn flakes. Inmates sensed he'd been singled out. It was the instinct of the tribe.

I remember staring down at my father, asleep in his chair while an old movie played on the TV, looking at his face as you might any other thing. I felt the same strange objectivity about Shay. I took in the clarity of his simple good looks, the definite outlines of him, tight muscle and bone filling the white T-shirt. He shifted in his seat. The easy, sly grin he turned on me became uncertain as his blue eyes ran out of data to work on. He looked away and shrugged and caught Bentley's eyes on him.

That evening, I found Nando outside the treatment room, waiting for Tanya to come back from the staff lounge.

"Eric says, 'They're keeping a close watch on Shay.' "

"So what? What do I care?" He splayed his hands to show the frustration of working with idiots.

"Eric says, 'There just isn't the money to move the stuff. They want to slow down delivery.' "

"If he can't move it, maybe he should check, see if he's got competition," Nando growled.

He pushed off the wall. Tanya was on her way down the corridor. For a moment, we listened together to the friction between her thighs.

"They're asking for more time," I said.

"Maybe someone else is selling on their turf," Nando said. "Maybe they should consider that."

Eric could hardly wait for me to step onto the block before waving for me to come up.

"Nando wants to know, 'What is it with this Shay shit? What are you watching him for?' "

Eric and Bentley exchanged looks.

"What else are we going to do?" Eric complained. "We got to watch him first. We got to figure out what he's about."

"That's what I told him," I said, "but he's got this attitude, like, 'What do these guys want to see? Why don't they get on with it?' "

"That's what he said? 'Why don't they get on with it?' " Eric asked.

"He didn't say that. It's his tone I'm talking about. The way he said it. Like, 'What are they *watching* him for?' "

I waited for this information to sink in. It was becoming clear to them what they had to do.

"I asked him for more time," I said, and they nodded their heads, eager, as if I'd done them a big favor. "He said, 'Maybe someone's selling on your turf.' "

I could tell this was a possibility they'd already thought about, but from the way they avoided looking at each other, I thought it hadn't been discussed out in the open until now.

"No way!" Bentley said.

He seemed confident. Eric gave him a little sideways look, evaluating him. The first cool draft of suspicion.

"We got control of the minimums," Eric said. "We got it sewn up. Total."

"I just didn't like the way Nando said it," I said.

"What do you mean?"

"I don't know—something about the way he said 'Maybe.' 'Maybe someone's selling on their turf.' "

"I don't get it," Bentley said.

"He just threw it out. 'Maybe.' Sarcastic. You know how he is."

"Who the fuck are you?" Bentley demanded. "Maybe this, maybe that?"

"Wait!" Eric told him. "He was hinting at something?"

"I guess."

"Hinting what? He was hinting at what?"

I shrugged. "I don't know. The way he said it, it was like you'd know already."

The next evening, almost as soon as I arrived on Medical, I was ordered back to the block for a lock-down. Shay had been found strangled in his cell, and there was a big investigation going on.

The next evening, when I told Nando that Shay was dead, the news had already reached the maxes.

"Good," he said, indicating that he was glad not to be distracted by the internal politics of the minimums.

"Nando said 'good,' " I told Eric, and he let a little smile escape him and nodded his head a couple of times.

130

After this, there was no talk of my smuggling syringes. I carried the messages back and forth as before, but I kept my editorials to a minimum. The communication between Eric and Nando was going farther and farther off kilter, like a wheel in an engine that is slightly misaligned and pushes more and more components of the mechanism away from their centers. They didn't seem to be able to make themselves understood to one another anymore, and this through no help from me.

Eric and Bentley looked edgy together, too. Bentley was rarely in Eric's cell when I came to make my report. If he was there when I arrived, Eric made small talk about sports until Bentley pushed off the wall and left of his own accord.

But I was still, against my will, a central part of the drug trade in Denning. I had no way out. I was too useful for Nando and Eric to simply let me go. Even to suggest that I didn't want to be part of their business anymore would have been lethal. I carried too many of their secrets. My life on Medical was good; I saw Carol almost every day, and my work with the AIDS patients made me feel I was contributing something. But I couldn't continue as their go-between. It was like participating in the slave trade. I couldn't be part of it, but I didn't want to die, either.

Carol and I had avoided saying anything about our lives outside Denning. Carol asked me about my family once. I talked about my sister, though there wasn't really much to say, since she'd left soon after my mother.

"No one else?" Carol asked.

"No, we never had any children."

That "we" was a gap in the paving that you had to be careful not to step on. But this time, I didn't want to obey the rules we'd silently arranged.

"Maybe it's better that way, given the circumstances," Carol said.

"I ask myself: Would it have made a difference? But I don't think so."

Carol was silent. She kept her head down, carefully filling out the dietary forms for Food Services. To an onlooker, it would have looked as though she was humoring me, tolerating the conversation only because she was too polite to tell me to go away.

"I loved Janie," I told her. "I know that sounds crazy, coming from someone who killed his wife. But I think at that moment, at the instant I sent her on her way, I loved her more than at any other time."

Carol didn't look up. She was nodding her head as though she could understand. I was thinking of Janie, and I couldn't trust my voice to tell her anything more.

"I had a kid," Carol said softly.

"What happened?" I asked.

"I had to give it up. A little boy. I had to give him up for adoption."

"I can't imagine how hard that would be." I was shocked.

"He was only a baby. I was in nursing school. It was the only way I could go on. Otherwise I'd have had to drop out."

"You had to do it."

"At some level, I know I did the wrong thing. You know?"

"I guess. I don't know whether you had a choice."

"Would you get some fresh towels?"

"Yes," I said.

This was her right. This was Carol's power, to cut me off, to change the subject, without notice, or apology, or even explanation. She owed me nothing. A few minutes of intimate conversation didn't build anything resembling a relationship. In prison, words do not leave a trace in the heart. There is nothing you can count on.

This is where I was with Carol after Shay's death. Relations between Eric, Bentley, and Nando were precarious enough that they didn't have time to think of ways of enlisting me in their schemes. For several months, I reported everything strictly as it was said. Most of their messages had to do with the decline in business. Before, the problem had been in getting enough drugs into Denning to meet demand. Now, according to Eric, no one seemed to have the money to buy; or, according to Nando, they were buying elsewhere. I let them argue it out, and watched uneasily as the relationship gradually righted itself again.

I planted the idea of the Shang with someone of low status. George worked for Food Services; he had a lot of mobility throughout the institution and ran a one-man operation, a kind of unofficial a la carte service. I talked to him while he was laid up on Medical for a couple of days with a scald on his arm. Eric collected a tax on everything, he complained, even on the small sideline George ran.

"And you have to take care of the Shang, too?" I asked him.

"Who?"

I ignored him, as if I shouldn't have mentioned them to him if he didn't already know who they were.

"Just watch out you don't get caught in the middle," I told him on my way out.

"What? Wait a minute. The who?"

I was at the door of the cell, and I glanced down the corridor. "The Shang?"

"What are they, Chinese?" George was annoyed he had to ask.

"Yeah, they're Chinese," I said dismissively. "Forget it."

There was an outbreak of flies at this time. No one knew where they came from. All at once the prison was full of them, buzzing against windowpanes, landing on exposed skin, then taking off again, too quick to swat. I read once that these sudden increases have to do with the mathematics of their reproductive cycle. But inmates talked about a plague. There were rumors that the flies were breeding on long-forgotten bodies that had been disturbed. It was said they'd eaten human flesh. Men were afraid to come into contact with them. If a fly landed on them, they flinched and jumped up.

It may have been for that reason, for the purpose of keeping the flies off the head and shoulders, but it may have been coincidental, that about this time men took to wearing towels over their heads like sheiks. There was a hunger for new fads. There was always some new way of dressing, a certain pattern of lacing your sneakers, which brought a weird novelty to the uniform blue denim and T-shirts.

One day, some of the black inmates would be walking around on the flat wearing towels on their heads like sheiks; and it would go on for a week or two with only the black inmates dressing in the new way, while everyone among the Hispanic and the white prisoners would be watching the leaders to see if they would go with the style. And if they did, for a week or two, only the leaders

133

would wear towels on their heads as they strutted along the upper tiers, because it would be a mark of rank—and a mark of disrespect for another prisoner to assume their headdress.

Then, bit by bit, the second rank of prisoners might take it up—in the beginning only within their own cells, then when they were visiting, then out on the flat in the open, with bright-colored headbands to hold the towels in place when they turned and let them swirl about their shoulders. This was the midpoint of a fad, when everyone who mattered flaunted the new style. There was a sense of being part of something, a community of men who chose to wear their towels around their heads like sheiks. It was a sign of solidarity among these men of shifting loyalties, signifying nothing in particular.

You never know with rumors, how they'll turn out, because it's part of their nature that they disappear underground. And you can't go asking around to find out whether the story's spread. A rumor must have a life of its own. For a while you can't tell whether it's died or is gathering strength and will soon emerge in the chow hall as news everyone wants to know the latest on.

No rumor can make it on its own. It must be nourished by circumstances, by real events, to make it swell and take on substance, and in this case, it was Eric himself who lent a hand. He'd become obsessed with what he called market share. When he discovered people who had smuggled small quantities of drugs for their own use, he hunted them down. But instead of making sure that everyone knew why these people had been hurt, Eric kept it secret. He worried about the impact on consumer sentiment if he was shown to be anything less than totally in control.

So every week there occurred some attack executed by figures whose heads were swathed in towels. There were no shouted threats, no warnings of what would happen if, no "This is for . . ." Men were beaten in silence, or shanked, or piped, for reasons that were mysterious. The result was a level of hysteria that put the whole institution on edge. No one knew who would be next, or why.

"Nando says it's got to stop," I told Eric. "He says it's bad for business. Everybody's jumpy. They're instituting extra checks. It's tough getting stuff in."

134

"He started it," Eric said. He seemed desperate, even then, thrashing around without any idea what target to hit. "It was Nando started this whole thing off, putting out the contract on Ralph."

"That's what *he* said," I told him with a puzzled look on my face.

"There! You see?" He looked around, but there was no one to witness this moment. "I told you," Eric said, disappointed that I was the only one he had to tell. "I told you all along it was Nando."

"He said it *started* with Ralph. He said—and this is Nando—if you'd taken care of things when Ralph was hit, we wouldn't be having this trouble with the Shang now."

"That's bullshit! There is no Shang. They don't exist."

"If you'd stomped on them in the beginning, when they were weak."

Eric and Bentley went among their people, asking about the Shang. And the more they asked, the more the Shang seemed to grow. The Shang ran protection; they taxed prostitution; worst of all, they sold drugs. Such was the power of the Shang that no one had ever dealt with them directly. Whoever their leaders were, they were modest men who didn't need the trappings of power that Eric flaunted. They didn't need to be recognized. And that gave rise to the speculation that perhaps they didn't have leaders, that they were more of a brotherhood than a gang, that they were not trafficking at all, but were in fact against drugs. No one knew. Instead, the rumors swirled about like smoke. Then there were the flies. They were everywhere, landing on people's bare skin and making them jump up suddenly.

One day, on another cell block, a sneaker was found outside a man's cell. A single sneaker. It wasn't the kind of thing someone would leave outside a man's cell by mistake. Nothing happens for no reason. Everything is purposeful. The men on that block took it to be a sign that that inmate was marked. They stopped talking to him. It was as though a spell had been put on him. A voodoo hex. They waited, turning their heads so they wouldn't see him, leaving any place he entered so they wouldn't witness whatever was going to happen to him. Nothing happened. And

135

the fact that nothing happened only made the inmates believe in the subtlety and patience of those who were acting against him.

Nando wanted to kill a Shang. He wasn't particular. A Japanese inmate, halfway through a five-year sentence for attempted murder, had his head half severed from his body in the kitchen where he worked. Nando's point was made. No action could have more powerfully legitimized the Shang. If they didn't exist before, they had been summoned into existence now.

Everyone waited for the inevitable retaliation. Two days went by without any response. A week passed, and still nothing had happened. Eric looked as though he wasn't sleeping. Nando was tight-lipped and snapped at me when I asked him if he had any messages for Eric.

"Why the Japanese?" I asked Eric.

"We're sending them a message."

"What if the Japanese hasn't anything to do with the Shang?" I suggested.

"We're still sending a message. If you're clued in, it's obvious."

"I don't know. Ralph—he's history now."

Eric gave me a peculiar look. "Not to me," he said.

"It's been a while. People may not make the connection."

"There's a lot of loose connections. If you don't see how it comes together, that's your problem. That's the reason you're there, and I'm here."

Eric was staring at me, breathing through his mouth. When he moved his head back and forth, scanning my face, his eyes narrowed and shrank behind the glasses.

"Ralph was a good buddy to me," Eric said. "I'm not about to let it go."

"Well, you're the boss," I told him.

"I already know that," he said, quietly and stealthily. I heard the threat rumbling in the background. "You think you're pretty smart, don't you, Cody?"

"No. Not really."

"You think I don't pick up on the bullshit you're feeding me?"

"I'm only the messenger," I said.

136

"You only deliver the message, right? You're always at the right place at the right time. You're always where the action is. Have you noticed that?"

"Not especially."

"Not especially." He nodded his head thoughtfully, taking me in. "You were here when Ralph got it."

"A lot of guys were."

"Not so many. One guy besides you remembers Leon on the flat. No one saw him go into the showers."

"I did."

"Except you."

"So what? He's not going to advertise. He slipped in, he did Ralph, he's out of here. Leon's good at what he does."

"Are you good at what you do, Cody?"

"Yeah, I guess. What are you getting at?"

"Because I figure, if it wasn't Leon, it must have been you."

"That killed Ralph?"

"Right."

"I don't think so."

"You drift around like a ghost. You're the gray man. No one sees you come, no one sees you go. No one pays attention. You're invisible. You don't matter. Except you're everywhere. Anything that happens, you're there."

"That's what makes me useful. To you and Nando."

"Prove it. Prove to me that you're useful."

"How?"

"Kill Leon."

"What for?"

"Someone's got to do it."

"But what's that going to do? OK, I kill Leon. But what's it going to accomplish?"

"Then I'll know I can trust you."

"Nando'll kill me."

"It's him or me. You choose."

That evening I didn't have a chance to speak with Nando, because Tanya took him into the treatment room as soon as he arrived. This was a relief. I was afraid what I might blurt out when he turned his eyes on me. When I returned to the cell block, I found a shank under my pillow. It had been a metal spoon; there was a bandage wrapped around the broad end for a grip and the original handle was sharpened to a point.

"Have you ever been caught in the middle of something?" I asked Carol.

"Yes. I guess," she replied cautiously. On the other side of the steel mesh, she was sorting out some blood samples in plastic tubes, matching them to the test orders. She wouldn't look at me.

"Between a wrong and a wrong, and there's no way out?"

"Yes," she said more certainly. She put the tubes in the metal container for transporting and paused for a moment.

"I'll take that to Control," I said, indicating the container.

"We've got some more to come."

"I have to kill someone," I said. I saw fear come into her eyes. "Not here. It doesn't involve Medical."

"Can't you tell someone?" she asked.

I looked away. But we both knew that she had to say something like that. It was a move in the game. She had to start from her position as staff.

"Who?" I asked with a bitter smile. "Who am I going to tell?"

I wanted the silence in all its meaning to work its way into her. There was no answer. And the reason there was no answer was because of where I stood, alone, on the wrong side of the mesh. I could never cross that gap. Only she could.

"Couldn't you speak to Sergeant Baruk?" she asked.

"You know I can't do that."

"Off the record?"

"I'm not a rat."

"I know. I know that."

"I'm not a killer, either," I said. She avoided my eye. I suppose she was thinking of Janie.

She should have walked away at that point. She wasn't stuck in the trap. If she'd wanted to, she could have recognized what was coming, that it was something she shouldn't get involved in.

"I don't want to do it," I pleaded with her.

She'd taken out the book we recorded vital signs in, and I was afraid she was going to leave, even though it wasn't time to do the rounds.

"The man isn't even threatening me. Probably, he hardly even knows who I am."

Carol was flipping through pages in the loose-leaf binder. She nodded her head as if she wasn't paying attention, but I knew she was listening. I clung to the mesh. My lips almost touched the mesh.

"I can't kill him!"

"Do you owe them money?" Carol asked. "Is that why you have to do it?" She looked up at me. Her eyes were cold. She flipped another page: It was a brutal, dismissive gesture that hurt me. "Do you?"

"No."

"Then why do you have to do it?"

"Because if I don't, they'll kill me."

"There must be a reason," she said accusingly.

"No, they just pick you. It's like a lottery. It's luck. Bad luck."

She didn't believe it. She kept busy. But she didn't send me away.

"Because I've done it before," I said at last. "They think, because I once killed someone, it's easy for me."

I saw the question come, involuntarily, to her eyes, "And is it?"

"I'm not cold-blooded," I told her. "I'm not a hit man. You know me. I'm a high school teacher, for God's sake! How am I going to kill someone?"

I was waiting for her to tell me, "Don't do it," but she asked, "It's you or him?"

"Yes."

"Or Segregation."

"I can't live the rest of my life with perverts."

She stared at me, but she didn't say anything.

"What would you do?" I asked her.

We heard Baruk coming, and I let go of the mesh and stepped back. She could have ignored me then. She was free to go, and that made her answer all the more precious.

"I'd escape," she said, and came out of the trap with the container

139

of samples in the metal basket hanging from her arm, letting the trap door slam behind her.

After supper, when I returned to work on Medical, I brought the shank with me. There was no way out.

Nando hated receiving insulin, depending for his life on a substance someone else doled out to him. He was always impatient to get it and go, so it was unusual to find him leaning against the wall by one of the cells instead of outside the treatment room. He strolled away when he saw me come around the corner. When I caught up with him a little way down the corridor, he jerked his head back in the direction of the cell where he had been.

"That Diego?" he asked.

"Yes," I told him. "He just got here."

"How come he's on Medical already?"

"He's pretty sick."

Nando made a face. "He's faking. I know him. He wants to stay out of population."

"I don't think so."

"You think he's going to die?"

"Yeah. He's not going to finish his sentence."

"Too bad."

"If he's a friend of yours, I'll keep an eye out for him."

"He owes me money."

Nando had people who collected debts; it wasn't something he did himself. But Nando seemed preoccupied with Diego and several times glanced in the direction of his cell.

I brought the shank down into my hand from my sleeve and held it out to Nando with the handle toward him. He took hold of it without comment, as if he was accepting no more than a cigarette. His face changed as he turned it over in his hand, feeling the texture between finger and thumb; his lips grew tighter and his nostrils flared. Diego coughed, a dry, irritated sound that seemed hard for him to stop, and Nando was immediately attentive. I thought he would go to him.

"I'm supposed to kill you," I told Nando.

"What for?" He turned back to me, and I saw the cold fire in his eyes. "You want to kill me?" he asked.

140

He kept the shank down low, along the seam of his pants. I felt his body in front of me coiled like a spring.

"No," I told him. "That's why I'm telling you."

"You don't have the balls."

"You're right," I said.

"So why'd they send you?"

"Because I meet with you. You wouldn't suspect me."

"Why?"

"I don't know. They want the business. I suppose they want to take over the business."

"I am the business. There is no business, except what's connected to me. In two weeks I'm gone. I max out. I'm back on the street."

"It doesn't make sense."

I think he was considering whether to stick me to deliver a message to Eric, but it wasn't worth a murder charge with only two weeks to go. He passed the shank back to me underhand.

"What am I going to tell Eric?" I asked.

It sounded stupid, even to me, and Nando gave me a look of contempt. "You want me to give you protection because you don't have the balls to stick me? You're on your own. If you've got any sense, you'll use it on Eric."

When I returned to the block that evening, I sat at the table on the flat, and Eric had to come down and talk to me there, in full view of the guard.

"I'm waiting," he told me. "Leon looks pretty healthy, I'm told. Did real good on the basketball court this afternoon."

"I had to talk to Nando first," I said.

That took his breath away. "You did what?" he demanded.

"Leon's his man."

"I told you to do him."

"I'm not suicidal."

"I ought to do you."

"Nando said it was OK."

"To off Leon?"

"Nando said if Leon is Shang, he has to be shanked. But it has to be on his say-so. No one touches Leon till Nando gives the word."

I'd bought myself some time. If Nando had Eric killed promptly, I was off the hook. Or in two weeks, when Nando left, the equation would shift again. The order was breaking down. Already, people were jockeying for position to take over what Nando left. Leon was one of those, and there was a chance one of the others would kill him before I had to. But it was just as likely that none of this would happen. Eric was closing in. If, in spite of my efforts, he overcame his mistrust and thought it worth his while to find another way to communicate with Nando, he'd find my fingerprints on everything.

All these possibilities were pressing in on me. Sometimes it felt as though we were part of some great machine, that we were involved in a process that churned out the events we lived. When events moved in a direction I wanted, I felt as though I'd found one of the controlling dials. In moments of elation, I seemed to control Denning. And, to some extent, I did. It wasn't as if I played on the thoughts and emotions of a thousand men like the keyboard of a gigantic organ. It was far more chancy, more precarious than that. And the chain of events was liable to reverse direction at any moment and trap me in my own schemes.

With the drug wars rising to a crescendo, you could feel a charge in the air, like electricity from the emotions of one thousand men rubbing together. The inmates were restless, on edge, waiting for it to happen. Whatever it might be. You could almost hear the faint hum, like the sound of the wind blowing through power lines high above, as if the space about us was strained taut, holding itself back from coming into being, tensed to the utmost with the effort of containing itself as no more than a possibility, on the brink of spilling into reality. It was the sound of a generator. A deep, deep rumble at the farthest edge of hearing. It vibrated through us, resonating so closely that it felt as if it was our own emotion. You could hear it when movement began on the hour: There was a surge of sound as the main corridor filled with inmates; they were shouting, running to catch up with one another, towels flapping about their shoulders, arguing, laughing, name-calling. That was the melody, the surface. Underlying everything was the bass part, the low rumble of possibilities shifting against each other, of events tilting into existence.

This was the reality that was closing around me, a reality of my own making. At the same time, Carol was so close to acknowledging what existed between us. Love lay beneath the surface, ready to break through into words. This was the point at which my life was in greatest danger, when I most risked losing everything. It was Carol who put the idea of escape in my mind. Carol gave me the opening when everything else was closing in around me in the most lethal way.

This is how you have to understand what happened next. I didn't have a lot of choice in moving Carol to the final jump. It was going to happen anyway, but it had to happen sooner than it would have if the emotions had been left to take their natural course. Some weeks before, we'd been talking about William Blake. I mentioned that there wasn't anything by him in the prison library. A couple of days later, I tried to give her ten dollars to pick up a paperback copy of his poems for me.

"Look," I told her, "if you're not comfortable with it, don't do it."

"Dan, I can't take money from you. It's a criminal offense. You know that."

"It's a technicality."

"It's the rules."

"I'm sorry you think so much of them."

"I don't."

"Surely you can decide for yourself what's right or wrong? You can't let your life be dictated by rules."

"I can't," she said. She made a helpless, unformed gesture that ran from her shoulders to the tips of her fingernails, and I knew I had her. "I just can't."

"OK," I said, resigned, my face registering nothing. "Stick to your rules."

"They're not my rules."

"You chose them." I raised my head so that she could see the anger in my eyes.

"I didn't choose them. They come with the job."

"OK. It's just a job. You've got to do your job."

"Why do you have to make such a thing about this?"

143

"It's the principle. This is a matter between you and me. It's simple. What does it have to do with anyone else?"

"Because it's not simple."

"You're always pulling this job thing. Like it's some latex glove you have to put on before you can deal with me!"

"That's not fair!"

"Life isn't fair."

"It's not even true!"

"The truth is, I'm an inmate. That's what the truth is."

"I try to treat you like a human being. It doesn't matter to me what you've done."

I stared into her eyes as she said this, trying to find something that wasn't there. I smiled sadly and shook my head.

"It's OK," I said gently. "I'm sorry." I took a couple of paces and turned to her again. "I put you on the spot. I had no right to do that. I apologize."

I kept to myself for the next few days. I didn't ignore her. On the contrary, I made a point of saying hello, asking about the weather, and so on. I was mild and respectful. But I avoided getting into conversation with her.

Then, on the Monday after her weekend off, I found hidden under all the paraphernalia on the trolley I took around to measure vital signs a beautiful old copy of Blake's *Songs of Innocence and Experience*.

"I'll put it in the refrigerator until you're ready," Carol said, as if it was nothing.

"I feel like a fool," I said.

"Don't think anymore about it."

"I feel like a fool for not trusting you."

"Don't trust me," she said.

"Don't be silly," I whispered through the mesh. I was singing to my songbird in her cage. "I do trust you."

"Don't trust me," she insisted. "I think it's better that way."

Blake had a fine understanding of what it was to be caged. Whenever I could find an opportunity, I reminded her of what she'd done by thanking her for the book. I reminded her of the crime she'd committed. This is how you go about blackmailing the woman you love. I knew what I was doing. I'm not giving

144

myself any place to hide. When I think of my manipulations, I disgust myself. There are reasons for what I did, but no excuses.

One day, after she'd raised the idea of escape, I brought out the book to read to her one of his poems I particularly liked. I came into the trap and leaned against the counter. She lined up the stapler, then some pencils. Once or twice when I looked up, I saw her glance at the book in my hands, and I know she would have given anything to get it back.

To make the point, in midline, I pushed off the counter and began to pace back and forth as I read, oblivious as it were to where I was, deep inside the trap. I had the run of the place.

"What do you think?" I asked her when I had finished.

"Great."

It was a couple of weeks after this that we consummated our relationship.

This is loathsome, this calculated manipulation of a woman's emotions. And all the time, I have been writing to you about love! I can feel your contempt. But remember that you judge me by standards that are grounded in your own comfortable life. You have never faced what I have had to deal with. Please God, you never will. But unless you've been where I have, please believe me when I tell you that you can't possibly understand what reasonable, civilized people will do in order to survive. Not to live—we're not talking about some pathetic biological existence here, although most people are satisfied if they can cling to life in nothing more than a medical sense. But to survive as a human being, however I wish to define that.

Perhaps you think you would have rather died. Than what? Rather died than been raped? Is the anus such a sacred part of the body that you would lay down your life rather than have the holy ring defiled? Ralph's sadistic thrusts in the metal shop did no damage to my soul. Ralph, R.I.P.

I could have dealt drugs, but I didn't. True, my record is not entirely clean in this regard. I took the cocaine from Vera. A few times Eric got me to deliver heroin for Nando to sell on the maxes. I brought half a dozen syringes from the infirmary. It was the very least I could do. I feel a sense of doom about those syringes, even though I gave Eric a container of bleach to sterilize them with. If I had done any less I would have been beaten until I did what they wanted.

It's not a question of guilt. I accept that narrow, legal concept. Guilty. There! Guilt is easy. I don't care about laws. That isn't what bothers me. I wish I could make amends to Carol. I would do anything. Now that we're free, I don't want the past to stand between us. Although she won't come out and say it, she believes I used her. I can feel it. And I did use her. I manipulated her, because I was going to be killed if I stayed in Denning. I only did what I had to do. I want her to understand that what I did only hurried the inevitable.

FIVE

Dear Sandy:
   We drive around a lot, Carol and I. We watch TV. She doesn't like me writing to you, Sandy. She says I have a death wish. But I don't think I've ever been happier, even if it's stolen happiness. It can't last for long. But I have it now, and I'm sorry to say that nothing much else matters.

   Carol has something on her mind, apart from the letters. She wants a commitment from me. I've already given her that. She's after something more. She's reaching for a sense of security we can't ever have. There is so much between us that goes unsaid. This is not easy when we live on top of one another in tiny motel rooms.

   We are not like lovers. We don't declare our feelings for one another. (If you can, read this part on your show.) In these cubelike rooms, every insignificant action becomes a gesture loaded with significance. There is no such thing as a simple movement. Every

147

motion of any part of our bodies is a revelation and a mystery. Anything we do will send out ripples of expression through the room. Sometimes the implications are so complicated that we're deterred even from beginning to talk. There's no knowing where they will lead, the implications of implications. Sometimes we're in conversation, and talk stops for no apparent reason. When we do talk, the words are overloaded with significance, or else they leave our mouths too light—like throwing feathers—too trite to move much beyond ourselves, across the gap that separates us. There is so much to understand and misunderstand.

We are not like usual lovers, because we touch only rarely. I never place my hand on any part of Carol unless it's understood that she gives permission, although I ache for her every minute of every day. I tingle for her in the same way that someone charged with static electricity, passing close by, sends a ripple of sensation across your bare arm or the fabric of your shirt, making the hairs stand on end.

I was never using her. I'm sorry I ever sent you that letter. I was trying to keep her out of it. I wanted to save her from what is coming to me. (I know this can't last.) I wanted to show you I was tough and callous, that I controlled her. The letter will only hurt her. She doesn't understand the wrenching tenderness I feel. What I am afraid of most of all is that I have prevented her from understanding the truth. I feel her eyes as I write, trying to penetrate me. At times, her face is composed and hard; she thinks she can protect herself by giving nothing away, except that her spirit leaks through in the gleam between black lashes. She reminds me of that first moment, through the bars, in the murk of J Block, when I thought life might be possible.

Carol has security on her mind. She thinks this way of life can go on forever if only we have the resources. She thinks we can escape and live somewhere like the Bahamas. She thinks I can do this because I know where Diego's money is.

Diego was a patient on the unit. He came straight to Medical from sentencing in superior court six weeks before I escaped. Everyone seemed to know about him even before he arrived. He wasn't exactly a celebrity, like a big figure of organized crime, but there were touches here and there, like not going through Classification, which indicated he was special.

Carol and Tanya had been notified to expect him, and both were standing by, waiting, when two officers brought him along in a wheelchair at racing speed. He was sweating and he had difficulty breathing.

"Not a pretty picture," Sergeant Baruk said, shaking his head.

The doctor diagnosed pneumonia and told Carol to put up a bag of IV solution. Diego was one of those men in the advanced stages of AIDS who wasn't wasting away. He looked sick but not dying. He had a seven-year sentence for drug trafficking, and Tanya said, even with good time, he wasn't going to see the light at the end of the tunnel.

"Give me a cigarette," Diego said. "I want a cigarette."

"Not with oxygen, you can't," Tanya told him, but politely.

There was a sense of excitement in the air. We were doing something important. Carol took charge of us. There was a flush to her cheeks. She was in her element. She told Tanya what to do, and Tanya did it without a second thought. We all caught it from her, the intense purpose. I'd never seen her so alive. I handed her the nasal catheter she'd asked for; she took it from me with a quick smile and then, the next beat, turned her attention back to Diego. The needs of the situation held her tight, compressing her and centering her after all those empty afternoons at the counter in the trap. Baruk stood in the background, easing things along, watching to see there were no snags.

That was the evening I found Nando outside Diego's door. He didn't go into the cell. A couple of times he glanced in and then pulled back his head, as if he didn't want the person inside to see him, though Diego wasn't in any condition to recognize him. The fever had him confused, and he mumbled to himself and twisted in the bed restlessly. Later, Baruk had come to his cell, too; he stood by his bed and looked down at him for several seconds while Diego shook his head in his sleep.

On the second day, the antibiotics seemed to kick in, and Diego was more in touch with his surroundings. He'd messed his sheets in the night, and Tanya sent me in to clean him up.

"Oh, man, look at this!" He held the sheet tight up to his head.

149

"Look at it," he groaned and turned his face away. "How can you let me lie in this shit?"

"We got to get you cleaned up," I told him.

He looked at the bowl of water and the towels I'd put down beside the bed, and his eyes came slowly over to me. "What are you going to do, a bed bath?"

"Right. Wipe that stuff off you."

He stretched out, watching me fuss with the water and the soap. When I came toward him with the wet towel, he still had the covers up to his chin. He was waiting, his eyes flicking from the towel in my hands, back up to my face. There was something about his face, his upturned eyes, that made me think of a picture in my grandmother's parlor of Jesus on the Cross.

"I got to be cleaned now. Like a baby." He sounded despairing. His eyes glistened, and he looked away. "Leave it," he said. "I can do it myself."

Diego got steadily better. Everybody on Medical seemed to take an interest in him. He drew people to him. He had large, deep-set eyes and a knowing smile, and he made you feel seen and understood. We were surprised how quickly he regained his strength. In ten days, he was sitting on the side of his bed to take his meals.

"He's weak, though," Baruk advised.

He and Carol were standing outside the officers' trap, discussing whether to move Diego to population. Baruk had a couple of fingers hooked into the steel mesh and his other hand on his hip, dangling himself before her.

"He can't defend himself," he said. "He couldn't intimidate a kitten."

"Okay, if you want, we can keep him," Carol said.

She had on a new uniform with a tunic top that accentuated her figure. When she took off to return to the nurses' trap, I thought she swiveled her hips more than usual, and even though this was for my benefit, Baruk watched her walk away. I couldn't claim her, as another man might claim his woman, publicly, with a simple touch to her arm. I had no access to the two-thirds of her life she lived among normal people outside the prison walls. This was a month before we escaped.

That night was Nando's last in Denning. He'd served almost the whole of his sentence on the maxes, without any attempt to get parole for good behavior. I thought he would be happy. Instead, he seemed on edge. He waited outside the door to the treatment room, turned away, walked a few paces, turned back, stood facing the wall with his head down, bouncing the toe of his sneaker off the bottom wall tiles.

Then they brought in Eric with blood spurting from a stab wound in the neck. Everyone dashed into the treatment room to try to keep him going long enough so that if he had to die it would be in the ambulance and not in Denning.

In the commotion, Nando took the trolley I used for the vital signs and wheeled it to Diego's cell.

"Stay outside," he warned me. "This is private."

I heard Diego gasp when Nando went in.

"Hey, Diego," Nando said quietly. He switched the light off.

"Nando, I swear to you!"

There was the silence of Nando waiting. "Yes?" he asked finally. "What do you swear?" He was calm. "All I want to know is where the money is at."

"I don't have it!"

"But that's the problem. Isn't that right, Diego?" He sounded very patient, talking to a sick man. "Isn't that the reason you and me are having this talk? I figure there's about one million two hundred and fifty thousand dollars you don't have."

"Not so much. Not one and a quarter."

I heard the sound of Diego trying to move in the bed, maybe trying to sit up or twist around, before Nando shoved him back down.

"More like one." Diego sounded tired and weak. "Come on, Nando. I'm sick. I can't think straight."

"I'm in here running the business on the ground, watching my back every minute so someone doesn't shank me. You're coming and going, doing anything your heart desires."

"It wasn't so easy. We got tough guys on the street now, just like in here. You been away so long you don't know what it's like."

"Vera says the last time the two of you made a deposit, it was little more than two hundred thousand dollars. There was less than a million in there!"

"Ask her about that."

"You're the one with access!"

"She helped herself. Ask her!"

"Don't act stupid. How can she get into the money without you? You were supposed to give Vera access. On the last day of the trial, you were supposed to give her access. You never gave her access."

Down the corridor, there was a sudden flurry of shouted orders. The door of the treatment room banged open. Someone called for the crash cart.

"Where is it?" Nando asked.

He was doing something. I heard movement. Friction. A ripping sound the blood pressure cuff made when the Velcro separated.

"Hey!" Diego cried out, scared and weak. "What is this?"

"I want to know where it is," Nando said. He sounded preoccupied, as if he had to pay attention to the other thing he was doing.

"I gave it to Vera!" Diego said hoarsely, the words coming out in a rush of fear. "I gave her access just like you told me to."

Something got in the way of his speaking. Diego was gasping. I heard dull blows fall on a solid part of someone's body, then the more resonant sound of a punch to the chest, none with much force. I heard the chair scrape as Nando drew it up to the bedside.

"If you cleaned it out, I want to know where you put it. If there's a numbered account, I want you to tell me that number."

"I'm sorry, Nando. I'm really sorry."

"All I want is the money. That's all. It doesn't matter why you did it, the excuses, the bullshit. Just tell me what I need to know."

"It's gone," Diego pleaded.

"Don't tell me that."

I heard three puffs as Nando compressed the bulb to inflate the blood pressure cuff.

"How's that?" Nando asked.

"Don't do this!" Diego begged hoarsely.

There was another puff, a pause as if Nando wanted to see the result, then two more. Then two more.

"Now I want you to tell me," Nando said.

152

I waited for Diego to say something, but there was silence in the room. I waited, but there was no sound. I risked a look into the room, and quickly pulled back before Nando saw me. Diego lay on the bed with the cuff inflated around his neck. Nando sat in the chair. He was bent over the bed, holding his ear to Diego's mouth as if he was hearing confession. I waited outside the door for what seemed like a long time. No one said anything. Then I heard the long sigh of Nando letting the air out of the cuff.

Diego gasped, "Huh! Huh!"

"You had a chance to think it over there," Nando said. "That was just a taste."

"Oh, God, Nando! There's no money, man!"

He started to say something more, but it was choked off, and I heard the puff, puff, puff as Nando squeezed the rubber bulb, pumping in quick succession.

"Cody!" Baruk roared from down the corridor. He beckoned impatiently. "Get your ass down here!"

They wanted me to help lift Eric onto the trolley. He looked white and dead and was covered in a slimy kind of sweat, so that my fingers couldn't get a purchase behind his shoulders when it came time to lift him off the table and onto the trolley. The doctor was doing CPR on his chest, but he seemed only to be going through the motions. Once Eric was on the trolley, we had to wait while everything was loaded onto the trolley beside him and the IV pole was slotted into place. Baruk was on the phone. The gate hadn't received clearance to let the ambulance into the compound.

"This is on you, pal! What's your name again? Figueroa? OK, Figueroa, this guy dies, it's got your name on it . . . No! Your name. And I'm telling you, he doesn't look so great . . . Then call Control and get clearance!"

He slammed down the receiver.

"OK, let's move him out. We'll meet the ambulance at Receiving. Let's go!"

I moved with them down the corridor, holding back to let them pull farther in front of me. Baruk was out in front like a motorcycle cop clearing the way for a presidential motorcade, with two officers pushing the trolley and the doctor running alongside and jumping periodically on Eric's chest. While everyone else seemed to be running, Carol walked extra fast, pumping oxygen through the Ambu bag as if nothing else in the world existed. As they went by, no one so much as glanced into Diego's cell, and Nando glided into position right behind them and rode their slipstream up to the front trap.

I was afraid what I'd find in Diego's cell. I was ashamed, in case he was dead, that I'd done nothing to help him. You quickly lose a sense of responsibility for other people in prison. It shrivels up in the space of a few days, like the umbilical cord on a newborn. Except, in Diego's case, I felt protective. We all did. Baruk, even. So although the impulse was foolish, although it had no right to exist in that environment, I felt that I'd betrayed him.

I switched the light on. Diego looked as though he was about to burst. His face was swollen and black. He was unconscious, but his eyes were open, almost popping out of his head in amazement, staring far off to some place beyond the ceiling.

The bulb was hanging over the back of the bed. Nando had screwed the valve so tight I had to use both hands to undo it. I ripped open the Velcro fastening and watched the blood drain from Diego's face. It seemed to jolt a mechanism into action, because he began to breathe again, making small barking sounds.

By the time I'd untied Diego's hands, I heard the sounds from the other end of the corridor of the nurses and officers coming back from the ambulance. Diego was still unconscious, but he seemed to be lightening. He coughed once, jerking his back off the bed. His eyes were closed, at least. A hand came up uncertainly toward his throat and fell back again onto the bed. I moved out of sight from the door.

They came past the door with the trolley. They weren't talking, which meant that Eric was dead. Tanya called me from the treatment room to help with the cleanup. I waited. Diego's eyelashes flickered. He groaned and tried to sit up. Then, as if he was suddenly remembering something, his eyes opened wide and alert and fixed right on me standing at the foot of the bed.

I've never seen such unearthly, bloodshot eyes. Except for the dark pupils, they were a bright red. It was impossible to read the expression in them. We stared at each other, intent, focused, and without any understanding, for several seconds. Diego seemed to be having diffculty with the idea that he was still alive. He moved his lips. Cautiously, he cleared his throat and tried again to speak. I poured some water into a paper cup and held his head in the crook of my arm and helped him drink.

"Where is he?" he whispered.

"He's gone back to the maxes," I told him.

I was still holding him, like a child. Like something precious and easily broken. He looked at me with those awful eyes as though I'd forgotten what I was about, because I was still holding him. I lowered his head back onto the pillow.

"He's going to be released tomorrow," I told him.

Baruk was at the door. Diego shut his eyes; he was smiling as he turned over. Baruk waited a moment, to watch, to take in the scene between me and Diego.

"I want a word with you," he said.

We walked for a few paces in silence down the corridor, then he turned on me.

"Where the fuck have you been, Cody?" he shouted. "You want to keep this job? Do you?"

"Yes."

"Then get with the fucking program!"

He was short of breath. He'd lost his sleekness and looked ruffled and disarranged, as if Eric's emergency had unnerved him.

The next day, Diego told me, "I got a eye infection."

I put the thermometer in his mouth. With his unearthly eyes, he watched my face, while we waited for the tone that signaled his temperature had come up on the screen.

"It's normal," I told him.

I reached down to remove the thermometer. Diego held it for me between his teeth.

"Like what?" he asked. "What's the number?"

"Ninety-eight, four."

"Ninety-eight, four," he said. "That's good. That's three days in a row."

I was sitting on the side of his bed to take his blood pressure, and he put his hand on my shoulder.

"What d'you think? Ninety-eight, four. Maybe it's my lucky number."

I felt his fingers move over my shoulder, measuring me, absent mindedly feeling for some landmark, then, as it were, coming back to himself, remembering who and where, and patting me in a friendly way.

I took up the blood pressure cuff, and the ripping sound of the Velcro made him whip around. He looked at the cuff, then at me.

"You have a problem with this?" I asked him.

"How do you think I got this?" he said pointing to his eyes.

I was ashamed to speak.

"You ever see conjunctivitis like this before?"

"No," I said.

"The doctor, neither. He thinks it's some weird virus only people with the disease get."

I pulled away, wanting to break from this subject, but Diego misread me.

"Don't worry, it's not infectious," he said. "Last night a guy tried to strangle me." He nodded to the blood pressure cuff in my hands. "With that."

I wound the cuff around his arm. Diego lay back and stared at the ceiling.

"It was a guy who wanted information," he said. "He put that thing around my neck." He laughed. "Around my neck!" He turned to see my reaction. "You know? He pumped it up real tight. Then he let it out. Then, you know, he pumps a couple more times. I'm about to pass out. I start to go, he lets some air out. I come back, he pumps it up some more. All the time he's asking me this question."

I must have paused for a moment in what I was doing.

He shook his head. "That you don't want to know," he said.

His hands were always in motion when he talked, and one of them would light briefly on my arm and as quickly fly away again into the air before I thought to say anything about it. Everybody craves the human touch.

"We're just friends, right?" I'd remind him.

"Whatever," he'd say, with an ambiguous grin and a shrug. "Whatever you want to call it."

"Because that's all it's ever going to be."

"I know. I know. I'm never going to beat out that nurse. I know that."

"Carol?"

"You think I don't see it? You can't take your eyes off her, man!"

"It's just because we work a lot together. We've got a rapport going."

"No, you love her. I can see it in your eyes. You want to be with her. You want her for your woman."

"Forget it. That's not going to happen."

"Why not? Go ahead. Break my heart."

"Not in here. Not in this lifetime."

"You ever think you're getting out of here, let me know. Maybe I'll give you a wedding present."

He was fanatical about his weight and insisted on weighing himself every day, at the same time, wearing the same clothes. He put a hand on my shoulder to help himself step off the scales, keeping it there a moment longer than he needed to. He shrugged and smiled with an inner sunny peace, which I believe had always been there, a disposition in love with life. He drew Carol in. I think he did this for me. It got to be a routine, at the end of her shift, that we'd come together in his room. The two of them flirted with each other, Carol with her way of doing something and at the same time making it seem that it wasn't happening, hand on hip, mock haughty, eyebrow raised, telling Diego, "Oh, is that so?" in response to something outrageous he'd said. I miss him.

Diego liked to talk about the old days. He was only thirty-five, but he'd already lived two lifetimes. He and Nando came from the same town in the Dominican Republic. They came to America together to work at Suffolk Downs and ended up dealing cocaine in Lawrence. I tried to stop him telling me about their business. Any knowledge of Nando's dealings was dangerous.

"Nando was the one who tried to kill me when I first got here." He squinted at me, smiling, as if this was one of those quirky, ironic facts of a person's life you tell once you have gotten to know someone. "What do you think of that—my best friend, from when we were kids?"

"I was the one who found you."

"And you never said anything," he said. There was glint in his eyes, fond and secret.

It was against the rules, but they let Diego smoke in his cell. It wasn't because he was dying. Everyone in Denning was moving toward death, however slowly. Baruk gave Diego a break because he was special. He made himself special, lying in state propped up in bed with half a dozen pillows, bestowing his smile, the light in his eyes, on whoever came to visit him. He had a knack for making people come to him. I watched him, but I don't know how he did it. Sergeant Baruk would come almost into his cell and lounge against the door, and Diego would exchange a few words before something emerged in his manner that, without coldness, would gently induce Baruk to go on his way.

I timed my vital signs so that Carol would be giving Diego his AZT when I came to him. He put me forward to her in a teasing, irreverent way that brought Carol out of herself.

"You ought to send this guy to medical school," he told her.

Carol gave a small, tight smile, but wouldn't look at me. This was the day after I'd walked around her trap, flaunting the book she'd given me.

"You see the way he takes the blood pressure?" Diego said. "He's real good. It doesn't hurt at all."

"Stop fooling around," Carol told Diego, but not sternly. "Take these with the water. Every day I give them to you, it's like you've never done it before."

"Every day is a new day," Diego said.

"You're full of it," Carol said. She was smiling now. She tossed her head back. "What is it?" she asked me in a controlled voice.

Her eyes came up to me, impossibly vacant in front of a third party who saw everything. I gave her the numbers, while she looked at a point on the cheek below my left eye.

"You've got a slight temperature," she told Diego.

"Yeah? And who's to blame for that?" he said suggestively, and looked past her to me. He didn't behave this way when we were alone.

158

Carol turned, curious in spite of herself, and a little alarmed.

"Why'd you say that?" I asked him when she'd left.

"So what?"

"The way you said it." I thought suddenly I'd made a mistake about what I'd heard.

"What's the matter with the temperature? It's too hot for you?" Diego laughed. "Me, I like it hot." He shifted in the bed.

"Listen," I told him. "Don't go getting any ideas."

"But I like you." He reached up lazily and took hold of the muscle of my upper arm. "I really like you," he said and let his hand drop back.

"I don't want you to say it that way."

"Why should it be a problem for you, if I like you? I don't understand that."

"I don't want you getting ideas, that's all."

"I got all sorts of ideas." He was laughing at me. "I got nothing to do all day but think up ideas."

He made me feel that simply meeting his eye made me part of what was going on.

"Look, I'm not into it. OK?"

"Hey, what am I going to do?" Diego beat his chest like Tarzan dying of AIDS. "What am I going to do, jump you?"

"I got to tell you, this kind of stuff makes me nervous."

"You think I'm going to give you what I got by looking at you? Huh?"

I started to say something to brush it away, but he held up his hand.

"I know," he said. "I shouldn't have said it with the bitch there. What I'm saying to you is, I can look after you."

"I don't need it."

"You don't think I can do it?"

"I don't know what you're talking about."

"You don't know what I can do. What I got."

"I have this job," I said. "I'm all set."

"I'm not asking you to do anything you don't want to do."

"No?"

"We're buddies, right?" He wanted to shake my hand, very serious all of a sudden.

159

"Yeah," I said. He held my hand in both his own. He held me tight as if I could keep him from slipping back beneath the surface.

Diego let go of my hand and fell back onto the pillows. He let out a deep sigh, and his eyes closed. I sat with him and watched him fall asleep.

"You know," he said, as I was at the door, "you can't take it with you."

When I wheeled the trolley back to the treatment room and knocked on the door, Carol let me in, then walked away from me, to the other end of the room where she'd been stacking specimen containers in the cupboard. I began to tidy up the equipment, throwing out the dirty sheaths for the thermometer and arranging water jugs on the bottom level of the trolley. She was still angry with what I'd done with the book and wouldn't look at me.

When two people pretend they're unaware of each other, there's a quality to the silence. It takes on substance. As we went about our tasks, each of the small, mechanical movements of our bodies were like lines in a hard-to-understand poem. I had to concentrate—focused and at the same time wide open to possibilities—to allow the meaning to emerge, to detect the signs of feeling that escaped her. I listened to the obscure relation between sounds—the clink of metal to metal, the rub of a paper towel pulled from its dispenser, the fine squeak of a rubber sole, the rustle of her clothes—which could only be understood in the context of the whole, at the end of the piece.

The room was thickened and made dense with swirling, unowned intent. We were robots. We held back meaning. We resented words. Even thoughts gave succor to the enemy. Actions came to the brink and were cut off before they could begin. In this substance there was the danger that words would form spontaneously, without our will, of their own accord: the spontaneous combustion of the obvious breaking out into sound.

She cleared her throat to prove that she was not beholden, that even in this medium she remained free, that she could breathe underwater. I concentrated on nothing more than being with her, on the pure, physical sensation of being in her presence.

160

"You do good with him," I heard her say.

When I turned around, I realized that she'd been facing me for some time. She was resting against the edge of the counter below the cupboard, checking off items on a clipboard.

"I'm sorry about what happened," I said. "Waving the book around. It was stupid."

"You have a good influence on him," she said. I must have been looking at her with a blank expression. "Diego," she prompted. "Sometimes they can't get him to do anything. There's an incident report every time he refuses his medication. Then his blood count drops, and they blame us."

She turned and lifted a white polystyrene cup from the counter.

"I'll do what I can," I told her.

She held the cup close to her and eased the cover off with her thumbs and then brought it up to her mouth with both hands. She sipped the coffee while she looked at me over the brim.

"I really shouldn't be telling you this." She looked away, choosing her words. "But in a way you're part of the medical staff. Not really staff. But you know."

"Sure."

"You do the vital signs." She spoke carefully. "You're part of monitoring his condition."

She was looking down as if she wasn't sure what she should say.

"Yes?" I tried to coax her.

"The thing is." She looked up. "Diego doesn't have very long."

"We've sent guys back to population looking worse."

"You'd have to see his blood counts to know. He doesn't have any T cells."

"That bad?"

She nodded her head. She was measuring me for what she wanted to tell me.

"You want me to look out for him?" I thought she'd be better off getting Baruk to beef up security.

"He's lonely," Carol said. "In that room all by himself."

"I suppose."

161

Everyone's lonely, I thought. I wanted to break through this conversation to the conversation behind it, but Carol controlled the situation. She held it firm at exactly the level she wanted. And I had no way of knowing who might be hanging around outside the treatment room door.

There was more she wanted to say, but I wanted to break the hold she had on me. I took the plastic sack out of the trash can and put a new one in and moved around the other side of the room dropping rubbish into the half-full sack.

"Hold on a minute," she said.

There was a little milky coffee in the bottom of the cup, which she swirled around. She tilted back her head and poured the coffee into her mouth, and I watched her throat move upwards as she swallowed and then her tongue poke out and curl the slightest bit over her upper lip.

"There," she said, dropping the cup into the sack I held in front of her.

I watched it fall and tumble into a corner between a crumpled piece of paper and an orange juice container.

"Anything else?" I asked.

"Not for now."

Everything she said echoed with further meanings. I started to go.

"Dan?"

It was the first time she'd used my name in many days. She said it softly, shyly, and my heart turned over. It felt like an embrace. I came back to her. I would have come to her, but she had her hands on the back of a chair, keeping it as a safeguard between us. She was wearing a new lipstick that made her lips dark and exotic.

"Be good to Diego," she said.

"Tell me what you want me to do. I'll do anything you want."

"All I'm saying is, be nice to him."

"Is there something special about him?" I asked.

"No," she said quickly.

She smiled and her lips came all the way back and exposed her teeth and pressed the skin tight against them, but her eyes weren't in it.

162

"OK?" she asked.

I smiled back at her, trying to melt her, trying to engage her eyes, to awaken her through her eyes. The professional smile faded, and gradually the corners of her mouth turned down and her cheeks puckered. Then her face came alive to me, and I knew I'd broken through.

I stowed the polystyrene cup behind a row of containers in the broom closet. When I'd put it away, there'd been a teaspoon of milky coffee in the bottom, but when I took the cup out of its secret place at the end of the day the liquid had evaporated down to a single viscous drop. I rolled it around the bottom seam so that it dissolved the dried stain there and when all the liquid had collected, I held back my head and the single drop fell onto the front of my tongue and rolled back, spreading and seeping, hinting at sweetness until it disappeared like a river in the desert. I held off as long as possible. When I swallowed, the flavor was so faint that it could have been another person's experience.

The lipstick on the rim was lush and dark. It was a graze, where the skin has been brushed away to show the blood beneath it. The imprint of Carol's lower lip was sharp at the outer edge and then increasingly smudged closer to the rim. I put my own lip where hers had been and tipped the cup back, as she had, trying to imagine her presence. Her flavor was there. I ran the tip of my tongue across the crimson stain and absorbed her spicy, perfumed stuff, my eyes closed, my mind curled about this sensation, until it filled me and that was all there was.

"Give me a good number," Diego said a couple of days later when I came to take his temperature.

"What kind of number do you want?" I asked him.

"A number that'll get Nando off my back."

"Nando's gone."

"His friends are here. Sooner or later I'm going to get a visit from one of them."

"Then give him what he wants."

"What if I don't have it?" He was smiling. He thought he was teasing me.

"I don't know what you're talking about," I told him.

"Sure you do."

163

"I don't want to know."

"It's a lot. A lot of money. I'm talking about a real lot of money."

"I want to stay out of that stuff."

"You think I don't know you worked for Nando? You think I don't know about you and Vera? She put her tongue in your mouth? Right? Hmm! It was good, huh? The lovely Vera! It had been anyone else, Nando would have killed you. But it was business. Right? Strictly business. So it was all right."

He laughed and let himself fall back onto the pillows, all the time looking at me to see my reaction.

"Anyway," he said, "you're not Vera's type."

"I didn't want to do it. They didn't give me a choice."

"That's good. If Nando thought you were enjoying it, Vera putting her tongue in your mouth, he wouldn't have liked it at all."

"Why didn't he do it, then?"

"Too obvious. Far, far too obvious. That's why we chose you," Diego said. "Because it's obvious you don't have the street smarts. You can see it right off."

"You weren't even here then."

Diego grinned. "I set the whole thing up." He seemed pleased to be recognized.

He stretched back against the pillows, then turned his head slowly from one side to the other to rub the back of his neck.

I try to give the appearance of calm. There are times when I was so hopeless in Denning that I wanted to bounce my head off the wall of my cell. Even now, outside prison, in motel rooms made of flimsy plasterboard, there are times when I want to feel the solid thud of myself against a thing that will not give. I want that dazed feeling before pain and the thick salty taste of blood trickles into my mouth. I want to hear the crack and feel something shift inside me and know a part is smashed. There is a piece of J Block embedded in me.

How can you possibly understand this? You are a pretty woman, Sandy. What could be farther from your mind? You have to understand that it's not a face I'm talking about: It's the fearful, hopeful man that hides just a millimeter beneath the skin,

164

not the deeper being, the one who peers out from behind the eyes. It was that thin layer of feeling between me and the world that I bashed against the wall in J Block.

Imagine your "me" shrinking down to something so dense as to leave no room for lightness, humanity. A very heavy, dark being. When I hammered my head, it was not much more than skin and gristle that was caught between the cold wall of the cell and this hard place inside me.

I can't stand being at the mercy of someone who might change her mind at any moment. I don't want to end my life. I don't want to destroy myself. I want to inflict damage and to experience it. I want the wildness of pain and damage. There's a freedom in that. You can cancel things out to the point that they don't matter anymore.

Today, Carol has been gone for almost six hours. I've been writing all day. I couldn't stand it anymore, alone in the motel room, waiting for her. I hadn't realized until now how little Denning mattered. I am free, but Carol has been gone six hours, and I am as much a prisoner as I've ever been.

I get up and go to the window that looks onto the parking bays. It's not a good idea to open the blinds, but I line up the slats so that I can see out. The sight of the outside world, the walkway, the parking bays, the traffic rushing by on the street, does not relieve me. There is a feeling that goes beyond the anguish of loneliness, of missing her, to the mindlessness of a crazed animal.

I stand in front of the window and let the impulse rise almost to the point of action and then wane. It is like nausea rising almost to the point of vomiting and then moving back from that point, back to a state that is no more than feeling, something you could be distracted from. I stand in front of the window and almost let my face smash through it. So close. I can feel the shards come through the gaps in the blind to pierce me and the terrible edges open a dozen floppy smiles in my cheeks and over my eyes.

The rush-hour traffic is roaring past my room, and still Carol has not come back. I love Carol, even though I am afraid the likelihood of pain is far greater than the possibility for happiness. I'm not sure I would recognize happiness anymore. It's something I've seen portrayed in TV ads. I know she will not leave me.

It was soon after this conversation with Diego that Carol asked me to clean up in the treatment room. There was a wedge that held the door open, but she pulled it out with her toe and let the door swing closed.

"Do you think that's a good idea?" I asked her.

"I meant what I said about getting you out of here," she said.

I was disappointed she'd brought it up again. It was a fantasy, too delicate to be handled.

"It's going to take a lot of money," I told her.

"It can take different things. It depends how you do it."

"You have to have the money to pay people off."

"Not if you're smart."

"Well, we're smart, but I think you have to have more than that," I said. A soft, fleshy part of me wanted to remain in Denning forever and never put at risk what I already had.

"You have to tell me now, before we go any further, whether you have what it takes to escape from here."

"I can do anything I need to do."

"I don't want you changing your mind, getting tenderhearted at the last minute."

"I'll do anything," I said. "I'll do anything I have to do to be with you."

That night, at the end of my shift, I heard singing in the squeaking of the steel gate as it closed behind me on Medical. It was a jubilant sound of sudden soaring. A crying upwards. There was joy in the sound, and abandon, as you might feel launching from a mountain face into an updraft, dropping in doubt for one terrible moment, in dread of gravity, before you feel the lift of air. I was soaring. I was sliding forward along some invisible, inevitable line. Against all the odds, my wings had found a crease within the air.

The next morning, I was prepared for Carol to ignore me. It was her pattern—reaching out to me without warning, on her own terms, and then drawing back as if nothing had passed between us. Instead, she wanted me to do rounds with her, dispensing the medications at the same time I measured the vital signs.

"That way, we'll be more efficient," she said for Tanya's benefit.

166

The corridor was just wide enough for us both to wheel our trolleys side by side.

"Did you think over what I said?" she asked as soon as we'd turned the corner.

I couldn't resist turning to look at her, to see in her face some of the excitement I felt. But Carol was always in disguise. She stared straight ahead with a sleepy, far-off expression in her eyes.

"Don't you know me by now?" I asked her. "I wouldn't change."

"I know," she said. The corners of her mouth were dimpled in a secret smile.

I wanted to hear her say it again, to listen to her taking me for granted in the best possible way.

"We've got to be together in this," she said. "We've got to give our trust. I'm in your hands. I'm completely in your hands. That's how much I trust you." She spoke softly, with a tenderness that melted me.

We went into the first cell. I gave her the numbers. She doled out the medications, and we moved on to the patient in the next cell. From her manner, I might as well have disappeared from view.

"We have to get Diego's help," she said when we were moving down a longer stretch of corridor.

"What for?" I asked.

"He's got money."

"I thought you said we didn't need money."

She sighed. "What's it going to take to get new IDs? How are we going to be able to pay for places to stay? Haven't you thought of that?"

"I guess." It was too much to imagine. A journey to the sun.

We went into another cell. I gave her the numbers. She doled out the medication. We went on.

Diego looked at us hungrily.

"Ah, the beautiful Carol," he said stealthily, spreading his hands in welcome. "And Dan."

"What's new with you, Diego? Anything I should know?"

"I don't know," he said, starting to act up, suggestive, coy. "How much do you want to know?"

167

Carol looked down at the Cardex, pretending not to notice, and Diego gave me a sultry look.

"I want it all," Carol told him. Her face didn't show any expression, and Diego couldn't tell whether she was being stern or playing along with him.

"I wish that I had something to tell you. Truth is, I'm not getting what I really want."

Carol stood with a hand on her hip, ready for something outrageous. "What's that?"

"Chocolate pudding," Diego said with a bland smile.

"Yeah? That's what you really want?"

I put the blood pressure cuff around his arm.

"Hey, not too tight," he told me.

"You got any problems, though?" Carol asked him.

"I get by with a little help from my friends," Diego said.

I told Carol the numbers, and she gave Diego his medication. He was the last patient.

"He's coming, too?" I asked her as we went back to the treatment room.

"He's too sick."

"Why would he help us, then?"

"I don't know," she said. Carol pushed her trolley with her arms rigid so that she walked almost upright, eyes fixed front. "Think about it," she said as the trolleys diverged. "You'll find a way."

"You can't take it with you," Diego said that evening.

"What makes you think I'm going anywhere?" I asked him.

I tried to laugh, to make light of it. I was sitting on his bed. There was a tension in the air that made it difficult to breathe.

"Wherever," he said. "You can't hold onto it forever."

"What?" I asked him.

"Your virginity." He gave me a roguish smile, dangerous and promising at the same time it was only make-believe. "Sooner or later you're going to give it up. I know it."

"I don't think so."

We could hear the sounds of the inmates watching the baseball game in the day room. His fingers touched the back of my hand.

"You are a virgin, aren't you?"

168

"I was married, remember?"

"You know which way I mean."

His fingers ran in the grooves in the back of my hand. He said something; then after a pause I replied; then he waited; then he said something else. In the gaps, I tried to breathe.

"Nothing wrong with that." He moved my hand. I felt his thigh beneath the blanket. "Except sometime you have to give it up."

"I don't know," I told him. He flattened my hand against his thigh. I was afraid to look at him.

"How long you been inside, Dan?"

"Four years."

"And all those four years, you never had a friend?"

"No."

"I don't believe it. Never?"

"I never did."

"Because you're a good-looking man. Very good-looking, in fact. No one ever said that to you?"

"No. I don't think so."

"Sure they did. You're playing with me! Making out you're a virgin just to add some spice. I bet some big stud came and whispered love words in your ear. Am I right? Come on. You don't want to say?"

"I never did any of that stuff."

"You don't have to act shy with me. I don't think that's the way you really are. I know you. Because I watch you. Did you know that?"

"No."

"When you're around me, I watch every little thing you do."

"What for?"

"Because I like you. I really like you, Danny."

I looked into Diego's hungry eyes. He searched for something in my face. He was soft and open and full of need. I could tell he wanted to kiss me. He looked at my lips. From my eyes to my lips and back again. I clung to the image of Carol, the sound of her voice. I wanted to say something, anything, to break the silence.

"I like you, too," I told him. It was an effort to speak. I had to look away.

169

Diego laughed. I'd hurt his feelings. "You're telling me you never did this with anyone before?" he said.

"I don't do that stuff."

"Then how come you got a hard-on?"

"I haven't."

"I do."

He moved my hand up his thigh. He held my hand in both of his. I let it go with him, wherever he wanted to take it. My will was gone. I had this almighty fear I was going to turn into something else.

"You've always got a hard-on," I said.

I was afraid I would feel it through the blanket. I was afraid that as soon as I touched it I would be different and I'd never be able to go back to the way I was before.

"You're right," Diego said. "But how d'you know that, Dan? Huh?"

"I don't know it. It's the way you talk all the time. You always talk like you've got one."

"I bet you been checking me out when you come to do those vital signs. You've been peeking, right?"

He must have been aware of the trembling of my hand between his own. I no longer owned that hand. I wanted to tell him the trembling was a lie, but Diego kept up the bantering tone as though what was happening wasn't really important. There were too many layers of meaning to mind them all. I felt dizzy. I felt myself falling behind.

Diego brought my hand to the top of his thighs and left it there. I felt his cock beneath my fingers. It wasn't so bad. Nothing happened.

I felt it out. I looked at the wall so that I didn't have to look into Diego's face. I was walking this narrow ledge and I thought, if I looked into his eyes, I'd lose my balance and fall into space. I let my fingers curl around his cock so that I could feel its outline. I heard Diego let out his breath all of a sudden. He turned his face aside on the pillow.

Diego closed his eyes. "Oh, God," he whispered.

I could have walked away then. He wasn't looking at me. His head was turned away. I heard the voices of the men in the day

170

room rise up over something that was happening in the game. I could have got up then and walked out of the room and taken my place at the back of the day room with the rest of them.

I hadn't moved. Maybe Diego felt me start to leave. I felt his fingers on my cheek. I realized I'd closed my eyes. He smiled when I looked at him, a hopeful, tender smile. He reminded me of one of the sixteen-year-olds at the high school who'd get a crush on me, their faces lighting up in expectation when I looked in their direction.

"I really like you," he whispered.

He was going to say more but stopped himself. His fingertips followed a line on my face that only he knew. They went along a secret, curving route that ended at the corner of my mouth. They hesitated at my lips. I thought of Carol ten miles away in her apartment, sitting on a couch in her bathrobe with her feet pulled up under her, her eyes on the TV, slowly spooning yogurt.

I felt his fingers begin again, then he took his hand away. There was a shyness about him I hadn't seen before.

Diego said, "We can do it any way you want." He seemed to be having trouble talking. "You know me. I'm ready for anything." I felt his hand on my head. He stroked my hair. I felt his fingers linger in my hair. "But it's different for you."

"I can't," I told him.

I wanted to explain, but I couldn't reach the reasons. He didn't say anything.

"I can't do it," I said.

Diego had hold of my wrist with both hands. I hadn't realized until I began to pull away. He wouldn't let me go.

"Please," he whispered, very close. "Stay."

I started to say something, but the words wouldn't come. My voice was clogged. In my mind, I'd made the decision to go, but I felt no relief. The sadness was lead inside me, weighing me down, stopping me from moving. I tried to clear my throat, but I couldn't get deep enough.

"It doesn't matter," Diego said. His voice was flip. "Hey. I figured it was worth a shot." He still had hold of my wrist. "You can't blame me for trying. Right?"

171

"I'm sorry," I said.

"Stay with me a minute," he said. "Just for a minute." He put his hand on my shoulder. "I won't do anything."

He raised himself on my shoulder, and it was natural for me to put my arm under him to support his body. I held him, and he turned and rested his head on my chest, then shifted a couple of times to find a position of comfort before he lay still. I held him to me. I felt the warmth of his body and thought of what a traitor I was and wondered what Carol was doing, so far away.

A couple of days later, I told Carol we were set to go.

"You're sure?" she asked.

I saw doubt lingering in her face. She began to say something, then changed her mind, because there wasn't anything she could ask that could settle her.

Carol has come back. She is sleeping now. I don't know where she goes. I never ask her. Other things are happening around us that are meant to be hidden from me. When we return to our car, I memorize the cars that are newly parked on the street, especially the ones with people inside them. I keep track of the taxis around us. I look for coincidences. There are wheels that move within wheels. There is not one thing going on. There are a lot of little things. Taken together, they don't yet add up to any single thing. At this point, it doesn't serve my purpose to be any more specific.

When I said before that Carol wasn't a hostage, I wanted to make clear that she wasn't in any danger. I didn't want some state trooper, stopping us by chance for a routine traffic violation, blowing me away to save the lady. I meant also that she has always been free to come and go. I am the prisoner who has to hide in motel rooms. I only go out when we drive around for a couple of hours to give the maid time to clean the room.

According to the original plan, Carol's plan, I was supposed to take her with me, out of the ICU, down the stairs, and through the emergency ward to the parking lot, where we'd separate. There was a car there for me, with keys in the ignition. While the police searched for a man and a female hostage, Carol would be back at her job at Denning.

172

But I'd have been a fool to walk away from her outside the emergency ward. Anything can happen when you're on the run. I might never have seen her again. I thought, at least I can be with her for—who knows?—a few hours, a few days. We've been lucky. I never expected it to last so long. I had Carol and I kept her.

Carol struggled when I kept hold of her arm in the parking lot, but not hard. What could she do? She was in no position to make a scene, to draw attention. And I had the gun. When I forced her into the car, she was frantic. I made her drive anyway.

"Where?" She kept staring into the rearview mirror. "Oh, God!"

She was close to panic. We almost went into the back of a car stopped at a red light.

"What do I do?" she asked. She couldn't think.

"Wait for the light to change."

She let out a deep, shuddering sigh. "OK," she said.

"Then we do what we were going to do before. We go to the room you rented."

"That won't work. It's a single room in a hotel. They don't let visitors stay overnight. It's that kind of place."

"What about the address you told me—if I had to leave a message for you?"

"Forget that."

"What is it—a bar? A store?"

"Forget it."

"Someone lives there?"

"It's someone I don't want involved. She's confused. You can't tell how she's going to react. That was just if you had to get a message to me, if there was no other way. Only as a last resort."

"Well, that's where we are."

"No."

"If this place is your ace in the hole, we need to use it now."

"No! No! No!" she shouted.

There were tears in her eyes, and I put a hand on the steering wheel, because even though she still stared straight ahead, she didn't seem to see what was in front of her.

"I didn't go through all this to go back there!" she said through clenched teeth. "That is not what this is about!" She shook her head. "Oh, God, what have I done?" She hit the steering wheel with the flat of her hand. "I must be out of my mind!"

"Slow down," I told her. "You're doing forty miles an hour."

Tears rolled down her face. She put her hand up to wipe her eyes and realized she was still wearing the glasses from the ICU. She snatched them off and rolled down the window and hurled them out backhand.

"Fuck you!" she yelled.

A kid in the car alongside laughed and pointed us out to his friend sitting beside him.

"At least roll the window up," I said. "We don't want people to remember us."

We made a turn into a residential street and stopped. There were only a few cars parked because everyone was at work. Carol took some deep breaths. She screwed the back of each wrist into her eyes to clear the tears; when she looked down, she saw they were smeared with makeup.

"Look," she said. "Dan. There's still time, if you drop me off at my car. Then you go to the room and wait for me, just like we planned, and I'll be back at Denning for my shift."

"We can't go back now."

She turned in her seat and put her hand to my face. "Don't you see what this does to me?" She held me with her eyes and ran the tips of her fingers down my cheek. "The whole point is, I'm not involved. Don't you see that? I can't be involved. How can I help you if we're both hiding from the police?"

"I want you with me," I said. "I don't want to lose you now."

"You won't. We're together. You know that. We've always been." With her left hand she reached behind her for the door release. "It can still go right. But I have to be on the outside of it."

"If you want to go," I told her, "you're free to go. I'm not going to keep you against your will."

She turned away and looked ahead through the windshield, trying to come to a decision. She gripped the steering wheel and rocked herself, pulling and pushing herself against the seat in frustration.

174

"Don't you get it?" she cried out. She hit the steering wheel with the flat of her hands.

"I did this for one reason: because I want to be with you. If you don't want to be with me, then go now."

She went very still. "You know what you're doing, don't you?"

I adjusted the gun in my belt. "We're losing time," I said. "We have to find a place."

Carol had put clothes under the seat for me, and I changed into them. But she was still in her nurse's uniform and looked very conspicuous. We parked in a small shopping mall, and she told me her sizes.

"You don't need that in there," she said, looking at the gun.

I pulled out my shirt so that it hung over the trousers and pushed the gun down deeper. "Look," I said, "it doesn't show."

"But you don't need it. Why take the risk?"

"You never know," I said.

I didn't feel sure of her. I thought that if she saw the gun as a kind of hostage, something she was responsible for, there was a better chance she'd be in the car when I came back.

"You can't be too careful," I said, and got out straight away and walked across the parking lot to the store without looking back.

Finding a motel wasn't easy. Being the July 4th weekend, most motels had "No Vacancy" signs lit up. We drove for a long time. When we found the right sort of place, Carol parked to one side of the office, so they could hear we arrived by car, but not see much of it.

"I'll get us a room," Carol said. "I wish I hadn't thrown those glasses away."

"You think one room is all right?"

"Why shouldn't it be?"

"I don't want you to feel . . ."

"Two people, a man and a woman—it's normal. Anyway, we only have money for one room."

They gave us one at the back where we could park the car out of sight from the street.

We'd never really been alone before. Immediately, she pulled the drapes and turned on the TV.

"Why'd you put that on?" I asked her.

"Place like this, most of their business is extramarital affairs. That's what they do, people who go to motels. So they're not self-conscious about making noise when they have sex."

"How come you know all this?" I asked.

"I do. OK?"

I meant it as a joke, but it had one of those sharp edges that catches a person in a tender spot, and she turned away.

Your show came on, and we watched the segment covering the escape. Carol stood without moving, frozen in the act of taking the ticket off the jeans I'd bought her, until the end. Then she sat on the end of the bed with one hand over her mouth.

"It doesn't seem real," she said, staring in front of her. "When you see it on TV, it doesn't seem like it can be you." She turned to me. She was shocked. "I can't believe what I've done." She was a mystery to herself.

I came to her to comfort her, but she put up her hands to keep me back.

"No," she said. She was bewildered. "I have to think."

"They don't know who you are," I told her. "They showed the wrong photograph. They think you're someone else."

"I just need some space, that's all."

"There's still time," I said, "if you want to go back."

She thought about it. Anyone in her position would think about it.

"I'm going to take shower," she said. "I need to relax. I'm going to take a nice, long shower."

Carol kept the shower running all the time she was in the bathroom. I left the TV on. After a while, I didn't hear it anymore, but I was never without awareness of the rush of the shower.

I sat at the table by the window. It was a round table with a wood grain in Formica, with a lamp suspended from the ceiling by a brass-colored chain hanging low over it. There were a couple of steel-framed chairs at the table, and against the wall was a chest of drawers with the TV set on top. A shaggy brown rug covered the floor. Most of the room was taken up with the queen-size bed.

I looked out through the gap where the curtains didn't come quite together. The sun was bright outside and seemed to bleach

176

all the color out of things. Only the maroon Dumpster parked against the picket fence seemed to keep its color. It glowed in the sunlight. I let my fingers rest on the sill in the gap in the drapes so that the sunlight fell on them. I thought that I must be as pale as one of those larvae that survive the winter underground, and I wondered if I would live long enough to get a tan.

The shower stopped and Carol came straight away out of the bathroom.

"Look," she said.

She wore a stern expression that seemed to say she'd made up her mind. She took a deep breath. Then she let it out, and her shoulders dropped and the tension went out of her body.

"Look," she said, "I have to go out and get some things."

"All right."

I stood up, and then I saw in her face that she'd meant to go without me.

"It's better if I go by myself. Don't you think? They're looking for you, not me."

"Maybe tomorrow," I told her.

The gun was on the table beside me. I saw her glance toward it, involuntarily. It was the center of gravity in the room.

"What are you saying?" she asked. "That I can't walk out of here on my own?"

"Why not wait till tomorrow? Let things calm down a bit out there."

"Because these are things I need today."

"What things?" I asked her.

I felt helpless. The gun made me weak. I felt the connection between us pulling apart like chewing gum, getting thinner and thinner. I could have kept her with the gun, with my bare hands. I could have done anything with her I wanted, except I didn't want her as a prisoner.

"Now is that any way for a gentleman to behave?"

She was trying to finesse the situation, hamming, exaggerating. There was something old-fashioned about the words she used, as if she were borrowing them from someone she knew who used them to good effect.

"What things?" I insisted. I pulled out one of the chairs

177

and sat down to break the momentum of the questions rising in me.

"Girl things. OK?"

"Why today? Why now? What's the rush?"

"I don't have anything, remember?" She came toward me, and I felt the power of her presence. "I didn't expect to be here. There was a change of plan." She stopped at some critical distance from me, powerful but beyond reach. "For one thing, we don't have any money."

"I can always get us money."

"How?" She nodded in the direction of the gun on the table. "That?"

"Why not?"

"You wouldn't know what to do, would you?"

"I talked to guys in Denning who did it for a living. I don't think you need a Ph.D."

"Dan. The cops are waiting for you to hold up your first liquor store. That's just what they want. They'll be right down on top of you."

"Not if we keep moving."

"No!" It came out louder and angrier than she'd intended. "Look." She clenched her hand and opened it again. "This is something we've worked for for a long time. Right? There's been a change of plan, and we have to deal with it. It's the unexpected. It's bound to come up."

"I want us to stay together."

"We are. We are together. But this is not Bonnie and Clyde. OK? This is a whole different kind of thing. We can't run. We can't hold up banks and liquor stores and so on, and keep moving. We're not looking to go out in a burst of glory. Right? The idea is, we live happily ever after. Right?"

She saw she couldn't reach me with words alone. I sat on the edge of the chair and waited to see how close she'd come. She wanted to touch me, to convince me with the touch of her hand, but she was afraid what it would allow me to do.

"Please!" Her fingers rested on my shoulder. She was pleading, her eyes close to mine. "We've got something good here. All we have to do is not screw it up. OK?"

178

She searched my eyes for signs that I'd come to the truth of what she said. She saw it there even before I felt sure myself.

"How long will you be?" I asked her.

She straightened up, and I felt a bitterness I tried to push aside.

"A couple of hours. Maybe three."

"I don't get it. What's going to take so long?"

"I have to dump the car, for one thing. That could take longer than three hours."

"It's risky. I should come with you."

"It's less risk by myself. You've got to remember what the police are looking for. They're looking for you. Think about that."

I hated the idea of her leaving. I hated myself for doubting her.

I switched off the TV when I heard the car leave. Then I turned off the lights. After a while, my eyes adjusted to the gloom illuminated by triangles of daylight that came in around the drapes. I lay on the bed and listened to the sounds of normal life going on around me. When you've been shut away, very ordinary things take on an exotic flavor, like the slight vibration from a truck passing nearby, or the sound of children's voices, or old people grumbling at one another. I listened to all the cars pulling in to park, and as the tires scratched on the hardtop as they made their turn into a parking spot, my heart beat faster at the thought that it was Carol returning, or the police.

By the time Carol came back, the headlamps of passing cars made crossing patterns on the ceiling.

"Everything's fine," she said. She seemed pleased.

It unsettled me to see her out of uniform. I felt I'd lost hold of her. At that moment, I wondered if I'd ever really had a good grasp of who she was. There'd always been this other side, her life outside Medical, that I knew nothing about.

"I've got enough money to keep us going for a while."

"Where'd you get it?" I asked.

"From an ATM." I thought she hesitated.

"They don't give out more than two hundred at a time."

"I thought you'd be pleased."

"I am. I'm surprised, that's all."

179

"Actually, I borrowed it from my mom."

"What did you tell her?"

"What do you think? I told her it was an emergency. She's my mother. What is it with all these questions? Do you have to know every little detail?"

I'm my own worst enemy. I'm possessive. That's the problem. I'm thinking as though I'm still in Denning, where you have to keep a tight grip on everything you have every minute of the day. Give it time. I want to hold her, to contain her in my arms, and it's too much for Carol. It's smothering. I can't help myself. I want too much from her all at once. We're strangers to one another, really. I can't own her. Love is such a fragile thing. I'm afraid I'll crush it out when I try to grasp it. We're on edge. I see Carol's lips tighten. I would sooner hold my hand over a flame.

Motels eat up money. I don't care about it. Carol does, though. She worries about it a lot.

"We can't keep on this way forever," she said on the second day. "We just can't. We're going to run out of money."

She had a wild, frantic look in her eyes. I held up my hand to slow her down.

"OK." She took a deep breath. "OK. It's just you and me. We have to make our own way. We've got to get money. I mean, real money. Now's the time to start thinking about getting Diego's money."

"It's Nando's money. Diego was keeping it for Nando."

"Whatever. We have to get it."

"I don't know where it is."

She didn't believe me. "You're joking."

I didn't say anything.

"Tell me you're joking," she demanded. "For God's sake!"

"Diego never told me," I said.

"You let him fuck you, and you don't know where the money is?" She laughed. "We're all fucked. Do you know that? I refuse to believe it. I do. I refuse."

She looked at me again as if she was trying to see me afresh, trying to compose her mind to look at me as though she'd never set eyes on me before.

180

"This is a test, right?" she asked, still unable to believe what I'd told her. "This is some kind of a test of true love?"

"Yes," I told her.

"Oh, God."

She sat on the bed. She looked scared. Her eyes moved back and forth across a patch of the shag rug in front of her, searching for a way out.

"I don't know, Dan," she said. "I can't read you. I don't know what kind of mind games you're playing right now. I don't know what you're about."

"The money's not the important thing," I told her.

She looked at me pityingly. "Don't you see what this is all about?"

"It's not about money."

"No, it's not about money. But we have to have money. Otherwise we're not going anywhere, except back to Denning. Don't you see, we're not going anywhere without the money?"

"All in good time."

"What's that supposed to mean?"

"What I say. We'll have what we need when we need it."

"So what you said before, about not knowing where it is, that's not true?"

"Why is this so important to you?"

Carol got up and came to sit on the corner of the bed closest to me.

"We've come so far," she said softly. "We've done the hard part." She put her hand on my arm. "We've got you out of Denning. The last part should be easy—getting the money and taking off. You can do anything with money."

She got up abruptly and paced, her arms curled tight around her chest, back and forth between the end of the bed and the chest of drawers. There was a violence in the way she twisted her body through the turns that I hadn't seen in her before.

"Christ, I want a cigarette!" she said. "Why didn't I get any cigarettes? Because I knew I wanted to smoke, that's why. This is how it starts, isn't it? Stress. That's how you pick up again." She stopped her pacing. "Aren't you scared, Dan? Aren't you afraid the cops will get us? Going away for the rest of your life? Tell you the truth—yesterday?—I didn't expect you to be here when I got back."

"Where would I go without you?"

"You tell me."

"I don't know. There'd be no point."

"You don't need me now." She perched on the chest of drawers and stared at me with her hands clasped across her chest. "I got you out. I've served my purpose. That's it, isn't it? You got me to do what you wanted."

"That's not it at all."

"Now you want me to put out, right? You want something up front?"

She unzipped her pocketbook. She was searching in the bottom for something small.

"I don't know why you're talking this way," I said. "What's gotten into you?"

"Here!" She tossed a condom in silver foil onto the bed. "You want to do me?"

I didn't understand why she was crying. "What is it?" I asked her.

She threw another condom onto the bed. "You better put two on, just in case."

The tears were coming harder. It wasn't the tears that affected me so much as the terrible expression of pain on her face, as if something inside her were being forced open.

I held her in my arms, and brought her to the bed. I held her tight to me. I felt her rocking, and let myself be moved back and forth by her rhythm.

"I never wanted it like this," she sobbed.

"I should never have gotten you into it," I lied.

She cried bitterly. I felt her pain as if it were my own. I wanted to absorb it into my body, to take it into myself and drain it from her.

"I've been so selfish," I whispered.

"No," I heard her murmur.

"If I really loved you, I'd never have gotten you mixed up in my life. If I really loved you, I'd have done my time and left you alone to get on with your life."

I felt her twist in my arms and loosened my hold on her. She turned to see my face. "Do you really love me?" she asked.

"Yes," I said. "I love you."

"You're not just using me?"

"Never," I told her. "You're the whole world to me. There's nothing else."

Her eyes stayed on my face. "There's no way of knowing, though, is there?"

She lay quietly in my arms on the big, flat bed. She was on guard, and it took a long time until she would let her body relax and mold to mine. I waited for her and watched the patterns from the streetlights between the top of the drapes and the ceiling.

After a while, our bodies being so close, with the small shifts to change position she made from time to time, we came together. It seemed natural. From lying beside me, she turned so that first her head was resting on my chest, then as she turned some more, I felt her breast touching me just below the ribs. She put her arm across me to hold herself to me.

"Hold me," she whispered.

My arms were already around her shoulders. I moved them lower to take the weight of her body. She murmured something I couldn't make out, sleepily it seemed, and at the same time slid her knee over my thigh. She wore black slacks of a thin, summer fabric that had a slickness to it when my fingers brushed across it. She pressed against the thigh between her legs so stealthily that I wasn't sure she was encouraging me until she backed off and the pressure came again.

"You'll wear something, won't you?" she asked, speaking, not whispering, talking into my chest.

"Yes. Sure," I said. I felt jolted, unable to think in step with her. "Are you sure this is what you want?"

"Of course I do."

Her hand ran down the side of my chest to my hip and came across, hovering so that only the tips of her fingers made contact with the denim of my jeans. She found me.

"Isn't this what you want?" she asked, sure of herself.

I didn't trust myself to speak.

"I think you do," she said.

183

Her fingers slowly traced my outline beneath the cloth. I didn't know it was possible to move so slowly and still convey the sense of motion, the slightest hint of friction. I existed only at her point of touch. I held my breath and trembled while the touch of her fingers held me at the edge of sensation.

She curled around my body. She brought her head up to kiss me below the corner of my mouth, and I felt the warmth of her breath against my skin. I saw the reflection of the streetlights in her eyes. Otherwise she was dark and deep, a shadow made real in the greater darkness of the room.

"Sometimes, I hardly know you," she said.

Her finger followed the line of my jaw, the outline of the ear, from the bone beneath the eyebrow around the curve to the cheek.

"Then I feel like I've always known you."

"I feel I've always been waiting to know you," I told her.

"It's funny, isn't it? Like the feeling you've been here before?"

"I've never been here before," I said, and she laughed.

I was afraid to touch her clothes. All the time I'd known her, she'd been set apart, and now I couldn't put aside that sense. She undid my belt, pulling up hard with determination to release the buckle. There was so much that was new about her. She looked up at me to see my reaction, and I kissed her on the mouth. When I put my tongue in her, she pulled away.

"You won't be rough?"

"It's not my way."

"Because I don't like that stuff. I know some women say they don't like that stuff, but they really do. But I really don't."

"I promise."

The spicy flavor of her lipstick was in my mouth, familiar and strange, just like the déjà vu she'd spoken of, because I couldn't for a moment remember the place I knew it from. I reached for another taste, and she met me.

"You won't forget who you're with?" she whispered.

"Never," I said.

She clung to me and pressed her head against my chest. I held her head between my hands. I held the world: her hopes and thoughts and feelings. I held infinity between my hands.

184

"I know who I'm with," I told her, stroking her hair. "I know who you are."

That seemed to soothe her. She crept up my body again to my face, stealing up on me. I raised my head to kiss her, and her lips met mine for a moment and then brushed by to the corner of my mouth, to my cheek, to my throat.

Very carefully, I turned her on her back. She couldn't look at me for more than a second. She glanced at me with scared eyes, placing me in space, finding the exact location of my mouth and eyes in relation to her mouth and eyes. My eyes never left her.

She turned her head, and I couldn't see her. She reached back; her hand groped the air to make its way toward my face. Her fingers found the side of my nose and slid down to my mouth. They touched my lips as if she could read there the truth in Braille. I kissed the tips of her fingers.

"I promise I'll never hurt you," I said.

She nodded several times, trying hard to believe.

"Wait," she said.

Carol pulled the T-shirt over her head. Without thinking, she started to fold it, then realized what she was doing and tossed it aside. She unhooked her bra and shrugged her shoulders and it fell halfway off her and her breasts came free. I cupped one breast and let it run through my fingers. Her creamy skin was soft, but the nipple was dark and hard, an alien presence. It was a mysterious substance that had flowed up from some deeper source inside her. I rounded the nipple with my fingertip and heard her take in breath sharply. At the same time, she watched to see the power she had over me.

"You're beautiful," I told her.

Her eyes had grown darker. I couldn't read them. They had turned to liquid.

Her lips were open, and I kissed her now without resistance, putting my tongue between her lips and bringing it back into my own mouth with the spice of lipstick on it and saliva that held the distant flavor of coffee.

I stretched myself beside her and kissed her breast. I wanted to explore her body inch my inch. I wanted to delight her. I put my lips about her nipple and sucked gently on it, pulling away from her

185

and feeling her back arch as we reached the high point of tension, and then letting it slide back from between my lips.

She sighed. "That's nice."

I did it again. I felt her back arch, coming partway with me, and then the release of breath she'd been holding.

"Nice and slow," Carol said. She put her hand on my head and stroked my hair to show what slow was. She was rediscovering her command of me.

When I turned to undress, she curled away from me, stripping off her pants and slipping under the covers in one fluid movement. I stood naked beside the bed, trying to cover myself with my hands. I pulled the blanket slowly off the bed. Carol had hold of the sheet. I pulled on it gently, and she released her hold of it.

"Please don't hurt me," she said.

I knelt beside the bed and kissed her feet. I was afraid of myself, the surging mixture of animal excitement and reverence.

"I worship you," I breathed.

Carol was looking down at me from the other end of the bed. I could hardly make out her face. She held out her hand to me and drew me up, alongside her thighs and past her navel and the darkness of her nipples. Her face was too dark to recognize. A truck rumbling by on the street outside reverberated in the room. I ran my hand across her belly and at the bottom felt the silkiness of her hair. She opened her thighs, and I dipped my hand down where she was soft and wet. I was afraid what I would do, even though I didn't know what that was—the crude and violent act of an angry inmate.

She slipped a condom on me and pulled me to her. As I slid inside her, she gave a soft cry of something like regret, of falling.

No one can tell the meaning of a person's struggles in the act of love. Passion is a kind of panic. Carol was like a drowning woman. She writhed and cried out. She clung to me as if I was her only hope to live, encircling my body and gripping me tight with her thighs with the desperation of someone who must keep from sinking. And at the same time, she fought me and pushed against my shoulders and twisted in my arms as if she was struggling to break free, to be released upwards to a surface from which I held her back.

I reached into this drowning woman as far as I could go. To save myself, I held her tight and wouldn't let her escape me. I was a lost soul, striving for an impossible union, reckless, eager to lose myself, overcome with the pagan wonder of entering another body.

I felt a peace I have never known before. I lay on my back. After a time, Carol propped herself on an elbow to look at me. Her face was a mystery in the shadow. Several times, I thought she was about to tell me something but stopped when she couldn't find the right words to begin. When I touched her face, she lowered herself onto my body. Her breasts were damp with sweat and cool at the point they touched my chest. The streetlights cast an amber sheen on her shoulder, and when I kissed her there I came away with the bitterness of salt upon my lips.

There are times when I can't bring Carol's face into focus. Once, during spring break, on a class trip to the Metropolitan Museum with some of the seniors, I fell in love with a pastel by Degas of a woman crouched in a bath. I went closer—I thought I'd see the picture better—but the woman disappeared. All I could see were smudges of chalk and cross-hatching laid over a surface that wouldn't let my eyes pass through. I stepped back, and there she was again, curved and wet and pink, but out of reach. Carol disappears in this way. I hear the words she speaks, I see the contours of her face, I experience the feelings she evokes in me, but I'm not used to such close encounters, and there are moments of panic when I don't recognize this person. Then, with a gesture I've seen a hundred times, she comes into focus again.

How long do I have before I'm captured? Or killed, in a shoot-out with the state police? One week? Two? Two months? Who knows how lucky I'll be? When you live in the present, these things don't matter. Nothing has any meaning beyond itself. It's a relief to live without hidden significance. Every event, every touch of Carol's hand on my arm, is a point; there are no lines that connect one point to another, no lines that refer back to points long ago that you would never have thought of, or forward to another point you can't yet see, or sideways, by a knight's move to one you could never have foreseen. Or if there are these

187

implications, I don't have to find them, here, wherever I am, outside Denning. You take, gratefully, what you can get. Each precious moment. It's true, what they say about living under sentence of death.

SIX

Dear Sandy:
    It's all come apart. I've been living a dream.
  I'm a fool. It's been a charade from the start. I don't exist. I cling
to the pain. It's the tether that jerks me back when I'm about to lose
my bearings. It's not real pain—it's more the thought of what the
pain would be. The real pain doesn't bear thinking about. It's a void
without feeling. It's falling in blackness. I'm floating in space with
a puncture in the suit, feeling the momentary suck—and pulling
the thought back just before the chest and guts explode into a
fine mist.
  Instead, I think about a small, real pain. It's manageable, and
it distracts me from the dangerous tip into anguish that is like a
free fall. If I walk carefully, placing the heel of one foot in front
of the toe of the other, I can follow this small pain like a yellow
line, and not fall off.
  I am sitting in a corner of a town library, scribbling furiously,

trying to keep up with the images and emotions that swirl through me. If I write fast enough, I can slow the flow to manageable gulps; I can swallow pain without drowning.

I am concentrating on the lash that caught in Carol's eye. It was driving her crazy, that day on Medical, but I couldn't help her unless I entered the nurses' trap. That's where I was, in the forbidden zone, when Baruk appeared.

I was furious with myself for putting everything at risk. I dreaded losing my job on Medical. Far worse, I was afraid Carol would be fired. For the rest of the day, I kept her lash folded in a piece of tissue in the chest pocket of my shirt. That night in my cell, in the minutes before the lights were switched off, I took out the tissue to look at this tiny piece of her. You don't realize how exquisitely tapered a lash is until you examine it up close. I was afraid it was all I would have of her. When the lights went out, I lay awake thinking of what I would do—anything—not to lose her.

The next morning I woke well before it was time to get up. The lash had curled almost into a circle during the night. In the bathroom, shaving with no one else around, I balanced it on the tip of my finger, and brought it up and touched it to the white of my eye. The moisture took it. I tried to hold back the blink, but the spasm broke through my fingers. I blinked again and felt the lash drawn across the surface. When I looked in the mirror, I saw it lying on the eyelid's pink inner flesh.

When I tried to keep the eye open, it flickered and twitched and a tear broke lose and ran down my cheek. I closed my eyes and brought up a vision of Carol, and I let myself flow into that image, breathing slowly and deeply as the face composed itself around the new element. I waited until the twitching had ebbed entirely. Then I slowly let the eyelids open on their own. I let them float up, not fighting the reflex that would clench the eye shut, but counterbalancing it, soothing it, entering into it and negating it. That's the way with pain: you have to enter it and make it part of you.

The officer called me to go to work. Throughout that day, whenever I felt the approach of the twitch in my right eye, I stopped what I was doing and looked far into the distance. It was like staring into the sun. I went through the pain, and when I came out on the other side, the reflex had faded away. Sometimes I caught my hand as it moved automatically to rub the eye. I raised it close to what the fingers wanted to do. I let them come within an inch of my face before I forced them down. I teared and blinked and went on. Over the day, her lash became sheathed in a strand of mucus. I liked the idea of secreting myself about the irritation like an oyster around a piece of grit. But the lash slowly dissolved, and her tissue became part of my body, dispersed and consumed, lost. On the third morning, the lash was gone.

I remember the torture from that small part of her inside me, edging its way like a splinter into my flesh. I think of it now, fighting the body's command, stifling the simple backhand smear that could have wiped the speck clean out, and I harbor the memory of the pain. I hold it close. I like the sensation's sharp edges, its definition. It is precisely here. It is a presence instead of an absence.

For the first two days after we escaped, I didn't go out, except to get into the car to drive to the next place. Carol chose where we went next, and she was very particular, even though the qualities she said she was looking for seemed to change from day to day: this one was too expensive, that one too cheap-looking; this one was too close to the highway and so too conspicuous; that one was too far from the highway and so more likely to stand out. I left it to her. I was busy looking out for trouble, counting cars, memorizing patterns, watching to see who might be following us. Every afternoon we rolled into some out-of-the-way motel. I thought she had an instinct for locating the right place. I didn't realize until I saw the map in my mind's eye, that in all the places we stayed, we were circling around a general area Carol had chosen for us.

On the second day we got into a car I'd never seen before, a Grand Prix.

"Where'd this come from?" I asked her.

"I got it last night."

She was leaning forward with her head turned sideways into the steering wheel. Her arms were stretched under the dash and there was a far-off look on her face. She touched wires together and the engine coughed and died. She tried it again. The engine turned over and caught finally as she gave it some gas.

She wiggled in her seat and lined up behind the steering wheel. She gave it gas again and listened to the response. "Good buddy," she said and patted the top of the dash proudly.

"How did you get it?" I asked her.

"I stole it," she said.

"How?"

We were pulling out of the parking lot, and she leaned forward to see if there was any traffic coming from my side.

"The usual way."

She glanced at my face to see my reaction as we set off down the road. She was pleased with herself, the happiest I'd seen her since we escaped. We drove a couple of miles. I turned on the radio, flicked through the stations, switched it off.

"You don't like that?" she asked.

"I don't like country and western," I said.

"It's a nice song, though."

She started to hum the tune.

"Where'd you learn to steal cars?" I asked her finally.

"I had a boyfriend who taught me." She looked over at me, checking my reaction. She reached down to turn the radio back on and moved her head in time with the music. "I was sixteen. He went into the Air Force, and that was the end of it."

I nodded. I felt her changing, becoming unpredictable. "People get into a lot of things when they're sixteen," I said. "It doesn't mean anything. Not necessarily."

"We used to do it all the time." She smiled through the windshield and swayed in time with the song, hands high on the wheel. "Pick a car for the evening, take it out onto the highway, see what it could do. We'd dump it off in a lot or something on our way home." She glanced over at me. "I never sold any, though. I never did it for money."

That evening she disappeared again without telling me where she was going or, when she returned, what she had done.

"I don't want you even to ask," she said. "It's better you don't know."

It was torture for me not to know. But I knew I couldn't control her every move. I'd lose her if I tried to put her in my own prison. I don't understand trust. It never made any sense to me. Why

192

assume something about someone when you can check it out? And if you can't check it out, why make the assumption? I tried not to think about it. That was a mistake. Of course it was. I wanted to avoid pain. I fear myself, my own energy turned back on me, more than anything else. In a frenzy of doubt, I could tear myself to shreds. Everything is obvious afterwards—that's what "afterwards" means.

The next morning we drove out of the motel court in the same car, but I noticed we had a new license plate. I didn't say anything. It made sense. It was too risky to steal a car every day, so why not switch plates? The next morning, the car had a different plate, even though Carol had been with me all evening, except for half an hour or so. Should I have figured out that someone was "helping" us? Some things are too close to see. I was delirious, being with her. If cracks were appearing in the picture, if they were opening up wider and wider, I didn't want to see them. Besides, we were on borrowed time.

I wasn't ready for the brightness of the summer sun. I wasn't used to the wide open space of the street, vehicles and people coming from all directions, more than I could ever keep track of. In prison, you know your surroundings, minute by minute. You know where everybody is. Every inmate walks with his own zone around him.

That day, instead of going to the drive-through window at a McDonald's or Burger King, we stopped for breakfast at a Howard Johnson's. I got out of the car slowly, looking around. The light was stark. There were no shadows. A car pulled into the lot and made straight to a parking spot, without pausing for us as we crossed toward the restaurant. It nosed by a few inches from us. We went into the restaurant and waited at the notice that tells you a hostess will seat you. I waited, standing exposed in front of the whole restaurant. I felt I'd arrived from Mars. I felt people saw this in me.

I was watching the people eating at the tables in front of us. There was a woman who every now and then looked in our direction, and I thought that at any moment the light of recognition was going to come into her eyes, and she'd identify me.

"You're staring," Carol said under her breath.

A man walked past us. He came from behind, and I hadn't registered his approach. I think he was returning to his seat from the bathroom. He brushed me with his sleeve as he went by. I wasn't prepared for someone coming up behind us, and I jumped back.

He said, "Sorry."

Without thinking, my hand went to the gun in my belt beneath the plaid shirt. He looked at my hand move; then his eyes came up to my face, wondering, sorting this out. But it wasn't in him to come to a lethal conclusion in Howard Johnson's, at breakfast time.

"I think there's a table opening up over there," Carol said, and he passed on.

A waitress came with menus and sat us in a booth. I took my time, wanting to see if the man would glance back, but he didn't. The waitress came back with coffee, and I ordered a western omelet.

"I wish you'd give me that thing," Carol said. "We don't need it anymore."

"I feel better with it," I told her.

"What use is it? It's only going to cause trouble."

"You never know."

"It makes me nervous."

"It makes me calm."

"I thought you were going to pull it on that old man."

"I wanted to make sure it was tucked in OK."

"Didn't you see the way he looked at you?"

"He came right up on me. What was I going to do?"

"Dan, this isn't Denning. This is general population. This is the real world."

I shrugged. "I wasn't ready for him, that's all."

I wanted her to be carefree. If she was, I could be, too. I didn't want her to spoil the moment.

Carol stared at me with a blank, objective expression on her face. She leaned forward over the table and lowered her voice. I saw an old woman across the room turn our way.

"You're going to blow someone away because he comes too close to you?" Carol asked.

I glared at the old woman, and she looked quickly away.

"You have to take control of a situation," I said. "You can't leave it till it's too late."

194

"But we're doing *fine*," she said, still leaning close to me. "You are in control of the situation. Everything's . . ." she paused to touch the back of my hand, to give the word its meaning, ". . . *good*." She sat back. "Don't you think?"

"Yes."

I wanted to start over with her. So easily, she slipped away from me. She changed shape so that I didn't recognize her. Sometimes she was like a double, a stand-in for the real Carol. Then she'd show through again.

"It's very good," I told her.

We looked into each other's eyes. I felt a depth of communion with her then that I had never achieved before. Carol was smiling. She was radiant with happiness. There was a dimple just beyond the corner of her mouth that made me melt with tenderness. I can't believe this was illusion.

The waitress arrived with plates of food. I played with the omelet, picking out the red and green specks with the fork, too filled with love to bother about eating. We were tuned to one another. I thought we were. Whenever I looked up, she would, too, and we'd exchange a smile. If she was shy and had to look away, it didn't matter. We were beyond words.

I think back, now, to those days and try to find the places in our conversations where she was trying to let me know what was going on. A certain inflection. The choice of one word rather than another. I blame myself for not realizing sooner. Should I have known? I believe she tried to tell me, even against her better judgment. What she thought was her better judgment. I didn't hear. I wasn't listening in the spaces between the words.

"We have to get some money," she said.

"Something will show up."

"What?"

"I don't know." I was beyond hope or fear. When you're in a free fall, it's easy to sustain the illusion you can fly.

She was silent for a few moments, her head down, playing with her fingers in a spill of milk, moving it one way, joining up the dots of liquid.

"You don't care, do you?" she said finally.

I hadn't known how upset she was. I thought she was angry at first, then it seemed more that she was hurt.

"I put myself on the line for you." She doodled with the drop of milk, then glanced up at me, said what she had to say, then looked down again. "I threw away everything for you. Apartment, job, career. What's happened to my cat? I'll lose my license. They'll pull that. I'll never work as a nurse again."

"I'll do anything for you," I told her. "You know that."

"No, I don't know that."

There was a sharpness to her tone. She looked up, and I was the one who looked away. She'd yanked at what connected me to her. I hadn't noticed how she'd been taking up the slack.

"You've said things." Her voice was controlled. "You've talked about how you feel. But it hasn't come to anything. We're still here, almost out of cash."

"What do you want me to do?"

"When we run out of money, that's it. We've nowhere to go."

"What about the place where I could leave a message?"

"No."

"No? That's it? No?"

She looked away.

"What is it you want me to do?" I asked her, though we both knew.

"When the money's gone, you're going back to Denning. That's a certainty. They're going to put you in J Block for the rest of your life. When the money's gone, we have no money for gas. We can't keep moving. We have nowhere to go. Do you get the picture? When the money's gone, it's all over. You. Me. Everything. It means we went through . . . this whole thing for nothing. Nothing, Dan. We went through this whole thing for nothing."

"You want Nando's money," I said.

"We have to get it." She reached across the table and took hold of both my hands. "Dan." She squeezed tight. She held me in her gaze. The emotion had come back into her. "We need it now! I don't want to have to beg you."

"Don't. I don't want you to do that."

"I've done everything I can do. If you want us to go on, you have to do this."

"I told you before, I don't know how to get the money."

She looked at me with pity in her eyes. Her lips were pursed tight, close to contempt. But I was stubborn. I was terrified she'd give up on me, even as I tested her love to the breaking point.

"You told me . . ." she began. She had to stop to bring her voice under control. "You told me you knew how to get the money. You told me this before I put everything together to get you out of Denning. I trusted you on this. Now you're saying you lied to me?"

"The money's in a bank," I said at last.

"Where?"

"In the Caicos Islands. That's in the Caribbean somewhere."

Carol watched me. She didn't know whether to believe what I was saying.

"It's not going to do us any good," I said.

"Give it a chance."

"If we don't have the money for gas, how are we going to get to the Caicos Islands?"

"We'll find a way."

"The account has a number. It's like opening a safe. You have to know the number to get to the money."

"What's the number?"

"That's all I know. Diego never told me the number."

"Don't you trust me, Dan, after all we've been through?"

I felt I was dangling, my whole weight swinging far out over the abyss, by a fraying thread.

"I trust you," I told her solemnly. I meant it to be true. In the way I meant it, it was true. I meant, I trusted the part of Carol that she herself isn't totally aware of, the part of her that hasn't yet come into being.

"You owe me, goddamn it!" she snapped.

Then her face broke, and she looked down and away. Her eyes were clenched shut, and her lips were drawn back tight against her teeth. She shook her head, as if she wanted to deny the way she appeared, but a sob caught her and brought her shoulders up in a sudden spasm.

"I know," I told her. "I owe you everything."

I was wrenched by her feelings. I felt her despair as if it were

197

my own. All along, I'd been blind to her unhappiness. I'd already accepted my fate, but even at this stage, Carol hadn't given up the hope of living a natural life.

"It's all falling apart," she whispered, not trusting her voice. She was talking to herself, staring at a space between the plates in disbelief. The mascara around her eyes was running, and she seemed blurred and out of focus. "It was going to be a new life. But it all turned out wrong."

She took a deep breath and held it. Her face was re-forming: the jaw, the cheeks, the lips were tightening and returning to their definition. I felt the effort as she clenched inside to bring herself back under control.

"I shouldn't have said that," she said. She'd regained herself. She dabbed at her eyes and looked at the result on the napkin. "About you owing me? I didn't mean it. I lost it. I totally lost it."

"I don't want to lose you," I said.

"You'll never lose me," she said. She smiled reassuringly. A brave smile. A cabin attendant telling the passengers the captain turned on the seat belt sign only as a precaution. I should have known then.

"At least give me the gun." She suggested it as an afterthought, it seemed. She found a mirror in her pocketbook and was examining her face. "I'm going to fix myself up." She got up, looking for the direction of the ladies' room. "I wish you'd put my mind at rest."

In the car, sitting in the parking lot, we settled on a compromise. I wouldn't carry the gun; instead, I'd leave it hooked under the driver's seat.

I'd intended to follow Carol when she went out that evening. But in the afternoon, after Carol checked us into the new motel, I pulled her down with me onto the bed and we made love.

We were still shy with one another at these moments. I was afraid of myself. Naked, we were unknown to each other, and our coming together was filled with mysterious possibilities. When I touched her, I believed in magic. I still believe. Her nipples are dark and distinct against milky skin. She tastes of a rare fruit never encountered before. At the point of orgasm, she turns away and shakes her head, as if she refuses to come. She will submit to the sensation only if it overwhelms her, and then she cries out, once, as if she is afraid. I am writing these things to keep the pain localized. Like a lash between the lid and the white of the eye. If I do it to myself, I know where it is.

She was fully dressed when she came out of the bathroom. She quickly collected the clothes that lay scattered on the floor. Carol is a neatnik who insists on ironing T-shirts. We had to wash our clothes, she said. She'd take them to a Laundromat she'd noticed a couple of blocks away. I said I'd come with her, and she told me it would look suspicious, two people at the Laundromat when only one was needed. Especially with one of us in the buff. She pulled it off so naturally that it wasn't until she'd closed the door that I realized she'd taken every piece of clothing I possessed.

She came home with the clothes in the duffel bag still warm from the dryer. All the time she was gone I'd rehearsed questions I'd spring on her when she came back. Devious, oblique questions that seemed innocuous when put casually. Questions that would have tied her down to coordinates of time and place. Then, when she returned, smiling, slightly out of breath—"Well? Did you miss me?"—my suspicions melted clean away. There is something very reassuring about putting on fresh clothes that are still warm.

The next day, the license plate was the same, but the car had changed. I won't bother to tell you what kind of car. I'm sure you've found out by now that the previous ones weren't a Grand Prix or a Monte Carlo. Please don't make me out to be a liar. I'm not going to give you information that will get me arrested. I don't have a death wish, in spite of what your psychiatrist had to say on the show the other night.

When I mentioned a Monte Carlo (and a couple of other things), that was disinformation, not lies. Disinformation is different from lying. Disinformation is when you tell someone something that isn't true because you have to. Lying is deception pure and simple—taking someone along for the ride, taking them in, getting their emotions mixed up with yours, so that you can use them. They're different.

You get out of the habit of money in prison. Carol kept our money and bought the things we needed on her excursions. By then you'd exposed the "hostage" story and shown her real photo

199

on TV, but Carol claimed it was a terrible picture that didn't look anything like her; her disguise was more effective than mine she said, so she should be the one to take care of business in the outside world. I didn't think much about not having money, until I wanted to keep closer tabs on her. I know now this was another layer of her control over me. It tied me to her. When I thought about it, I figured she'd set it up that way because she was afraid I'd leave her. Later, when we went to restaurants, I pocketed the tips.

The next time she went out the back way to the car—she was going stir-crazy, she said—I went out the front and stepped right into a cab.

"Where to?" the driver asked in a tone full of resentment at the world. He reminded me of the guards at Denning.

He didn't bother to turn around, but instead fixed me in the mirror, so that I was looking into the slit that framed a piece of head with eyes and the skin around them. Carol was stopped in the forecourt, waiting to join the flow of traffic on the road outside. I slid down deeper into the seat, and the driver adjusted the mirror so that he could follow me down.

"I want to follow this black car that's coming out of the motel right now," I said.

He blew air out through his lips as if I'd just made him tired and disgusted. "I get it. You're a private eye, right?" he asked sarcastically.

"No. It's my sister." I didn't know what else to say, except something like the truth. "I'm worried about her."

"What is she, hooking?"

I hadn't thought of that possibility, that Carol would sacrifice herself for us in this way. I felt ashamed for doubting her, even though I didn't know what I suspected her of. The disembodied eyes saw some of this. The man in front of me with the thick neck settled back in his seat. All I could see in the mirror were lips.

"These girls." The lips were moist and moved hungrily. "They'll do anything—*an-y-thing*—for a snort of cocaine."

"I know," I said.

"*I* know," he said, "because they sit right where you are. I see it. I hear what they say to the johns. The kind of stuff—it'd turn your stomach."

The man shifted so that he could get a look at me. The eyes stared far beyond, frowning. They kept flicking back to me. I watched the road. "You're going to lose her," I told him. He was hanging back. There were three cars between us.

"You know, don't you, this isn't going to make a fucking difference?" he said. He might have been talking about the prospects of the Red Sox. "If she's on cocaine, if that's what this is, forget it."

"I don't want you to lose her."

"Hey, you want to drive?"

"No."

"Do you?"

"No, I don't want to drive."

"All right, then. Let me handle this."

Carol made a right on a green light. The light changed to yellow, and the brake lights of the car in front came up red. The driver pulled the cab left around the car and accelerated through as the traffic lights changed to red. After we made the turn and straightened up, he stretched back in his seat, pleased with himself.

"See, I done this before," he said. "When I was a cop." The piece of head glanced up to see my reaction.

"Is that so?"

"I ever see you before?" he asked.

"I don't think so."

"Why not?"

"Why not what?"

"Why d'you think I never seen you before?" The eyes were narrowed, troubled, concentrating.

"Because I've never seen you before."

"That isn't what I said. See, I said I never seen *you* before. I never said anything about you seeing *me*."

I didn't want to lose sight of Carol. To finish the conversation, I said, "I've been living in Florida. That's why you've never seen me."

"Florida, huh?"

"Yeah."

"That where you got the tan?"

"I've been sick. I just got out of the hospital."

201

"Just in time so you could help your sister out of her jam."

"Fuck you," I told him.

"You want me to drive past?" he asked, concentrating on the job at hand, matter-of-fact.

Carol had pulled up to a Dunkin' Donuts in a small shopping mall and taken a spot on the lot close to one of the exits, away from the shops.

"Pull into the Osco lot," I told him.

He parked the cab among a group of other cars, with our backs to Dunkin' Donuts. I started to turn around so that I could see Carol.

"Don't," he warned sharply. "Don't turn around."

I thought he was slumped against the door frame, but he'd changed his angle to the mirror so that he could view Carol's car.

"She's waiting," he said. "She's smart, this one. She's not getting out of the car. She's having a good look around first."

I was impatient to see for myself. I didn't want to hear about the woman I loved through the eyes of this man.

"You don't want to turn around," he said. "She's looking this way now."

"Turn the car around," I told him.

"Lean forward. Like we're talking. I'll adjust the side mirror so you can see her."

I hunched over with my face up to the window cut in the Plexiglas. He breathed heavily when he shifted himself over a few inches and lurched sideways to reach the lever on the side of the door.

"How's that?" he asked.

I saw a square of brown roof. "Lower," I said. "And to the left."

He struggled and panted and rolled on the seat. His shirt came loose from his pants top. He looked helpless. I wondered what he'd do once he found out I didn't have the fare. I thought I might have him drive me to a quiet spot among the warehouses on the other side and break the news to him there.

"How's that?" he asked. He was short of breath from the movement.

I could see the car now. It was empty.

202

"What happened?" I asked. "I can't see her." I wanted badly to turn around.

"Shit."

He jacked himself up bit by bit on one arm. I listened to the regular sound of the breath sighing through his open mouth while he adjusted the mirror on the windshield.

"Uh-huh. Yep. There we are. She's gone inside."

He was silent for a long moment, studying the mirror with his face so close it looked like he was trying to look through his eye into his own mind.

"You know that guy?" he asked finally.

"Who?" I asked him. My hands pressed against the Plexiglas. "Which guy?"

He leaned sideways again, and we went through the laborious process of adjusting the side mirror.

"No," I told him. "More to the left. More."

"What is he, a dealer?"

"Which one? The one in the baseball cap? No? Back to the right. Up a bit. I see her! Back. Back more! I saw her! There she is! That's it!"

Carol was sitting in a booth. I could see her in profile. She was talking to someone sitting in shadow. I caught glimpses of his hands. She was very animated. She'd say something and move her hands toward him in an abrupt gesture and then look quickly to the side in case she was attracting attention. She looked around a lot, out the window, too. I wondered if she was checking to see if there were police around, or if I was.

I couldn't make out who she was talking to. There was a large reflection of sky with a big, white, reflective cloud that stopped my gaze from penetrating the inside of the shop where she sat. I saw her hands go into this reflection, to reach for something across the table and pull it toward her. I saw his arms in black leather come from the cloud, and it was his hands she clasped and pressed her lips to, her eyes closed, her head down in prayer to him. He started to take his hands from her, and as he pulled away she held the hands tighter, harder to her. Her face had a stricken look, finally, as she gave them up.

I found it hard to breathe. I find it hard to breathe. I have to adjust the flow of pain.

"Ah, shit," the cabbie said.

My world was turning inside out. The light was stark and unwavering. Time slowed. I could see the infinite detail of each moment. Everyday things seemed more substantial, infiltrated with an unnatural heaviness.

"You don't need to see this, right?" the driver asked. "You know the guy?"

"They won't be long," I said.

"You done this before."

"I guess," I said.

"Walk away from it. It's the only way."

"You don't know until you see it."

"No one can tell you." He shifted his bulk, and the eyes in the mirror stared at me. "You have to see it for yourself, right? They don't believe it unless they see it for themselves."

"We'll wait," I told him.

He shrugged. He took a roll of bills from his pocket and set to work straightening them out, unfolding each one where the corners had become dog-eared.

I stayed fixed to the mirror. They were talking still. Carol was disappointed. Her head was turned down and away from him, toward me. She shook her head at something he said. I couldn't be sure, but I thought she was fighting back tears. From the cloud, his hand, comforting, came slowly toward her face, and she brushed it away, but slowly, reluctantly. Perhaps I'm imagining this. She said something angrily, accusing him. She looked up to see his response, then away again.

She stared out into the parking lot, looking and not looking, not seeing. She seemed tired and defeated. She surveyed her bleak landscape: the facade of the drugstore, a stray dog with time on his hands, the cluster of cars, a woman in a Buick Regal talking on a car phone, two guys sitting in a cab, the passenger leaning forward to talk to the driver. I longed for her eyes to linger on me, even if I was invisible to her. Her eyes passed over, beyond me.

Did she make a decision then? His hand came slowly toward her again, and she let it approach her face. The fingers touched her cheek. She didn't pull away. The hand closed on her, the whole surface of it molded to her and cupped her face as if it were a precious liquid it must hold. It melted her. She closed her eyes in her hunger for the hand's touch, and a bliss close to anguish, a joy, feather-light, balanced on the razor edge of pain, overcame her, her mouth open, head back, eyes closed so that the tears spilled from them.

If you know a face, there are points, secret catches that need only the gentlest pressure, something scarcely more than a fingerprint, to release emotion. I could have been that hand. I could have tamed her with this touch and brought her to the point of surrender.

I try to remember her as she gazes out the window of the coffee shop, blinded by her emotions, and the slow wander of her gaze as she picks out objects near, far, at the corners. She wasn't looking for anything. She scarcely knew that her eyes were open, even. Could the sun at that moment have glinted off glass and caught her eye? She didn't know what to look for. Then how could she have found that pinpoint of vision, that unique angle through the tunnel, a single car mirror in a parking lot, that led her to me?

Because that is what happened. One moment she was gazing, without any apparent direction, the next her eyes fastened on the mirror. Her eyes narrowed suddenly. You might have thought the sunlight dazzled her momentarily so that she narrowed her eyes. But I saw her vision sharpen. It was uncanny. The alignment, the angle, was fantastic: She had looked through the pipe in the tunnel and threaded the needle. She had looked into the parking lot, looked into the mirror, and caught sight of me.

A miracle occurred, and then it was over. The world re-formed around it. Even though the contact had lasted only a moment, it lingered in my mind like the afterimage from a flash of intense light. It still does. I wonder if it even entered Carol's awareness. I think a lot about this, arguing back and forth with myself about the nature of the other person, the possible but unrealized person who is inside each of us.

Carol turned again to the person who sat opposite her. The hand returned behind the cloud reflected in the window. Carol tugged a napkin from the dispenser on the table and dabbed at the tracks of her tears. She glanced around to see if anyone had noticed as she touched the napkin gingerly to the corners of her eyes, opening them extra wide, careful not to smudge the makeup that was in place.

I think he asked her if she was all right, because she nodded her head several times, and I saw her mouth say yes.

She gave him a quick, brave smile and said something like, "I'm fine. Really."

I think he got up from his seat at this point, because her head came up for a moment. Then she looked down again at the piece of table in front of her. It must have been hard for her. I saw her shoulders move in a deep, slow sigh. She shook her head at something he said and wouldn't look up at him again as he stepped away. I saw his form pass behind her in the gloom of the interior, and after a moment she relented and glanced over her shoulder to catch a last glimpse of him, but by then Baruk was already through the first door.

It was too warm for a leather jacket, and I thought he was wearing it to cover a handgun tucked into his waistband. In the space between the two glass doors, he ducked his head to slip on aviator sunglasses. He didn't look back. He came out into the sun and paused to survey the world before him, and his hands started to go up to his head where his hat would have been, in the gesture he had of bending it so that it curved around the badge in front. Out of uniform, he was unfamiliar to me, as if he might have been someone with a family resemblance, a brother, maybe, or a cousin. In that moment when he stood outside the door, stretching and rising a little on his toes, I doubted that it could really be him.

Baruk was taking his time. He looked left and right at the parts of the lot he hadn't been able to check from inside the coffee shop. I'm sure he didn't like the sight of the cab with two men sitting in it, but he must have known that if we were a police surveillance detail, he would have been surrounded long before he got a chance to come out into the open space of the parking lot.

Carol was working at something on the table, wiping at a spill with a napkin. She looked up quickly from time to time to steal glances of him all the way to his car.

"You got twenty bucks on the meter," the driver said. "You had enough, or what?"

"Wait a bit longer," I told him.

Baruk was stopped at the exit, waiting for a gap in traffic. I could see him by turning my head slightly and watching out of the far corner of my eye. There was no break in the traffic, but he pulled out anyway, with his tires making an abrupt screech.

"Give me something up front, then," the driver said.

"What?"

"Give me the twenty."

Carol was getting ready to go. She looked straight ahead as she thought something through. She was tightening herself, closing the places she'd let the emotion leak from. Was she thinking of returning to the motel, to me? I was afraid to take my eyes off her. I was afraid if I took my eyes off Carol I'd never see her again.

"You haven't got it, have you?" the driver said wearily.

"No," I told him. "All I've got is ten."

"Give it to me, then."

In the side mirror, a tiny Carol was clearing up. She dropped her coffee cup into Baruk's and moved out of sight toward the doors. I passed a handful of singles to the driver through the slot and dug in my pockets for the change I'd collected over the last few days.

"Here," I said.

He counted the notes. Then he looked over his shoulder and saw the coins in my hand.

"You sorry piece of shit," he said.

Carol came out. She didn't look about her. She walked slowly to her car as if she was in a daze.

"Keep it," he said. "I don't want your fucking change."

She passed close to us. I was afraid he'd turn me out of the cab right in front of her, but I think he wanted to get a look at Carol up close. I didn't look at her, but I listened to each one of her footsteps, a scuffing sound of leather against the blacktop of the lot, as she approached and then receded.

Faith is not a natural impulse. Mistrust is our natural condition. We have to overcome suspicion if we're to form a bond with another person. It goes against the grain. You have to go against your nature

207

to love completely. Love is always on trial. It lives from moment to moment. It hangs, precarious, in the balance.

She'd kissed Baruk's hand—or his fingers, anyway. So what? I'm trying to get the image, to hold it in my mind as it really happened. I can't let it in all at once. You have to set the aperture, you have to time the exposure just right to get the true picture. Yes, I saw her do it. It happened. It was real. But what does it mean? She touches her lips to the back of a man's fingers. It could mean nothing at all.

I'm on the edge of something I can't define. Everything is part of something bigger—I can sense it, even if I don't know what it is. I can't see the whole picture, so the pieces don't make sense, each one by itself. Without the context of the whole, it's easy to misunderstand the significance of one small piece—one incident, say, in Dunkin' Donuts. Only when you put the piece together with another piece do you begin to see a pattern. Or the beginning of something that might be a pattern. There's never certainty. I'm struggling to bring it into focus. I can't get the pieces to stay together. Why is it that the most important things are so often too big to fit into the mind, too big to swallow in one gulp of understanding? I'm taking a deep breath. I'm going to start over.

When you look back, you can see a pattern that wouldn't have occurred to you before. Incidents fall into place, slowly at first, and then in a rush, making connections like a pinball machine ringing up points. Baruk was always there. I'd mistaken him for part of the background.

Once, Carol was walking along the corridor on Medical while I was mopping the floor. She hadn't talked to me since I'd taken the lash out of her eye. As she came closer, I had the feeling she would stop to say something to me, some words with no significance of their own, a secret smile perhaps—any sign that would give me hope that I hadn't destroyed what we had.

The floor was wet. I wrung out the mop to make a dry path for her. I was the beggar man. She was the lady. I leaned on the mop and lowered my head. I thought I might sense a pause in her step, a hint of hesitation. All I needed was a glance from her to slant a ray of sunlight into my existence.

But she went by full of some other intention that made no room for me. I breathed in the fresh smell of soap or body lotion that always surrounded her, and she was gone. I crouched to find the angle. I went down on my hands and knees and turned my head to sight along the reflections to find the trace of her footprint on the damp floor, before this sign of her presence evaporated and was lost.

I was on my belly, moving closer to the spot where she had walked, when I became aware of a soft approach from around the corner and saw the black lace-ups with the quiet rubber soles that belonged to Baruk.

"What's up, Cody?" he asked. "Sleeping on the job?"

"No, Sarge," I answered promptly.

"You looked like you were all ready to curl up in the fetal position."

"I was checking out the floor."

"Yeah?"

"I wanted to see if it needed stripping."

"You stripped this floor last week."

He waited for me to speak.

"Right," I said.

Baruk stared into me, as if I was a view from the top of his hill. He considered me with a small smile. He took his time. There was a glint in his eye of amusement and contempt.

He shook his head wonderingly. "A mind is a terrible thing to lose, Cody."

"I know, Sarge."

"You're the best worker we ever had on this unit, but you're fucking crazy."

"Whatever you say, Sarge."

"Crazy like a fox."

"That's me."

I see now the sneer that lies behind his grin. I can hear laughter far off and low. This has been nothing more than a joke to him! How long has Baruk looked on from his vantage point, his hiding place of secret knowledge, superior and smirking, while I struggled forward an inch at a time, a snail across his path, trying to make my way toward a life?

Was it by coincidence that he happened to stroll along the back corridor the night Carol and I made love for the first time? I can't

209

bear the thought that he knew, that he cheapened us, that he defiled the moment with his presence!

Baruk has drawn us into his own squalid schemes. On Thursday nights, he watched the baseball games with everyone else on Medical, sitting in a wheelchair at the back of the dayroom. For Baruk, this was not a simple spectator sport.

"Who d'you fancy?" Baruk asked me one night.

"I don't know," I said. "The Indians maybe."

"Nah. No chance. It's the Red Sox all the way."

"The Indians won their last four games."

Baruk turned around to look at me. He seemed annoyed. "That's the point." He turned back to watch the game. "Sure, the Indians won their last four games, so everybody thinks they're on a roll. That's why there's a three-point spread. The Indians have peaked. You could see that in their last game. That's why the smart money is on the Sox."

The game went on, but Baruk couldn't let it go. He had to make his point.

"You see what I'm saying?" he wanted to know.

"Yeah." I nodded my head, concentrating on the game. "I know what you're saying."

"Anyway, you go with the herd money, you can't get the points. There's nothing in it for you."

The Sox never seemed to get into the game. As they went down, Baruk sat hunched forward, elbows on his knees, rocking back and forth in the wheelchair. He smoked cigarette after cigarette, drawing on them so frequently that they came to sharp points.

"Don't trust him," Diego told me.

The idea of trusting Baruk would never have occurred to me, but Diego liked to draw me in by starting conversations that didn't make sense. He kept giving me gifts of information. He'd tell me, "This will be useful for you sometime," but I didn't understand.

"He goes easy on you," I said. "You got an air-conditioned room. He lets you stay on Medical."

"He gambles too much," Diego said. "He's in over his head. He owes a lot. I mean, *a lot*."

"So what?"

"I still got some friends left."

"And what do your friends say?" I asked.

"Someone just bought up all Baruk's markers." He peered at me out of the corner of his eye, looking for my reaction. "That person was Nando. Nando owns him now."

Baruk is playing with us—Carol and me both! You must read this part, Sandy. Baruk is using us both!

Where is tenderness? Where is reverence? I can't believe fate led me to prison for no purpose. There are no accidents. I didn't escape for the sake of a life of motels, for nothing. I refuse to believe in "no reason." Even at the bottom of despair, I've found reason to keep faith. On the damp concrete floor of the Medical corridor, I located the drying outline of Carol's footprint. I lowered my cheek and pressed it to the place where her foot had been. I have lived on the mere scraps of her presence! I existed from day to day on fragments that could not have sustained life outside of Denning.

There is nothing I have that anyone else would want. Except the police, who want my body. And they will have it, in due course. I want all other concerned parties to realize that I do not know where the money is. And by "concerned parties" I mean everyone I have mentioned in passing in this letter—they will have recognized themselves, even though no one else may have noticed their presence at the edge of the picture. I swear to you all, Diego told me nothing that you do not, collectively, already know. I have never known where the money was. Leave me alone. Leave Carol alone. She has nothing you want, either. To the police, I say, watch Baruk. Baruk. Baruk. Baruk. He's involved up to his neck. Pick him up. Lock him up. Give him what he deserves.

In the silence of this town's library, amid the stir of paper and throat clearings and the creak of chairs, I can tell you this: I am not nothing. However concentrated I may be, however compacted and dense my humanity has become in order to survive, I will not be nothing. I will love her. In essence, if nothing else. She is mistaken. She is misled. She is misled by her feelings more than by his manipulations. He's clever, I grant him that. But cleverness can't change the truth.

In essence, she is unchanged. A deeper part of her remains true—cannot be false. She doesn't even know this. Carol doesn't know herself. It's one of the things I recognized about her at once. It was the door that let me in.

SEVEN

D ear Sandy:
     I'm waiting for you to read the last letter. I want Baruk
out in the open. I want the spotlight on him. I've been waiting
for news of his arrest, but it hasn't come. Why not? What's so
difficult? All the police have to do is pick him up. At his home. At
Denning. I like the thought of Baruk doing time. Will he live out
his days with the rapists and child killers in Segregation? Maybe
one of his old buddies will get him a job on Medical. Is it possible
that you've already received the letter and that Baruk's evaded
arrest? It's easy to underrate him. Baruk wears his blue collar as
if it was a Purple Heart. He's dumbed himself down. He's worked
on it. Even he doesn't remember anymore how smart he is. He's
the classic underachiever who realized early on he was too restless
to sit behind a desk for the rest of his life. He's cunning. If he's
escaped, it wouldn't surprise me. Either way, I'm going to meet
up with him eventually.

I worry Carol's getting in too deep. She doesn't know there are cross-currents. These didn't become clear to me, until I'd spent days in public libraries turning over in my mind the permutations of who and what and why. Only now do I see how all the motives can be brought to a single focus. I believe there's been a purpose to the suffering of these terrible days, tugging me toward this realization.

I admit I gave up on her to begin with. My faith was tested. I couldn't bear the thought of being shut inside a motel room with Carol after what I'd seen. But she doesn't know herself: I have to say that over and over to keep the thought in front of me. Whatever I felt when I saw her with Baruk is not important. Hurt feelings are not important in the long run. Feelings are fleshy. My love must be hard and enduring. I came to this only slowly, painfully.

For several days I drifted. I sank into the despair I know from J Block. I spent my nights in shelters with other lost souls. In the darkness, people prowled between the rows of beds: men searching for the bathroom, people with brain damage who'd lost their way coming back from the bathroom, thieves looking to take watches off wrists or lift sneakers that aren't tied to a body part, lonely people looking to be invited into another bed, children in adult bodies who are afraid of the dark. There was a retarded man who cried out in his sleep and wouldn't stop until someone beat him up. Men masturbated with difficulty, straining after a tiny spark of pleasure. Old men coughed through the night, carefully, patiently.

I stayed awake and slept during the day. I lay awake and considered how the world might be changed if a fire raged through the shelter and destroyed all these people who slept inside its locked doors. Would destiny be deflected by the loss of these souls? I wondered if God's plan was so intricate that it depended on every interlocking piece of humanity on the planet. Or whether fate was composed of a track through the human race, like a lightning strike that finds its jagged way along a thread of molecules out of all the vast number in the atmosphere. I thought of Carol and me finding each other in Denning and the routes that had brought us both there. I wondered at her finding my eyes in the sideview mirror of a cab. Simply by being in this place, I have put myself in the path of destiny, of that lightning strike.

I am part of something. I don't see it or hear it. I feel it, though, like the faint trembling in the vicinity of machinery. I know I am not being followed. I've done everything possible to bring a tail out into the open. I've spent afternoons pacing empty suburban streets where no one could walk behind me without being conspicuous. To be thorough, I stripped naked and went through every piece of clothing, every item I carry with me, to exclude the possibility that I'd been bugged in some way. In extreme situations, you have to be rational in the extreme. It's essential that you think clearly. I have to exclude each logical possibility one by one, until all I'm left with is certainty.

All the same, I can't shake the feeling that I'm not alone. I have to resist the urge to glance over my shoulder. Sometimes I give in and turn quickly, hoping to catch whomever in a wrong move. But no one behind me is interrupted, changes direction, or turns away. Everyone acts normally. I know, in a literal, physical sense, there's no one with me. But I sense a presence. You know when you're being watched. There's a vague unease, like an itch, at the back of your head and between your shoulder blades. This doesn't make sense, because in the most important way, I am lonely. I was so alone in the libraries and shelters that my life had no meaning. I existed only at the point of painful memories. I had no purpose, until I began to sense the bigger picture that I was a part of.

I miss Carol. One day, as I wandered aimlessly along a street, I thought I caught sight of her getting into someone's car. I ran up to her, but she turned when she heard me running, and I saw it wasn't Carol at all. I know we remain connected. I feel her straining toward me. She calls to me from a dream in which no sound emerges from her mouth. We are moving toward each other. The fantastic machinery of destiny turns, connections tighten, and slowly and with great difficulty we are drawn to that point in time and place where our paths intersect. Along with all the others, like Baruk, who don't know that the parts they play are minor ones, who do not realize they are walking up a down escalator that, in spite of their efforts, in spite of the illusion of freedom, will bring them to the appointed spot.

That is why I have come here, to the address that Carol said was to be used only as a last resort. I have this bursting sense of something trying to happen. It's a pressure around me, like a black sky, the fullness before a thunderstorm breaks. Energy is pent up. It's barely held back. There's a joining together of situations. People and places and motives are sliding into a configuration: The details are hidden from me. I watch for signs, but I'm not sure what to look for.

When I first arrived here, I slept in a big old Cadillac. It's like a boat. It must be twenty years old. It has forty-two thousand miles on the clock and hardly ever leaves the garage. It has the original leather upholstery. I can stretch out in the backseat and drift off to sleep with that reassuring old car leather smell. I haven't come across the scent since I was a kid, and it's kept its closed meaning of childhood. It gives me the illusion of being safe and secure!

I spent my summers in the backseat of a Ford, not a Cadillac. My father was a silent, reckless driver. I could never guess from his face what his intentions were. On a trip to York beach he took me with him into the ocean. I was seven, excited by the water, even though I was intimidated by the larger waves. But my father held my hand, and we rode them as they came in. He hauled me by the arm as each one reached us, and as I rose up the wave pushed my legs out from under me. The icy water was up to my chest when he decided to let go of me; I don't know why. The next wave knocked me off my feet. I went beneath the surface, but I began to kick and flail beneath the dark, silent water, and one of my blows connected with my father's body. I struck out again and made contact. I grabbed hold of a handful of skin and pulled myself toward him. I wrestled my arms around his neck and clung tight. It was not a feeling of safety and security. I would have strangled him if that was what it took to get me back to the beach.

At night, the garage is perfectly quiet and dark. It's very hot, with the smell of leather and oil filling the air. I'm not used to silence. It's too open. The darkness contains too many possibilities. The first night, I heard whispering. The words were indistinct, and I couldn't make them out. When I listened more closely, the sound disappeared, as if whomever it was stopped speaking as soon as they sensed I was paying attention. I let myself drift off to sleep,

216

and the sound began again. It seemed to come from one side. Slowly, making as little noise as possible, I sat up and leaned my head out the window on the passenger's side. What I had heard was a dry scratching sound by the side door to the garage. When I moved, it stopped. I waited and finally heard two deep sniffs from the bottom of the door.

I knew the dog had my scent, because he became eager suddenly, and I heard him scrape his claws on the concrete step. He worried at the bottom of the door. He thrust his nose at the crack, and I heard him suck in the familiar mixture of oil and cigarettes and leather upholstery and, mingled inside these pungent odors, the scent of a man's sweat. He whined, frustrated because he couldn't get to me. At any moment he was going to bark.

I went head first out the window, and when my hands touched the dusty floor of the garage I walked forward on them until my legs were free of the car. The dog was silent all this time, listening intently to my movement. I put my hand to the gap at the bottom of the door. He was skittish. His nose came down and he sniffed, then he jumped back, then came forward again to smell me, finally wedging his nose into the space beneath the door for a long, definitive sniff. Then he licked my fingers.

I know now Gypsy was lonely. When I opened the door, he came forward with his ears back, wagging his tail uncertainly. A black dog, part Lab, eager to please. I let him come to me. I let him see my hands before I reached out to stroke him. As I was about to touch him, he moved his head anxiously aside, peering up at the hand approaching him, but willing to accept what the human wanted to do to him. He carried his name on a circular disk on his collar, but it wasn't Gypsy. He's probably registered, and I know you want me badly enough to look through applications for dog licenses.

There was a walkway leading from the garage up to the back door of the house, and I called Gypsy's name softly and backed through a gap in the hedge that lined the walkway into the darkness of that suburban backyard. I crouched on my heels with my back against a tree, and Gypsy came up to me, more confident this time, to taste the various parts of my face. He licked my cheeks, and I felt his warm tongue cross the space between cheek and eyebrow,

217

lingering momentarily in the corner of my closed eye. I have rarely been touched these last few years. I have not felt a caress conform to the shape I am. I have never been tasted in the corners of my body. I think about this and wonder if, for Carol, I've been seamless, without the breaks in the surface that would have let her penetrate appearances, that would have let me be known.

Gypsy was a warm hole within the darkness of a world gone dead. Occasionally a fragment of distant light caught on the surface and revealed to me his glistening eyes. For the first time, I heard the steady din of insects and let myself merge into the sound, only to find its gaps and irregularities. Gypsy paused at a precise point in the shadows nearby to spatter the earth with a few drops. Later, I heard the rustle of last year's leaves as he walked the boundaries of his territory beside the chain-link fence. I stared up at the night sky, at the immensity.

Above the hedge, in the direction of the street, the sky was lit up with the orange glow of the city. I wondered where in that glow Carol was. I considered the possibility that, during the day, I'd breathed in one of the molecules of oxygen that had passed through her body. I wondered if, walking in the shopping mall, I'd put my hand on a spot Carol had touched. Whether the FBI, backtracking, desperate to make a case, would find somewhere on a brass railing or a store window where I'd rested my hand for a moment fingerprints, his and hers, overlapping in the magic of destiny, merged into one.

I looked up into the night sky and could have howled like a werewolf or screamed out like a man becoming a ghoul, a man whose soul is being torn from him. I stood beneath the tree and raised my hands into blind nature: I stood at a cliff top and prepared to launch myself, to surrender myself to any benign forces in the universe that might save me, to risk my life if that would gain me a new start.

I spent the day in the crawl space above the garage. It was cramped and uncomfortable, and I sweated in the hot air trapped beneath the roof. Most of the space was taken up with a small boat they'd stored there that was covered by odd lengths of lumber left over from a carpentry job and by curtain rods. Beneath the dust, the paint kept its original gloss, and it must have been an

218

expensive gift for a child that had gone unused. When I crouched on the side of the boat, I had a good view through the skylight of the rooms at the back of the house.

The house was a big Victorian that had once been renovated and had fallen into a second period of dilapidation. It was clad in dark shingles with a green trim that was chipping and showed the white primer underneath on the peaked eaves and around windows. Only part of the house was in use. I could see into the kitchen and a kind of den on the first floor, and also a bedroom on the second floor where the lady of the house slept at night. In the shadows of the old house she looked to be in her early fifties. She was a good-looking woman with fine cheekbones and bold lips. She spent a lot of time on her appearance, sitting at her dressing table in the morning in front of the mirror to apply foundation and lipstick and various touches to the rest of her face I couldn't make out. She'd dyed her hair a strawberry blond. When first she got up it was flattened at the back of her head and stuck out around the sides, but she worked at filling it out and getting it to settle in the spots she required.

She rarely seemed to eat, except a piece of toast now and again. At regular intervals throughout the day, she went to the fridge to pour herself half a glass of Perrier water, which she then topped up from a container of orange juice. I didn't understand this at first, until I saw her replenishing her daily supply, hauling up from the cellar a gallon container of vodka and filling the empty Perrier bottle with liquor.

She set a time for the first drink. I saw her checking her watch more and more often as the hour approached. It wasn't until I entered the house that I found out she set a kitchen timer to go off when it was time. Until the buzzer sounded, she was at a loss as to how to occupy herself. She stood on the back step and called for Gypsy to come to her. I saw him look up and regard her for several seconds from behind the hedge, then continue with his investigations. She went back inside, and I saw her wandering from room to room. Once she stood in a silk kimono at the bedroom window with her arms wrapped tightly around herself. She stared out the window angrily, shaking her head occasionally and muttering to herself. Then she turned suddenly, startled by the buzzer.

It isn't until the buzzer sounds that Debbie's day really begins. She'd been startled that first day, because according to her own rules, she has to be dressed in day clothes before she allows herself a drink. When the buzzer sounds, she places two cubes of ice at the bottom of a tall glass, pours in vodka, then orange juice, swirls the mixture around with a long spoon she uses for this purpose, then raises her skinny arms to hold the glass up to the light to judge its color. After this ritual she's ready to retire to the den, where she switches on the TV and settles in the armchair with her feet up on an ottoman. Gypsy has usually returned by this time, and she gives him an affectionate pat on the head before she raises the glass to her lips for the first time.

It is a quiet neighborhood that has come down in the world. In the morning, there is almost no traffic on the street. A brown UPS van comes around at ten, delivering packages people have ordered from catalogues; then the mailman makes his rounds an hour or two later. There are rarely any kids on the street. This is a neighborhood of older people, where the women stay home and a lone man strolling the sidewalks is sure to attract attention, which means that once I was in the garage, I couldn't easily come out until after dark.

Debbie wouldn't have noticed. She was fully involved in *The Young and the Restless* and *The Days of Our Lives*. During the commercials in the middle of *The Bold and the Beautiful* she ran out to the kitchen for a refill. Then she let Gypsy out again at the beginning of *As the World Turns*, and after it was over she began to doze.

I'd lived hand to mouth the last few days. In the evening I drank hot water that had sat all day in the coils of a garden hose. The last time I'd eaten had been two days before, from a Dumpster behind a Chinese restaurant. When I saw Debbie doze off in the armchair, I knew it was the only chance I'd get, unless I wanted to wait through the day until nightfall. Gypsy came up to me as soon as I stepped out the side door to the garage. He sniffed at me and wagged his tail, but was still a little skittish when I stooped to stroke his head. Then he followed me happily up the path to the back door and made no protest when I opened the screen and stepped inside.

In the kitchen, Gypsy observed me for a moment, but when I didn't move about, he went to his bowl and began to eat what remained of breakfast. I should have taken what I needed and gone back to the garage. I needed food, but that was just bait to lure me back to my destiny, to lure me into the current, into the middle of the stream where events flowed most swiftly. I knew what I was doing. I knew the risk I was taking in setting foot inside that house.

I stepped slowly toward the den. The house, even in July, had a musty, neglected smell to it. Applause from a game show came from the TV and masked any sounds that could have told me about Debbie's state. When I turned the corner, I found her splayed out on the armchair, sleeping with her mouth open. While I stood over her, something clogged in her throat and she caught her breath almost to the point of waking, but it passed and her regular breathing began again.

She was ten years older than she'd seemed when I'd observed her from the garage. The skin at the edges of her mouth was lax. There were bags beneath her eyes, which she'd shaded with makeup, but the trick didn't work close up, with her head thrown back. Her appearance was more fragile and desperate. The audience burst into applause, and Debbie stirred and sighed. I stepped around the armchair to stand behind her. I hadn't noticed the TV until then. It was an old model with a big screen set in a wooden cabinet with angled legs. The picture she'd settled down to spend the day in front of was in lurid hues of green and pink, so that the contestants looked like they'd been recruited from another planet.

I left her and went back to the kitchen. Gypsy came up when I opened the door to the refrigerator, wagging his tail hopefully. There was some baloney that had a sharp smell to it, and I gave him a slice. He grappled with his teeth, sucking and snapping at the slice, inch by inch, while I drank milk out of the container. I folded two slices of bread and twisted them into the mayonnaise. With a finger, I scooped peanut butter right out of the jar. I had found some toaster tarts in the bread box and was stuffing one in my mouth when I became aware that Gypsy, who'd watched my every move until then, wasn't paying attention anymore.

I didn't look around right away. I thought back, trying to figure out how long she'd been there, standing in the doorway. Finally, I swallowed the mouthful of pastry and turned. There was no one there. I heard her footsteps at the front of the house, then the sound of the front door opening. Then she closed the door and locked it. I thought she must have walked right past the kitchen without noticing me; but that wasn't right, either. She came back through the hall with a couple of letters in her hand and the folded newspaper and glanced into the kitchen. She stopped and looked as though she was going to say something, then changed her mind and went on into the den instead.

She switched off the TV, and I waited in the sudden silence, imagining her with the phone tight to her ear, listening to the ringing, waiting for the police to pick up at the other end. I heard the crackle as she folded back the newspaper to the obituaries, then silence again. I could have slipped away through the back door, but I have no other place to go, or any other future. This is not a time for running, but for moving deeper into what surrounds me. I heard Debbie sigh in frustration, then bunch up the newspaper and throw it aside.

She stood in the kitchen doorway. Her eyes were narrowed in an expression that could have been puzzlement or shortsightedness.

"Don't you at least have something to say to me?" she complained.

"I'm sorry," I told her.

She seemed to think about this. "Well, at least you have the decency to apologize."

"He looked hungry. And you were asleep."

She bent down, and Gypsy wagged his tail at the attention. "Were you hungry, Prince?" He cocked his head to one side when she called him Prince, and his tail sagged. "Were you?"

"I thought his name was Gypsy," I said. "That's what it says on the tab there on his collar."

She messed with the skin of his neck and ruffled his ears. "Prince. Gypsy." He looked up when she mentioned his name. "Whatever. He has different names. Don't you? You're a prince to me, though, aren't you?"

When she straightened up again she gave me a long look as though I ought to be familiar to her.

222

"I always have a nap in the afternoon," she told me.

"I didn't want to disturb you. I looked in the fridge and saw some luncheon meat. So I gave him a piece."

"Now he's your friend for life."

She was looking at my clothes. I could feel her growing suspicious, checking my hands, glancing up at my face.

"Where are your tools?" she demanded.

"They're in the cellar."

She started to say something, then stopped to give it further thought.

"The dishwasher's over there," she said. She waited to see if I'd followed her so far.

"Right," I agreed.

There was a glint in her eye. "So what are your tools doing in the cellar, when the thing that needs fixing is right here in the kitchen?"

"Because of the connection. Part of the problem is in the hook-up down in the cellar."

She nodded. I glanced at the two doors and wondered which one was the pantry and which opened to the stairs to the cellar.

"It's just I thought you'd be finished by now," she said.

"Not quite," I told her. "There's a bit more."

"Well, how much more? We don't have all day, you know."

Her mouth opened in a slack smile. She was looking me up and down. She was sixty years old and she was checking me out. "Just so you know I'm not paying by the hour."

"It's a bit more difficult than I thought."

"Don't get me wrong. I don't object to a man around the house." She smiled and shifted her hips. She'd kept her figure. I let her see me look at her.

"If I don't sort out this connection, I may have to come back tomorrow to finish the job."

"You can come back tomorrow, but I have to have you done by three-thirty today. I have my hairdresser's at four, and I have to have you done by three-thirty." We both turned to the clock above the stove. "Oh, my God!" she exclaimed.

"You've still got time," I told her.

"Now look!" She turned distractedly to the door.

"You'll do it."

"I've only got five minutes to get ready! It's not enough time. And the car has to warm up."

"I'll drive you," I said.

She turned to me, abruptly hopeful. "I don't think I could go in your car. I'm old-fashioned that way."

"All right. We'll go in yours."

"Would you? It's not too much trouble?"

On the way, Debbie told me she'd been going to the same beauty shop for twenty years.

"They understand my skin type," she said.

"It shows," I told her.

"Ooh, you are a liar!" she giggled.

The beauty parlor was in a small plaza containing a dry cleaners, a discount shoe store, a hobby shop, and a store that sold baseball cards and comics, almost swallowed up by the shopping mall that had been built in front of it.

"You sure you don't mind waiting?" she asked.

"No problem. I got some things I have to do in the mall."

"It could take a while. Miracles take time, you know."

"No way!"

She laughed, her eyes lingering on my face. "You know," she said, "for some reason I keep thinking your name is Jack. In my mind, I keep calling you Jack."

"Dan," I said, as though reminding her, though she'd never asked what my name was.

We got out of the car and she waited for me to lock up. She held out her hand for the keys. "Well, see you later."

"Wait," I said as she started to go, and she turned around, startled. "When they're done, how am I going to recognize it's you?"

She smiled, but I saw I'd overplayed it. As I left her, I had the uneasy feeling that everything in her head could come unraveled under the hair dryer. It didn't trouble Debbie that what passed back and forth between us was missing a beginning, but the future, and me with it, was just as liable to disappear from her view. As I watched her hurrying to keep her appointment, tripping on her pumps, with her pocketbook clutched tight to her chest,

I wondered whether she would have noticed if I'd kept the keys. I've never felt that my fate rested so precariously, so open to small random influences as it did then on Debbie's fragile faculties. I went in the back door of the mall with the feeling that my life dangled by a thread.

The mall was a very dangerous place. So many people to recognize me. It was a bit like Denning. They even had security guards hanging around the exits, though these were young kids who spent most of their time talking to their friends. They had nothing more than nightsticks, and they didn't look as though they could use them.

On the surface security was lax. It wasn't the people in uniform who worried me. Beneath the surface the mall was a very difficult place to figure out. Nothing was happening. Everything was happening. It was an enclosed space with lots of people milling around with nothing much to do except get into other people's business and cause trouble. Most of the men looked soft and meaty in their summer shorts, milk-fed, as though they were being raised for food. The women strutted, aloof and purposeful. They strode through the crowds with their bags; they brought their feet down hard on their high heels with a heartless click on the floor, or moved stealthy in sneakers.

Beneath the surface the mall swarmed with signals. It was hard to keep track of the people who might be connected, because at first I wasn't sure I knew how to spot them. Two or three people would converge in what looked like a prearranged pattern. Then they'd go walking off in different directions without so much as a look at each other. I had the overpowering feeling that something was going on. But whichever way I tried to figure it out, I couldn't get the hang of it. I told myself it didn't necessarily have to do with me, but whenever I succeeded in talking sense into myself, I was pulled back by the feeling that something very important that did concern me was going on behind my back. I'd catch sight of the tail end of it out of the corner of my eye—it might be a look passing from one person to another—but that was it.

I had the constant, nagging feeling that I was missing a message that was crucial to my future. I thought that meant Carol. It was like living in the middle of one of Debbie's quiz shows, with everything at stake. I had the vowels, but they didn't mean anything. I was on the verge of understanding. All I needed was one good consonant, and I couldn't get it.

There's a strange ability people have for recognizing when someone is looking at them. You pick it up immediately. And yet the precision needed to detect, at a distance, the fact that someone is looking at you, rather than the person standing next to you, is phenomenal. When a person looks directly at you, you see their pupils as perfect circles; when they look at something to one side of you, what you see of their eyes is an ellipse. And the difference between a perfect circle and a very fat ellipse half a millimeter away from a circle? To the naked eye? At thirty feet? By purely physical criteria, it's impossible. It's beyond the resolution of the human eye. It borders on the uncanny.

Under the right circumstances, this phenomenon of knowing when someone is looking at you can cause even reasonable, sensible people to wonder about the possibility of telepathy. I know it's ludicrous to *believe* in telepathy. But it's not crazy to consider the *possibility* of telepathy. And to guard against it.

A lot of people in the mall looked at me. Usually it was nothing more than a brief glance. People stroll in the mall and they look at the people who walk past them. But when a lot of people glance in your direction, you have to wonder why. It can make you self-conscious. You wonder what it is about you they're picking up. You find yourself considering, against your will, against your better judgment, even, the possibility of *prearrangement*.

I memorized faces. I tried to remember who was with who. I scanned everyone walking toward me, then everyone walking away, and always people who were loitering, who appeared to be looking in store windows. I switched back and forth in unpredictable patterns. If something was going on, there'd be a slipup sooner or later, and I'd spot it.

Most of all, I looked for very specific faces in the crowd. You know who you are. You know you weren't there. I'm still one step ahead of you. That's all it takes. One step is all I need.

I was still hungry. I had an hour to kill until Debbie would be ready, and I had enough money for an ice cream. At Brigham's, I waited in a line that stretched from the end of the counter to the door. I lounged against the counter and tried to block out the voices of the happy people in the booths behind me. They looked up when I came in, but not all at once; one person glanced in my direction, then back down; after that, another person would raise her head and look away again almost immediately; then another person who was talking would seem to hesitate in finding a word, and his eyes flicked over onto me, and then began talking again where he'd left off. You could almost see a sequence, like a relay team. I don't know how they could have coordinated it. I do know this: Whenever I glanced up, there seemed to be someone who was looking in my direction.

Directly behind where I stood at the counter was a booth filled with girls, of college age, I'd guess. They were confident and pretty. They smiled at each other with a hundred secret understandings. I turned my back on them. I tried to ignore them, but they were smirking. I thought they were taunting me because I was alone, but I wasn't going to be drawn into that. I didn't respond, even when one of them put the name Carol into the middle of whatever she was telling her friends.

"No!"

"That's what she said."

"She didn't! She'd never do it. I don't believe it."

"I'm only telling you what Carol said."

"Then what?"

"They went to a motel."

"Oh, God!"

"It's true!"

"She's not the type."

"Bobby saw the cars parked outside the room. His and hers."

It was gossip. I couldn't hear all the words, but I caught the stereotyped back and forth, the chorus of chiming disbelief, and always the plea for more. It was a facade. The tone of the sound was light and laughing, but I knew that if I could see behind me, if I could whirl around with such unexpected speed that they'd have no time to recompose their faces, I'd catch the expressions of contempt, and I would glimpse the fact that they were speaking not to one another but tossed their words like gobs of spit at my back.

There was nothing very subtle in the sorority sisters' message. They were calling me a fool. They were telling me Carol had used

227

me. They were trying to provoke me. They thought that if they tormented me I'd show myself. And any public move would send me back to Denning. Everybody in the place seemed to know what the stakes were.

When my turn at the counter came, the conversation behind me stopped, as if they wanted to hear my voice, without the background noise, to analyze the nuances of expression for weakness, for foolishness. I ordered chocolate chip in a cone. Immediately I spoke, I heard the tittering behind me start up again. I felt their ridicule as a physical sensation on the skin of my back, an itching, crawling glow like a sunburn, a burn of shame. But I refused to be provoked. I wouldn't turn to face them.

"The other one."

"What other one?"

"She's going with both of them at once?"

I pulled a napkin from the dispenser. I was going to turn away and walk out of the restaurant, but I stayed to fold the napkin around the bottom of the cone and to listen. I shouldn't have given in. It was weakness.

"He's got money," one of the girls said.

Or, she could have said, but didn't, because she didn't need to spell it out, "He's rich." Or, "He's Rich."

Do you see what surrounded me? They were lies, but I let them enter my mind.

"She says she loves him."

"Oh, yeah."

"Which one?"

"The one with the Mercedes, of course."

Gradually, the conversation shaded off into talk I couldn't follow, like looking over the edge of a boat as you're pulling away from shore, when you reach the point where you can't see the real substance of the bottom anymore, only the dancing reflections on the surface that throw the sky and the clouds back in your face.

After Brigham's I wandered without direction. I walked around in this gigantic pretense. The air was dense and controlled. I felt I was moving through a dense psychological medium, as if humanity were a substance. I stopped in front of store windows and tried to

228

catch sight of strollers who also paused. I had the overpowering feeling that everyone knew who I was, that everyone knew the others knew, but that no one would acknowledge it. I wandered within a diagram in which lines connected each person to every other person in silent, implicit undestanding. I stood alone. The pressure was almost unbearable. Several times I came close to breaking down. Carol was true to me; she loved me with the same fierce religion with which I cherished her. I clung to this.

I went out the back of the mall and walked over to the plaza. I thought Debbie was liable to forget I existed and drive away without me if I wasn't at the car before her. I know now that it was touch and go whether she'd even remember who I was when she saw me. I browsed the model airplane kits in the hobby shop where I had a good view of the parking lot and Debbie's Caddie. There was a good flow of traffic coming and going so that it was easy to spot people who lingered, and I didn't recognized any of the cars. There was one van with the name of an electrical contractor on the side that was a possible surveillance vehicle, but I didn't think the police would try to take me with only one vehicle, and the other people wouldn't be so subtle.

The man in the hobby shop had asked twice if he could help me when Debbie came tripping into view. She was moving fast, and from the determined set of her head I thought she must have in mind a refreshing drink from the refrigerator.

"You look great," I called to her from the other side of the car.

She had her back to me, trying to sort out the key to open the door. She turned around, not sure who had delivered the compliment. I stepped around the car to her side, so she could get a better look at me.

"Oh, you!" she said fixing on me.

She was smiling expectantly, vaguely, hoping I'd fill in the blank.

"Well, you don't think I'd leave you to drive yourself home, do you?"

"You never know," she said carefully.

She was suspicious, but she didn't want to give offense. She seemed experienced with this kind of situation. Feeling her way, stalling, not giving anything away. Sooner or later, she'd discovered, if you're prepared to wait them out, people explain themselves.

"I got to get back to that dishwasher," I said.

"That's right."

She looked hard at my face, but I don't think it jogged loose any recognition. She smiled up into my face anyway, and I reached out to take the tangle of keys, but as soon as she felt me start to pull them from her fingers, she tugged them away.

"It's about time we got back," I suggested. "Don't you think?"

"I know that."

"I'd be glad to drive, if you want me to."

She was still undecided. "But can I trust you?" she asked. It started as a thought stumbling into speech, but she pirouetted into a flirtatious moment. She had a hand on her hip, a thin smile on her lips. "That's the question."

"I don't know," I said. "You want to live dangerously?"

She tossed me the keys. "Just remember, I'm not paying you by the hour."

"Relax," I told her as I swept open the door, "everything's under warranty."

In the evenings, I while away the time in the cellar looking through boxes of old photographs, high school yearbooks, and other memorabilia. Strange, I can't find any trace in the house of the person in the yearbooks. Apart from Debbie's room and one other on the second floor, the bedrooms are anonymous. Even as guest rooms they lack charm and warmth. The other bedroom on the second floor belonged to Jack, Debbie's last husband. Jack was a man of expensive tastes, judging by the clothes that hang in his closet. There is a rack of fine shoes that fit me perfectly. Everything in the house is of the best quality, but twenty years out of date.

Periodically, throughout the evening, Gypsy snuffles at the bottom of the door to the cellar, and I hear Debbie yell, "Prince, get away from there! You'll get rabies!" He ignores her, though he is surprisingly obedient when she calls him by his real name. I wonder who trained him. Not Debbie. I'm sorry to say he's too young a dog for it to have been the person in the yearbook. I hear footsteps, slower and more shuffling as the evening progresses, of Debbie's trips to the refrigerator. Finally, when I think she must have fallen asleep, I emerge. I have taken to carrying her up to her bed and tucking her in. She scarcely wakes. The gesture appears perfectly natural to her. In the morning, she has no recollection. Every day is a new day for Debbie.

I let Gypsy out last thing and look up into the night sky while he goes about his business. Inside, he accompanies me while I secure the entrances to the house. The windows are solid and can't be forced without noise. The front door is oak and could have been built for a castle. In the cellar, the bulkhead looks strong; it's steel, but one of the hinges has almost rusted off. I'm mainly concerned about the kitchen door. The lock is flimsy and would give with a quiet shove, so I hook one of the chairs under the handle to brace the door and remove it first thing, before Debbie gets up.

Before I go up to the third floor to sleep, I walk through the silent house. The orange light from the streetlamps at the front gives the rooms an eerie appearance. They are not quite real, as if they'd been assembled for an exhibit at the Smithsonian: "Living room circa 1970, American Northeast." It's very difficult to put together something that is flawlessly typical. The slightest detail punctures the surface. During the day I think of how I want to arrange events, and then at night, as I walk about this house, I wonder if I'm living in the middle of an elaborate hoax. There is a ticking clock in the hallway. While everyone in the house sleeps, the clock ticks through the night. There is something reassuring and homey about the sound. But in a time when we have silent clocks powered by electricity, why is there a clock that ticks? Things can be so typical that they cross a line into strangeness. As I walk through these eerie, orange rooms, it strikes me that you could easily be taken in by the edges of things, fooled by their clear, square endings into missing altogether the fact that a given situation curves ever so slightly. That the cozy scene curls around, like the twisting and stretching from a blemish in a pane of glass. That it curves around all the way to a back side that is far more sinister, if you could only get a look at it.

Baruk wants Nando's money. There are a lot of wheels turning.

Baruk is only one small cog. Here's something to open up the throttle of the destiny machine.

"You do massage, Dan?" Diego asked me. He was stretching, looking at me through drowsy eyes, a small, secret smile on his lips.

This was around the time Carol began talking to me about escaping.

"No," I said. I'd been doing his vital signs, and I started to gather my things together on the trolley.

"I was going to tell you something," Diego said. "Something that could be good for you."

"It's not good to know too much," I said.

"This is good, believe me. It's what everybody wants to know."

He saw that I didn't understand enough to be teased with small pieces of information.

"I'm going to have to go soon," I told him. "I've still got to check out the other guys."

"Listen to this," Diego said. "This could be useful to you. You don't know yet, because you don't know what's going on around here, but what I'm telling you could be important at a certain time."

I perched at the end of the bed. Diego moved his feet aside to make room for me.

"This was something we had to put together while Nando was out on bail," he began. "Nando had decided to plead out to the trafficking charge, so he was going to be out of circulation for three, maybe five years. Nando—because of who he is—he was going to stay in for five, because he wasn't going to get any good time.

"So a week before the hearing, we met in this restaurant on Route 1. Vera chose it. It's a dumb place. It's set up like a French cafe. Waiters in striped shirts. It's inside, right? A restaurant? Every table's got an umbrella!

"Nando's unhappy already. He feels out of place. The restaurant's half empty. The waiters are standing around, looking at us, because they've got nothing else to do. Vera's light. She could pass as Italian. Nando's dark. He stays with his own people. He thinks the waiters are looking down on him.

232

" 'What is this?' he wants to know.

" 'What's wrong with it?' Vera asks. 'What's wrong with something with a bit of class?'

"Nando's angry. He can feel the operation slipping out of his hands, and they haven't even put him away yet. Vera's making the moves. I'm keeping quiet. Just the three of us sitting under that stupid umbrella. Vera in the middle.

" 'If I want to better myself, if I want something more upscale,' she says, 'there's no harm in that.'

"She's messing with the white Russian she's ordered, stirring the cubes around with a swizzle stick shaped like the Eiffel Tower. Nando's looking into the glass, following every move of her fingers, watching the cubes of ice turn over. He's disgusted she's drinking that shit. It hurts him.

"She's his cousin and he loves her. He's old enough to be her father, and Vera's his cousin. It's not a good situation. She needles him with her Italian boyfriend with his Corvette and big muscles. She doesn't know what she's doing. She thinks Nando's like her uncle. She has no idea how he feels about her. Even Nando, half the time, doesn't know what's eating at him. It confuses him, the tender feelings. And if he made the Italian disappear, sooner or later there'd be another one. It drives him crazy. He should have fucked her, got it out of his system that way. But he loves her, so he never does it.

"The reason Vera's there is she's family. I'm the closest thing Nando has to a partner. If he doesn't trust me, I don't blame him. I use the product. That's a problem. But I take care of business, too. Nando knows he can trust me to run the operation, up to a point.

"Nando knows he shouldn't trust Vera, either. Vera's got ambitions. She has the idea she can make money from the operation that will get her into high society. Until this meeting at the French restaurant, Nando's kept her out of the dirty end of the business. He had her do book-keeping and whatnot, but she never saw the product. He wanted her to stay clean. Vera the princess.

"We didn't want to send her those times she passed it to you. We didn't have any other way. Nando was very nervous. He

233

handpicked you. You were perfect. You were like a virgin, Dan. No one was going to suspect you. The thing that worried him was if you'd screw it up for Vera. If you screwed it up, if Vera got caught with the drugs because of you, Nando would've gone to the end of the world to kill you. You didn't know that? Good thing.

"That day in the restaurant, we set it up so I'm taking care of the merchandise; the buys, cutting it, packaging, putting it out on the street, paying people off. All the dirty stuff. Vera's Nando's watchdog. All the cash is going by her. But she isn't going to touch the money. I'm there to see she keeps the accounts straight, and she's there to see I put it in the bank. The idea is, we'd watch each other.

"Nando's talking to me as if Vera isn't there. Maybe he'd gone over all this with her before, but I don't think so. He can't even look at her.

" 'You remember, this is my operation. Even in prison, I got the telephone. I'll have visitors every week. I'm going to know everything.'

"He's restless. He can't settle. He keeps telling me things twice, reminding me about things I already know. It's understandable in a guy who's looking at five years. Vera reaches across him to catch the waiter, handing him her glass as he walks by, like this is the only way she can get a refill.

" 'What about her?' I want to know.

" 'Yeah, what about me?' Vera says, looking at me directly. 'Don't think you're going to be calling the shots when Nando ain't here no more.'

" 'I'm calling the shots,' Nando says. 'You two got to work together.'

" 'What does she know?' I say. 'She doesn't know the business.'

" 'You're going to tell her what she needs to know,' Nando says. He says it quietly, like a confession, and I know she's been working on him.

" 'I don't need no favors,' Vera says.

"She puts her drink down hard on the table and people at the other table look around. I can tell Nando doesn't like the situation, but he doesn't have many options. He doesn't trust us,

234

but he needs us, because he's going away for three to five. He's looking down, lining up each finger on one of the squares at the edge of the checkered tablecloth.

"I say, 'You're crazy if you think I'm taking orders from her.' I push my chair back from the table to show I don't want any part of it. 'I don't even know what the fuck she's doing here.'

" 'Watch your language,' Nando says, like a growl. He looks around. He's ready to stare down anyone who turns to watch. 'Don't talk that way around my family.'

"I say, 'Oh. She doesn't know what "fuck" is? Vera hasn't been introduced to that idea?'

"Nando won't touch that, but it really sets Vera off. Something ugly comes into her face when she's mad.

" 'Yes,' she says, 'I know what fucking is. Because you ain't never going to be a woman, Diego, whatever you do to yourself. You know what? I got something you'll never have. That's why I fuck real men.'

" 'Yeah, I know,' I say quietly. 'I had some of them.'

"All these wise remarks Vera and me trade back and forth are hurting Nando like an ulcer burning in his stomach. But I think the fact that Vera and me are uneasy around each other—and that's on a good day—makes Nando feel better about the business side. It isn't like there's any chance of a romantic interest bringing the two of us together. Nando figures if he adds together all the fear, the loyalty, the family ties on Vera's side, and the old times' sake on mine, the two of us won't get together to double-cross him for the money alone. We were oil and water, Vera and me.

"It worked. It worked pretty good. Every six months, whatever, Vera and me got on a plane and went to the bank. The way Nando had me set it up, there was one key and one signature. I kept the key to the box, but to get into the vault, you have to sign, and the only signature that would let us get to the box was Vera's. So neither of us could get to the money without the other one. It was a nice arrangement. It was pure Nando."

Diego lay on the pillows, grinning at me. He was tired. He was dangling something in front of me.

"You got no idea the tricks Vera tried to get that key from me. One time, I thought she'd try to kill me. She thought about it. She talked to someone, who talked to me. But she isn't cut out to be a gangster. With Vera, there's too much drama. Going into the bank, she'd wear a long raincoat and some kind of hat and dark glasses to cover her face. She doesn't want to be recognized, she says. She doesn't want people to remember her. She scrawls her signature all over the card; meanwhile, everyone's looking around in case she's Jackie O reincarnated.

"There's a lot of money in the box. A million dollars. Not as much as there's supposed to be. According to Nando, there's supposed to be exactly one million, two hundred and five thousand, three hundred dollars in the box, because that's what Vera told him we put in. He's been counting on the money. He's been living on it. The idea is, when Nando's released, he opens the box, packs up the money, and retires to some nice little Caribbean island. Part of the idea—he's never told me this, but I think it's there, in the back of his mind—is that Vera comes with him.

"The problem is, Vera's been skimming money all along. The second time we go to the bank, I take the money out of the bag and start putting it into the box. Vera picks up a wad of bills. She opens her pocketbook and drops the money in and snaps it shut again.

"I say, 'What are you doing?' I can't believe it.

" 'Commission,' Vera says. 'We ought to get something for what we do.' She takes out another wad and stuffs it in my shirt pocket.

"I say, 'Are you out of your mind?'

" 'It's a loan,' she says. 'We can pay it back later.' She stares at me through the big sunglasses. 'OK with you?'

"I say, 'No, it's not OK with me.'

" 'Tell Nando, then,' she says. 'Or I can tell him.'

"She knows Nando won't believe it from me. She knows Nando has some special feeling for her because she's family, like an uncle with a sweet spot for his favorite niece.

" 'We'll put it all back before Nando comes out,' she says. But of course we never did. If I hadn't been there, she'd have cleaned him out.

"When Nando came to take my blood pressure that time, I told him what happened, but he couldn't hear it. He doesn't want to believe Vera would do that to him. Nando's an old-fashioned guy. Family. Loyalty. He believes in things like that. He can see what she is, and he doesn't want to know. But Vera can't be sure this Uncle Nando stuff is going to last. She's scared shitless he'll open the box and find the money missing. She's the one who's been telling him how it's been mounting up for five years. When he finds out, he'll kill us both. As long as the box stays locked, he never knows for sure. And I have the key."

Today, as I am writing this in the cellar, Debbie is calling me. It's the moment I've been waiting for, for better or worse. I placed myself in fate's hands when I sent the last letter to you, Sandy. Now what I started must play itself out, even though I can already hear in Debbie's tone of voice that this is not the outcome I hoped for. What will be, will be. I'm going to put this installment with the utility bills on the plate on the dresser in the hall, so that Debbie will give it to the mailman when he comes.

It takes several tries, searching the kitchen and dining room, calling up to the second floor, for Debbie to remember where I am, and then she stands in the kitchen at the top of the stairs and yells down to me.

"Hey!" There's a brief pause while she remembers that she won't remember my name, then she calls, "Someone to see you!"

EIGHT

D ear Sandy:
      "Your social worker's here," Debbie said as I came up the
steps from the cellar.

When I came to the top, she looked at me as though she hadn't
examined me properly before.

"You didn't tell me you had a social worker," she said
accusingly.

"I've got two," I told her. "A man and a woman."

She looked up into my face. There was fear in her eyes. Her
world was going to change and she didn't understand.

"It's a man," she said.

I took a deep breath. I thought I was calm, but I had to lean for
a moment on the kitchen table. I was light-headed and my heart
was thumping madly in my chest.

"Where is he?" I asked.

"I told him to wait at the front door."

But when we came into the hall, the front door was closed. Debbie wandered anxiously ahead of me, and I took the letter out of my pocket and slipped it between a couple of bills on the dresser.

"I took the liberty," Baruk said. He'd been waiting in the parlor, listening to my movements, and now he stepped into the doorway where we could see him.

He had on a big, ingratiating smile for Debbie, and his eyes flicked nervously from her to me. He came into the hall with his arms crossed loosely across his chest and the right hand tucked into the leather jacket at the level of his waistband.

"Hey," he said, turning to me, "it's been a long time, buddy."

"It sure has."

I came toward him, holding out my hand to him, and he watched me carefully, smiling all the time. As I came closer, he shifted his right hand under his jacket, releasing the safety and freeing the weapon from his waistband. He let me approach, and when I was in reach, he raised his left hand and slapped mine away in slow motion.

I wanted to kill him then and there, to keep on coming in spite of the gun, to move quickly to trap his right hand in the leather jacket so that I could get to his face and throat. Baruk knew that. He stood his ground and waited for me to make my decision.

"We've been looking for you," he said. "We even called here a couple of times, in case you'd left a message."

"What are you talking about?" Debbie demanded. "He's here to fix things. He came to fix"

"The dishwasher," I said.

"Exactly!"

"Then I thought, maybe I ought to come and see for myself," Baruk continued smoothly, "on the off-chance."

"So what does he need a social worker for?" Debbie asked.

"He's a person with a problem," Baruk said. "He's got a big problem. He's lucky I showed up. I'm the only person who can help him deal with it."

"You wouldn't have been my first choice," I said.

"That's the risk you took, though. Right? It could have been her. If everything'd gone according to plan, it'd be her. But it's not. It's me here."

"Hey, what's going on?" Debbie asked, shrill and frightened.

Neither one of us took his eyes off the other.

"You lose," Baruk said. He stared at me, nodding his head slowly, daring me to attack him. It was what we both wanted.

I let the tension drain from me. I made a silent pact with myself to let him live until he brought me to Carol.

When I stepped back, Baruk let out the breath he'd been holding very slowly. He wanted me to see the movement of his right hand fitting the gun snug into his waistband. He didn't need it, he wanted me to know. His hands came out, open and empty. He didn't need a gun when he out-manned me.

"Will somebody please tell me what's going on?" Debbie asked. She was unsure of herself, uncertain whether she ought to understand, from common sense alone, what passed between us.

"Debbie, don't worry about this," Baruk said. "It's old stuff between him and me, that's all. We'll be going soon, anyway. We'll be out of your way."

"Going where?" Debbie asked. "I need him. He fixes things."

"Look, when we've had our session, I'll bring him back. How's that?"

"I don't have what you want," I told Baruk.

"Maybe you do, maybe you don't. You're still my best bet."

I considered walking away. I thought of turning from Baruk and walking out the back door, down the concrete path to the garage. There wasn't a lot he could do. I didn't think he'd shoot me in front of Debbie, and I didn't think Baruk could summon the coldness to shoot her, too. But my freedom wasn't worth anything. Outside the back door, the world stretched off in all directions, the entire planet; but it was a world of glances, gestures, uncertain meanings, meaninglessness. I felt the narrowing of destiny. I'd come to the point of no return. I felt the pull of the machine I myself had set in motion.

"Where are you taking him?" Debbie asked. She sensed there was something about the setup that wasn't right, even if she couldn't put her finger on it.

"See," Baruk mumbled, biting his lower lip, too obviously

thinking hard. "I didn't want to say this. But I'm not really his social worker." He sighed, reluctant to go on. "I don't know what he's told you."

"What?" Debbie asked. She looked at me as if I'd become a different person, as if I was changing before her eyes with each sentence Baruk spoke.

"The fact is, I'm his probation officer," Baruk said.

"I see," Debbie said, but the truth had not relieved her. Everything had not come clear.

"I wasn't able to say anything before."

"I know that."

"I'm still not meant to. So, if you wouldn't mind not mentioning it?"

Debbie nodded. "All right," she said.

He turned to me. "So. We got a lot to talk about."

"You're not taking him . . . back, are you?" Debbie asked.

"I don't think that's necessary. But, like I say, we got a lot of talking to do."

Baruk stood solidly, his feet planted wide and his hands crossed over his crotch and the gun in his waistband, letting the heavy words sink in.

I let myself go, and I was taken up by the flow of events. Once I'd resigned myself, I fell into the convict's way of thinking, or not thinking. All Baruk had to do was to jerk his head slightly to one side, and I moved. It didn't matter that we were standing in Debbie's hall and not Medical. We went out the front door and down the steps. I walked in front of him at the regulation pace. Two men walking along a residential street, one man three feet behind the other: It would be obvious to anyone who'd had anything to do with prisons.

Baruk had parked around the corner, on a side street. He had an old two-door Monte Carlo. It had been painted gray over the original black, and I wondered how many times it had been stolen and restolen. I wondered if Carol had stolen this car for Baruk as she'd stolen cars for me. I stopped two feet back from the passenger door and waited.

"Keep going," he said. "I want to show you what I got in the trunk."

241

When he unlocked the trunk and lifted the lid, there was nothing there except a bottle of water.

"What?" I asked, though I knew what he was going to do. The only question was whether he'd hit me over the head.

"Wait," he said.

We stood staring into the empty trunk while a six-year-old boy rode along the sidewalk on his bicycle. He stopped alongside to peer into the trunk. Then he looked at us closely, trying to see in our faces what was missing from the trunk before he went on his way. We waited for him to turn the corner.

"Get in," Baruk said, and I heard the creak of his leather jacket as he reached for the handgun.

I thought maybe the kid would turn and ride back toward us, buy me more time. Baruk took out the gun, and I saw from the way he was holding it that he'd club me with it if I didn't do as he said.

"Get in now," he said without emotion. We could have been back at Denning, as if he had the whole weight of an institution to back him up.

I climbed in, and as I turned over I had a brief glimpse of the peaceful suburban street, with light filtered through the trees forming dappled shadows on the sidewalk, before Baruk brought the lid down hard. Then he locked the trunk.

Time passes slowly in darkness. It seemed that we drove for a long time. At first, I tried to figure out our direction from the turns Baruk made, but I soon lost track. He was a rough driver who made sudden, lurching turns without warning, as if he was trying to shake a tail. Several times we came to a complete stop, and I thought we'd come to our destination, only to have Baruk take off again with a squeak of rubber as the traffic light changed. He'd turned the radio to a station that played oldies, and I listened to the Beach Boys sing about life on another planet as I was bumped and rolled from one side to the other.

The car was parked for several hours. It was hot in the trunk, and I used up all the water in the bottle, but it wasn't unbearable. I couldn't hear a sound, not voices or even distant traffic, and I thought I must be in a garage. Sometimes I wondered if Baruk had changed his mind and dumped me in some isolated spot, but I convinced myself that didn't make sense.

I was dozing when I heard the door open and then slam, and we got moving again. We drove farther this time, most of it on highway. Finally, I felt the car slow to a stop, then carefully back into a space, and I knew we were there. When the lid opened, I was dazzled by the light, even though it was late in the afternoon. I tried to sit up, but Baruk stuck me in the chest with a club like a short baseball bat.

"Wait," he commanded. He held the club ready while he reached round to a rear pocket. "Hands out," he said. I was moving too slowly for him. "Come on, for Chrissake! How many times've you done this? Put your fucking hands out."

I reached up my hands toward him automatically, wrists close together, and he hooked the cuffs around them and ratcheted them tight. He looked quickly left and right.

"Out," he said, and hauled on the handcuffs.

I was off balance and almost falling, as he wanted, when my feet met the ground. I stumbled forward the few steps to the door of the motel room, and it opened magically as I reached for the handle to steady myself. The lid of the trunk slammed, and then I felt Baruk give me a shove that sent me tripping into the room. I fell forward sprawling and helpless, catching the corner of the TV painfully in my ribs and rolling sideways, my head hitting the side of the bed, and bouncing out of control, trying to break my fall with my forearms and the sides of my hands.

I lay where I was and didn't try to get up. My chin rested on the shag rug and I breathed the deodorant powder they'd put into it.

"It went good," Baruk said.

The other person didn't reply, but walked away quickly; when they tried to close the bathroom door it stuck, and they had to pull it back and slam it to get it shut. I heard water running, splashing into the basin for the sake of the sound it made. I knew it was Carol. In my heart, I saw her staring at herself in the mirror, her thoughts drowned out by the rushing water swirling aimlessly around the bathroom sink.

I started to get up, but Baruk put a foot in the small of

my back and pushed me down so that I lay with my face in the rug.

"Wait," he said.

He stepped over me to turn on the television, then sat down on the end of the bed, his foot resting on my back. It was a soap opera, and after a few seconds he got up again and clicked through three more channels.

"You like TV, right?"

When I didn't answer him, he pumped on my back with his foot a couple of times.

"Yo, Cody! I'm talking to you." He was silent for a moment, and I could feel him staring at me. He wanted to get into something with me so that he'd lose his temper. He leaned over me and his voice came closer. "You're a ghost, aren't you, Cody? No one sees you come. No one sees you go. No one notices you, because you don't matter. You sly shit! You killed Ralph Mandell, didn't you, Cody? They read your letter on TV."

"If you heard it on TV, it must be true."

He gave me a sharp kick in the ribs. "Don't get smart with me, Cody. You're too damned smart for your own good."

He shoved with his heel on my shoulder to turn me over so that he could see my face. When he leaned over me I saw how furious he was.

"Do you know what you've done to Carol with your celebrity turn on TV? Do you? Do you know what those letters have done to her? Everything out in the open?"

"We've got nothing to lose," I told him.

"We? Huh? Excuse me?"

"Carol and me."

"Carol and me?"

He rocked back on the mattress, limp, with his mouth open and his head hanging back, mocking, breathing like laughter. When he rocked forward again he kept on going until he leaned down close to me. He was tight and focused and he held the gun between his hands, high and up and close, like a pointed part of his face.

"What is it—you're in your own special world? You're too fucking paranoid to see what's going on?"

"Things aren't always what they seem."

244

"Is that a fact?"

"The truth's going to come out, in time, if you give it a chance."

"What? Like the truth about Carol and you?"

"If you like."

"How do you think you got here?"

"I was waiting for you."

"How do you think I knew where to find you? Huh? Who do you think told me that?"

"She did what I expected her to do. I don't blame her for that."

"See, Cody, I don't believe you're crazy. I think you're a sly bastard. I think you use all that psychological mumbo jumbo to bullshit the system. And it's worked for you. Up to a point. It didn't get you off when you killed your wife. Almost, though. Very close, they tell me. It worked on the shrinks and psychologists who came along after you escaped. They came up to Denning and interviewed everyone who'd ever had anything to do with you. They'd got themselves convinced you were nutty as a fruitcake. They said you were irrational. They said there was no telling what you'd do, because you were irrational. Those letters to Sandy? That was a nice touch. And all the time, you were working on Carol. Love letters through the TV. Trying to get her sympathy."

He kicked me hard below the ribs. It was a western boot, and the hard, pointed toe went in under the ribs. It took the breath out of me.

"But that's all you got from her. Sympathy. Nothing else."

I lay on my back and tried to believe that I wasn't going to suffocate. Slowly, I became able to draw deeper and deeper breaths. When I opened my eyes, Baruk was looking down at me. For a long moment, we studied each other silently.

"You have no idea," I told him.

"Is that so?"

He seemed to lose interest in me. He glanced impatiently toward the bathroom. Finally, he got up and went over to the door. I saw him take a breath and raise his fist to knock, then change his mind and walk back to the bed.

"Don't you move," he ordered me. "You got that?"

245

He wanted an excuse to hit me. He needed me and he wanted to kill me by mistake. He fingered the gun in his pants and looked around for the billy club. He was restless. In the bathroom, the water was still splashing into the basin. Baruk walked over to the bathroom door and back, clicking his fingers. I was afraid he'd kick me in the head, just for the hell of it. He went to the bathroom door and lowered his head to listen, then straightened up when he saw I was watching him.

"How long you going to be in there?" he called.

The door opened all of a sudden, in front of his face.

"What?" Carol said.

She had a cigarette between her fingers. I twisted around so that I could see her. She took a puff on her cigarette, and as she blew out the smoke, at the end, as her breath and the smoke gave out, her eyes involuntarily flicked over to me.

"This is a no-smoking room," Baruk said.

"Hello, Dan," Carol said, looking at Baruk, through him.

She took another drag on the cigarette and exhaled. Her eyes followed the smoke as it wafted to the top corner of the room, and at the end she gave a little shake of her head, almost like a shiver.

I felt confident of her. I said, "Hello, Carol." I wanted her to hear the absolute trust I had in her.

"This room is nonsmoking," Baruk said.

"No one cares about that," Carol said. She came into the room, careful, as if she might step on something, and looking about everywhere for an ashtray except into my eyes. She was cold and drawn into herself.

She waved irritably at the walls. "All the rooms are the same. They just ask which kind you want so you think you have a choice."

I sat up with my back against the bed. "I missed you," I told her and saw her mouth open as if she was going to tell me something. Then she looked away. She couldn't bring her eyes to me, but it seemed better that way, because there was no opportunity for deception. It didn't matter that Baruk was in the room with us. He was like someone waiting on our table who heard the conversation but wasn't part of it.

246

"We don't want the management coming around, do we?" Baruk told her.

"Management!" she said. "You saw the management when we signed in."

"It doesn't matter who he is. We don't want him snooping around right now."

"Well, you're the security chief."

"Come on, Carol, give me a break." He looked over to where I was sitting. "I thought I told you not to move!"

He started over to me. Carol caught at his arm. He pulled himself loose from her, but he stopped when he came to me.

"Leave him be," she said sharply.

I heard the hidden nuance of concern in her voice, and I was strengthened.

He came back to her. He was angry and confused by his own impulses. He wanted to talk to her privately, softly, but he had difficulty keeping his voice low.

"Come on, Carol, put out the cigarette, for God's sake. Sue smells it in my hair. She smells the nicotine, whatever, on my shirt, and she asks me where I've been. I can't keep telling her I was in a bar. I tell her I was here, I was there. She knows there's something going on. She lets it go; then she thinks my guard's down and she says, 'Who was you with? Come on, who was you with?' "

"Well, you're going to have to tell her sooner or later."

"Yeah. But when the time is right. I want to break it to her—" He looked over to see if I could hear what they were saying. It humiliated him that I could hear what he was saying about his family. "—You know, gently."

"That's what you've been telling me all along."

She turned away from him and started back to the bathroom, but he snatched her wrist. She twisted around on him with fire in her eyes.

"Don't you ever grab hold of me again." She wrenched her wrist from him, even though he was ready to let her go. "Who do you think I am?"

"OK. But let's not do this now, OK?"

"Tell her, then. Tell your wife you're not coming back."

"All right. But not now. OK? I don't want to talk about it now."

"Break it gently! That means never."

"What the fuck are you looking at?" he shouted at me.

"If you're going to leave her, you've got to tell her. It's only fair."

"I said not now! OK?"

"When, then?"

"Later."

"Not now. Later." The flash of anger in her eyes gave me life. "You're always giving me the brush-off when I want to talk. Then when you've got something to say, it's got to be right away."

"How can we have a conversation when he's here? Answer me that."

Carol still hadn't set eyes on me. She was walking a narrow path high up along a steep slope. If she looked down at me, she'd lose her balance.

"When is there going to be another time?" she asked.

There was a dark question buried beneath the surface of the words, and it stopped them both.

"Anyway," Baruk said, "it's time for his program. You want to watch TV?" he asked me. "You send any more of those letters to Sandy?"

I didn't say anything.

"You've still been sending them?" Carol asked. Her eyes came onto mine and away again. "I thought you'd stopped."

It was the first time she'd spoken to me directly. There was a coldness in her manner that I knew she managed only with an effort. She worked to block me out. I wanted to signal to her that everything would work out all right, but her face stopped me short. I couldn't get through. She looked through me, as though I didn't quite exist for her, something shimmering like a mirage at the end of the road that evaporates before you can reach it. It hurt, even though I knew it was a disguise. These letters, Sandy, are the only way to get through to her. Letters on television are more real to her than any words I speak.

The signature music for your program came on. You had the letter in your hands, ready to read, teasing the viewers.

248

"Oh, no," Baruk groaned. He turned to me angrily. "What does this get you? Huh? You think you're a fucking folk hero?"

I wanted to see Carol's face when you read about the meeting in Dunkin' Donuts. I had to know the effect it had on her. But as soon as you started to read, Baruk sat himself down on the bed above me and made sure I didn't move from the floor.

Carol sat on the side of the bed, behind us. All I could see of her was a fragment of her face in the corner of the mirror to the right of the TV set, a side view of her lips and chin. She'd put on fresh lipstick during the time she'd spent in the bathroom, a crisp, lustrous maroon. Lips are full of tiny movements of hesitations and second thoughts. I watched Carol's lips in the corner of the mirror. They were uncertain and slightly open. When you read about my getting into the taxi to follow her, they opened more and she turned away and looked down. I glimpsed her tongue, which showed for a moment. Her tongue was delicate and pink between the maroon lips, as though it belonged to a different animal. Sometimes I feel that the face with the maroon lips is a mask and that there's a being inside that was never meant to be exposed to light. Its tissue is delicate and is not made to reach the surface and be seen.

The sound of your voice, Sandy, filled the room and bound the three of us to the story. No one looked at anyone else. No one moved in a way that indicated the presence of another person in the room. Until you came to the part where Baruk emerged through the front door into the sunlight, and I named him for the second time.

Baruk grabbed hold of my hair and jerked back my head.

"No!" Carol cried out, to stop him.

"You ratted me!" Baruk hissed in my ear.

He'd pulled the gun and held the barrel against my cheek under the eye, pressing hard on a nerve, causing real pain. I could feel the shaking of his hand, and I knew how much he wanted to pull the trigger and how hard he fought against the impulse.

"Don't do it, Rich," Carol said in a voice that was perfectly calm. She'd come off the bed and stood somewhere nearby.

"You see what he's done?" Baruk was almost helpless. He was clogged with anger. "The cops know about me and you. The way we worked it. They'll put the whole thing together in three seconds."

"You should have told Sue while you had the chance."

"What do you mean?"

"You're not going home to her tonight, are you?"

He took the gun away from my cheek, and I knew he'd let go, that he'd let the impulse to kill me control him. He raised up the gun to smash it down on my head, but Carol put her hand there first. She spread her hand across my forehead and over my eyes, to save me.

"It's no good taking it out on him," she said.

"I can't go back!" Baruk shouted. "Don't you get it? I can't ever go back to my family!"

One hand still gripped the hair behind my head. He was shaking, I thought in anger. I thought he might smash Carol's hand if he could smash my head, too.

"We can't any of us go back!" Carol said.

"I have a family. How can you know what that's like? I have a kid."

"This has been a game to you, hasn't it?" Carol said. "Now it's real. Live it!"

"I'll fucking kill you!" he said, shaking my head. The words were strangled, as if he was fighting back sobs.

"Anyway," Carol said. She was very cool, observant. "We need him. Remember?"

I felt the hesitation in his hand. The words bound him tighter than any cuffs. He was a prisoner of reason, and his fingers clenched in my hair.

"He's going to pay," Baruk said, and threw my head forward. "You'll pay for what you did to my family."

"Well, it was going to happen sooner or later, wasn't it?" Carol asked. She'd walked away to light a cigarette.

Baruk didn't have anything to say. I shifted away from him, but he didn't notice.

"What?" Carol asked him. "Did you think you were going to float around free and easy, above suspicion, while I did all the dirty work?"

"I took my share of risks. I put my neck on the line."

"It wasn't quite the same, though, was it? Not compared to what I had to do."

"Don't keep talking about it, for Chrissake. You think I want to hear about that?"

"Then don't go on to me about risks."

"I've lost fucking everything!" Baruk said. He jumped off the bed and paced back and forth to the door. "My house, my wife, my kid. Pouf! In one second of TV. What've you lost? You never had anything. You never had a fucking life."

"I had a life. What do you think I did until you came along?"

"Your mother the alcoholic. The baby you gave up. Your step-father."

"Stop it!"

"Is that why you loaded the gun? Huh? To even out the risk?"

"I put a couple of rounds in it. There wasn't even a round chambered."

"No one said anything about a loaded gun. When I gave you the gun, it didn't have any bullets in it. Right? I didn't give you a loaded gun. Where'd the bullets come from?"

"I bought them in a store. What do you think?"

"You made a special trip to buy bullets to put in the gun I gave you?"

"How's he going to use the gun to escape if it isn't loaded?" Carol asked. "Does that make sense?"

"You don't use the gun. That's the point. It's a threat. He wasn't supposed to fire the gun."

"And what if someone tries to stop him?"

"They did. Fairburn did."

"Right. So? That's the point."

"Fairburn is dead."

"And you're alive. You're here with me. Aren't you lucky!"

"He could've shot me. He's a fucking lunatic. He could have taken me out with the bullets you put in the gun."

"Maybe he's not so crazy. Whatever, he deserved a real shot at it. I wasn't going to let him do it with an empty gun."

"Oh, he got a fair shot at it. Fairburn's dead. I could have got it, too. Then it'd just be you and Cody, working your magic together."

"Don't throw that in my face!"

Baruk sat on the side of the bed and held his head. Then he got up without saying anything and paced eight feet to the door, back again, then six feet to the chair, then back to the bed again. He sat on the bed and gnawed at the dead skin on the side of his thumb. He wasn't good alone with his own thoughts. They were like flies buzzing in his head, unwilling to settle. Finally, he seemed to have come to a decision and he stood up.

"We got to do it now," he told Carol.

She was leaning against the farthest wall. He stared at her hard, as if he could strengthen her and give her will.

"This is real," he said. "That's what you said. Well, this is a piece of reality we got to take care of."

Carol glanced at me and turned away, but there was nowhere to go. She held her arms crossed tight across her chest, and from behind I saw the fingers working, picking and clutching at her own body.

"It's the only way," Baruk said. He sounded kind, cautious, considerate, out of character.

Whatever it was, he needed Carol to say something, but she didn't turn around or move in any way.

"You got something better in mind, let's have it," he told her.

She shook her head.

"Because you're part of it. This is it. This is what we talked about."

She turned around at that. Her face showed fear, and she looked from one to the other of us, back and forth.

"Don't get any ideas about that. Your fingers are just as dirty as mine. You're in it, girl. Up to your neck."

"I don't know"

She pulled herself together. Her face tightened and she went quickly to the dresser and lit herself another cigarette. She blew the smoke out in a long, thin stream with her lips pulled back in something like a smile.

"That's your department," she said dismissively as she hung her pocketbook on her shoulder and looked around for the keys. "Not mine."

I was still sitting on the floor, blocking her way to the door.

252

She couldn't find the keys because Baruk had them. I think she must have known this.

"You're in, whether you like it or not," Baruk said. "You think I'm enjoying this?"

"You're used to it. You're trained not to feel."

"You're the nurse, though, aren't you?" Baruk asked. "You know how to do things."

"What things?"

"Stuff you can do."

"What do you think I am?" she shouted. "I can't do that!"

"You've done a lot of things you've gotten used to. It ain't so hard."

"What do you know?"

"I heard it on TV. Sandy said so. From her special correspondent."

"Don't push it."

"I am pushing it."

"You don't know where the edge is."

"Why stop now?" he said, grinning.

Carol had gone as far as she could go toward the door, but she wouldn't step over me.

"Go in the bathroom, babe," Baruk told her gently. With his eyes, he was urging her to go. "We got to do it. We got no choice now."

I watched the heavy swing of the pocketbook as Carol turned to go into the bathroom. It was always by her hand, but I knew it was too early to expect her to help me. The thin door closed behind her.

"We got to talk," Baruk said.

"You heard the letter," I said. "I've got nothing you want."

He'd drawn his gun. "Assume the position," he ordered.

I got up and rested my cuffed hands against the wall. Out of the corner of my eye, I saw him crouch and unzip a red duffel bag. He did it slowly, with one hand, feeling his way, always with his eyes on me. I thought, if he looked down into the bag for a second, there was a chance I might be able to kick him in the side of the neck, but he never did.

I heard a metallic chink and saw him lift leg irons out of the bag, and I knew that it wasn't killing that he had in mind. He threw them at my feet behind me, and they landed with a jangle on the shag rug.

"Put them on."

When I reached down to pick up the shackles, Baruk moved quickly past me to a new position on the other side.

"Stay down," he said.

There was tension in his voice, as if the situation was precarious. But if there was a way out, a way to resist him or defeat him, I didn't see it.

"Don't stand up. There's no need to stand up. Put them on now, where you are."

I ratcheted them loosely about my ankles. He saw this, but it didn't bother him.

"Get on the bed." He was sweating, even with the air conditioner.

"You horny, Baruk? Is that what this is all about?"

"Shut the fuck up and get on your back."

"You said we had to talk."

"When I say. Now just do what I tell you."

"You're not getting it. That's your problem."

"I get it three times a day, pal." He grunted as, above me, he pushed the bed out from the wall. "Is that getting it, or what? Huh? What do you think? Put your hands above your head."

I twisted my head to see what he was doing at the head of the bed. He'd tied nylon cord to the top of the bed frame.

"She fakes it," I told him.

"Yeah, sure. For you, maybe."

When I raised up my hands above my head, both Baruk and I knew that he'd reached a danger point. However carefully he'd managed me until then, now he had to come within striking distance, to come inside my zone with his hand, his arm, his head, in order to tie the cord.

I said, "Does she cry out, 'Oh, Rich. Oh, Rich. Oh, yeah, yeah, yeah'? Is that what she does? Is that what you're getting, Baruk?"

I tried to locate his head above and behind me, but he wouldn't speak. I knew he'd put the gun back in his waistband, because he needed both hands to tie the cord. I felt him hovering, waiting for the right moment.

"Did you ever wonder about that, though?" I said. "How come, if someone's really in the middle of a great orgasm, how they have it together to do all that talking? Did that pass through your mind, Rich?"

Quickly, he passed the cord between my wrists and over the chain that linked the cuffs and pulled tight. I let him do it.

"It's all right," I said. "Carol told me." He was pulling to knot the cord, and I felt the tension go off it for half a second as my words went into him.

"None of this bullshit's going to do you any good now," he whispered close to my ear. "You're nothing to her. You're just a piece on the chessboard. All that had to happen was for you to move from one square to the next square. For you, that's all there was to it."

He sat on my knees and tied another piece of cord to the chain of the shackles, taking his time to show he had me exactly where he wanted me. Then he looped it through the bottom of the bed frame and hauled on the cord and knotted it so my legs hung off the end of the bed.

He stood up then, feeling his power over me as he walked around the bed surveying his handiwork.

"Not a pretty picture," he said, grinning and shaking his head.

But he was faking it. He was tight and nervous. He couldn't stretch the grin all the way across his teeth.

"Oh Carol!" Baruk cooed at the bathroom door. "You can come out now."

There was no sound from the bathroom. Baruk rummaged in Carol's overnight bag. He had his back to me, and I couldn't see what he found. He stooped and plugged it into the electrical socket beside the dresser.

"Lover boy's ready on the bed here," he called again.

The door opened a couple of inches, but Carol didn't come out.

"He's all set," Baruk said.

"You don't need me," Carol said.

Baruk reached into the bathroom. "Babe." I think he put his

hand on her. He was half coaxing her, half pulling her. "We got to use everthing we got. If you can talk to him, maybe that'll do it. Maybe we won't need to use anything else. All right?" He waited to see her response. "Wouldn't that be better? Now, wouldn't it?"

Baruk stepped aside, and Carol walked out of the bathroom. She kept her head down and she seemed resolute as she came into the room. Then she stopped when she saw me tied to the bed.

"Oh, my God!" Her hand went to her mouth and she turned away. "That's obscene!"

"I haven't done a thing!" Baruk burst out. "He's just lying there on the bed, for Chrissake."

"I can't handle this."

"Babe, we're in too deep." He took her by the shoulders. "We got no choice now."

She'd left her pocketbook in the bathroom, and I knew I had to play it out to the bitter end, if that's what she'd decided. Carol let Baruk hold her and put his arms about her body. Reluctantly, she let him soothe her, allowed the soft words he murmured in her ear to influence her.

"There's no way back, babe. We got nowhere to go. We got no money. There's the police. There's the other one. We can run, but the odds are stacked too high. He's our only way out."

Carol broke away from Baruk's embrace. He wanted to hold her, to bring her back inside the power of his arms, but she pushed his hands down. She came over to the bed and looked down at me long and hard. She crouched beside the bed, with her face close to mine. She held her hands together as if she were going to pray. The appeal in her eyes was clearer than if she had asked me aloud to keep faith in her.

"Cody," she whispered. "Please give him what he wants." Her eyes glistened. "Please!"

"Is that what you want?" I asked. I watched her face very carefully so that I would be able to tell, ignoring her words, what it was she wanted me to do.

"Yes. That's what I want. Just tell him. And get this over with."

"OK."

She closed her eyes and nodded her head once very slowly. Her lips were slightly parted, and I heard her breathe a long sigh of relief. It was a soft, intimate sound, our heads close, almost lying together on the bed.

"Tell him how to get the money. Tell him about the money in the Caicos Islands."

"I don't know."

Baruk slapped his thigh and turned away.

"Dan, please," Carol whispered. "This is the time. I know you've been holding onto it, but this is the time to let it go. Believe me."

"If I knew, I'd tell you."

"Please!"

"Forget it," Baruk said, like a dark echo in the background.

"Tell us how to get the money that Diego put away," Carol persisted.

She was trying hard to stay calm, to be patient. I heard the fine vibration of fear in her voice, and I longed to reassure her. But I knew that whatever I told her, she wouldn't be able to see as far down the road as I did.

"Time to try the other way," Baruk said. He crouched down over the thing he'd plugged into the electrical socket.

"Before he died, right before he died, Diego told you the number of the account, isn't that right? That's what you told me."

"He never did. I thought he would. I thought he was going to. But he didn't."

"That isn't what Diego told me," Baruk said. "Diego said he told you how to get the money. He said you'd been good to him. That was the deal."

Carol put her hand on my shoulder. "Wasn't that the deal you had with Diego? He was lonely. He liked you. Wasn't that it? It's OK with me. It doesn't change anything. You already know that."

I heard something rip on the other side of the bed. When I turned to the sound, Baruk covered my mouth with duct tape.

"You said you knew how to get the money!" Carol said. She was wild-eyed, scattered, close to panic. "You promised me!" she cried.

She glanced over her shoulder. She hadn't noticed that Baruk

257

was standing behind her. He had her traveling iron in his hand. He touched her shoulder.

"Careful," he said, as she got up.

Carol went over to the dresser and lit a cigarette. She held the cigarette between two outstretched fingers level with her right eye and supported her elbow with the other hand. She strolled up and down in front of the mirror as if she were alone in the room.

"I want you to feel this thing, so you know how hot it is," Baruk said. In his eyes, I saw he was afraid how hot it was.

He held the iron up to my face, an inch away from my cheek. It was very hot. After a few seconds it began to scorch the skin, and I moved my head away.

"That's how hot it is. OK? You got that straight? That's not touching. That's not even touching you." He wanted me to respond, so he wouldn't have to do what he was thinking of. "I'm sure there's a way we can avoid all this unpleasantness," he said. I think he'd heard someone say that in a movie. He couldn't bring himself to the action. He had to be someone else.

Baruk took the Swiss Army knife out of his pocket and opened up the main blade between his teeth. He hooked it beneath the top of my T-shirt, and when he slid the blade downward, the T-shirt opened like a zipper. He closed the knife with a snap and dropped it into his pocket. I wasn't ready when his fingertips lightly touched the bare skin of my chest, and I flinched from him.

"Jumpy?"

I stared at Carol. I concentrated on her. She was in her own world. She paced the length of the room, holding an elbow with one hand, arms tight to her body, the cigarette and the other hand hiding her face. She paced five steps, swiveled on her heel, then paced five steps in the opposite direction, like an automaton, like a pendulum. Sometimes, in the middle, she took a pull on the cigarette.

Baruk peeled back the duct tape from my mouth.

"We don't have to go through with this," he said. He fussed with the tape. "All you got to do is say the word."

His eyes were pleading. I was stronger, because my will was stronger. I composed myself. I felt myself growing compact, dense and hard and enduring.

"I don't know," I said. My voice sounded weary. I listened to it as if it came from another person. "If I knew, I'd tell you."

Everything about Baruk was stretched taut. His jaw clenched. His fist was tight around the handle of the iron. Then something broke in him. He smoothed the duct tape back over my lips. He placed the iron on the left side of my chest, over my heart, and let the weight of it rest on my chest. He watched my face.

At first, I was surprised that it didn't hurt at all. Like putting your hand into a basin of scalding water, you had to wait for the pain to catch up. It took me by surprise. I was knocked out by a blast of the purest form of nerve hell. It was pain stripped of fear or sense of injury or any other emotion. It was an abstraction on the other side of pain. My body screamed.

I was pushed aside. I couldn't catch up with what was happening. All I knew was the pressure on my chest that blotted out everything else. It was a white water of sensation that swept me in it, tumbling, always off balance, too late, clutching and losing footing and grip.

Then Baruk took the iron off my chest, and I was left only with the familiar pain of being burned. The pain was strong enough to make me want to cry out, but it was a known quantity, and I was there at its center, not annihilated, not in hell.

"I can't stand it!" Carol cried. She held her hands tight over her ears to block out imaginary screams. Her face was hardly recognizable, so distorted with anguish and disgust. She shook her head to free herself from the screams.

"You think I like this?" Baruk asked. "You think I feel good about what I'm doing?" He peeled the tape back from my lips and waited to hear what sound I might make.

"Then stop it!"

"Then what? Then where are we going?"

"I don't care. If we have to do this, it's not worth it."

"You think this is worse than fucking it out of him?"

He watched her. "It wasn't like that," Carol said.

He watched the pain come to her abruptly, in a sudden expression, and she turned away to hide her face. "Because that's all it was," he said to me.

"We made love," I told him.

259

"Oh, please!"

Carol had recovered, and her eyes appealed to me not to go on, but I said, "We made love right under your nose."

"Is that so?" Baruk asked, nodding. "Right under my nose, and I didn't know anything about it?"

"That's right," I said.

"That was the through the door routine—is that it? That's the love you're referring to?"

"She told you. So what?"

"She?" He moved his hand in a flowery gesture of incomprehension. "Who do you think was on the other side of the door?"

I wouldn't look at Carol. I refused to weaken. Baruk was so sure of himself that he didn't even need to see the effect he'd had on me. He was walking away.

"See," Baruk said. He was stooping. I heard him plug in the iron again. He stood up and came back. "That was my deal with Diego." He stood over me. "Was it good for you?"

"You're bluffing," I said. "I know who it was."

I had to see her. I knew the instant our eyes met it would be clear and certain. But she was out of view. She was leaning against the wall where I couldn't see anything of her, and her only presence was the thin stream of smoke she forced between her lips.

Baruk, above me, stared at Carol fixedly. He tried to hold her against the wall with his eyes. Even though he spoke to me, he didn't take his eyes off her. "After a few years in stir, you don't know the difference between a man and a woman. That's what they say."

"Diego wouldn't do that," I said.

"Diego'd do anything," Baruk said. "For you. And you got something out of it. You got as far as this. Everybody got something." He turned and walked away to get the iron. He wanted me to see how confident he was, but the iron in his hand unmanned him. "Problem is, everybody got what somebody else wanted. Like under the Christmas tree? With the labels on the gifts all mixed up? But it's over for you now. This is as far as you go, Cody. There's nothing in it for you anymore." He showed me the iron. "It's pointless."

We both knew the iron was cooling as he tried to persuade me to surrender, but still he hesitated.

"Don't be an asshole," he said, confidentially. He wanted to confide in me. He wanted me to help him. "Give it up."

"Gestapo!" I whispered. "Gestapo man! You can take care of this little problem."

"You don't get it, pal, do you? You're going to make me do it."

"Do it, then, Gestapo man. Let's see you do it."

He was afraid. "I'm really going to do it this time." He put the tape back over my mouth and smoothed it down.

I locked onto his eyes. He looked at my chest for a spot to put the iron and when he looked up, I was still looking at him. He put the iron on my chest, and I would not take my eyes off him. He leaned his weight on the iron, with his arms straight down from his shoulders, and I stared back at him, and when our eyes met I saw the terror in him at what he was becoming. He took the iron off my chest.

I passed out. When I opened my eyes, Baruk and Carol were standing over me. Carol was waving a hand in front of my face. She bent down to take my pulse and held the cigarette stiffly out behind her in her other hand.

"I thought he'd killed you," she said.

She looked at the burn on my chest, and I knew from her face it was bad. Carefully, wary I'd scream for help, she peeled back a corner of the duct tape.

"Just give him what he wants," she whispered. She ran the backs of her fingers down the side of my face. "Do it for me." She turned to Baruk. "We're going to have to get him to a hospital."

"Later," he said. He was plugging in the iron.

"It's a third-degree burn."

"People get those all the time. You can survive burns covering most of your body. What percentage is it, when you die of it?"

"Sixty. Seventy. I don't know."

"What do you say, Cody?" he asked me. "That was five percent. You're good for another fifty-five before you croak. You want to go all the way? Do you?"

Pain is defining. Baruk was unnerved by his own actions. He wanted me to fight him, to save him. He was evaporating, while I was made more dense by what he did to me.

"I don't have what you want," I told him.

Baruk reached over Carol's shoulder and put the tape back over my mouth. They stood together at the foot of the bed and studied me with worried expressions while the iron reheated. Carol walked away to light a fresh cigarette off the one that was half-smoked in her hand. I craved a cigarette. I wondered what would happen if Baruk came to the point where he believed I really didn't know how to get the money.

Torture is very stressful. Not many people are suited to it. It certainly took its toll on Baruk. His hair was untidy and dried out; the sleek look he cultivated was gone. His hands were sweaty, and he kept wiping them on the front of his sport shirt. He licked his finger and crouched to test the iron. I heard the sizzle of saliva and Baruk's grunt of surprise and pain. He came back slowly to the bed with the iron in his hand, the cord trailing. His will was failing him.

Carol was alone, away from us. She didn't turn her head or react to the sounds the iron made. The hand that held the elbow was a fulcrum on which her whole body turned; she paced back and forth, staring straight ahead to her new life, and when she came to the wall or the bathroom door, the hand on the elbow steered her through the turn.

I brought myself to a point of focus on the smoke from her cigarette. I was the cigarette smoke she pulled deep into the farthest corners of her lungs, eddying and lingering, feeling the warmth of her rushing blood all around me, before being expelled, rushing through the tubes, the cavity of her mouth, and squeezed into a tight stream between her lips. Baruk pushed the iron onto my chest.

He leaned on me as if the iron was a defibrillator that would shock my body into truth. I was afraid the agony would become a permanent part of me. The pain, when it came, was no longer sharp and startling. I knew it, and I anticipated it. Baruk saw how afraid I was once I came to know the pain. He played on the fear. I hoped to become confused. I tried to find my way to delirium, groping for the exit.

Then the smoke detector went off.

Baruk was the first to react to the sound of the siren. He had

262

the gun raised in his hand and immediately took up a position to the side of the door. He was crouched in a firing stance, looking about him, confused by the noise and trying to figure out where it was coming from. Carol came out of the bathroom where she'd been throwing up. She shouted to Baruk, but he didn't hear her. He was fixated on the idea that a SWAT team was preparing to assault the motel. She got his attention and pointed to the ceiling.

"Get the fucking batteries out!" Baruk shouted.

He twitched open the curtains to see if anyone stood outside the door, but the setting sun was in his eyes, and he shook his head and turned away.

Carol stood on the bed. She towered above me as she strained to reach to the ceiling. She seemed very far away. I felt her moving her weight from one foot and then quickly to the other in order to keep her balance, and the mattress rocked under me like the swell beneath a boat.

The noise was deafening. I could see from where I lay that the smoke detector was wired in. Baruk went to the bathroom to turn on the fan. There was a loud knock at the door, but I was the only one who heard it.

Someone outside yelled, "What's going on in there?"

It was hard to make out the individual words. All I really heard was the tone of protest. They banged on the door again, and I saw the security chain jump. Baruk was coming out of the bathroom, looking around for a switch to turn off the alarm, when we all heard the crunch of a key going into the lock and saw the handle start to turn. He got to the door just in time to drop the end of the chain into the slot.

The person with the key opened the door as far as the chain would allow. Baruk faced him through the four-inch space. He kept the gun out, resting in his hand against the door.

"What's going on in here?" he demanded.

He was a man in his late sixties. I could see half of his glasses. He peered over Baruk's shoulder, screwing up the eye to see into the dimness of the room.

"I don't see any fire," he shouted into Baruk's face. "You got a fire in there?"

Carol dropped a shirt over my wrists to hide the cuffs and removed the tape. She pulled the torn halves of the T-shirt over the burns on my chest.

"No," Baruk told the man. "There's no fire."

The old man turned aside to signal to someone to turn off the alarm, then peered again into the room. Baruk tried to block his view, but he bobbed his head and changed the angle suddenly and could have taken in the whole scene if Carol hadn't come up behind Baruk.

His nose was twitching. He turned his head this way and that, like an animal scenting, trying to poke his nose into the dark room, sniffing, inquisitive.

"You've been cooking!" he shouted. "You can't cook in these rooms," he bellowed through the gap in the door.

Somewhere, someone switched off the alarm, and in the silence he noticed me for the first time. In a slow count, his eyes went from Carol to Baruk, and back to me again.

He nodded toward me. "What's he up to?" he demanded.

The scene was slowly, bit by bit, giving up its meaning to the man. You could almost see the movement of comprehension as he took in each fresh aspect.

"What do you think?" Baruk asked nastily.

"He's having a rest," Carol told him.

"It's only two people to one room," the man said.

His eyes stayed on me. I troubled him. Baruk turned from the door to see what I would do.

"I work nights," I said. "I'll be out of here in a couple of hours."

"How come he keeps his arms up like that?" he asked Carol. It wasn't so much suspicion as a growing disgust that was forming on his face. "How come he doesn't move them?"

"He's got a back problem," Carol said. "He has to stretch."

"You're perverts, aren't you?" he said finally. His lip curled. He wanted to say something, but he was taken with shortness of breath.

"Hey," Baruk shrugged, "everyone's got to express themselves in their own way."

"This here is a family motel," the man protested. "We don't

want your kind here. You want to act perverted, go down the road to the Bel Air. They don't care what you do there."

"Well, we're here now."

"You get out of here, or I'll call the police!"

"We've already paid for the night," Carol said. She spoke mildly, and he heeded her.

"You think I want to clean up your filthy mess?" he complained to Carol.

"We're not that kind," Baruk said.

"There won't be any mess," Carol said. The man looked to Carol for reassurance. He wanted to believe her. "Honest," Carol promised him.

He breathed heavily, considering, softening. "And no cooking."

"OK. No more cooking," Carol said.

" 'Cause we have trouble with the fire marshal if there's cooking."

"All right."

"They could close us down."

"There won't be no more trouble," Baruk said, but it was Carol the man looked to for acknowledgment.

"As for you," he said to me over Baruk's shoulder, "I feel sorry for you, letting yourself be used this way. I really do."

He was still looking at me and shaking his head when Baruk shut the door on him.

Later, Baruk couldn't decide who should go out for food. "I'll toss you for it," he suggested.

"You should go," Carol told him.

"They're onto me same as you."

"But they didn't show your picture on TV."

Slowly, reluctantly, Baruk went out the door to get some subs. Then, a couple of minutes later, without warning, he came back into the room because he'd forgotten his keys.

"You don't need the keys," Carol said. "You can't take your car anyway. You'll have to dump it when it's dark."

"Right." He frowned.

After the escape, Carol and I had been with each other for entire days and nights, but now it bothered him to leave us alone for a few minutes. It humiliated him to come back to the room on such a flimsy pretext, because we knew he hadn't been able to resist checking on us.

He patted his pockets. "You going to be all right?" he asked Carol.

"Sure. Why not?"

He smiled. It was a very good smile. It was probably the thing Baruk did better than anything else. It was a confident, honest, open smile that Carol couldn't help responding to. It lit her heart like a match lighting a candle, and its glow stayed on her face for several moments after Baruk had swept up the keys to the cuffs from the dresser and closed the door behind him.

I was alone with Carol. I waited, totally aware of her. The air conditioner came on. The front of my chest was very painful. If you let it, pain drowns out everything else, obscuring feelings, preventing you from following a thought. But ignoring it is like treading water, a constant effort to keep your head above the surface.

She didn't speak. We were too conscious of each other to know how to begin. She sat on the far corner of the bed. She could have turned on the television, but she didn't. She sat very still, trying to control her breathing. Any movement she might make would become an un guarded gesture. The tension of things unspoken built in the silence. It was a lovely moment of pure, unspoken intimacy. The moment stretched on and on, far beyond its natural breaking point.

The silence was too strong. It was too ambiguous for Carol. She wanted the safety of something she could be sure of hearing or seeing. She got up to light a cigarette, and the ripples of her movement off the mattress rocked me. Then she came over to where I lay and placed the cigarette between my lips, looking not at me but down at the large raw area on my chest. She pulled the chair over and sat beside me and took the cigarette out of my mouth and took a drag on it herself, and we shared the cigarette that way.

"I don't blame you," I told her. "Don't for a moment think that I blame you for this."

"I don't care if you do," she said.

She was cold only to control her feelings, to keep the emotions solid, like ice, to stop them flowing and melding. She gazed far off, blowing the deeply inhaled smoke slowly in a fine mist from between her lips. She tapped the cigarette hard, twice, on the side of the ashtray, even though there hadn't been enough time for ash to form.

"I did what I had to do," she said, as if she were talking to herself.

"I'd do it all over again," I said.

"You got something out of it. You got your freedom." She wanted to look at me in the hope my face might show some sign of gratitude, but she couldn't risk what the glance might do to her. "Well, anyway, you got out of Denning."

"You still don't understand. I'm with you. That's what I want."

"I'll make sure Rich lets you go. I promise you that. It's only fair."

"Maybe he'll let us both go." She glanced at me, wondering. "Somehow, I don't think so."

"I think you knew, all along, what was really going down," she said. "I mean, we're both grown-ups, right?"

She turned to look at me, really look at me, for the first time since Baruk had left. She looked into me, as if she wasn't sure I was the person she'd thought I was, as if I might have changed and she needed to check what she saw, feature by feature, against memory.

"You knew, didn't you?" she asked.

"Yes," I said, because it was what she needed to hear, and because it contained a deeper truth that she would come to by and by. "I always knew."

She let out a small sigh of relief. She brightened. "I thought you did. But I wasn't sure. We used each other, but, in a way, we helped each other. You know what I mean?"

"Sure."

She picked her way carefully between the words. "What Rich said. About who was on the other side of the door."

"I know," I said quickly. "I always knew it was you. I never doubted it was you."

267

"Good." She laughed nervously. "I feel better now. You know, I didn't want you to think I'd taken advantage of you."

"You couldn't have done that. Love isn't something you can take advantage of, because it's a gift. It's given freely."

"Cody, I want you to forget about me."

"Whatever you do, I'll still love you. Nothing can change that."

"I'm not worth it."

"You're the world to me. I couldn't forget you, even if I wanted to."

"I *want* you to forget me."

"I'll never do it."

"Rich set the whole thing up. Right from the beginning."

"He's using you."

"*We* used you. Rich and me."

"You had to do it."

"Yes, I had to."

"There you are, then."

"I had to do it, because it was the only way I could keep him."

There are moments in time that are waves breaking over you, that can wash you off your feet and pull you backwards, downwards, under, forward in the undertow, out to the great, empty ocean.

"He was there for me during a very difficult time in my life," Carol said.

I tried to cut her off.

"I want to explain it, though," she said. "I want you to understand why I did what I did. Then maybe you won't think so badly of me. I don't know if you can imagine what it's like to be the only woman surrounded by a thousand men. It's not easy, I can tell you. Then someone put out the rumor that I was a plant for the state police. Whenever I came into the staff lounge, everyone stopped talking. I was totally alone. I don't know if you can imagine what this is like, in a prison, surrounded by men. I didn't have anyone to turn to. But Rich was there for me."

"I saw some of what you were going through."

"I know. But you were an inmate. It's not the same."

"But . . . Rich was there for you."

"Then, later, he had his problems. His little boy is developmentally disabled. Rich wants him to go to a residential school where he can get the special therapy he needs. I had to help Rich get the money he needs."

"He's a gambler. He loses a lot."

"How do you know that?"

"You think I don't know what's going on?" I asked her sarcastically. "He owes Nando."

Baruk came back with two large meatball subs and a bottle of Tylenol. He joked with Carol about dividing them up between the three of us, giving her a minute portion and watching to see how she laughed, gauging the spontaneity. Making a move, watching, making another move. In his own way, he was sniffing the air for signs of intimacy that might have lingered.

He undid the cord that tied the handcuffs to the bed frame so that I could sit up. My shoulders were stiff, and my hands were swollen from the tightness of the cuffs. Carol didn't mention this, leaving it for Baruk to notice, so that he could be the one who decided to take them off.

"We're going to need dressings for his chest," Carol said.

Baruk waved the problem away. "Tomorrow," he said through a stuffed mouth.

When we finished eating, I was in their way. In an elaborate, logical sequence of orders, which Baruk must have choreographed during his trip from the sub shop, I moved from the bed to the bathroom. In the bathroom, under Baruk's direction, I locked one of the handcuffs around the cold water pipe behind the ceramic support of the washbsin. Quickly, he stooped to test that it was secure, and then he was out of range again.

"Aren't you going to take off those leg irons?" Carol asked him.

"Later," he said.

When Carol gave me the extra blanket and the pillows from the closet, Baruk scowled but didn't object.

I found a way to curl around the toilet with my right hand above my head so that I could lie without too much contortion. I wasn't going to sleep. Through the cheap panel door I could hear every sound in the bedroom. They whispered at first. It was difficult to make out the words, and all I could hear were suggestive, taunting hints in the darkness. There was the deep murmur of Baruk, as he cajoled her toward something she wasn't inclined to do. Of Carol's voice, I heard only the hissing part of her whispers, sudden and rapid and urgent, following periods of silence, protesting, warning. There was the dull krump of the mattress as Baruk changed position heavily. There was the spring as the pressure was released when Carol got up to turn on the TV. Most of all, I was tantalized by the anonymous movements signaled by the tiny frictions of skin against fabric. I had to guess what these sounds meant. I tried to remember their exact starting positions at the time I left the room and then added the major sounds of movement, allocating each one to Carol or Baruk as best I could.

Baruk got up and turned off the television. He was stealthy climbing back onto the mattress. He was kneeling on the mattress, crawling across it to her, coming to her like an animal.

I heard Carol say, "No!" quite clearly, then his low murmur, muffled as it would be if he held his mouth close to her ear.

"No!" she said again, not quite seriously.

Baruk said something and laughed.

"You're terrible," she said, forgetting to whisper.

"That's because I know you," he said. "I know a thing or two about you."

"That's what you like to think."

"I'm right, though, aren't I?"

"You think you are."

"I am, though, aren't I?"

"Sometimes."

"Like no other?"

She didn't answer him. He'd gone too far. He'd pushed too hard, and even though he'd pretended to be joking, he'd broken the connection.

They were quiet for a while, then Baruk said, "You know, it's just you and me now."

"What about Sue?" Carol asked.

He didn't answer immediately. "I can't go back," he said. "It's just you."

"What about your little boy? You won't see him."

"Maybe later. Maybe after a while I'll find a way. Right now, we've got to move out of state."

"Won't he miss you?"

"Sure he will."

"Won't he miss his dad?"

"Will you get off this?" he snapped.

"I'm only trying to help you talk about it."

"You're not my fucking therapist, OK?"

They were silent for several moments, then I heard Baruk sigh in irritation. "What can I do? I show up there, I'll get arrested. They're waiting for me at the house. They'll have an unmarked car parked across the street twenty-four hours a day. They expect me to show up. That's how they get people. Sooner or later people weaken. The heart wins over the head. They get emotional and they get arrested."

"We'll make our own home," Carol said.

In the silence, I heard movement on the mattress of people coming together.

"Yeah," Baruk breathed, loosening.

I thought they lay on their backs, staring into the future on the ceiling above them.

"Maybe something on the beach," he said.

"Yeah?"

"Sure. Some little Caribbean country where they don't extradite people. Get a place on the beach."

"A nice house."

"Oh, yeah. We're not living in any shack. Once we get into that account, we're set for life. We'll get something real nice. Simple, so it doesn't draw attention. But nice."

They spun out their fairy tale.

"We'll sit on the verandah."

"Drink pina coladas."

"Watch the sun go down."

"Yeah."

There was the sound of Baruk turning, then silence. I think he kissed her.

Then he said, "Look what I got."

271

"Oh, God." She gave a laugh that was tight and uneasy. "You're too much."

"No one ever complained about it before."

"Stop it!" I heard her slap him lightly. She was playful, but it wasn't spontaneous.

"You stop it. You're the one that's getting me going. Look at you!"

"We can't!" She whispered now, even though they'd been talking, forgetful of me, for some minutes.

"Sure we can. Relax. Let me take care of you."

"Rich, he can hear."

"So?" he asked coldly. "Some people like that." He didn't bother to whisper now, even when Carol did.

"It makes me feel funny."

I heard bodies shifting, a zipper running, the swish of fabric slipping quickly over skin.

"Lift up a bit," he told her.

"You didn't have to say that, about Diego."

He stopped. "Hey. Where are you? Are you with me, or him?"

"You, of course," she said doubtfully. "It's just, it doesn't feel right."

"Well, I think it feels OK. I think it feels damned right."

"I don't like it."

"If you don't like it, what's this I'm feeling here?"

"Oh, don't do that," she moaned.

"You tap me on the shoulder when you want me to stop." I could imagine his grin. "All right?" he asked, confident she wouldn't complain.

They were quiet. I heard the sharp intake of her breath as though she'd been touched in an exquisite, tender spot, and then the long, slow sigh as she let it out.

"I can't think straight when you do that," she said, still with the troubled knot in her voice.

There were adjustments.

"You don't have to think." He was serious and intent. He was breathing regularly, focused on his destination. "Huh. Yeah," he said in a different voice, to himself.

272

The regular, liquid slap began.

"Now what do you say?" he asked her in a clear, calm voice, as if he was above and apart from what they were about. "You want me to stop now?"

The rhythm never varied. The slap of their bodies was relentless. They grunted with the effort of finding pleasure in each other, searching and straining to find the beginning pull of the current, the first tug of delight that would take them to the point of inevitability, push them off the edge, over the edge into soaring, annihilating flight.

I yanked at the handle on the toilet. I held onto the cold, white ceramic for dear life. It was hard and real. I leaned to rest my face on the rim so that I could be close to the circling, panicked water. There were sounds within the rushing swirl, voices that were lost before they could call to me, echoes of memories, words snatched away. I clutched tight to the cold ceramic. I hugged it with my one free arm, careless of the mere agony on the front of my chest as the water sucked itself down and was gone. And at that point of balance, defenseless and emptied of all hope, I distinctly heard Carol sob.

It wasn't much more than a slight cough, cut off quickly. But so much was concentrated within that sound of a woman at the brink, spilling into mindlessness, helpless as emotion was unlocked and surged for release. People don't know themselves until the critical moment surprises them. You never know when this moment of birth will come. I heard in her cry the sharp pang of regret, like a stab wound, as she lay on the mattress where I had suffered to keep our secret safe. I heard another person breaking through, a possibility that had been invisible to Carol, even though I had watched for signs of it all along. There comes the moment of realization, the turning point. The instrument, who brings it forth, is not important.

You think she betrayed me. But love is not about surfaces. Carol had to find her way. She had to be released from the day-to-day concerns that preoccupied her—money, Caribbean sunsets, appearances. There is within a person a slower, deeper process, like water trickling underground. It will find its level. It will inevitably make its way. Everything she took from me I gave

273

to her willingly. You cannot steal something that is given freely. You cannot use someone who wants to serve. If I refuse to condemn her for what she did, there can be no crime. Betrayal is an abuse of trust; but I made no demands of her, I expected nothing from her, while I waited for my love to make its way within her.

NINE

Dear Sandy:
   Rich came into the bathroom in his Jockey shorts the next morning. He flipped up the toilet seat and directed a thick stream into the middle of the water so that it made a deep bubbling sound close to my head. He leaned back and sighed and looked down at me out of the corner of his eye.

"Don't get any ideas, Cody," he said.

He wanted me to lose myself in some hopeless attack, to pull his legs out from under him, even though I was chained to the pipe. He'd been so careful up to that point, I knew he was ready for me.

"You've got it all figured out, Rich," I said without looking up.

I didn't have to see his face to tell he didn't like me using his name. I would always be an inmate to him, even though we were both fugitives now, living in the same motel room.

"Your chest hurt?" he asked casually. He shook himself off.

"Yes."

"You still got a lot of skin left."

He flushed the toilet with deliberate precision, staring down into the bowl to watch the mechanism do its work.

"Whatever you do to me, it's not going to make any difference. I don't have what you want."

"You told Carol you did. You swore to her you knew how to get Nando's money."

"I lied."

"You lied to Carol?"

He put the seat down and sat on the toilet, leaning with his elbows on his knees, and studied me. Then he tipped forward, closer to my face.

"I thought you loved her."

"What do you know about love?"

"You'd have to ask Carol that. My impression is she thinks I know a thing or two."

"She's been asleep. She'll wake up eventually."

"Yeah, and the police are going to catch up with us eventually—you, me, and Carol—unless we find our way to that money. Right, Cody? You see that, don't you? You're not so dazzled by love you can't see we have a survival problem here? Food, shelter, *then* love. Right?" he demanded.

"Those are your priorities."

"That's the way it is: survival first."

There are things you can tell people, but they won't hear them, because they can't see what's happening around them. They can't see the predicament closing in around them. I wanted to tell him it didn't matter to me whether I survived or not, if I could take him with me. But I wanted Carol to live. I wanted her to go free.

He stepped back toward the door and switched on the fan. "Move over to the toilet," he told me.

As I shifted position, he passed quickly behind me to stand by the washbasin. I sat with my back jammed against the toilet while Rich washed his hands.

"See, all three of us, we have this one thing in common." He glanced down to see if he had my attention. "I know you and I've had our differences." He waved a towel in a dismissive gesture. "But we have the same basic interest in common. We all want to survive. There's no real conflict, not basically."

He stared at my face to see if he was making any headway, but I stared far off through the opposite wall, and there was nothing for him to read either way. On the other side of the door, I heard Carol stirring in bed, padding over to the dresser, and the burst of a match as she lit her first cigarette. Rich sat down on the side of the tub to bring himself closer to my level.

"Cody, I don't want to hurt you. Why would I want to do that?"

"From where I was, it looked like you could develop a taste for it."

He got up. He had to move. There was room for two and a half paces along the side of the tub. He was full of bluster, selling, explaining, excusing from long practice, almost without having to think about what he was saying. But in the gaps, in pauses in his smooth flow, I saw a hunted look in his eyes.

"You've known me—what, three years? OK, so we're on opposite sides of the fence, in a manner of speaking. Some officers are goons. I'll admit it. Control freaks. Guys who get off on it. But me!" Instinctively, he put his spread fingers to his chest in a stagy gesture of authenticity. "It doesn't come natural. It just ain't my style."

"What were you doing yesterday, then?"

"That's my point!" He leaned forward and thought better of it. "That's what I'm trying to tell you. I did what I had to do. No more than that. No less, because we have to get that money, or we're fucked. But no more than I had to. Right? Wasn't I always fair to you on Medical? Aren't I a fair man?"

He'd started out trying to convince me with his sales pitch, but he'd become the audience. His face was filled with an expression that was simple and earnest.

"You used to be," I told him.

"I'm still the same guy. In or out of uniform. It doesn't make a difference."

"You can look yourself in the eye, after what you did with the iron?"

He glanced aside, without thinking, into the mirror.

277

"I got nothing to hide. I did what I had to do. Soldiers do that stuff every day."

He couldn't resist looking at the three-quarters view of his handsome face. He drew himself up, patted his stomach where it was starting to fill out below his chest, and nodded hello to himself. Then he met his own eyes. He met his image peering into the darkness of himself, in doubt.

"It doesn't mean anything," he said. "A man can do things. It doesn't change what he is. It's just something you do."

"I was watching you."

"That was playacting to make it look good. I can tell you that now, because we're both in this together. It's over, that stuff. I told Carol. I'm not doing it anymore."

"Do you know what I saw in your face, Rich?"

"No, I don't. What did you see in my face, Cody?"

He was composed, gathered into himself with his arms folded over his chest. He stood over me, feet apart.

"You were afraid of what it was doing to you."

"Is that so?"

"Because every second you held that iron on my chest, you were changing. You knew it. You could feel it. You were turning into something, weren't you?"

"I know who I am. You think you can play mind games with me, Cody?"

"You've got a tough decision coming up."

"Oh. You got it all figured out."

"You have to decide what you're going to do with us."

"We're all going to jail, unless you tell us where the money is. It's as simple as that."

"But you're starting to realize, we're not going down that road anymore. It stopped working the way you told Carol it would a long way back. There's no Caribbean vacation for the rest of your life. All it is now is whether you're going to jail, or whether Nando's going to kill you. Nando watches TV. He knows you're trying to steal his money."

"You've screwed it up for all of us, you crazy mother!"

"You've only got one move left, Rich. You've got to decide what you're going to do with me and Carol."

278

There was a noise in the bedroom, and we heard Carol's voice. Rich opened the door a crack. I recognized the manager's voice.

"I want you out!"

Carol was placating him. "All right, all right. We're out of here."

"If you're still here when I come back, I'm calling the police."

Rich closed the door.

"You hear that?" he asked.

"He's not running off to dial 911," I said. "He doesn't want the police around his motel, giving the place a bad name."

"You get the message, though? Sooner or later the police are going to arrest us in some place like this."

"You, maybe," I told him.

It was cool in the bedroom, where the air from the conditioner could circulate. I stretched out on the bed while Carol looked over the burn on my chest. I lay on her side of the bed, I knew, because when I turned my head slightly, I could pick up the scent of her hair on the pillow.

Carol tore open the paper bag of medical items she'd bought at the drugstore down the street. I didn't want to look at my chest. I watched her face as she worked at the cut edge of the T-shirt. The burns had been weeping the previous evening, and during the night the surface had dried to a crust that stuck the cloth to the wound. Carol frowned, turning her head to view the area from different angles, and glanced quickly up to my face to see what I knew.

"I'm going to have to soak it," she told me.

"Well, don't make it too long," Rich said. "We got to get out of here before the old guy gets antsy and calls the police."

"We should take him to a hospital," Carol said.

"And say what? 'Oh, he tripped over and fell on this iron that was lying on the floor?' I don't think so."

"We could take him to a hospital and leave him there."

"The police'd be down there in a minute."

"We'd be long gone."

"Yeah, but he could tell them things about us."

"Like what, that he hasn't already?"

"I'm all right," I said. "I don't need a hospital."

Carol looked at me doubtfully. She rested her hand on my forehead. Her hand was cool. The fingers curved around the side of my forehead and held me, and I felt their pressure as an immense comfort. I felt she had found me. I closed my eyes and gave myself up to the moment.

I think I fell immediately into sleep. But her hand was gone in a few heartbeats, and I was jolted, blinking at the light and confused as though breaking surface back into the present, back to a motel room.

"Well, you don't have a fever, anyway," she said.

"See?" Rich said.

"I have to take the T-shirt off," Carol told me. "It's going to hurt."

"That's all right," I told her.

"Just do what you've got to do," Rich said.

He watched the procedure over her shoulder. When Carol lifted up an edge of the cloth, he grimaced and looked at my face to see what effect it had on me.

"Do it quick," he advised. "It's the only way. Like a Band-Aid. Pick off one corner, then rip the whole thing off in one go."

Carol ignored him, but Rich couldn't let it go. He was fascinated by what he had wrought, repelled and awed.

"Jesus, when I was sixteen I had a sunburn as bad as that! Believe me, I know."

Carol took her time, wetting the shirt with warm water she sprinkled from her fingertips, then gently tugging more of the fabric loose. At every step, she paused to look into my face so that she could gauge how much pain she was causing.

"I'm sorry," she whispered over and over. Her eyes were moist. I'm sure they were. "I'm so sorry."

I didn't know whether she was apologizing for the pain she was causing me then, or in the past. I wondered how much longer we were going to live.

"It's all right," I told her. "It's not your fault. Do what you need to do."

When a corner seemed stuck and she leaned closer to see what was snagging it, a lock of her hair fell loose, and I saw up close her mannerism of hooking the hair behind her ear.

280

"We need to get you some paper clips," I said.

"What?"

"Some paper clips. For your hair."

"Oh, yes."

Finally it was done, and the torn flaps of the T-shirt lay separated. Rich came back to peer over her shoulder, then turned away quickly. He sat in the chair and played moodily with his gun, taking out the clip, squeezing off the rounds into the palm of his hand, then putting them back into the clip.

Carol glanced over her shoulder at the sound, then up to his face. Rich avoided her eyes. He squeezed off the rounds one after the other into his open hand, and each bullet made a monotonous click as it dropped among the others.

"Do you have to do that?" she asked. I'd never heard her speak so sharply to him.

"You want me to do something else with them?"

He smacked the clip into the grip with the heel of his hand. Then he went over to the window and delicately pulled the drape back between finger and thumb to get different views of the parking lot.

Carol watched him for a moment, but she didn't read the signs. She hadn't thought things through far enough to be afraid about what was going to happen. She was ashamed. Without thinking, she put her hand on my arm. She was staring at a point on the pillow beside my head. I saw her draw breath and her lips open to speak, and her eyes came to mine. I waited, never showing my hunger, though I could have sucked the words from her mouth. Then something stern clamped the lips shut. She squeezed my arm, and her fingers lingered there an extra moment before she withdrew again into herself.

Carol smeared some antiseptic cream on my chest, dabbing at a spot here and there, drawing back with her head tilted to one side to regard her work from a certain angle, then reaching forward to touch up some spot that wasn't quite to her liking. She taped a dressing to my chest, then helped me ease into a fresh shirt she'd bought for me that morning.

Rich had already thought out how I could be safely transported. He attached one of the manacles to the framework under the front

281

passenger seat, then he had me get in and clip the other around my right ankle.

It was hot in the car. We drove around aimlessly, it seemed. I found a way to lounge in the backseat so that the leg iron didn't pull on my ankle. In that position, I lined myself up so that I was close enough to Carol for the wind blowing through the window to bring me the scent of her body. At the same time, I had an angle on her side mirror so that I could view the cars behind us.

Rich made a big fuss of checking to see if anyone was following us, leaning almost into the mirror and then announcing, "We're clean." But he didn't do it regularly, and after half an hour of this, he forgot to check at all.

Surveillance is something you don't notice unless you watch continuously. And you have to have a good memory. All taxicabs look the same, until you really take the trouble to look at them. Rich didn't bother.

Lounging in the backseat, with the wind blowing through my hair, I watched a black Chevrolet maintain its position two cars back. I wasn't sure at first whether it was following us, because we stayed on main roads and it could have been going in the same general direction we were, if we'd had a destination. But when Rich went through a yellow light and I saw the cab whip out from behind a pickup truck and surge through on red, I knew we were being followed. He hung back, just out of view behind another vehicle, and I couldn't get a look at the driver.

"Do you know where we're going?" Carol asked, after Rich had made what seemed like another turn on nothing more than impulse.

"Can't you see I'm thinking!" he said.

He hit the top of the steering wheel with the flat of his hand and went clear through a red light without noticing.

"You just ran a red light," I told him.

"You shut the fuck up!" he said, glaring into the mirror.

I looked away indifferently out the window. Rich's plans were falling apart. Mine were falling into place. The cab waited on the white line, in clear view at last, for the light to change. There was only one person sitting up front, the same woman who'd followed

282

Rich to the parking lot and waited while he'd had his rendezvous with Carol in Dunkin' Donuts.

"We've got to have a plan," Carol said. "Otherwise, we're just going to run out of gas."

"I *know* that! What do you think I'm doing?"

"Rich can't decide whether he's better off without us," I said.

"Shut up!" he yelled into the mirror.

"Or what?" I said. "What's he going to do?" I whispered, to taunt him.

He made a right turn, then a left, abruptly, randomly, then turned again in a pattern that seemed increasingly desperate. Finally, he must have come to some kind of decision. He began to make turns as though he really knew where he was going, and in a few minutes we drove along a narrow causeway with water on either side and the ocean farther out, beyond the bay.

"You're right," Rich said. "We can't go around, the three of us, forever, two guys and a woman."

"Why not?" Carol asked. I liked the coldness of her manner toward him.

"I don't know. A man and a woman up front. Another guy sitting in the back. It doesn't look natural."

"Maybe he's my brother."

"It's the kind of thing, if you have to explain it, it's already too late."

"So what are you saying we do?" Carol asked.

I heard resistance in her voice. I wondered if she thought he was going to turn me loose, or whether she was starting to catch on to what Rich was screwing himself up to do.

We went through a gateway into a park. Rich drove slowly, looking for something. The cab stopped at the hot dog stand at the park entrance and didn't follow us in. That left me and Carol alone with Rich at a moment when I needed the situation to become suddenly complicated for him.

Rich put his hand on Carol's knee. "Babe, we got to talk, you and me."

"Sure, Rich," she said uneasily.

There were people about. Not many, because it was a weekday, but enough to make it likely someone would hear a gunshot. I wondered if there was any chance the driver of the cab had followed us into the park on foot.

The road was empty when Rich suddenly veered off into a gap between the trees. We stopped twenty feet into the forest. Rich turned in his seat with his gun drawn.

"Let's make this fast," he snapped. "Put your hands out."

He had the cuffs on me in an instant. Something came in the air at my face, and I clutched at it instinctively at the same moment that I knew it was the key to the leg irons. I bent down and unlocked the manacle around my ankle.

"Quick!" he said.

By the time I straightened up, Rich was already standing outside the car. He held open the passenger door so that he could see my hands, then backed off a couple of paces.

"Out."

He'd crouched to peer out to the road, quickly checking back to me. The gun stayed on me.

Then Carol was shifting across the front seat.

"No!" she cried.

She grabbed his left arm and tried to pull him back into the car.

"Please, Rich!"

She shook his arm. He shrugged her off, but he had to take a step back to keep his balance, and I stepped out of the car. He pulled back the slide, and I saw him tense around the gun, and I know he wanted to shoot me. But he couldn't pull the trigger. Carol grabbed him again, coming at him from the side. He turned to her, wild-eyed, then back to me.

"Let go of me!" he said in a strangled voice.

He tried to shake himself loose from her, but she clung to him.

"Don't kill him, Rich. Please! Don't!"

I risked another step when he glanced at Carol, but he saw the movement. He almost lifted Carol off the ground to bring up his left hand to shake her loose.

"Stay put!" he ordered me.

He looked scared half out of his wits, and I knew that at that moment, if he had to save himself, he'd pull the trigger. Carol had an arm around his neck, and in a few seconds she'd tighten her grip enough to cut off his breathing.

"Don't! I won't let you do it!" she cried.

He watched me all the time, even as he staggered and struggled to break Carol's grip about his throat. He lurched suddenly to one side as Carol's foot caught between his legs and tripped him. I saw in his face a look of astonishment and the clear realization that he was going over. He toppled, but even as he went down, the gun wavered only for a moment from my chest.

I was already coming at him. He fell ruthlessly, his eyes and the gun on me the only priority, and when he hit, he landed heavily on top of Carol and knocked the wind out of her. At the moment I committed myself in a lunge at him, he rolled away and came up on one knee, all in one smooth motion. I was off balance, with all my weight going forward, and he checked me, the point of his shoulder slamming into the burn on my chest.

I was dazed by the pain. I lay on my back, but Rich took hold of the chain between the cuffs and hauled me to my knees.

"Move!"

His blood was up. If he couldn't bring himself to shoot me before, he could now. I saw it in his eyes. But he let the moment pass. He half-dragged me to the car and pushed me against the side. When I turned to look for Carol, he slammed my head against the side of the door. Carol was still on the ground. She turned and moaned and kept her knees up to her stomach.

"What the fuck were you trying to do?" he spat at her. "All I was going to do was put him in the trunk so we could talk!"

"Oh, God!" Carol moaned. I don't think she heard what he said.

"You almost got us all killed."

He took hold of a handful of hair at the back of my head and hauled me around to the back of the car. Then he unlocked the trunk and gave the lid a push so that it swung up. He stood behind and to one side while I unloaded the two duffel bags and the plastic bags of dirty clothes.

"Everything," he said.

Carol was on her feet. Rich kept track of her as she walked slowly around the front of the car. She held herself tightly with her arms crossed over her stomach and didn't look at us. I reached in deep for a set of jump-starter cables, a brush, a plastic folding seat, and a child's stuffed rabbit.

"Give me that," he said.

Some people went by in a car. If they noticed us among the trees, they must have thought we were unpacking for a picnic.

"You want me to get in there?" I asked him.

"Oh, no," he said. "I'm not stupid."

Watching me with that alert, vacant stare people have when they do something difficult with their hands without looking, he reached under the mat, into the well that held the spare tire, and extracted the tire iron.

"I reckon you won't be needing this."

He hefted the black metal bar in his hand, testing its weight. I kept my face turned to him all the time, because I didn't want to offer him the back of my head. He was pale and strung taut. He wanted to hit me with the tire iron, but he was afraid what he might do if he let himself go. I watched him look at my face, and I saw in his eyes what the metal would do to my forehead, or the side of the head above the ear, or the cheek and nose. Carol had changed the balance, and now he couldn't find his way back to the point of decision. He heaved the iron backhand, and I heard it crash through the trees.

"Now get in."

As soon as I drew in my legs and rolled over on my back, he slammed the trunk shut. I could hear them arguing. Rich wanted to walk a short distance so they'd be out of earshot, but Carol didn't trust him. She didn't know what other plans he might have. The rules were changing in unknown ways. Maybe she was starting to wonder what value she had.

"He could suffocate!" she said loudly.

"Never mind him! What were you trying to do?"

"What were you going to do?"

"I was taking him out. I was going to have him kneel down in behind those trees with the cuffs on, execution-style. Stand behind him. Put the gun to his head. Make him think it was his last chance. Scare him a bit—that's all."

"You were going to shoot him!"

286

Rich didn't say anything.

"Were you?"

"Carol, sooner or later we're going to have to do something."

"We've got to stop this, Rich. It's getting out of control. Look what it's doing to you!"

He wanted her to move away from the car so I wouldn't hear.

"Leave him," he said.

"I don't want to leave him."

"This is Cody's bullshit!"

"No, this is me. I don't know who you are anymore. I don't recognize you."

"You let him mess with your head."

"Don't be ridiculous."

"I should never have left you together."

"Nothing happened," she said wearily.

"I only have your word for that."

"That's all you need, isn't it?"

Neither of them spoke for a while, and I sensed the struggle of wills.

"Well, isn't it?" Carol insisted.

"Why do I get the feeling there's something you want to tell me?"

"There's nothing!"

"Then why is he so full of himself?"

There was a pause I had no way of understanding.

Then Carol said, "He's playing with you, that's all."

I heard Rich let out a long "Oh, God!" from a different spot, and I thought he must be pacing back and forth beside the car. "Have you thought what it's like for me?" he asked. "Knowing the two of you were together all that time? Who knows, maybe some of what he said in those letters was true?"

I waited for Carol to reply. We both did. Everything, the entire meaning, lay in her hesitation.

"You know that isn't so," she said at last.

She spoke more softly, as if closer to him. I struggled in the darkness, turning my shoulders painfully in the confined space to bring my ear closer to the sound. She murmured something. I strained to hear.

I heard Rich say, "Yeah. I know, babe."

"You've got to promise you won't do anything to him."

"We've got to go the other route now. Plan B."

When Carol didn't say anything, he said, "Well, we got to get going."

"Where?"

"You know where. Your mother's. It's the only place left."

"There's got to be somewhere else."

"It's just to get us back on track," Rich said. "Cody was there for days. If they'd traced her, they'd have picked him up."

"I don't know what I'm going to say to her."

"Come on—it'll only be for a couple of days. We'll make our best deal. Then we're out of state. West, maybe."

"Not the Caribbean?"

"Not straight off," he said uneasily.

"It doesn't matter."

She paused to gather herself, as if conviction came trickling slowly and she had to wait until she had enough to fill the smallness of her feelings. I waited for the rest of the corny line.

"As long as we're together," she said.

It seemed that we drove for a long time, but perhaps that was because I had a fever that made me thirsty. My pain was centered at the point where Rich had blocked me with the point of his shoulder, and any movement was agony. I tried to brace myself, lying on my back with a hand pressed hard against the lid of the trunk, against the threat of movement, but the sway of every turn and stop was exaggerated, and however strongly I tried to contain it, at the last moment the force would often break my grip, and I'd be shifted and jarred in ways that started the throbbing again.

Carol and Rich talked occasionally, but the muffler was bad and I couldn't make out the words. Most of the time Carol searched restlessly through the radio band, changing stations every few minutes as she had when she and I had first started out.

As time passed, I wondered if I'd get so sick that Rich would have to dump me somewhere and leave me to take my chances, but I didn't think he'd do that. I was the only thing of value he had left; and I was of value only to Nando.

We stopped once, almost at the end of our journey, and Carol

288

got out. Then we drove on for a short time. I thought maybe Rich had dropped her off to prepare the way with Debbie, but all the same, I was afraid to be alone with him without Carol. I wondered if I'd misjudged the situation and that he was, after all, taking me for a ride from which I wouldn't return.

But he only drove around the block a couple of times. We made a slow turn and bounced off the road into a driveway, then waited while a door or gate was opened. We maneuvered slowly into a confined space and came to a stop. I heard Carol's voice and knew I was safe.

"It's all right," she told Rich. "But we can only stay two nights."

"That's enough."

"She's in a rotten mood. I was lucky to get that."

"We'll be out of here tomorrow."

"I told her we'd just got married."

"She thinks I'm a social worker."

"She won't remember. She mixes me up with my sister most of the time."

"I don't know. She got a pretty good look at me."

"You'll look familiar, that's all. You can tell her she met you when I brought you over at Christmas."

"Who's he, then?"

They were quiet, considering this question.

Rich opened the trunk. The air was hot and close. In the gloom, I recognized the bicycle hanging on the wall and I smelled the familiar, musty odor of Debbie's garage.

I tried to sit up, but my balance was off. Rich stood by the side of the car. I think the fever was disorienting me. Even if I'd been in perfect shape, I couldn't have surprised him. He looked down at me with professional interest, evaluating me as a threat to his security.

"Not a pretty picture," he said, shaking his head.

Carol came forward, but he held out his arm to stop her.

"Let me check him out first," he said. "He's tricky."

"You can't fake the way he looks," Carol said, and brushed his arm aside.

I was dizzy and had to support myself with one arm over the

side of the car. She touched my cheek with the inside of her wrist, and I saw a look of concern pass over her face.

"He's hot," she said. "We'd better get him inside."

Rich put the handcuffs on anyway. It was agony climbing out of the trunk. The pain made me feel weaker than I really was. Rich had to help me step down. He put a shirt over my wrists to hide the cuffs.

"That's not going to work," Carol told him. "You're going to have to take those off."

Rich didn't like it. He studied me. He narrowed his eyes and blew out his cheeks.

"OK," he said finally.

Without warning, he reached out and pushed me on the shoulder to test how weak I really was. I staggered back against the car and almost fell over.

"All right," he said. He seemed satisfied. "We'll put them back on when we get him up to his room."

"She wants us to wait," Carol said. "Ten minutes. She wants to fix herself up first."

"Who is he going to be?" Rich asked.

"I'm who I was before," I said. "Don't worry about me."

Rich looked to Carol. She shrugged. "He's only been gone a day. She probably never noticed he left."

"If you just got married," I told Rich, "she'll need a ring."

They looked at each other, waiting for the other to speak first. I saw how they balked at the tie to one another, even if it was fake.

"If you just got married, that's something Debbie's going to want to see," I said. "It's her kind of thing."

Perhaps, in the gloom of the garage, each caught a glimpse of what a life shackled to the other would be like.

"Don't you have something you can put on?" Rich asked her.

Carol shook her head.

"It could be anything."

"She could wear yours," I said.

He looked at his hand as if that was the only way he could understand what I was talking about.

"No, I don't think so," Carol said. She shook her head as Rich squeezed the ring off his finger. "I don't want to."

"It's only temporary," Rich said. "Just for a couple of days." He held out the plain gold ring to her in the palm of his hand. "If that's what it takes."

She shook her head and mouthed, "No," silently.

Rich flared suddenly in anger. He'd kept back his emotion while he squeezed the ring off his finger, and now he let it go.

"Here!" He shoved the ring at her. "You got us into this!"

"I never wanted to come here."

"You were the one told her we were married."

"I thought it would make it easier. She's always on me about it."

"The least you can do is wear it."

We went along the walkway from the garage and entered the house by the back door. Carol held the hand with the ring away from her body as she walked. She took us through the kitchen to the hall, and we stopped there and stood about uncertainly by the door to the living room. She became more and more uneasy as we came closer to her mother. Gypsy padded silently to me along the sides of walls, wagging his tail. He inhaled delicately at Carol's ankles and looked up at her face, but didn't seem to recognize her.

Debbie wore pink. She had composed a still life in which she stood beside her recliner chair with a hand casually resting on its back to steady herself. She smiled graciously and inclined her head in welcome as we came into view. Her lipstick was applied slightly off center, so that from several feet away she looked as though she had a thick lip from someone punching her on the side of the mouth.

"Mom, you remember Rich," Carol said, stepping forward awkwardly.

"Why, yes, of course," Debbie said. She held out her hand, palm down, for Rich to take. "You handsome devil! How could I ever forget you?"

"Nice to see you again," Rich said. I think he wondered if he was meant to kiss her hand.

"You know, I feel so badly," Debbie was telling him, not letting

291

go. "You know I would have come to the wedding if I could have? You know that, don't you?" She shook his hand for emphasis. "But I couldn't, you see, on account of my hip. You understand, don't you?" She pointed at his face, teasing, flirtatious. "I can see you understand."

"It was only a small wedding," Rich responded gallantly. "Just family and immediate friends, that's all."

"But I'm family!" she said, letting go of his hand abruptly. "I still am, aren't I?" she asked Carol softly, with exaggerated mouth movement, as if Rich and I couldn't really hear their conversation.

"Of course you are! Always."

Debbie patted Carol's cheek absentmindedly, turning away already.

"They want to put me in a nursing home," she told Rich in a stage whisper, "so they can get their hands on my money." Her eyes passed over me, triggered a recognition, and came back to my face.

Rich chuckled uneasily.

"Oh, yes!" she said, in case he wasn't taking her seriously enough.

"This is my daughter and son-in-law," she told me, "come to stay for a few days."

"Very nice," I said.

"Perhaps you would bring in their luggage from the car?" she suggested.

She looked at me closely. The social context was throwing her off. For a moment she looked into my face with a puzzled frown, but it led nowhere, and she was quickly distracted by something else she noticed there.

"What happened to you?" she asked.

"He looks a bit poorly," Carol said. "Maybe he should lie down."

"She's a nurse," Debbie said. "My daughter."

She was looking around to see where she'd placed her drink. Rich came around quickly behind her and held it out.

"There you go!" he said, smiling into her eyes.

They recognized each other immediately: He was the man with the ability to charm, and she was susceptible.

292

"Maybe," Carol said, "Dan should lie down before dinner."

"Off you go, then," Debbie said, with a flutter of her hand.

Rich stood indecisively. Debbie stole his arm and looked slyly to Carol.

"As long as you don't mind leaving me alone with this gorgeous thing!"

"I should help," Rich told Debbie weakly. "We don't want Dan falling down the stairs or anything."

Debbie held him tight. "Now, he doesn't look to me to be quite that badly off."

"I can manage him," Carol told Rich.

"I'll be all right," I told him.

Carol led me to the top of the house, to a small, out-of-the-way room under the eaves. I lay on the bed for a while and tried to see how the intersecting planes of the ceiling might represent the converging destinies of different people, all coming together at a single line at the apex.

The air was hot and used. We needed rain. I got up carefully from the bed and opened the window to get some fresh air into the room. I brought a chair over to the window and leaned on my arms on the sill. A faint breeze moved the leaves of a maple outside. On the short stretch of street that was visible, I watched as a teenaged boy came by on a bicycle that was too small for him and threw newspapers onto front porches. A green Volvo station wagon drew up to the sidewalk a few doors down and waited; the rear door opened and a small girl dressed for dancing class ran down the driveway and climbed in. A German shepherd slunk along by the fence on the opposite side and turned suddenly to sniff at one particular spot he had almost passed by. And on this quiet suburban street a cab cruised by slowly, twice in fifteen minutes.

I lay down on the bed and must have fallen asleep, because the next thing I remember was being woken by the movement of the bed as Carol sat down beside me.

"Take these," she said. Two dangerous-looking capsules lay in the palm of her hand. "It's an antibiotic I found in my mom's medicine closet."

I put them in my mouth and swallowed them with some water from the glass she handed me.

She put her hand to my forehead to feel the fever and held it there longer than she needed to and let her fingers drift down the side of my face. She weakened me with her tenderness. My eyes began to close as the pleasure stole over me like sleep. Like opium. I covered her hand with my own at the moment I sensed she would have taken it away.

"Don't," she said, without force.

Sometimes love needs a physical medium to convey it from one heart to another. I kept her fingertips to my cheek, prolonging the moment that was all the more precious because she could reclaim her hand with the slightest impulse of will. She took her hand away.

"You've got to put me out of your mind," she said.

"I can't. Even if I wanted to, I couldn't do it."

"You've got to save yourself now."

"Is that what you're thinking about?"

"You frighten me when you look at me like that."

"Why? It shouldn't frighten you."

"It's too strong."

"How can it be too strong? How can it be too anything?"

"When you look at me like that, I'm afraid you don't know who I really am."

"Yes!"

"I'm afraid you'll wake up and really see me . . . and then what?"

"I know you," I told her. I wanted her to hear the certainty in my voice. "You don't know how well I know you."

She sighed and looked away. "I'm glad someone does."

"You don't even know yourself, half the time," I told her.

"Look. You have to go before something bad happens."

"Not yet. I'm not ready yet."

"This is your last chance. Do you know what Rich is going to do?"

"Rich wants to sell me to Nando."

She was surprised I knew.

"It's obvious, isn't it?" I said. "There's nothing else he can do."

"You know Nando. You know what Nando'll do."

"No one knows what Nando'll do."

"You know the kind of thing, though."

"It's not going to happen."

"You have to take off now, while you can. You can go down the back stairs. Take Debbie's car. I got the keys for you."

"Where will that get me?"

"Here. I saved this. Rich doesn't know about it."

She wanted to give me a thin roll of banknotes, but I wouldn't take them. She looked around for a pocket to tuck them into and finally squeezed them into my jeans.

"There isn't much time," she said. "You've got to get going."

"I know. They know we're here."

"Who do? The police?"

"No, not the police. Nando."

"Don't do this!"

"You didn't see the cab that followed us from the motel?"

"Rich was watching. If we were being followed, he'd have seen it."

"They've been following Rich for days, waiting for him to lead them to you, then to me. You didn't see them outside the park when we came out? A woman driving, and Nando sitting in the back like a passenger?"

"You were in the trunk. You couldn't see anything."

"You should come with me. I can look after you."

"No one knows we're here. That's the only way Rich is going to make a deal."

"You and I could make it, if we slipped out the back in Debbie's car."

"I don't know."

"They're here already! You think I'm making this up to get you to come with me?"

"No, I think you believe it."

"You think I'm paranoid!"

"You're thinking like you're still in Denning. You've forgotten what it's like. There're lots of taxicabs. They go by all the time. It doesn't mean anything."

I lay back on the bed and stared at the intersecting planes of the ceiling.

I asked her, "If I told you where the money was, would you come with me?"

Carol looked down at me for a long time. She looked down into me as if she was staring into a deep pool, trying to see past the pieces of her own reflection that shimmered and danced apart and magically joined again. I tried to make myself transparent to her, but still she couldn't see.

She said, "You don't know where the money is," as if that was a way to close off a hope she'd already resigned herself to living without.

We heard a creak halfway up the staircase. Then there was the sound of normal footfalls as Rich gave up any attempt at stealth and climbed the rest of the way up the stairs.

He came into the bedroom without knocking, but Carol had already got up from the bed.

"Your mom is something," he said, shaking his head in disbelief. "She's driving me crazy."

He reached in his back pocket for the handcuffs, then unhooked the bunch of keys from the clip on his belt to unlock them.

"We don't need those," Carol said.

"Says who?" He came toward me.

"Take a look at him," she said. "Where's he going to go?"

Rich looked me over, measuring my strength. He nodded his head as though he was still making up his mind. I saw myself becoming merchandise. He rubbed his hands together, fingers pointing vertically to the ceiling, while he swayed back and forth like an athlete warming up. The bustle, the forward motion, the easy self-assurance were coming back. Rich had plans.

"You feel as shitty as you look?" he asked.

"Pretty much."

"She looking after you all right?"

He took hold of Carol's arm in a proprietary way, to show me it didn't matter to him one way or another what we'd been talking about together.

"She's a good nurse," I said, looking at Carol only.

"Yeah, you said it."

He had an arm around her shoulder, and he leaned in with his lips straining to kiss her. But they weren't in the same context.

Carol was looking at me, and he caught her off guard, so that without thinking she wriggled her shoulders and tried to pull away, saying, "Rich!" drawing the word out in protest.

He let her go. For a moment he was troubled.

"Don't," she said quietly, though by then he wasn't near her. "Not in front of people."

"You hear that?" he asked me, grinning as if he and Carol were newlyweds. "What you are now, Cody?"

I nodded. I saw him weakening before my eyes.

"People!" he said.

I thought maybe Debbie had given him a drink and he'd put it away too quickly on an empty stomach. I smiled back at him. I wasn't used to it, and the movement of my lips felt strange and difficult to carry out.

I watched the gap widening between Rich and Carol. Carol saw it. She looked frightened. The world beneath her feet was breaking up like an ice floe.

"Your mother said something about making supper," Rich said. "I don't know, though. The way she was going about it, maybe she should stick with liquids."

"I can cook," I said. "I don't mind doing it."

"You always have to have an angle, don't you, Cody?" Rich said. "Nothing's ever straightforward with you."

"You should stay up here and rest," Carol said. "You didn't listen to what I told you." Her eyes were telling me to escape, but I ignored their message.

The kitchen was a shambles. Debbie wandered around with a glass of orange juice in her hand. When Carol opened the refrigerator, she tripped quickly around the table and leaned her hand against the door so that Carol had to step back, out of its way, as it swung shut.

"Out. Out. Out!" Debbie sang, and Carol sighed as if this was a piece of theater that had been repeated many times before.

"I thought it would be easier . . ." she began.

"This is my kitchen," Debbie declared, walking away. She found a metal spatula, which she flourished to accompany her speech. "I am the mistress in my own kitchen, thank you very much!"

Debbie had eyes for Rich, who lounged against the corner of the counter, keeping tabs on everything that passed between us.

"This one looks like he could boil an egg," Debbie said. "What do you say?"

Her fingers danced lightly on Rich's shoulder. As she walked behind him, she let her hand trail down along the curve of his back, and he had to pull away to prevent her from encountering the gun stuck in his waistband.

"Ooh, jumpy!" she said playfully.

I saw Carol look away. She stood uncertainly in the doorway, at the margin. I opened the refrigerator, and Debbie turned her attention to me. She sidled around the counter to see what I might try to reach for inside.

"I'll make a salad, maybe," Carol said to no one in particular. She seemed adrift, lost.

"And what's your specialty?" Debbie asked me coldly.

I saw a pack of gray hamburger alone on the wire shelf. "I do a good meat loaf," I suggested.

"You've got some tomatoes," Carol said. She crouched so that she could see between us into the bottom of the refrigerator.

"There isn't room for everyone," Debbie said impatiently, waving her away.

"I do meatballs," Rich said, from behind us.

Debbie turned away from the fridge to regard him. "Now that appeals to me no end," she said.

Carol tossed the pack of hamburger over Debbie's shoulder. We watched it spin in the air, suspended for a moment.

Rich leaned nonchalantly against the end of the counter, rehearsing in his mind the bargain he'd force on Nando, and the package caught him off guard. He had to come alive all at once to get his fingers to it before it knocked over a plant.

"Hey!" Debbie protested. She ducked her head, long after it had gone by.

"I'll slice the tomatoes," I told her, moving back to the counter where the cutting board was.

Rich came off the counter to make room so that I wouldn't pass behind him. Carol put two tomatoes in the air in quick succession, and I caught them and set them down one by one on the board.

298

Before Rich had a chance to say anything about it, I'd pulled the biggest, thickest-bladed knife out of the block.

"Knock it off!" Debbie cried.

"You're next," Carol told her.

"Oh, no, I'm not!"

"What's your contribution going to be?"

"I'm not playing your games. I'm not doing it. And that's that."

"What about some Perrier?" Carol dangled the bottle dangerously between finger and thumb. "Isn't that what they use in the best restaurants to cook their vegetables in?"

"I don't get to the store as easily as I used to," Debbie said uneasily. Her eyes never left the bottle. "That's all I have in the house."

The doorbell rang.

The three of them froze in position. Gypsy got up and padded to the front door.

"Who could that be?" Debbie asked in annoyance.

Rich looked questioningly at Carol. She looked scared. She glanced at me and away quickly, denying the possibility.

I tested the knife on the tense skin of the tomato. I moved the edge slowly forward, and with no more than the slightest pressure, it sliced down to the core. When I drew the knife back the tomato fell apart neatly.

"Well, couldn't one of you go see who it is?" Debbie asked plaintively. "I don't like them to know there's a woman living here alone."

Rich scratched his back, feeling for the reassurance of the gun. He looked to Carol, tilting his head in the direction of the door. "You want to get it?" He nodded, as if he was coaching her.

She looked to me, and I knew if she'd been able, she'd have told me that our gun was in the shoulder bag on the seat next to the table.

Abruptly, she started for the hall and made for the front door, as if everything had to be done very quickly now.

"Wait!" Rich said, to slow her.

He ran almost silently, crossing behind her, to the parlor, and positioned himself in the back among the shadows, at a point where he could make the angle through the window to see who was standing at the front door.

The front doors had panels of frosted glass, and we saw a gray shape that turned sideways impatiently, then leaned forward, looming but never achieving definition, to ring the bell again.

"What?" Rich asked from the parlor, disbelieving, bending and twisting for a better look.

Then he straightened up and let out a guffaw. He blew air out between his lips in a soft whistle of relief.

"It's a fucking pizza delivery!"

"Watch your language!" Debbie said, emphasizing each word. She held the Perrier bottle securely in her hands.

"Sorry," he said, turning to her and noticing me for the first time.

I stood with my hand on an armchair, no more than five feet from him. He looked for my other hand to see if I'd brought the knife, then lost interest—as far as he was concerned, I'd missed my opportunity. He strolled toward the hall, easy and full of confidence again, adjusting the gun in the back of his waistband, so that he brushed me with his elbow as he passed. It didn't matter that I was there. It went to show how he controlled the situation, that he could touch me, but I couldn't get closer than five feet to him.

"Open the door," he told Carol. He was grinning. The fear, the gun he'd held in his hand, were all part of a big joke.

She looked worried still. "Are you sure?" she whispered.

"Sure!"

Rich strode up to the door and pulled it open. On the threshold stood a nervous girl of about nineteen in the pale blue, white, and red uniform of Domino's Pizza. In her hands she held a large pizza box, which she offered to Rich.

"Large peppers and sausage with extra cheese?" she asked.

"You got it," he said, reaching for the box.

"We didn't order any pizza," Carol said.

The girl looked from Rich to Carol apologetically. "It's already paid for," she said, with a rising inflection, as if she was asking a question.

"It's OK," Rich said. "I took care of it."

"Maybe you've got the wrong address," Carol said.

300

"It's paid for already," Rich said, smiling and impatient. "Didn't I say it's all taken care of?"

He opened the box an inch and put his nose to the crack to sniff at the pizza.

The girl peered over his shoulder to check the number on the door.

"This is right," she said.

"Who paid for it?" Carol wanted to know.

"A secret benefactor," Rich said as he turned away from the girl, murmuring, "Drop it," to Carol.

"I wasn't there when she came in to place the order."

The girl stood awkwardly, with her weight on one foot, then the other, trying to remind Carol she hadn't been tipped.

"So it was a lady who paid for the pizza?" Carol asked her.

"I guess," the girl said, anxious to go. "I don't know. I wasn't there."

I stayed out of sight of the people who'd seen Rich and Carol drive into the garage, and who'd now seen Rich and Carol come to the door, but who hadn't seen me alive since we entered the park.

Rich closed the door. He balanced the pizza box in one hand as he locked the door and withdrew the key. Then, holding the pizza high on fingertips, he paced ceremoniously to the kitchen.

"Go now!" Carol whispered. "Please!"

There was laughter coming from the kitchen, and we heard the voices of Rich and Debbie fooling with each other. Carol hesitated.

"Doesn't this prove what I told you?" I asked her.

"It doesn't prove anything," she said, without conviction.

I took her face between my hands and held her like a precious liquid that might run between my fingers and be lost forever. I felt myself very close to the end. But everything that had gone before was made worthwhile by this moment. At last, she raised her eyes to me. There is a point of hope, infinitely close to belief, that is like physical pain.

"It doesn't mean anything," she said. She turned aside, taking herself back from me. "It's a mistake. It happens all the time."

"I'm going to get us the money," I told her.

301

"Hey!" Rich leaned out into the hall, hanging by one hand from the doorjamb. "We're serving up!"

No one seemed to want to sit at the table to eat. Debbie leaned against the counter and nibbled absentmindedly at the corners of a slice of pizza while she cradled the half-empty Perrier bottle in the crook of her other arm. Rich paced. He held the slice of pizza away from him and came at it from below like a shark to tear off the softest, most laden part at the center. He walked and made appreciative noises as he chewed. Carol didn't eat. She leaned moodily against the wall by the telephone.

"Well." Rich had to stop to swallow what was in his mouth. "For those that went without so we could eat, we give thanks, O Lord."

"Kind of late for grace," Debbie said. "Now we've mostly eaten it."

Rich wanted to say something, but his mouth was full, and by the time he'd emptied it again, Debbie had lost interest and was picking pieces of sausage off the pizza and dropping them vertically in the direction of Gypsy's mouth.

"I wonder," he began, swallowing, addressing Debbie with a new formality. "Would it be all right with you if I was to use your telephone to call my mother? She hasn't been right lately, and I wanted to check up on her."

"Long distance?" Debbie asked suspiciously.

"No. Oh, no. Local call."

"Where does she live, then?"

"My mother? Andover."

"All right," she said reluctantly. "But don't go giving out this number, because it's unlisted."

Rich wasn't paying attention to her. He seemed to be readying himself for combat. He took a deep breath and squared his shoulders and let it out again. He flashed Carol a smile, hasty and anxious.

"Thanks," he told Debbie, as an afterthought.

He went to the doorway and turned back to us indecisively, half in the room and half in the hallway. Debbie studied him carefully. I picked the last remnants of cheese and sauce from the crust of a piece of pizza.

"You'll keep an eye on things till I get back?" he asked Carol uneasily.

"Sure," she said, unsmiling.

"Keep an eye on what?" Debbie asked. "Where is he going?"

On the other side of the hall, Rich apologetically closed the door to the den.

"He wants to make a private call, I guess," Carol said.

"You know what it's like," I said, "when you're newly married."

Carol crossed to the telephone on the wall. She lifted the receiver off the hook and cupped the mouthpiece with both hands.

"Is he two-timing her?" Debbie asked me.

Carol stared at me from far off, listening and looking in an unfocused, all-encompassing way.

"If you're going to go, go now," she told me.

"I'm staying with you," I said.

"I can't look out for you!" she said angrily. "I can't save you!"

She was going to say more, but her body straightened and tensed as she became aware that Rich had picked up the receiver in the other room.

I read the dial tone in her vacant sideways gaze. Her hands were clasped tight around the mouthpiece. Then her eyes came quickly into focus and turned to me as the call was answered. I watched her eyes move back and forth as she followed the conversation and figured its implications.

Debbie got a container of orange juice from the refrigerator, filled her glass half full from the Perrier bottle, then topped it up with juice.

"They always have something on the side," she murmured to me, as if the idea was so beyond dispute that it was hardly worth saying aloud. She stirred the mixture then took a swallow from the glass. "Especially if they're at all good-looking. Like this one is. Some of the others weren't."

Carol replaced the telephone. "They're going to call Nando," she said, "and he'll call us."

Rich strode back into the kitchen. He was suppressing a grin, but he couldn't resist giving Carol a discreet "just right" sign with finger and thumb. He helped himself to a fresh slice and leaned against the counter to eat it.

"You think you're eating someone else's pizza?" I asked him.

"A gift of the gods!" He was eerily confident. "We're on a winning streak, I can feel it!"

He tossed Gypsy a piece of sausage and watched him snap it out of the air. Then he caught me glancing at the clock.

"Ah. It's almost time," he said. "It's almost time for my favorite TV show."

"You wouldn't like it, Mom," Carol said quickly.

"How do you know?" Debbie protested. "If he likes it, I rather think I will, too."

"It depends," Rich said. "Sometimes it's violent."

Debbie looked doubtful. "Oh, I don't know about that."

"Sometimes it's very violent," he said, already on his way to the den. "I'll check it out first. I'll let you know."

We heard the signature music for your show, Sandy. Then Rich came back and put his head around the kitchen door.

"It's going to be very violent, I can tell," he told Debbie.

He jerked his head for Carol to follow him, but she didn't make a move to go. Debbie studied him carefully. She turned around to see if there were signals being passed behind her back. I chewed on the remnants of cheese and sauce at the edge of a crust.

We could hear your voice, Sandy, but not the words. I picked at the pizza and wondered how much of my letter about Debbie and Gypsy you'd read. Tame stuff, mostly. But important as an insurance policy in case Carol or Rich hadn't figured out where I was. Then there was Diego's story. I was sure you'd read that part. I thought of Nando in a motel room nearby, or slouched in the back of a cab with a portable TV on his lap, and wondered how he'd react when he heard what Diego had said about Vera. He wouldn't believe it, of course. You don't believe something like that until you see it with your own eyes. Not even then. You have to be ready to see. But perhaps your show that evening made Nando a shade more vulnerable to my plans.

"There is no fucking bank account!" Rich burst into the kitchen. "It's all in a safe deposit box! All we need's the key. He's had it all the time."

He looked from one to the other of us, but no one said anything. We must have seemed like zombies to him. He threw his head back and let out a great guffaw.

"You don't get it," he said. He pointed behind him, to Debbie's sitting room. "You didn't hear what she said. Sandy read the letter. It was all there. The whole thing. They had a safe deposit box, and every six months they went out there and put more cash in it. It's beautiful! All we need—"

"—Is the key," I interrupted, "and Vera's signature. And a plane ticket to the Caicos Islands."

He came over to the chair where I was sitting. He put a hand over my shoulder, to the back of the chair. He waited, poised, as if the question were a dive from the high board that could, if executed perfectly, penetrate me without a splash, without any impedance.

"You know where that key is, don't you?"

"Yes," I said.

He straightened up slowly, staring down at me wonderingly as he moved farther away. "It doesn't matter," he said. "It doesn't matter whether you do or you don't. That's Nando's problem."

The telephone rang. I couldn't take my eyes off him. He was like an insect trapped in amber that you can turn and view any way you choose, a moment arrested for a million years that you can turn in your hand. It rang a second time, and I watched him turn to Carol with a triumphant grin.

"Well, isn't anyone going to answer it?" Debbie asked.

Rich held up his hand. "Wait."

He strode over to the telephone as it rang again. He stood with his hand hovering above it and let it ring once more before he snatched it up.

"Yeah, what's up?" he asked, then stiffened when he recognized Nando's voice. "Of course he is." He turned to me. "He's fine. Just fine. Yeah, you can, if you want." He seemed reluctant. "But what for? What's the point?" He held the phone away from him and shook his head, then brought it back to his ear. "Listen," he said forcefully. "If you want to see that key, you deal with me. You got that? You hear me, Nando?" He listened for a few seconds. "All right. If that's what you need, I'll put him on. Just so you

305

and I understand one another." He kept hold of the phone so that we could both hear Nando.

"I want this out in the open," I said, "in a public place. You get the key. Carol goes free. And I go free once you have the key."

"Hey, this is my deal!" Rich said. He snatched the phone away. "A hundred thousand," he said. "The markers, too. Tear up the markers. You get Cody for a hundred thousand plus the markers." He listened for a moment, growing more impatient. "He wants to speak to you."

"Tomorrow at ten-thirty," I told Nando. "At the toy store in the mall."

"I've got the goods!" Rich shouted. "I set the conditions!"

"He doesn't get it," I told Nando. "Why don't you tell him what kind of pizza he just ate?"

I gave Rich the phone. He listened for moment. "Fifty," he said immediately. "I'm not taking less than fifty." He waited while Nando talked, sticking his chin out, or shaking his head, or blowing air through his lips for our benefit. At the end, before he hung up, he was going to say something. I saw his lips prepare, then he changed his mind. "OK," he said quietly.

That night, I slept off and on. Rich had chained my wrist to a radiator, so I woke up whenever I tried to turn. An old house makes many noises during a night, and there's no way to tell which ones are innocent.

Carol came in the early morning, when it was still dark, to give me the next dose of antibiotic. Every six hours, she'd said, and she was like clockwork. We heard the rain begin on the roof outside the window. She switched on the small lamp on the bedside table and sat on the bed beside me.

"He's sleeping," she said.

She'd brought her pocketbook with her, and she watched me without protest as I lifted it from the floor. I felt the weight of the .38.

"There's a receipt for the dry cleaner's at the bottom," I said.

"I've got all sorts of junk in there."

"I put it there."

"If it's the gun you want, you can take it."

"I don't want the gun now. It's the receipt that's important."

"If you don't want it now, I'll hold it for you. I'll pass it to you tomorrow."

"Find the receipt," I told her. "I want to be sure you have it."

She stared, wondering, into my eyes while her hand unzipped the pocketbook and her fingers picked through vials of lipstick, eyeliner pencils, a broken necklace, and a hairbrush. The gun kept falling in her way, and she took it out and put it on the nightstand and returned to the jumble of change, hair clips, and casually folded receipts at the bottom. She tilted the pocketbook so that the light from the lamp reached into it, and parted its jumbled contents until she came to the bottom.

"It's yellow," I said.

"This?"

She turned over in her fingers the flattened wad that Diego had carried almost to his death. She looked at me as though I was crazy.

"You want me to pick up dry cleaning?" she asked.

"It's Diego's," I said. "They're storing a leather coat for him."

She started to see the possibilities. "What about it?"

"The key's in the lining, at the bottom on the right side. It's the key to the safe deposit box."

"A million dollars isn't any good if it's in the Caicos Islands," she said.

"The bank's in the same mall as the toy store."

She'd been deceived too many times. She studied my face and looked for signs that hadn't helped her in the past.

"Believe me," I told her.

"You said you didn't know where the money was."

"That was before."

"What's different now?" Her fingers turned the folded receipt over and over.

"You weren't ready. You're ready now."

I saw she didn't understand. She didn't recognize how far she'd come. She was within reach of love. If only we had more time.

"If you knew where the money was, you should have said. We'd have had a chance. When you were first out, I had to keep him from selling you to Nando right off. I had to convince him you were just about to tell me how to get the money. You don't know how close it was."

"It's better now. It's much, much better. It'll work out. You can't see it yet. But you'll see."

I was afraid the greasy piece of paper would become important to her. All the time, I'd tried to keep it from becoming what we were about. Now she had it in her hands. Afraid, almost, she took the edges in her fingertips and pried them slowly open, then carefully pressed it to the tabletop to hold it flat. She gave every detail of the receipt her careful attention, as if it was a map to pirate treasure.

"The cleaners are in a plaza at the back of the mall," I said.

I saw the possibilities strengthen in her mind. Her imagination ran ahead, leapt free into the future.

"You could do the whole thing—pick up the coat, practice the signature, clean out the safe deposit box—the whole thing in an hour, tops." She nodded, frowning, still looking at the receipt. "In fact, it's better you do it quickly. Specially the bank. Walk in, tell them you want to get into box 526, be brisk."

I waited for her to look up, but she was looking at the receipt, the money. I had a hunger for her and wanted to feel her eyes on me, to know that I existed in her eyes. She had no way of knowing how precious this time was, how little there was left. She sat on the side of the bed and smoothed out the receipt on the night table with the tips of her fingers.

"They don't let you into a safe deposit box with just a key," she said.

"They'll let you in with a key and a signature. You wear a raincoat with a hood, something on your head, glasses. You could pass as Vera."

She thought about it. "How old is she?"

"Early thirties."

"I guess."

"The bank personnel turn over all the time."

"How do you know?"

"I don't know. It's a risk. You've got a shot at it. People get away with using stolen credit cards all the time. It's a small risk for a lot of money. You've taken risks before."

"Where will you be?"

"I'll be waiting for you."

"Where?"

"There's a coffee shop by the dry cleaners. If everything works out."

"What if it doesn't?"

"Then I'll wait for you in Denning."

"You're taking all the risks."

"Everything I've done, I've done for you."

She started to say, "You were right not to trust me," but I put my fingers to her lips to prevent her confessing.

"The receipt's been in your bag all the time," I said. "You've always had it. Since the first day. And tomorrow I'm going to get you Vera's driver's license and her credit cards so you can practice her signature."

Carol stared at me, measuring me. She was thinking of what I had to do to get Vera's driver's license. I saw her lips start to move. She started to ask, then her lips clamped shut.

"I don't want you to do anything stupid," she said. She covered my hands with her own.

"If everything works out, you'll be set for life," I said.

She squeezed my hands. "It's not the money."

"I know," I said. I felt the words choking me. They were so close to the truth.

She was biting back tears, and I felt her struggle as a vibration through her body. I was afraid of her tears. I wanted her to be strong, and if she cried I'd weaken, too.

"Do you think, after all we've been through, I'd let you go now?" I asked her.

"No." She laughed nervously, something between a cough and a sob. I felt her gathering herself, concentrating her emotions. She let herself be reassured.

"As soon as we get to the mall, get away from Rich and me. It's dangerous, and it doesn't concern you. But don't go too far from the toy store. For a few minutes, it's going to be very confused. People running all over the place, scared. That's when you have to go in the store. You walk in quickly. You pick up Vera's pocketbook. Then you're gone. You walk out. You disappear.

309

Listen to me, now. Don't try to find out what happens to me. I'll meet up with you later. I'll know where to find you."

She turned this over in her mind, trying to make it work, trying to think it through so that everything came out all right.

"We can still walk away from it," she said at last. "Nando can pick up the dry cleaning."

"We're so close," I told her. "I've brought Vera to us. I made this happen. We're so close to pulling this whole thing off. All I need is for you to pass me the gun before we go into the mall."

We lay together on our backs and listened to the soft rain falling on the eaves and trickling into the gutters outside the window. After a while, our bodies rolled together, and we made love. We moved with difficulty, chained to the radiator, avoiding the burns on my chest, within the limitations of silence. I feared the incoherence, and I longed for it, too. I was afraid I'd never come back. We strained toward each other, and at the climax we clung hard to one another as if it was only through each other that we anchored ourselves to the world. Afterwards, she fell asleep beside me, but I made her go.

I felt a whole lot better in the morning. In the kitchen for coffee, I noticed that Carol always kept a piece of furniture between herself and Rich. He whistled and bustled about with phony bravado, as though he could evade gravity if he kept moving forward fast enough, with enough belief in what he was doing.

"It's going to be real smooth," he said. "This is it: You're cuffed to the shelving where he can see you. Nando puts the money on the shelf ten feet back from us. I check it out. If the money's right, I give him the keys to the cuffs. Then you take Nando to where the key is . . . , and you're home free. If you play it right, Cody, it's a win-win situation. If you're smart, you get out of it alive. If you've been bullshitting us all along, if you don't know where that key is" He grinned. "Let's just say I wouldn't want to be in your shoes. But you do know where it is. Right? So there's no problem."

"How much are you getting?" I asked.

He hesitated. "Ten grand."

"That's it? Ten grand?"

"Plus the markers. That's another ten."

We waited in the kitchen for time to pass. The minutes were empty but exquisitely precious to me. In so many different places, people were in motion, apparently at random but converging along their different routes on the toy store. And within the kitchen, I was aware of the intricate paths we wove: Debbie glancing at the clock, Rich preparing a peanut butter sandwich with careless edges, Carol sipping from a coffee cup between her hands, staring ahead, and Gypsy moving between us like a shadow, inhaling gently, inquiring, moving on.

Carol brought me a pair of slacks and a yellow jacket from her stepfather's closet, which fit pretty well.

"Jesus!" Rich said when he saw me in the jacket. "Why don't you just paint a bull's-eye on him?"

He was wearing one of the old man's blue blazers. The sleeves were too long, and during a moment when he thought no one would notice, I saw him practice a cross-draw, reaching for the gun stuck in the waistband behind the left side of the jacket, then putting his hand up and shaking his arm until the sleeve fell back, then reaching again.

We left Debbie watching television with a fresh glass of orange juice beside her.

"Back soon," Carol called to her, and Debbie nodded, taking her eyes only briefly from the screen.

"Why don't you drive, babe?" Rich told Carol.

He was nervous as I walked down the path in front of them without cuffs or leg irons. Inside the garage, he had me stand splayed against the back of the car while he patted me down, and I was glad Carol had kept the .38. Then he was quickly out of reach again. He waited until I was all the way in the backseat of the car and had closed the door before he leaned in the window and put one of the cuffs on my right wrist.

"Do you think that's really necessary?" Carol asked. There was an edge of sarcasm to her voice.

"You do what you've got to do, and I'll do what I got to do," Rich said. He meant to point his finger for emphasis, but the gun he'd kept low on the other side of the door was in his hand, and he was pointing it at her before he realized what he was doing.

"Come here," he ordered me, and hooked the other cuff through the armrest on the door and closed it.

He sat up front, turned sideways in his seat so that he could see me out of the corner of his eye. He glanced at me constantly, down at my hands and up at my face as though this would tell him what was about to happen.

Carol sat stiffly with both hands placed symmetrically on the steering wheel. She drove very precisely in the rain, coming to a complete standstill at stop signs and slowing when a traffic light turned yellow as we approached.

When we reached the mall, Carol turned off the ignition, and we sat silently for a few moments, without the regular thump of the wipers. I looked around at the slick, reflective surface of the parking lot and thought that these might be my last moments on earth. Time was slowed and made dense by a poignancy that was almost more than I could bear.

"It's too early," Rich said.

I didn't look at Carol, because it would make me want to live too much, and I couldn't afford to soften now. I felt her eyes come to me in the mirror, sharp stabs of contact. I concentrated on being in her presence and refused to let in any sense of the future.

Rich drummed on the dashboard with his fingers. He shifted and looked around, but there was nothing to see, except people coming to their cars, stooped in the rain, with bags from the mall. If you didn't know what you were looking for, everyone was suspect.

"At least inside we can move around," Carol said.

Rich bent forward under cover of the dashboard to check the clip in the automatic and then tucked it into the front of his waistband beneath the blazer. He took the keys off the clip on his belt and tossed them to me.

"Oh, no," he said when I started to unlock the cuff around my wrist. "Just the one on the door." He watched me a few inches out of arm's reach. "Then drop the keys over the seat."

We were parked beside a van that hid us from the mall entrance and half the parking lot. He wanted me to wait until they were both out of the car. He leaned against the van and looked around for signs of trouble, then he beckoned me out of the car.

The rain had stopped, and I looked around to see if the sun

312

would come out before we went inside. I was bidding the world farewell. For a moment, I wondered how Vera was spending her last minutes.

"Hold out your hand," Rich said.

He was very quick. He took hold of the cuff that dangled from my wrist and ratcheted it around his own, then his hand was back on the gun.

"You're my ticket out of here," he said. He jabbed me with the gun he held beneath his coat. "You're sticking with me."

He'd never been so close to me before. I smelled his sweat and felt each movement of his body, even premonitions of movement, transmitted through the cuffs. He didn't feel my movement, even though he was being swept along by it. He was a man who hadn't noticed that a corner of his sleeve had caught in the machine.

He'd brought along one of the old man's raincoats and a windbreaker to cover the cuffs, but they were still on the front seat.

"Hey, babe," he said. "Get those for me, will you?"

He knew his hold on her was loosening. She waited a moment, to show him that she was free.

"Come on—give me a break, will you?" he asked quietly.

Carol put one knee on the front seat and reached in, but the pocketbook on her shoulder swung in her way. She put both feet down on the blacktop again, and nothing seemed so natural than that she should turn and take two leisurely steps toward us and hang her pocketbook on my shoulder as if I were a coatrack.

"Here," she said. "Hold this a minute."

I looked away, over Rich's left shoulder. Carol brushed back her raincoat and raised her knee to the seat again, and I felt for her pocketbook with my free hand. Carol leaned across the seat. I glanced again over Rich's shoulder and reached my hand into the pocketbook and felt the gun. Rich looked quickly away. He kept his free hand under his jacket. I could feel the tension in his body as he scanned the parking lot, ready for an ambush. In the car, Carol had the raincoat and the windbreaker. She knelt on the seat and held the raincoat by the collar and shook it out. I took the .38 out of the bag. I had it in my hand. I could have killed Rich there in the parking lot. As Carol slammed the door,

I shifted stance so that Rich had to adjust, and under cover of the movement, I slipped the gun into the side pocket of my trousers and held it there.

Carol stood in front of us with the raincoat. She began to fold it across the shoulders.

"Not too neat," Rich said. "Make it look natural."

She tossed it over Rich's wrist and stepped back to look it over, then made some adjustments so that it fell differently. But this wasn't right, and she lifted it up and dropped it over the cuffs again, and in all this shifting and posing, I brought the gun out of the pocket and tucked it into my belt at the back. She put the windbreaker over my arm.

"That's good enough," Rich said impatiently.

Carol lifted the pocketbook from my shoulder, and I knew she must have noticed the change in weight, though she gave no sign. She walked ahead of us to the mall entrance and didn't look back. Rich made us stay close to the vehicles and crossed from one line of cars to another without warning.

The mall was busy but not crowded. Rich tried to keep track of the people who came at us from all different directions. It was noisy, with teenagers shouting suddenly to each other, and this kept him on edge.

I stopped by a cart selling magazines and browsed through a travel magazine. Rich tugged at the cuffs underneath the raincoat, but there wasn't much he could do. Carol looked through the section, touching some titles with the tips of her fingers. The man minding the cart was waiting for me. It's difficult to read a magazine with one hand, and I folded it back.

"You want to buy that magazine?" he asked.

I ignored him and turned away.

"No, he doesn't want it," Rich said.

"He's with you?"

Rich looked around for Carol to help but couldn't find her.

"Hey," the man said, "your friend wants that magazine, it's four-fifty."

"Give the man his magazine," he said.

314

"This is interesting," I said. "It's about where to stay in the Caribbean."

Rich thrust his free hand into his pocket and came up with a handful of bills, mostly ones. He dropped them on the magazines and looked frantically around. He picked out dollar bills, and as he handed them to the man, he searched for Carol.

"We got to get going," he said. "We'll catch her up."

"We're early. Remember?" I said. "She's gone to take care of some things. She'll meet us at the store."

"Oh. You think you know something I don't know."

He fussed with the raincoat and glanced to see if anyone was watching. He was pulling me to go faster. I spotted Vera staring in a window ahead of us on the other side. She broke away and sauntered across the concourse. Rich scanned the crowds, looking for Carol, or for Nando's associates. There was an Hispanic man on the other side who kept pace with us. Rich kept track of him at the same time as he scanned the faces of all the people who came toward us.

"Take a look at these Caribbean beaches," I said, handing him the magazine. He brushed it away. "Take a look," I persisted. I held it in front of him. "It'll calm you down."

Distracted, he took hold of the magazine with his free hand. Vera walked toward us. She wore denim shorts that were stretched tight against her hips and a white T-shirt and large sunglasses. She walked on high heels with a sulky, arrogant thrust. You'd remember the body, but not the face. On her shoulder, she carried a big straw bag like people use to carry towels and a book to the beach, and she kept her right hand deep inside it, holding the bag close to her hip.

She walked toward us, looking away, looking anywhere but at us, and we were about to pass her, when she changed direction, as if something had caught her eye in a shop window, and almost collided with us.

"Hey, Rich," Vera said. "Look what I got in my bag."

He looked down and saw the gun pointing at his gut. She came close and put a hand on his chest like an old friend. She could have been an old lover, running into Rich in the mall by chance, her fingers familiar and experienced as they ran

315

down the front of his body and found the automatic under his jacket.

"Deep breath," she said, and lifted it out of his waistband and dropped it into the basket.

She cuddled up to him and her arm circled his waist to feel for weapons underneath his jacket at the back, while Rich held the magazine stiffly away from his side.

"It's been a long time, Danny."

"Hi, Vera," I said.

"You got that thing, right?"

"I've got it."

She shook her finger, joking, like a scolding parent. "'Cause Nando's just going to kill you if you don't have it." Her face froze. "Lucky it's not me you're dealing with, repeating all those lies Diego told you." She was feeling about in the raincoat, but it was hard to search it systematically, and she lifted it up and was going to shake it when she caught sight of the handcuffs underneath. "Oh, my!" She dropped the raincoat back in place. "People don't trust you, do they, Danny?"

Her hand went straight to the key clip on Rich's belt, and she lifted all the keys.

"Wait!" Rich said.

"It's OK," Vera said. "You get them back when we're done."

"Wait a minute—this wasn't part of the deal!"

"What deal?" Vera asked, very cool. She gave Rich the losing-interest look I recognized from the visiting room at Denning.

"I set this up with Nando!" Rich insisted.

A man passing by glanced at him curiously, then looked Vera over.

"Meet Nando by the action figures," she said, and passed into the flow of people.

Rich wanted to go after her. He started to follow, but I held him back.

"She's got the keys!"

"Yes," I told him. "We're both in it together now."

I tried to coax him to move. He kept turning, looking back for Vera and the keys, as if he could change the past, even when we had begun to walk toward the toy store.

316

"Come on," I said. "They're gone now. The best thing is to keep going."

You know a man when you're connected to him by three inches of chain. I sensed each particle of movement in Rich's body, and I knew his fear. I felt ripples of it from time to time myself, but I had lived for days with the promise of death. I'd become reconciled to the idea that I was moving steadily toward it, insofar as it's possible to accept the idea of your own death. I had chosen this as my path. For Rich, the idea that his life would probably come to an end in the toy store was new and unexpected. All his life, there'd been so much stretching ahead of him that he couldn't let it go now, in the space of a few minutes. I felt his fear and anguish as we walked together through the mall, and when he had to stop and he hung his head and I felt his chest heaving with great gulps of life-giving air, I gave him a few moments to pull himself together.

Everyone else moved on around us. No one changed direction. The people who'd been looking in store windows before were in motion. I wondered where Carol was, but I knew I couldn't let myself think about her.

"We have to keep going," I told him gently. "We don't have a choice."

He turned to me, and I saw in his face the helpless, stricken look of a man who realizes that he is being pulled, slowly but inexorably, into a machine.

"The deal," he said. He saw the entrance to the store in front of us. "We had a deal."

He clung to Nando's promise as if it were a piece of furniture that would hold him back from the events that were taking control of him.

"You have to play it out," I said.

Now that we were so close to the end, now that Rich no longer mattered in the scheme of things, I felt a dangerous trickle, a leak of pity for him.

"There's no side deal, though?" he asked. "You don't have anything going with Nando I don't know about?"

"The action's between Nando and Vera. If he gets the key, he's going to find out how much she's been stealing from him."

"You know where the key is, though?" he asked uncertainly.

317

Once inside the machine, he was starting to understand that the key wasn't necessarily a good thing to have, if it brought you into position between Nando and Vera. Then again, if we couldn't deliver it up to Nando . . . "You know where it is," he insisted.

"Yes," I told him. "Carol's got it."

I felt him balk. We could see people standing at the cash registers and the brightly colored merchandise piled high behind them.

"You can't go in there if you can't get him the key."

"Don't worry about it," I told him. "This doesn't concern you."

"Are you crazy? He's going to kill you and me both!"

I brought him to a stop and turned to him. "You're irrelevant. That's your best shot. Your best shot is to stay irrelevant. If you try to get into the action, if you fuck things up, you're going to die alongside me."

The store is very large, with every imaginable thing a child could play with stacked fifteen feet high on warehouse shelving. We entered a giant maze that forced us around cash registers and past displays of special promotions, and then to the aisles that ran back a hundred feet. It wasn't crowded, but there were enough people around so that an aisle, as we walked past the cash registers, was rarely deserted for long.

Rich started to check his watch and realized it was on the handcuffed wrist.

"We're early," I said. "Let's check it out."

We walked away from the cash registers and started down one of the outside aisles. There were board games and jigsaw puzzles stacked on shelves ten feet high with boxes stored above them. Two boys left their parents and rushed by, then saw what the aisle contained and turned back, almost bumping into us, brushing past me. I nudged Rich to turn into the cross aisle at the back of the store. Three young girls wandered unattached, holding hands. I heard a father calling for a stray son. Kids argued with their parents over how much to spend. I looked for lone adults. I looked for Nando who wanted the key to his money and Vera who had to kill him before he got it.

We paused by stuffed animals at the back of the store, each one

318

with dark, frozen eyes staring straight ahead. A gorilla was large as life. A small girl came up and stood staring beside me.

"Can I touch him?" she asked.

"If you want," I told her.

But she didn't touch him. She looked at the gorilla and peered up at me, then ran happily away.

At the end of the aisle, by the cash registers, I saw Vera checking through a stand of batteries, spinning it around with a bored, casual tug of her trailing arm before sauntering on. There was no sign of Nando, but I thought he must be close by. He'd find us in his own time, when he'd had an opportunity to watch us move about the store and to see if anyone moved with us. I wondered how he'd take to Vera's plan to keep us together. We crossed to the next aisle and looked around the corner. There were masks and disguises and fantasy costumes on the shelves. I caught a fleeting glimpse of Nando walking fast in a cross aisle.

We came to an aisle with models and the action figures, but there was no sign of Nando. We started down it slowly, I could feel Rich clenching and unclenching his hands. He kept glancing over his shoulder. When we came to the end of the action figures at the next cross aisle, I knew, from the way Rich twisted around, that Nando had appeared behind us.

He'd been walking quickly, and now, as I turned, he slowed, taking time to look behind him, checking activity behind me at the front of the store, watching for figures who might suddenly turn into police or store detectives among the people waiting at the cash registers or walking the aisles.

Nando looked softened out of prison blues. In slacks and a sports coat he could have been the grandfather of one of the little girls who ran past him. He strolled with his arms crossed and his right hand inside his jacket and stopped ten feet from us. We each turned to examine the articulated aliens on the shelves until the mother of the girls had passed us and turned along the cross aisle after her daughters.

"You want to cuff him to the shelving, like we said?" Nando asked.

"Give me the keys, then," Rich said. Step by step, it was coming to him how badly wrong things were.

Nando looked at him warily. "What are you talking about?"

"You don't have the keys? I thought she was with you?"

"Just have him come here. You'll get your money."

"Wait a minute," Rich said, holding up his hand to stop things from happening.

Nando reached inside his jacket and pulled out a long, thick envelope. "Here," he said, holding up the envelope and waggling it in the air as if Rich might be able to smell the money. "This is what you want." He poked it between two boxes on the shelf. "Send him over." He beckoned impatiently.

I shook my hand loose from the windbreaker so that Nando could see the cuffs. "Vera has the keys," I said. "She didn't tell you?"

"If this is some bullshit . . ."

"Where is Vera?" I asked him.

"She's situated where I want her." He slowly came closer on the other side of the aisle.

"You ought to know where she is."

"She's waiting for us by the door."

"What about me?" Rich appealed to him. "I'm not part of this. Just give me the money, and I'm out of here."

Vera turned the corner at the end of the aisle, behind Nando. She dangled Rich's keys between finger and thumb, and as Nando turned to see what we were looking at, she tossed them so that they landed with a soft clink on the top of a box ten feet above her. Nando heard the sound, but he didn't see the motion that caused it. He looked at me suspiciously, then back at Vera.

"The plan's changed," I said.

He frowned and jerked his head for her to get back to where she was meant to be, by the door. Vera ignored him. She might have had no connection with him at all. She was picking over model kits at the end of the aisle. She took her time, stopping whenever something caught her eye, her hand always in the beach bag on her shoulder. I noticed Nando kept his back to the shelves, facing both of us.

He gave her a head signal, angry and abrupt, which she ignored. She was creeping along the aisle toward us, studying models of racing boats.

Nando started to say something, but a man with a six-year-old

320

boy turned into the aisle behind Vera. They stopped beside her to look at the models.

"Would you get to where you're meant to be?" Nando told Vera.

He'd raised his voice, and the man looked up, thinking that Nando was talking to him. "I was talking to my wife," he told the man, and I thought I saw Vera tip her head with a small, sour smirk on her lips.

"Would you get on the other side, where you're meant to be?" Nando repeated, but Vera ignored him.

The man looked at Vera ignoring Nando, then back at Nando. "Let's look at baseball mitts," he told his son and pulled him away. "Let's go," the father said. I waited for them to move out of the line of fire. The boy hung back, wanting to see the cars.

"It's a setup," I said. "She stole your money. Now she's going to shoot you with Baruk's gun."

"Come on," Vera told me. "Let's make it quick. Give up the key."

I reached slowly behind me, underneath the jacket. Nando released the gun from his waistband. We all heard the slide go back on the gun Vera held. Nando turned to her sharply. Rich's gun was very big in her hands.

"I got this," he said. "Put that away."

But Vera didn't move. Nando was calculating angles, possibilities, certainties. The way he was standing, I think he was mainly covering Vera.

"Give me the keys to the cuffs and get back to the front of the store," Nando said angrily.

"Let's see the key to the box first," Vera said.

They both watched as I reached behind my back. I thought of Carol and tried to control my breathing. I tried not to think of the bullet hitting me. My fingers curled around the butt of the .38 and slipped it out of the belt. A finger caught on the trigger guard, and I fumbled getting my hand around the weapon. I eased off the safety behind my back, already flinching from the bullet that was coming, wondering too late whether Carol had a round in the chamber. I was turned away from Vera, and so it was Nando who saw the .38 come out from behind the yellow jacket. He snatched out his

321

gun, and he was looking down, pulling back the slide, when Vera fired her first shot.

The noise was enormous in that enclosed space. Nando was thrown back against the shelving. Rich barged into me, and I had to twist and jerk the chain to keep him from running. Vera walked toward us. My gun was hidden from her, but Nando never took his eyes off it, even though he looked to be on the verge of losing consciousness. He was on the floor on his hands and knees, blood coming from his mouth. He held his head up to keep me in view, and his face was contorted with the effort. He seemed convinced I'd shot him. He managed to prop himself up and push himself upright so that he sat with his back against the shelving.

"Let's go, for chrissake!" Rich shouted.

Vera was still too far away for me to be sure of hitting her.

"You move, and you're next," I told him.

We watched Nando laboriously bring the gun up from the floor. He could barely keep his eyes open, but he managed to raise it to my chest, and then it wavered as his strength failed him. His face was full of hate. He was oblivious to Vera who walked quickly toward us, closing in. I forced myself not to pay attention to what Nando was doing.

Vera had her gun on Nando, but she didn't fire. She wanted to make sure. I wanted more than anything for her to shoot first, to kill Nando, to spare me the pain of his bullet going into me. I couldn't hit her yet, and I held off. I heard Nando panting with the pain and the effort of bringing his gun up on me, and I was afraid that after all I'd been through, he'd put me away before I could shoot Vera. But Vera kept walking closer with her arrogant strut.

We all seemed to be moving in slow motion. I was starting to raise the gun when Nando fired. I felt as though I'd been kicked in the chest. The wind was knocked out of me, and I spun around on the chain of the handcuffs. Vera fired almost at the same time, and blood spurted out of the back of Nando's head. Rich pulled me up. I hooked my arm around the metal upright of the shelving and clung there so that I could stay upright a few moments longer.

Vera stared at what she'd done, and I saw emotions flow across her face like electric discharges. As the horror filled her, and her

322

hand came up to cover her mouth to stop the escape of pity and protest, I shot her.

I had trouble breathing. Rich wrenched me away from the metal support. I lost my footing and stumbled to my knees, but he hauled me up. I tried to get up, but my legs buckled, and Rich pulled me across the floor to Vera's body. She lay against the shelving with her legs splayed. Her eyes were open, but they didn't move as he stooped to pick up the gun. Something gave way inside me, and I collapsed backwards and swung for a moment around his wrist. He was shouting something to me, but I couldn't hear what it was. I was fighting for air. My chest was growing tighter with every breath I took.

I heard Rich yelling, "For God's sake! We got to get the fucking keys!"

He was moving very quickly, but my legs had turned to rubber. There was a buzzing sound inside of my head. Rich was pulling on my arm, dragging me across the floor to the model cars where the keys were. He tried to jump to reach the packing cases, but he wasn't even close. As he jumped I was already sagging to the floor, and in midair the weight of my body on the handcuffs jerked him back to earth. He fell hard on top of me.

I wanted to look back, for Carol, but I was in and out of consciousness. Rich moved me as if I were nothing more than a mannequin. The last thing I remember is the sensation of being lifted to my feet by Rich hauling on my arm. He was trying to climb the shelving with one hand, clinging to the metal supports and pulling me up after him. I heard him grunt with the effort of climbing with the weight of my body holding him back. I was on my feet, but floating on the tips of my toes. I was dimly aware of Rich preparing for one effort that would take him within reach of the keys. I felt his arm trembling with the strain, but no movement came. He cried out, I felt him struggle, but we didn't move, and I lost consciousness for good.

The medics had me on a stretcher. They were giving me oxygen, and I found an IV tube in my arm. I moved my fingers lower, to the wrist, to feel for the handcuff, but it was gone. A crowd had gathered outside the store, and they already had police in place to hold them back. I must have been out for some time.

We had to slow for the police to open a path for us through the spectators.

I remember the medics wheeling me at a speed that made me dizzy, watching the ceiling tiles flash by, across the smooth floor of the mall. There was a sound that followed me, a rustling, billowing sound, like the breeze filling a silken sail. Everything else, all human noise, was unnaturally silent. I laid my head sideways and saw the running feet keeping pace with us. Other stationary legs came between us. Once I caught sight of a raincoat I recognized and over it a straw shoulder bag of the kind you might take to the beach. When we went by a knot of people who'd stopped to take in the spectacle of the wounded man, I'd lose sight of her for a moment. But in gaps between people, I'd see again the movement behind them, the running feet, the raincoat catching the air, and I heard the flapping, tugging sound of what she carried.

Once, I glimpsed Carol's face. She was staring intently ahead and turned at that moment toward me, but someone came in the way at the instant our eyes would have met. The wheels of the stretcher made no sound on the mall floor. Gaping faces stared down at me. Three police officers charged past us. We were held up at a door because the crowd was thicker, and there wasn't room for people to move out of the way. Then I saw Carol in front of us. Tears streamed down her face and spoiled her makeup. She held up Diego's coat for me to see. It swayed and shimmered in its plastic cover.

I nodded to her. I wanted to say, "That's it. That's good. That's what I wanted for you."

We began to move again, and she reached out her hand to me. I held up my hand to block her. I was afraid to implicate her. I moved my lips to tell her, "No, stay back!"

But her fingers touched mine. They brushed across my hand, and her strong fingers slipped between my fingers like water, the touch leaking away, and I lost her forever.

I felt myself sinking down into a buzzing blackness that I supposed was death. I accepted it: I had no further use for my life. I felt myself drifting down like a feather falling slowly to earth, floating sideways in eddies of consciousness. Death seemed fitting. I didn't fight it. I felt only the loss of Carol, and as I fell deeper into darkness, I struggled to keep in view my last glimpse of her face.

Most people do not know what is necessary to sustain life beyond mere subsistence, beyond brute existence. Freedom? Honor? Decency? Security from harm? The truth? I live day by day without them. They are luxuries that would make us soft. We cannot afford them here.

Love is the essential nutrient of the human spirit. Only love is the thing I cannot live without.

They tell me I'm lucky to be alive. The worker on Medical says Baruk is plea bargaining to do his time in a federal institution. They're threatening to hang Nando's murder on him. I often wonder what went through Carol's mind as she walked briskly through the melee in the toy store. Did she give any thought at all to climbing the shelves to retrieve the keys for Rich, to give him a life? Did she turn when he pleaded for her help, or hesitate as she stooped to gather up Vera's shoulder bag? If she did, it can only have been for a moment.

It looks good. There's been nothing about her in the newspapers. I have a TV set in my room so that I can watch your show, Sandy, and I know that if you had the slightest snippet to report on her, you would. Carol has disappeared. Fairburn's wife received a package in the mail, postmarked Miami, containing a hundred thousand dollars. I don't regret for a moment what I did, except for Fairburn—and I blame Baruk for his death. The rest of my life is fair exchange for two weeks with Carol. I'll never see her again. Wherever you are, Carol, on your Caribbean island, you will always be here with me.

Outside in the corridor, I hear footsteps and the swish of pantyhose stretched tight on meaty thighs. Any moment now, lazy Tanya will appear to change my dressing. But first, she will hold back at the doorway until her escorts have checked to ensure that I'm safely chained to the hospital bed. These men take no chances with me now. There's an element of respect in the care with which they approach me. I'm a celebrity, of sorts.

Tanya is not careful in the way she handles the wound, though lately I've noticed she's more sensitive to the possibility that she might be causing pain. Yesterday, I sensed a new and uncharacteristic gentleness in her fingers as she peeled back the dressing. When she thinks my eyes are closed, she steals a look at my face. One day I will catch her in this and look back into her eyes, with a gaze that is full and bold, and dazzle her with the full intensity of my soul. In time. I'm in no hurry. Signs of love are everywhere, waiting to be discovered, for those who want to see.